The Society

by
John F. Conn

Meisha Merlin Publishing, Inc
Atlanta, GA

THE SOCIETY

Published by Meisha Merlin Publishing, Inc.
PO Box 7
Decatur, GA   30031

Editing & interior layout by Stephen Pagel
Copyediting & proofreading by Josh Mitchell & Lorelei Feldman
Cover art by Kevin Murphy
Cover design by Kevin Murphy

ISBN: 1-892065-49-5

http//www.MeishaMerlin.com

First MM Publishing edition: January 2003

Printed in the United States of America
0 9 8 7 6 5 4 3 2 1

For my sons,
Winston and Ryan.

The Society

by

John F. Conn

"He who is unable to live in society, or who has no need because he is sufficient for himself, must be either a beast or a God."

—Aristotle,
Politics

Leavenworth Military Prison—1951

Dark shadows of gray covered the inside of the prison, not quite as rich as the night outside, but close. Within those shadows, voices of caged men scurried like so many vermin. Over the voices, footsteps began to echo along the tiers in a very distinct rhythm. The sounds of the sleepless and bored receded into the night, fearful of those steps. The footsteps walked on in the silence.

In a single cell, a lone reclining figure opened his eyes to the sudden retreat of the voices. He looked out towards the confining bars that he always faced. The footsteps slowed, stopping in front of his cell, their echoes dying quickly.

"They leave you alone, don't they?"

James heard the voice in the dark whisper across the length of the cell to him. No one was supposed to be along the tier at this time of night. The midnight rounds weren't due for another hour. Still, it came as no surprise to him. James sat up on his hard bunk, scrutinizing the dark outline of the man. He was tall, thin, almost skeletal within his clothes.

"They aren't all that dumb," the voice carried directly to him. "No," it paused, the body shifting its weight. "I take that back. They are dumb, but at times their instincts are good."

Getting up from the bunk, James walked over to the bars. Reaching out, he put his hands around the metal that imprisoned him, feeling their coldness. Automatically, his hands tightened around the painted metal, almost as if the slim bars were a throat. His court-martial had been swift and he was now entering his sixth month of imprisonment, closing in on his eighteenth year of life.

"They know when a *predator* has been dropped in their midst," the voice whispered on. "Perhaps a demonstration, an example. Not so much for them, but for me. Smoke?"

In the dim light of the cellblock, James made out the offered cigarette through the bars. Taking it, he was aware of a quick motion and watched as the match flared up, casting its light on the face of the guard. The thin face in front of him appeared crisp and spotless in the flickering flame that ate its way down the wooden match. From what James could see, the guard's face carried just enough flesh to give him a thin veneer of humanity. The illusion was good, but the guard's eyes gave him away. It wasn't hard for James to know which flame burned brighter. What he read in those eyes could never be covered up. James knew this man instinctively.

As the match burned, James took his time leaning into it. Touching the cigarette lightly, the flame danced, burning the tobacco as James drew the smoke into his lungs. Dropping his eyes he examined the guard. What he could make out of the Army uniform was, like the face, crisp and spotless. But James wasn't fooled. He knew the uniform for what it was, just another mask.

Drawing back from the match, he gave a quick "thanks" and watched as the flame continued its way down toward the guard's fingers.

"Moth," James barely whispered and reached out to smother the match between his fingertips.

"Wait...look." The guard's voice was suddenly anxious, stopping him from extinguishing the flame. "Can you see the tattoo here?" The match moved away.

"Yes," James said as the flame finally flickered and died. The darkness seeped back in with just the glow from the cigarette filling their shared corner of the night.

"That tattoo is a rare sight." The guard's voice, prideful, drifted in from the darkness carrying a distinctive stench with it. James knew the odor.

"I've been watching you," the thin guard confessed. "I read your record. I know what you did. I know your true *nature*. Leavenworth need not be your home for long." The voice sounded like it belonged exactly where it was: in the dark of the night whispering things that would stir the worst of nightmares.

James was taciturn, taking a small drag on the cigarette, keeping it aglow. He had known he was being watched, and not only by the other prisoners. This meeting came to him as no surprise. He listened to the voice, curious to see what else it had to offer. He didn't have to wait long.

"You know the prisoner they call Red? He's an embarrassment of sorts, a bit of a Bolshevik, if you get my meaning." The guard fell silent for a moment. He moved in to the bars, his voice a little more excited, death a little closer. "Do him like you did those Red Chinese soldiers. The word would travel far in here."

James knew that what he had done was under the guise of war, but he had given it no second thoughts, during or after. He understood the *nature* of war, and he understood his own *nature* better than anyone else. To him, there wasn't any difference. He didn't have any feelings about those soldiers he killed in Korea, nor did he have any feelings about Red. They all were just walking slabs of meat put on the earth for his taking. What he did know was that he wanted out. He wanted—*needed*—his freedom. He knew there was a destiny to be fulfilled.

"When do you want this done?" he questioned.

The reply was simple. "You've hunted. You'll know when it's right."

James was quick, hunting already. "If this is a setup, you know I'll kill you." He felt nothing as he said it, just knew it as a fact.

"Relax, kid. Don't be such a hothead," the voice came back, reprimanding. "I went *beyond* your normal records. I know when something has been doctored. How many years did you add to your birth certificate?" The guard laughed. "You're good for your age, I give you that much. A bit of a *natural,* if you get my drift. Besides, *kill me?*" The guard laughed again. "No, not at all. You need me as much as I need you. Unless, of course, you want to rot here for another ten years?"

James said nothing as another cigarette was suddenly passed through the bars—a peace offering. He took it, automatically placing it behind his ear. Nodding to himself, he knew he didn't have much of a choice.

"When I'm ready, then," he replied quietly, his mind elsewhere. He brought the burning remains of the cigarette closer to the bars and watched as the paint absorbed some of the heat, forming a tiny blister. James blew lightly on the tip to hasten its effect. He hated smoking. It was a foul habit, but cigarettes were an important commodity within the walls. A man's behavior could be controlled with just a few of them. *Silly little petty lives that they are.* Fear was the only commodity he dealt in. It was fear that was everlasting. In a way, he was insulted by the offer of the cigarette, as if he could be manipulated in that manner like the rst of them.

No longer caring for what the guard had to say, James turned his face away. Crushing the cigarette between his fingers, his anger rose. The gurat's voice droned on, irritating him. *Patience*, he cautioned himself. He knew that somewhere in that voice there was a fear to be found, a commodity to be dealt in. As every man had his price, every man had his *fear*. He had learned that it was useless to work with a man's surface fears—the obvious. At most, it confused them. Instead, he knew to go directly to the one fear that lay dormant beneath all the others. The one that gave birth, that gave breath. The idea was to find it, draw it to the surface, and in doing so, expose the fearful soul. And once that quivering entity was uncovered, he could confront it, feed it, take control and watch it grow. And the more it grew, the less of the man was left to contend with. *Makes it all so easy*, he thought. It was like being God—no, different. *It was better.*

James smiled in the dark. He knew that another true, yet undiscovered soul continued to speak from the other side of the bars. He also knew this one was Godless. And if he got the chance, he might show him what God could be all about. Slowly, James turned his head back toward the guard. *Yes, there is a fear there. That's why he came to me.* His smile widened. The guard's words drifted back.

"...all is said and done and you're out, thinking you've tasted freedom, I'll introduce you to The Society. You'll understand true freedom then."

James' interest was suddenly piqued. "The *what?*" he asked. James was met with silence, and wished once again that he could read the eyes of his jailer. Instead, he became aware of the guard's movement. The dark outline of the thin figure was starting to walk away. *Too soon.* "Say," he tried, "there a new guard called Jimbo here?"

"Don't worry about any of *that* now," the guard's voice drifted back, annoyed at his lack of attention.

James pressed the side of his face against the bars, trying to catch a last glimpse of the retreating figure. The coldness of the bars was his only reward. He started to question the guard about Jimbo again, but the man cut him short.

"Like I said, don't worry about any of that." The footsteps stopped, the silence embracing the guard's words. "That embarrassment of ours...*that's* what *you* worry about. Show me you're worthy, and...just one more thing."

James knew the guard was facing him again. "What's that?" he asked.

"I want a souvenir." And the footsteps were on the move once again into the night.

James turned away, facing the darkness and the silence of his own cage. Taking the extra cigarette from behind his ear, he rolled it back and forth in his hands before crushing it. Walking over to his bunk, he lay back down, facing out toward the bars once more.

Like crickets, the whispering voices began to fill in the silence of the night one by one. James closed his eyes and cocked his head, hearing nothing of the prison chorus. He had retreated to a darker confinement than the one that held him.

Jimbo—Two Weeks Later

Jimbo walked cautiously through the prison machine shop, the overhead lights flickering with the whims of the storm. The flashlight he carried seemed prey to those whims as well, leaving him, at times, in total darkness. *Par for the course,* he thought. His shift had been over for hours, and he knew he should have been catching some shut-eye instead of catching shit like always. And this was not only shit, but damn fuckin' *creepy* shit at that.

It was his second week as a guard. He didn't like the assignment, the training, or the people around him. That went for his fellow guards as well as the inmates. It seemed most of the other guards didn't like their assignment, either. If they weren't taking out their aggression on the prisoners, they were taking it out on each other in little ways. And with him being the new guy, they were always on his shit. *Always*. Still, it was better than being wounded and watching your blood freeze in one of those damn Korean winters. He knew that was a page of history for him that he had no intention of repeating. But now, things had taken a turn for the worse with that prisoner Red missing. The guy was a real commie. Having a prisoner get away was one thing, but having a *commie* prisoner get away was something else. The creepiest shit was the way the other guards said practically nothing about Red being gone. *Just ain't right.* There was an uneasiness throughout the prison about it, but no one really seemed to be looking for him. Jimbo didn't believe the man had escaped. *No way.* He rubbed the back of his neck. *Nope, no way. Shit just doesn't add up right.*

Jimbo turned the corner on a large piece of equipment and stopped dead in his tracks. At the other end of the machine shop, he thought he saw *something* across a drill press. But before he could get a better look, the overhead lights crackled and died as the lightning flashed.

"Fuck." His flashlight flickered and he gave it a smack, bringing it momentarily back to life. The light was weak. *Batteries. Shit!* He shined it toward the drill press; the light fell off quickly, leaving the press and that *something* covered by the darkness. Jimbo hesitated, squinting into the distance. He wasn't quite sure what he had seen, but whatever it had been, he knew it couldn't be good. He really had no intention of getting caught up in this by himself.

"Hey! I think I got—" Jimbo started to call, but his own light flickered again and died leaving him in darkness. "*Son of a bitch!*" he yelled, smacking the flashlight against his palm. Preoccupied, he took a small step, his foot shooting out from under him. Reaching out blindly, he grabbed for the machinery, missed and hit the ground.

Shit! Something's wet! Fuck! Cursing under his breath, he carefully got back up. The overhead lights crackled into life again. Jimbo looked at the dark stains on his clothing and back down toward the drill press.

Aw, shit!

The pale limbs dangled from the press, wilted stems no longer able to give support to the body. A thick dark trail of blood meandered from the bottom of the press, catching him in its path. His heart raced on as he looked around nervously.

"Hey! I got something here!" he yelled, his words ricocheting within the empty workshop. Stepping away from the blood on the floor, he continued to look around, a little more fearful now. *"Hey, got a body here!"* he cried out again. It was useless. He knew there was no one within earshot. No one else wanted to find this body. He was beginning to suspect that he—and only he—was meant to find the body.

Walking toward the nude form that lay across the press, he noticed that the drill was centered mid-chest. He wanted to stop, but found he couldn't as his mind flew back to those stripped enemy bodies his patrol had found that cold winter day in Korea. He remembered the silence of his men, the freezing winds and snow that screamed digging into them, sapping any warmth body or memory could hold. A cold memory of how they stood with not a word passing between the ill-fed and ill-equipped war-weary men. A freezing memory of how they stared down at the dozen nude bodies laid out in a perfect line, slowly being covered with snow. But what bothered Jimbo then hadn't been the vacant faces of the Chinese soldiers they fought. Nor the way death and the extreme cold gave them all a surreal, porcelain doll-like appearance. Nor the way they held hands like children off on a run through the park. No. What bothered him were the gaping holes in their chests. Holes in their chest with their hearts replaced upside down. What bothered him was the single bite in each of the dead frozen hearts. What bothered him was the way each of his men reached in and touched the heart of their enemy before the ragtag group of American soldiers continued on their way.

But there was more.

Shuffling away, he remembered how he had been the last one in that line when he had looked back over his shoulder and suddenly stopped. How something had seemed to seize him as he watched a figure materialize out of the swirling snow and move from one dead Chinese soldier to the next like a human vulture. How tired, frightened, and weary he was that day. How some of the captured Chinese soldiers had spoken of a "demon." Most of all, he remembered the relief he had felt when he had turned his head away, leaving cold death behind him and walking off into the pure white of the Korean snow.

He hadn't gotten far.

A few short steps and a bullet had taken him. He always wanted to believe it was the enemy. Maybe a sniper. He had lain there not far from the dead Chinese soldiers, the snow coming down thick. His blood had felt warm, soothing, before it froze, closing the wound.

Dragged.

He had had the sensation of being dragged. More shots. He had lain still. Suddenly his men were looking down on him, fearful.

A sniper...a vulture waiting for a straggler.

Yeah, a sniper.

That's what he wanted to believe, that's what he wanted to remember.

Thunder crashed in, filling the machine shop. Jimbo found himself staring down at another one of those gaping holes. The opening was neatly drilled and just big enough for a hand to reach in.

He stepped in closer and placed his hand over the dark hole in the body as the killing winter winds of Korea screeched across his mind, and wondered where Red's heart was.

James sat with his back against the wall, listening to the whispers of the men and the sounds of the storm. Both had been brewing for hours. The talk around him wasn't the usual boredom of the men before the silence of the night spread its blanket. The voices tonight were fearful, caged, with no place to escape to, nothing to cover them. Even the guards were on edge, keeping their distance from the cells and from each other. James smiled as he slipped the last small piece of tough, raw meat into his mouth. Chewing slowly, he got up from his bunk and walked over to the bars, taking hold of them. They didn't feel all that cold to him tonight. Slowly his hands began to open and close around the bars with the rhythm of a beating heart, the fearful caged voices falling silent. James closed his eyes, his hands speeding up their beat. He would lick the last of the blood from his nails later.

"Unfortunate accident in the machine shop," the voice whispered matter-of-factly. The storm was spent, and with it's passing, the prison seemed to be drawn deeper into the night. James pressed his head against the bars of his cell, half-listening to the dark figure of the guard. He didn't want to give up his souvenir. He was confined, his pleasures were few; but in the long run, he knew it would suit his purposes. Still, he had wanted to hold onto this one as long as possible. But as the guard spoke, he slid his hand between the bars and James placed the fist-sized object in the outstretched hand. As the guard's hand closed around it, James ran his finger along the tough tissue. *Gone.*

"...most want to get caught," the guard was saying. "They don't understand what they are." James could see his hands moving, caressing the heart, *his heart—a violation.* He waited to see if the guard would say anything about the piece of meat missing. He didn't.

"Like I said, most want to get caught," the guard continued, "but not all. Some understand and accept..."

James nodded. The two predators talked through the night. There were no other voices.

None dared.

The Guard's Parting Gift

James stood waiting outside the prison walls. The old clothes he wore were meant for a larger man, giving him a boyish, disheveled appearance. He didn't care. Things had moved quickly, and he'd had other matters to think of other than his looks. After three years, the confining walls were finally behind him. It was over, and his mind dismissed the last few years as if they were nothing but a passing dream. His attention was now drawn to the car coming up the road toward him.

A cloud of dust followed it, and James cocked his head to one side as the car skidded to a stop in front of him. The passenger door swung open. James stood patiently. The voice within sounded uncertain of its errand.

"I've been sent to pick ya up. Get in now."

A light covering of dust from the road caught up with the car, and James waited until it settled before looking in at the driver. Staring back was a clean-cut boy not much older than him, with a hard but nervous look. The young driver avoided eye contact. James turned away and looked back at the prison.

"Hey, Bud," the driver tried to assert himself. "I mean *now.*"

James' head snapped back; his eyes flashed for a second. Slowly, a very pleasant smile worked itself across his face.

"'Kay."

The car pulled up in front of a simple two-story family house. On the close-cropped lawn, two brand new bicycles lay side by side. The surrounding houses were all neat, sterile, with patches of green grass and concrete driveways. James turned to the nervous driver and watched him.

"Dis it." The young man stared straight ahead, looking out over the quiet neighborhood. His sweaty hands were busy along the steering wheel, almost as if he was polishing it. James kept perfectly still. The driver took a deep breath and turned to him.

"Said, *dis it—*" He reached across and pushed open the door. James sat there, feeling the fear that rode hard on the boy next to him as the young driver went back to staring straight ahead, his hands nervously working the wheel again. Finally, James spoke.

"We'll cross paths again," he told him. "I'm sure of it."

"Yeah, Bud, whatever ya say."

James smiled. Getting out of the car slowly, he closed the door behind him and took notice of the license plate as the car sped away.

Walking up the path to the house, he looked at the two bicycles as if they had just fallen out of the sky. It wasn't something he had expected. Reaching the front door, he was about to knock, when it suddenly opened. The tall, skinny guard stood there, dressed in a white, short-sleeve shirt worn outside his khaki pants. The guard didn't seem as sinister on the front steps of his home as he had in the prison. But James knew better.

"See," the guard said, appraising him cautiously, "all just wars come to an end, even this one. For what you did inside those walls, saved you what?"

"Seven years."

"Now, do you understand what was done for you?"

"Yes."

"You understand what *is* being done for you?"

"Yes."

The guard was satisfied, and nodded. "The wife and boys are away. We can talk. Come in." He stepped aside, and James shot a quick glance around the neighborhood before walking past him.

The living room was well-kept. Clean, neat, sterile. Nothing more than an extension of the crisp lawns and the barren concrete. James took in everything. Various sized photos of a family that showed an attractive wife and two teenaged sons next to a loving father. A few more pictures of the guard as a soldier in World War II. A gun cabinet with a collection of pre- and post-war German handguns. Plastic slipcovers that protected the flowery patterns of the furniture. Off in a corner of the room, a television. James had read an article in Life Magazine about them, but had never seen one before. From what he understood, it was a small Cyclops of an eye to the outside world. Right now, the curved glass screen stared back at him blankly; dead to the world he hadn't had the privilege of viewing in three years. He heard the guard laugh.

"You can watch some later. It's really entertaining. I don't know if there's much use for it beyond that."

James didn't care. Something else had caught his eye. He saw a thick book on a small table in front of the picture window. Most of the pages looked loose and mismatched, a haphazard collection. A heavy piece of worn leather acted as a cover, leather strips binding the whole thing together. James could tell that for the most part it was old, very old. He had always had an obsession with books, and this one intrigued him now. As he moved towards it, the guard's mood suddenly changed.

"That is our Journal. In it is our record, our lives, our beliefs—who we truly are. I brought it out to show you." The guard walked over to it and placed his hand upon it like a Bible. As he touched it, his eyes glazed and he seemed momentarily unaware of his surroundings, as if the book had drained a little something from him. James watched silently, but intently.

The guard took his hand away and looked at him. There was a fever in his eyes, a heaviness to his voice. "You know The Society has accepted you upon my recommendations. Do you realize how blessed you are?" he asked, his voice slowly clearing.

James stared at the book, curious about its contents, curious about the feel of it. There was life within its pages; he was certain of it. In all of their talks late at night, the guard had never mentioned this book. James felt cheated. He was wondering why, when he heard the guard's voice again.

"James, do you realize?"

"I have an idea." He took a small step toward the guard.

"Good. The meeting is next week. Can you acquire a *gift* in that short time?"

"Yes." James knew he was still being tested. "Yes," he said again, thinking back to the young, frightened driver and the license plate number. "Won't be a problem."

"That's good." The guard's demeanor changed again; now he was the smiling father of the family portraits. "Come on, let's go to the kitchen. The wife's cooking is a damn sight better than the chow you were getting in that stink-hole of a prison."

James nodded, stealing one more glance at the book, and followed the guard through an arched doorway into the kitchen.

Spacious and well-lit, the kitchen was as orderly as the living room. The guard went over to the fridge and started to rummage through it.

"Are you hungry?" he asked over his shoulder.

James noticed a set of kitchen knives in a wooden block near the sink and walked over to them. Fingering one, he watched the back of the guard.

"No...not yet, thank you," he said, and slipped the largest knife out of the block. The guard froze momentarily, then straightened up from the refrigerator. He kept his back to James, the disappointment evident in his voice.

"I had hopes for you—" The guard's hand traveled under his shirt and pulled out a large hunting knife with a serrated edge. Brandishing the blade, he slowly faced James. "You won't survive this." The fever was back in the guard's voice.

James stood there, oblivious to the threat. He turned the kitchen knife slowly, getting the feel of it. *Not bad; it'll work.*

The guard watched carefully, continuing with his threats. "I'll use you as a warning to the rest of The Society." His own knife gleamed, catching the light in the room.

James cocked his head, the knife in his hand picking up a little more speed. "I have no fear of that." His voice was indifferent, but the knife now moved with a life of its own.

"No, I suppose you don't, do you?"

Each waited for the other to move first. James smiled at the guard. It was a most enchanting smile.

Abruptly, the kitchen knife stopped. James' smile held tight.

Both men stood there within the neat quiet house that stood within the neat quiet neighborhood. Suddenly, there was a flash of movement, a clash of sharp metal against sharp metal. A snarl...

James looked out of the living room window. The neighborhood was peaceful. He watched as a couple down the block unloaded groceries from their new car. He knew he would need a vehicle soon, and made some mental notes. In front of him, the Journal lay open on the small table, its pages telling stories of lives lost and lives taken. Indistinct voices murmured from the television, its glass eye flickering, rolling, trying to catch up with itself. The guard's body lay sprawled out on the kitchen floor. His white short-sleeved shirt was no longer white, and like the flesh beneath it, was in tatters.

James placed a small strip of tough, raw meat in his mouth. His eyes took in every movement of the couple as they carried the last of the shopping bags inside. He placed another small strip of meat in his mouth. Finally, the reception on the television cleared. A voice rang out sharp.

"Loooo-cy, I'm hoooooome!" Canned laughter followed it.

James smiled. The following week's meeting would prove to be the start of a bloody but short battle. In the meantime, he realized the guard was right. He had never felt such freedom.

Chewing slowly, James placed his hand upon the Journal and viewed his world.

Peter and the Deer—1988

The deer was alone and, at the moment, it feared nothing. It walked through the dark woods under a full moon, its head close to the ground, grazing with a quiet ease. As it ate, something crashed in panic through the sparsely covered foliage. The noise was far enough away that even though its muscles tensed for an instant, it kept its head moving along the ground. The noise faded, and the deer continued to work the patchy earth.

Occasionally, as it moved, it would pick up an unwanted twig, working it out of its mouth without losing any of the nourishing grass. The deer was young, its seasons few, but it knew enough not to waste any precious food. Already, as it exhaled into the night air, a warm moist cloud formed, foretelling colder times to come. It knew, without the acknowledgment of knowing, of the hungry times ahead. For now, though, it had been feeding well, and its awareness was at a low. Nothing stirred in its immediate surroundings, so nothing stirred within it.

A sound in the distance made its ears flick, but the deer was familiar with this sound. A light moved along with it, but the deer was also used to this. The deer knew exactly where it had to stop.

As the light and sound drew closer, filling the space between the bisected woods, the deer, still relaxed, picked up its head as instinct dictated. The noisy light was close and caught the deer at the edge of the woods. As used as it was to this light, the deer froze in place. Without its knowing, in a fraction of a second its primal instincts searched its long inherited programming and came up with nothing. Just as secondary learned instincts kicked in, the noisy light flashed by and was gone. The deer blinked. As the darkness returned, it looked in the direction of the noisy light, watching it disappeared. Feeling no fear, the deer dropped its head resuming its eating before crossing the road.

As it worked another twig out of its mouth, a puff of warm, moist breath from its blood-enriched lungs hugged the cold ground and slowly disappeared.

Stephen watched the moonlit road ahead. His thoughts twisted and turned with each new curve that led nowhere. He knew that was the beauty of it; pick a direction and just go. The car that sped him along was one hell of a monster, an '85 Lincoln Continental. He loved the space it afforded him. He especially loved the trunk space.

The Society. The meeting had gone well, and he knew he was in. All he had to do was bring a gift to the next meeting. It'd have to be his latest to date. That was the deal. If they found his offering acceptable, he would then receive a gift from another member in return. That would be the whole of the ceremony and the acknowledgement from all. It was as simple as that. The next and final thing would be the tattoo. If, on the other hand, they rejected the gift, he would be dead. But he had no fear of that. No fear at all. His instincts were good.

His instincts were also good about meeting *Him*. Stephen had heard the rumors from some of the other members of what he had done in Korea. How sudden cold fronts would preserve the bodies, showing off his handiwork. How the the Red Chinese thought he was a demon, while his fellow American soldiers never spoke about him. Then, there were the rumors of how he had taken control of The Society and had never been challenged for it. Of how most of his kills over the many years have never been found. How he had come to be known simply as *Him* by The Society, with few if any, calling him James. Stranger still, how even law enforcement agents who thought they had come across some of his victims over the years mumbled under their breaths of a *Him*. Stephen understood that the cops knew nothing of who or what they were faced with. They would rather believe in demons or devils than something human running amok all of these years. He was their basic fear. Something they couldn't quite put their collective finger on. Something that stayed hidden, alive and well. The bogeyman of childhood nightmares. A piece of their fearful dream that didn't quite die as the sun rose.

Stephen smiled. He knew the truth about *Him* and all the others, and the truth was, the cops were right to fear. But Stephen felt no fear at all. None.

During the meeting, he had been talking with Candy. She was young, attractive, and an avid killer. A rarity of the species. And because of that, one of James' favorites. It was a standing that she used to her full advantage. Stephen suspected that if it hadn't been for James' watchful eye, she might have fallen prey to one of the others long ago. As with most good hunters, the rarities were most sought after. Many in The Society had an eye on her.

Candy had just finished telling him how James had killed seven members of The Society before the rest gave in to him. Stephen couldn't escape noticing the pride in her voice as she added that he took two more members to make sure the point was driven home.

"Took their hearts, you know," she had whispered to him conspiratorially. She had started to talk about some of the other members who, as it turned out, were very influential men, when James had walked over. Stephen remembered the change in her as James extended his hands, gently taking hers, his lips lightly grazing the backs of them.

"Candy, you've been out of contact much too long," James had said, smiling, but his words were meant as a warning and didn't carry the warmth, he was sure, that Candy had longed for. "A very poor example for all here," James added.

Stephen had watched as Candy withdrew into some hidden world, becoming a different person. But James had given her a kiss on the cheek, his smile deepening with a warmth, and the Candy that Stephen had been speaking with had surfaced again.

James had continued to hold her hands as he turned toward him. James' smile had never faltered, but the warmth was gone. There had been no protectiveness in his glare. Stephen had felt the eyes take him in as if he were a scent in the air.

"Ahh, Stephen. A true predator, I see." James had dropped Candy's hands, touching her face, her eyes half-closed with the gesture. Stepping away from her, both men had reached out to shake hands. As their hands locked, the others members had turned and watched.

Yes, Stephen thought as he drove, *James' instincts are good, but then again, so are mine.* Besides, time was on his side. James was getting old, and he couldn't maintain control forever. But it wasn't control of The Society that Stephen was interested in. It was something else. Something grander.

As the road came toward him out of the darkness at forty miles an hour, it felt as if the headlights of his car were pulling him along, burning him through the night; an unnamed comet lighting up the universe. *His universe.* Wherever he was heading now, he knew it didn't matter. He had a few days off from work and just wanted to travel north into the cooler night, letting the stars guide him.

Wandering within his thoughts, he had lost the sensation of the wheels turning over the empty road hours ago. He had also lost that other feeling, but that didn't matter; it was simply dormant at the moment. After all, this last incident was random; no pattern to it, just something that was needed at the time. And being the creature that he was, he gave into it without any resistance.

As the miles accumulated, Stephen knew this burning of his would change many things. He was experienced for his twenty-seven years. On the other hand, he understood he still had a lot of maturing to do, a lot to learn. That was one of the purposes of The Society: to allow one to grow, to realize one's full potential and to take care of one's kind. Yet, right from the beginning, all in The Society knew he was a natural, a rarity like Candy—like James. And, also like James, many of the members seemed to fear him. He would let that play on their fears. It would give him an advantage. Stephen knew it would take years to ready himself, but in the end, he'd be the brightest star in the firmament. The idea brought a smile to his face.

Watching the dark ribbon of road, he thought he heard a moan. Reaching over, he popped the tape, silencing the Bee Gees. A moment passed, and there it was again. A quiet sound confined within his trunk. He ignored it.

Straining against the tug of his seatbelt, he grabbed the bottle of Pepsi that lay on the passenger seat next to his sandwich. The drink was warm now, just about right. He could never drink anything cold, not liking the feel of it in his mouth. But he always got thirsty beforehand. *Strange. Maybe nerves.* He didn't know, but now he decided to wait. Jamming the soda between his legs, he licked his lips. His thirst was building.

The Lincoln cruised along, taking the twist and turns in the road like a hand sweeping over sand. Stephen's body glided easily with it. The silence continued. Finally, looking to fill the spaces around him, he pushed the cassette back in.

More miles passed. Loosening his seatbelt, he retrieved the sandwich. Careful not to take his eyes off the road, Stephen worked half of it out of its paper wrapping and held it above the steering wheel. At this late hour, he'd seen only one car so far, a pair of headlights passing him like the Devil himself was chasing after them. Nothing since.

Good.

Leaning against the steering wheel, he momentarily took his eyes from the road and speeding trees that gauged his passing to gaze up at the stars. But before he could think about the night sky above him and all of the brilliant pinpoints of lights, another moan from the trunk brought him back against his seat. He checked the rearview mirror. Nothing but blackness. Smiling again, he took a bite of the sandwich, feeling the texture of the two similar meats. The deli guy had done a good job slicing the tongue, but when he couldn't finish making the sandwich, he had taken over also doing a nice slicing job. He had plenty left over to put back into the glass fridge with…with…*what is his name?* "Oh yes," he whispered to himself as he envisioned the nametag that now stuck out of the remainder of the tongue. "Peter," he said out loud.

Yes, he thought, *Peter.* Such an easy name. He heard Peter again in the trunk of his car. He checked his rear-view mirror once more.

Nothing.

Stephen tossed the sandwich back onto the seat and pulled his seatbelt tight again. Squeezing the soda tight between his legs, he braced himself as he jammed on the brakes.

The tires screeched as the speedometer dropped from 40 mph to almost zero; the strain of the seatbelt tight across his chest. The Lincoln skidded to a stop, and the muffled moan from the trunk was replaced with a heavy thud.

Stephen waited a moment in the silence that followed. Leaning forward against the steering wheel, he angled his head, looking up at the stars. Everything was quiet. *Nice.* He sighed. *Such a beautiful night, so many points of light.* He cherished the moment. Sitting back, he looked at the black road stretched out ahead of him. The moment was short lived. He knew it was time to move on.

Bringing the Lincoln back up to speed, he loosened his seatbelt. Guided by the stars, Stephen traveled toward them, the full moon illuminating his way.

As the deer ran out of grass, the sound of yet another noisy light caught its ears. It stepped gingerly onto the road, its instincts now on mild alert. It knew it had to go to the other side of this hard space before the noisy light came any closer, or it had to wait until the noisy light was gone.

The deer stepped back from the road just as a branch snapped behind it. Another branch cracked off to its side and the deer's head flew in the direction of that sound. *A scent. Movement.* The frightened deer sprang forward onto the rock-hard clearing.

Its breath hot and its eyes wide, it whipped its head around at one more sound. This time from the dark clearing it was on. The bright noisy light was running quickly along it.

It now had a new fear.

Stephen saw the deer. It was out in the middle of the road. He pressed the gas pedal to the floor. It was his nature to do so.

The deer froze, trying to decide whether or not this noisy light thing actually saw it. Its nostrils flared wide, trying to get a scent in the night air, but nothing came. It turned its head away from the oncoming lights, its body tensed to spring. The safety of the woods was just ahead, but the speeding light separated the deer from the darkness leaving it with nowhere to go.

It was so close.

The deer was broadside to him, caught in the bright glare of the car's headlights. A puff of steam from its nostrils was high-lighted as it floated in the late autumn air. Stephen took in the small detail as he swerved the car sharply to catch the deer on the hindquarters.

He wanted it alive.

As the deer jumped, he hit it. In his mind's eye, the deer spun in mid-air, caught between light and dark, its body slamming into the side of his car, bouncing off. With its body broken, crushed, it skidded along the hard road, coming to a rest a few feet short of the woods. A flash, a single heartbeat; the image was preserved forever in him. Yet, with that heavy thud and jerk, all that he actually heard and felt was the screeching of his brakes as he whipped his car into a tailspin down the road.

The dented car stood still. The smell of burnt rubber wafted up from the abused tires. Stephen reached down to the floor-board for the Pepsi. It hissed as he opened it, as if in complaint. He took a long drink, but the soda didn't—couldn't—quench his thirst. Recapping the bottle, he let it fall from his hands. His heart beat heavily.

The deer lay there. Its front legs kicked and its head whipped around on the ground out of pain and fear for the thing that had done this to it. Its upper body twisted, heated breaths coming out of it like a steam locomotive barreling down the tracks. Stephen watched the bursts of steamed clouds and wondered if the deer knew that with each exploding breath, it came closer to its own death.

He ran his tongue over his lips. He was so thirsty, but it was a different thirst now. Wait, something told him.

Wait—

He felt a certain peace settling over him, a contentment in the scheme of things, a control over his life and others'. Within that sweet embrace, the night seemed deeper, the moon brighter, the stars more plentiful. It was a wonderful feeling.

The deer's struggling movements began to slow. Stephen revved the engine in his latest joy almost forgetting about The Society and his passenger in the trunk. Slipping the car into drive, he inched it forward, closing in on his helpless prey.

Stopping just short of the deer, he spotlighted the dying animal with the car's surviving headlight. Reaching under the seat for his knife, he watched as the animal continued its efforts to escape. He admired it for that, but for the moment he had to ignore the animal. Getting out of the car, he walked around to the rear and opened the trunk.

"Peter, wake up. It seems we've hit a deer. You must come and look." The body in the trunk didn't stir, but Stephen knew Peter was playing possum. Annoyed, he placed the knife down on the road, reached into the trunk, grabbed Peter by the hair, jerked his head back, and slapped him across the face. Peter's eyes shot open with pain and fear, and he tried to cry out. He managed nothing more than a sputtering moan. Stephen let Peter's head drop.

"Look at me, *Peee-ter*," Stephen ordered. "*Peee-ter*...show me those baby blues of yours. Come on Peter, show me those blues!" Weakly, Peter raised his head. "Good, that's better. Oh, by the way, name's Stephen. Pleasure to meet you."

Peter started to gag. He tried to spit something from his mouth, but found that he couldn't spit without his tongue. He tried to speak, but had trouble doing that too. The space where his tongue had been was extremely painful. His mind ran in circles trying to understand this nightmare, trying not to *believe* this nightmare. But there was no understanding it, and nothing else but to believe it. It was real. Peter started to cry.

"Now, now, Peter, that isn't necessary," Stephen said sympathetically. "I know it must hurt, just don't try to say anything." Stephen stroked Peter's hair as he checked the duct tape that held his wrists secure behind his back. He also checked the tape around his knees and ankles. Satisfied, Stephen stepped back.

"Peter, you're breathing so hard, I can see your breath. You must be cold. Need to get your circulation going. Here, let me help you out."

Grabbing Peter by the shoulders, he pulled the upper half of his body out of the trunk, wedging his legs. Easing him down, Stephen let him hang like a high jumper frozen backwards over the bar. Peter squirmed helplessly. A rush of blood filled his mouth, streaming down his face.

"Sorry it's so messy, but you know, Peter, how about a littlle music? Something classical maybe? Wait, be back in a moment." Stephen walked away whistling beethoven's Ninth. The Bee Gees came back to life. Interrupting his musical rendition, he yelled back. "I'm afraid I don't do it justice. hold on..." The harmonious voices of the chorus floated over in the starry night.

Peter heard the footsteps returning. Despite the pain, he whipped his head around looking for Stephen. No luck. The only thing he saw was the knife on the ground. He tried to angle his body, hoping to get his taped hands on the back of the bumper, freeing his legs. His fingertips had just touched the shiny metal when Stephen suddenly whispered in his ear.

"*Peee-ter.*" Peter froze, but his eyes slowly turned to Stephen. "Did you know it was based on a poem 'Ode to Joy' by a von Schiller?" Stephen asked. "It depicts an initial struggle with an adversity. Can you hear that?" Stephen paused, looking up at the stars. Letting out a sigh, he continued. "But don't be dismayed. When it concludes, it's with an uplifting vision of freedom and social harmony." Stephen looked back at Peter. "You know, I do have this *idea* about a gift," Stephen said. "Need your input."

Peter watched as Stephen reached over and picked up the knife turning the razor sharp edge toward him, fingertips lightly touching his neck. He understood the nightmare completely now. Angling his shoulder, he tried to protect the soft flesh of his neck. No luck.

Peter found that, even without his tongue, he could still scream.

The deer heard the strange cries. Its head thrashed about. The cries came to an abrupt end. All was silent. The deer was weak, exhausted, and laid its head back down on the road. A breeze whiffed along the black asphalt. Suddenly, its nostrils flared with a new scent. The deer slowly picked up its head again, the scent of blood overpowering. Its eyes grew wide. The deer saw something move toward it. Its instincts told it that it was next.

The gift on the passenger seat was the exact size of a head. As Stephen drove along the road, his single headlight flashed upon a sign. The white letters stood out briefly against the dark background.

Town of Tranquillity 1 mile
Population 1,635
Founded 1834

Leaving the sign and the bodies behind, Stephen continued his journey into the night. As the sound of the car died, silence held the area once again and the stars were as bright as they had ever been.

The Fat Cat—1994

Christian Lord and Nestor Diaz doubled back, watching the two and three-story brownstones alternate between sunlight and shade. The Brooklyn neighborhood was an equal mix of Hispanics, Whites, and African-Americans. The community had held steadfast like this for a number of years without adding another color to the face of it. In recent years, the only change had been the influx of Korean vegetable stores. The new immigrants worked long hours, keeping mostly to their own territories of twenty-four-hour stores. They sold their produce and the neighborhood gave them respect, but not too much acceptance. The first three races weren't ready to give in to another minority; there was an unspoken alliance among them. It was an understanding that covered a number of blocks before one or another race filtered in, holding domain. But all in all, it was a good mixture, a good neighborhood. Stable; only good things happened there. A balance all wanted to keep for as long as possible.

Things were about to change.

Sipping cups of hot coffee from a corner Korean store, Christian and Nestor overshot the address they were looking for by some thirty house numbers before they realized it.

"Hopper...Hopper?" Christian asked as they picked up the pace. "Would that be...*Dennis* Hopper?" The weather had been overcast for the last two weeks, but the sun was finally breaking through the gray clouds. Long, low, sharp shadows ran from building to building, covering each of them at a forty-five degree angle as if drawn by a draftsman's hand.

Nestor looked over at Christian. "Edward. *Edward* Hopper," he corrected. In his spare time, Nestor was a painter. Edward Hopper was his idol.

"Okay, *Edward*," Christian echoed. "So, now you're saying this is the type of neighborhood that you would catch Mr. Hopper in, painting away?" Christian grinned as he continued sipping his coffee. Both friends wore jackets as fashionable as their wrinkled ties.

"Sure. The light...the buildings...the color...the geometric design. It's all there. See?" Nestor pointed to a line of identical buildings, his voice growing earnest, excited. "Row after row of buildings breaking up the lines of light, and the lines of light breaking up the lines of the buildings." Edward Hopper was one of three people that could start Nestor's blood rushing. The other two were his wife, Gigi, and Christian. Nestor looked over at Christian. "*Yes...?*" he prompted. He knew what was coming. This had been going on for years.

"Oh, I don't know," Christian said with a smirk. Stopping short, he made a point of looking around at the buildings. "A fine Puerto Rican like yourself knowing all about the world of art. Amazing."

"I'm not Puerto Rican, I'm a Spaniard. My parents were born in Spain."

"Uh-huh."

"Uh-huh, *what?*" Nestor asked, pouring his coffee out along the curb. Christian did the same before falling back in step. Reaching over, Nestor took the empty cup from him, crumpling it. "Koreans can't make coffee worth a shit," he said, tossing the cups into an open garbage can in front of one of the houses. Coming to the street corner, they waited for the walk sign. There wasn't any traffic to be seen.

"I forget...where were you born again?" Christian asked, adjusting his shoulder holster underneath his jacket.

Nestor noticed the .45 caliber pistol. It concerned him, but he tried to play it off.

"Wiseass, you know where I was born." His voice a little uneasy now. "What number are we looking for, anyway?"

"Twenty-three. Light's green," Christian said, eyeing Nestor. "Now, where were you born? I didn't hear the answer before; must've been the noise of the traffic that's not here." He had been busting his friend's chops for years about this.

Nestor took a deep breath and let it out before answering. "My parents were on a cruise ship. I wasn't due for another two weeks—"

"Okay wait, the cruise ship docked in...*Puerto Rico?* And you were born *where?*" Christian started to look at the numbers. "Come on, four more houses," he said, pointing.

Nestor shook his head. "I'm an American of Spanish descent and proud of it! And besides that, I was named after my grandfather, God rest his soul." Nestor crossed himself as he spoke.

"Why do you do that?" Christian asked, perplexed.

"Do what?"

"Make the sign of the cross every time you mention your grandfather."

"Out of respect for the dead."

"Yeah, okay, but you said he never liked you."

"Still, respect for the dead."

"Any dead?"

Nestor thought for a moment. "Yeah," he said, "any dead."

"Hmmm, okay." Christian paused, quickly checking the house numbers. "All these years, didn't know that. But do you know what I do know?" The game was almost over.

"What? That my parents are Spaniards, and I'm Puerto Rican?"

"Finally got it right," he said. They slowed, stopping in front of a brownstone. "Here's the building, and I like 'Nighthawks' best." Christian added casually, turning to Nestor.

"Easy choice, everybody's favorite," Nestor replied. "Shows you know nothing of Hopper. So, this the place?" His demeanor was as casual as Christian's.

"Yeah. Not exactly something old Hopper would paint, is it?"

"No, but I would. And I *ain't* Puerto Rican." Both looked up at the building. "Coffee sucked," Nestor commented.

"Yeah, it was total shit, but they're nice people." Christian watched the windows at the top of the building. His mind was racing.

Light cut across the three-story building. Unlike the other buildings along the block, it had not aged well. Cracks ran through the façade's mortar like a maze, and stone-cut figures that had once been grotesque gargoyles and winged angels standing guard were now nothing more than rounded lumps beaten smooth by the changing seasons. Atop the building's steps, between the two first-floor windows, a metal "For Sale" sign hung, blistered with rust and held in place by two equally rusted screws. Across the "Call for Information" number, two illegible names were spray-painted in dripping red paint. Some of the paint ran over onto one of the windows, partially obscuring a fat cat fast asleep on the inside sill. Both of the first-floor windows were cracked, and like the windows on the second and third floors, heavily barred. The only thing that didn't look decrepit was the stained glass door.

"Yep, they are hard working gems, those Koreans," Nestor commented absentmindedly while studying the building with a painter's eye. "Just can't make coffee worth a shit." He paused, his mood changing, gears shifting. "He's up on the third?"

"Yeah, he's up there." Behind the bars, the third-floor windows were closed and draped in white. Christian cocked his head to one side as something caught his attention. He couldn't tell if it was a reflection off the glass or if a hand had moved a drape.

Nestor looked over at Christian. "What's this guy's name again?"

"Isaac," he answered. "A big, fat guy."

"Think he's watching us?"

"Don't know…I would be." Christian was trying to see if anything was moving in the windows again other than his imagination. "He knows we're here, though." It was almost a whisper, as if he was afraid that his voice would carry up the thirty feet to the window. Christian wondered who had tipped Isaac off. He had an idea, but kept it to himself. Reaching inside his jacket pocket, he pulled out his detective shield and clipped it to his breast pocket.

Nestor was still watching him.

He had been restless since Christian had called the night before. Gigi had picked up the phone, spoken briefly with Christian, and passed the phone on to him. She didn't ask him anything, and he didn't say. But Nestor knew the look on her face. That night, she had tossed and turned in her sleep. And now, as he caught another glimpse of the .45 under Christian's jacket, he knew this was all wrong. He needed to say something.

"How's your sister?" Nestor asked instead.

"Cecilia?" Christian continued to look up. "She's good. A little run-down lately, but good. Why?" Christian momentarily gave up on the windows and turned to Nestor.

"She's okay?" Nestor was genuinely concerned.

"Yeah, she has to have some blood tests, that's all." He knew Nestor wanted to say something. Christian's sister was the only other surviving member of his family, and the two of them were close.

"Hey, I hope she's okay."

"She'll be fine, she's a tough girl." Christian waited.

Nestor nodded. "Yeah…"

"Well?"

"What?"

"You're dying to say something."

"We have to talk, Christian." With that .45 snuggled under his partner's arm, Nestor knew Christian had no intention of arresting this guy.

"No," Christian disagreed. "We don't have to talk." He watched Nestor's face and knew exactly what was on his mind, but now was not the time for a pissing match. The time would, in fact, never be right. He turned back to the windows above. Christian was sure they were being watched. With the type of creature they were dealing with, there was no other way. He had to keep things moving.

"Thanks for asking about Cecilia, but I'm going in. You can come or not." Christian started up the steps. Nestor looked up and down the block, shook his head and followed.

Taking the steps slowly, Christian watched as the cat in the window stretched. It opened its eyes sleepily and, catching sight of him, quickly disappeared from the window, as if it knew this was a bad place to be now.

Coming to the door, Christian noticed that it looked like someone had tried to work it off its hinges. The weight of the door was off to one side and he had to lift up on the doorknob, pushing in with his shoulder to open it. It felt like someone was pushing back from the other side.

"Need help, old man?" Nestor asked, tapping his shoulder. Christian extended a single universal digit and shouldered the door one more time. It gave way, slamming against the wall. Christian stumbled, wincing in anticipation of the crash of breaking glass. But the door just hung on its hinges for a second, and, as they stepped into the small vestibule, started to close slowly behind them, sealing shut. Refracted sunlight from the stained glass bathed them in a kaleidoscope of colors.

"Feels like a colorful tomb," Christian commented surveying the entryway. Three numbered but nameless mailboxes hung on the wall to the right. Next to them was an intercom with three equally nameless buzzers. In front of them stood one more door.

"Yeah, not the biggest of spaces," Nestor agreed. "Here, allow me." Nestor slipped past Christian and tried the inner door. It was locked. "I guess buzzing ourselves in is out of the question?"

As he smiled at Christian, the door buzzed, catching him off guard. The two cops looked at each other.

"Don't like this…" Nestor said, keeping his hand on the doorknob. He waited, and when the buzzer went off once more, he turned the knob quickly. The door opened easily as the buzzer continued to sound.

"Seems we're being invited," Christian remarked as they stepped in. The buzzer echoed off the walls like a bee caught in a glass jar.

Christian slipped the .45 from his holster and slid back the slide, chambering a round as Nestor clipped his shield to his breast pocket, pulling his .38 from his waistband. The door closed behind them, muffling the buzzing.

Nestor looked back at the door. "That was a little too easy," he said, shaking his head. Christian knew he was right, but kept silent.

The lobby was small, with a staircase leading to the upper floors occupying most of the space. Off to the right of the stairs, the door to the first floor apartment blended into the wall. The only illumination came from a lone bulb over the base of the stairs that was buried in a small, tasteless chandelier layered like a six-tier wedding cake. The light it gave off was weak, confined to the chandelier itself.

Christian's eyes wandered up along the staircase. A threadbare carpet covered them as they took a left turn a few steps up. The finish on the wooden banister was worn smooth, and Christian could envision Isaac's hand moving along the banister not trusting himself on the steps without support. *Large. Slow moving. Dangerous.* But he didn't think that Isaac had traveled that much lately.

He looked toward the first-floor apartment door. He had noticed a musty odor when they had first entered. It was heavy, settled, well entrenched. It hung in the air reminding him of old clothing in an attic with nothing more than the aroma of deteriorating mothballs wrapping around them. It was elderly; something waiting to die, something watching itself decay.

"You smell that, Nestor?" he asked.

Nestor was quiet for a moment. "Yeah; this ain't good. We should call Martinez."

He walked over to the apartment door and ran his finger across it. A line cut through the dirt and dust. Shaking his head, he held up his finger for Christian to see. "We should call Martinez," Nestor advised again.

Ignoring the suggestion, Christian nodded toward the brass doorknob. It was rubbed shiny. "I wonder what the cat eats?" He knew he was playing his partner, but it was necessary.

Nestor looked down, not touching it. The buzzer finally fell silent. Both men glanced at the outside door. In the silence, Nestor pleaded with him.

"*Christian? Martinez…?*"

Christian wheeled on him, whispering hoarsely. "*Fuck Martinez!*"

Nestor looked at the .45 and back to Christian. He stepped in closer to his friend. "Christian, what are we doing?" Nestor knew something was spinning out of control here.

"Our jobs, that's what we're doing!" Christian no longer whispered.

Nestor shook his head. "No, Christian. No, we're not."

"Nestor," Christian stepped in closer as if sharing a secret, "he takes *children,* Nestor. *Little people.*" They stood nose-to-nose, like two kids in a staring contest. Nestor blinked first, bringing up his .38.

"Thanks." Christian turned around, starting up the staircase. The stairs squeaked loudly with each step.

"Good thing we're sneaking up on him," Nestor said.

"Yeah, well…" Christian began to move up the steps faster, and Nestor picked up the pace of his own squeaky steps.

The third-floor landing was damp, dark. The odor from the lobby drifted up, mixing with a stronger, pungent smell. There was no covering it. Neither man said anything about it. They faced a spotless apartment door. Christian fought the urge to touch it.

"*Hey, you know this is all wrong,*" Nestor's voice whispered over his shoulder like a guardian angel. "This whole case is Martinez's…and I won't even bring up the idea of a *warrant* or anything legal like that."

"I thought we had this!" Christian shot back impatiently. "This is *our* break; we can use this. I got the tip, and we're taking it." He brought his .45 up. Turning to Nestor, he cocked his head to one side, bringing a finger up to his lips. "*Shhhhh*...Nestor, did you hear that? Cries for help. Screw the fucking warrant!"

Nestor rolled his eyes. "Okay, okay, disregarding *voices* in your goddamn head," he said in a whisper, "kids or not, I still don't figure this tip of yours. You never said who—"

Christian's voice was hard. "*Hey*, it ain't important now, so shut up and let's do this, okay? I *want* this one! Look the *fuck* around, Nestor, are we here? You want to go home now and leave whatever he does in there? "

"You got a tip...or you took the tip?" Nestor asked pointedly.

Christian said nothing and turned back to the door. Nestor knew that when his partner got like this, there was no talking to him. He held his .38 high and looked over the banister to make sure there wasn't anyone coming up the stairs.

"Yeah, yeah, sure," Nestor said, turning back. "With you, it ain't like I'm gonna have a career left or anything. Me and Gigi, go on welfare or some shit." He shook his head and sighed. "Okay, nothing on the squeaky stairs, but this place gives me the creeps."

Christian nodded to him and they moved to opposite sides of the door. Taking hold of the doorknob, Christian tried to twist it. He shook his head.

Nestor gestured with his gun. "On three?"

"Three sounds like the number. Who kicks?"

"I'll kick," Nestor said. "Who yells *Police*? "

"No one. He knows we're here and the fuck knows who we are."

"Uh-huh...on your three—"

Christian held up his fist, hesitating. He looked back over at Nestor. Gun high, Nestor gave him a slight nod. *Good cop*, Christian thought, *but he always holds his gun too high. Blocks his line of sight.* He knew it was something to do with his left eye being dominant.

"Your gun is too high. Rest it on your big belly," he whispered to him.

"Fuck you. Go low, you emaciated prick." Nestor winked at his partner with his dominant eye and grinned. They had known each other off and on since the academy and were partners going on five years now.

Christian was a natural athlete. Graceful and muscular but lean, with dark serious eyes that took the warmth from his face. The sharp angles of his face gave it a hard look that was seldom broken by a smile. At thirty-three, his short brown hair was already starting to pepper itself with gray. Breaking five feet, nine inches, he stood an inch shorter then Nestor.

An ex-Golden Glover, Nestor had the look and grace of a pit-bull. His face showed the results of his opponent's gloves that, even at thirty-five, had never healed properly. His last three fights had seen his nose broken as many times, leaving it decidedly favoring his right. His years of being pounded had also lain his ears flat against his head, as if they had been beaten down into submission. Nestor's features were rounded, eroded. The green of his eyes softened them even more. The only thing sharp about him were his movements. He moved like he was still in the ring; each movement had a calculated look about it as if he was coming in for the knockout punch. The last nose-breaking fight had told him that his career was elsewhere. He joined the police force as soon as it healed. Together, Nestor and Christian hunted their criminal prey with a vengeance.

Christian nodded to his partner and turned to the door once again. He felt he was about to enter a new life. All of this was for Katie. She brought meaning to his life, a peace that he had never known before. He wanted a future with her, and this case, this break, could be the beginning they needed. With or without that asshole Martinez, he was moving with the information he had. This was more than a career maker. This had to be done.

His first two fingers went up one at a time. As the third was about to, a dull noise echoed from within the apartment; they froze. Nestor looked uneasily at his partner. Christian shrugged and on a whim, reached across and gently pushed the door. Giving way, the door opened a crack.

Light streamed out of the opening, cutting a sharp path into the poorly lit hall. It was as if he had opened a doorway to somebody's backyard on a bright sunny day. Christian almost expected the smells of sizzling hamburgers and chicken to whiff by, accompanied by the sounds of joyous children. *But no, not this time...not the smells, not the joyous voices.* He knew with Isaac, it would be a childless cookout. Isaac had other uses for children.

He looked over to Nestor and shook his head. The door had been locked a moment before, and now it was open, daring them. Christian felt the control slipping away. They weren't being invited in, they were being told.

Christian squatted as Nestor pointed to his eyes. Christian nodded and they quickly swung their guns around into the apartment, peeking over them. Just as quickly, they jerked their heads back. Christian spoke up first.

"See them?"

"Yeah."

"I saw six, maybe seven...one on a cross. Isaac?"

Nestor was a little shaken. "No, no fat man, just them and the black door. I'll cover the door." His fingers readjusted themselves over his weapon. It was a nervous habit.

Christian was wary. "You okay with this?"

"Yeah, I'm okay now. Let's do it." His hands were calm. Quickly he made the sign of the cross.

"For who?" Christian inquired. Nestor didn't say.

Reaching across, Christian pushed the door. It swung smoothly in, light pouring out, blanketing the rest of the hall. Nestor counted again and, on three, with guns pointing, both cops moved into the bright light of the apartment.

The sunlight on the weatherbeaten brownstone had shifted; the building was slowly being drawn deeper into the shadows, the big cat blending into the grayness. It had taken up its post once again, peering from the first-floor window. A black couple carrying some groceries made their way down the block, the cat's eyes trailing them until they passed from sight. Giving a little stretch, it settled into sleep. Suddenly, there was a muffled report of gunfire from the inside of the building, and the cat disappeared from its window.

Dull booms sounded from the third-floor apartment. A shattered window suddenly rained glass down onto the street. Sharp cracks of gunfire now erupted from the apartment, echoing through the neighborhood. A curtain-wrapped body slammed through the wooden window frame and against the metal bars. The bars held for a second before they pulled loose from the crumbling stone. From within the apartment, Nestor's voice cried out.

"Christian!"

The body fell from shadow into sunlight of the once-quiet neighborhood, adding another sound. It was a sound that a melon might make bursting open on the hard concrete, scattering its soft insides and seeds. To this, Nestor added one more cry.

"Christian!"

The Dream

The dream came and went, seemingly with a will of its own. Sometimes it would end as soon as it began, only to pick up at the point it had left off to continue its journey through the night...

"Shhhhh," she said. "You cried out. You were dreaming again."

"Sorry I woke you," he replied, concerned.

"'Tis nothing. You talked in your sleep, too."

"Did I now?"

"Yes."

"What did I say?"

"You said, 'He forgives you.' "

"Strange thing for a man to say."

"'Tis," she agreed. "Who is he?"

"I don't know." Confusion replaced concern.

"Were they there?"

"Yes."

"Strangely dressed?"

"Yes." He sounded troubled.

"How many this time?"

"Too many."

"Come then, try to get back to sleep. In time, it will pass."

"I don't know. I cannot be sure of that."

"Then sleep," she said...

Necessities—Present Day

Mondays were the pits. After a weekend of staying up late clubbing and then sleeping equally late to catch up on those lost hours only to have to wake up to all of this mess again, she hated to go to work on Mondays. Even worse was coming home to the mess after work. It invoked a feeling of guilt that had been instilled in her long ago by her mother about doing the 'necessities of life.' Those 'necessities of life,' as her mother so adamantly called them, stayed with her the whole week; she would wash only what was needed to go out in and live with the guilt of what was left dirty until that item was needed.

Well, it'll all be over soon, she thought, the guilt lessening with each shake of her head. Joey was moving in and her tiny Manhattan studio was about to become smaller. Now she would have to clean up her act. *Damn!* She knew he had his own way of doing things. She hoped that this wasn't going to be too hard, but the fact that Joey's friends had dubbed him *Mr. Clean* worried her. She loved him, or at least she thought she did. She really wasn't too sure. But maybe if living together worked out, she wouldn't feel so lonely. She was sure that whatever love she might lack would develop during the time they spent together. Besides, hadn't her mother always told her that one of the necessities of life was learning to love when there was no other choice? And hadn't she further told her that such things took time, and effort, and that the necessities of life weren't necessarily easy?

She sighed. She had to admit, Joey did fill a lot of time in her life. Maybe *that* was what love was about—filling in the blanks. *Is that really it?* Maybe her mother was right. She really wasn't sure, but she knew that he did keep her busy, and keeping busy passed the time. He'd even managed to start her jogging. God, if anybody had told her before that she would be out running around, sweating and smelling like who-knew-what, she would have laughed in their face. But what was really strange was that she'd begun to enjoy it. And, what's more, she seemed to have more energy since she'd started to run. And her sex life! *Talk about the necessities of life!* She grinned, knowing that if her mother ever found out she thought like that, she'd fall over dead!

Letting out a giggle, she flopped back on her bed. Overhead, she saw the spider-web cracks in the ceiling. *Damn, needs paint or something.* She quickly looked at her watch. It was getting late. She definitely wasn't going to do anything about the ceiling tonight—or any night, for that matter. And if she didn't get up now, she wouldn't make it out of this damn hot apartment, either. God, she hated Mondays. At least work was over.

Sitting up, she tied her sneaker and wondered if she could make it all the way around the track that circled the Central Park Reservoir. She had almost completed a full lap the other evening, but the summer heat took its toll, and she had walked the last few hundred yards. Tonight, though, it'd be different. She was determined to make Joey proud. She had had that special feeling all day at work that something would happen tonight.

Tonight will be it.

Falling back on her bed, she lay amid the guilt of the dirty laundry from the past week. *Feels sooooo good,* she thought. The temptation to stay home was strong, but...*the hell with it, I'll run tonight and make it around that damn reservoir and call in sick tomorrow and clean up this mess!* She sighed. *If that's not good enough for Mr. Clean, he's welcome to do the cleaning. Maybe he'll even paint the ceiling!*

Dragging herself off the bed, she spilled some of the guilt onto the floor. Leaving the clothes there, she grabbed her canister of Mace from the top of her cluttered bureau. At night she always took it with her—just in case. She found it annoying to run with, but Joey had insisted that she take it. Mimicking him, she spoke out loud: *"If you have to run at night, at least take some protection with..."* Hearing herself, she stopped. Whether it was out of guilt or because she felt foolish, she didn't know. He always worried about her. Maybe *that* was love. Still, she wished that he wouldn't be so bossy and set in his ways.

Holding onto the small canister, she gave her apartment one last look and wondered for the thousandth time how the two of them were going to fit into this space.

It will work…it has to.

A pang of fear and doubt swept over her. Closing the door behind her, she leaned against it. *Necessities.* She let out a long sigh. *Shit! Maybe Mom was right. Maybe it's all a learning process.* She tried to come up with some other insight, but failed.

Muted voices, arguing, worked their way down the hall from the last apartment.

Learning process?

"Okay," she said out loud, and made her way out of the building and along the few blocks to the reservoir.

The Track and the Seagull

A heavy mist hung over the track and reservoir, absorbing the fleeing light. Restless seagulls, wings spread wide, rode on currents of air that couldn't be seen or felt from the ground. Occasionally, a cry from a gull would travel out, echoing off the flat surface of the water, when the bird would suddenly dive, shattering the illusion of its suspended animation of flight. Just barely touching the surface of the dark reservoir, it would pull back up into the air currents that held it, to hang there, to wait. Below these waiting birds, the few joggers that remained made their way around the calm water. Most ran only their minimum distance and left the damp, growing darkness for home.

One figure, though, remained on the track. He moved along the darkening surface, waiting, wanting. He heard the gulls above, but he would not look up at them. He knew they were watching, also waiting. He loved the way they would suddenly cry out. Soon, he knew, another cry would carry out into the night. But that would be just for him. He smiled in anticipation of it.

As he walked along the track, he wasn't alone. One other figure moved, hidden even from the prying eyes of the gulls. The figure that followed him worked its way effortlessly through the trees and bushes that ran adjacent to the track, a dark shadow to the man matching his movements. He also waited and wanted. Both moved in tandem. Both had a purpose. Only one would live.

Coming to the graveled track, she thought about going home. The moisture made her jogging outfit cling to her like a second covering of skin. A chill ran through her body. God, she hated Mondays!

The track seemed empty, but remembering Joey's warning, she held onto the Mace canister tightly. Ahead of her, the track was a patchwork of dim yellow lights thrown out by the aged streetlamps. During the day, they looked quaint, but for some reason she couldn't fathom, stretched along the track tonight they seemed...spooky.

Go home! A voice in her head cried out. She turned and looked at the track behind her. *Spooky.* She turned back. She knew she was being silly. It was just the idea of covering all of that distance alone—that was all. But everything looked so far away, spooky or not. She sighed. Maybe she should just tell Joey that she had made it all the way around the track. She could, but...no. If she lied and he somehow caught her, he'd be pissed. Besides, lying wasn't a good way to start a lasting relationship. God, She *really* hated Mondays!

Taking a deep, damp breath, she decided she just needed to move, to get going. Foregoing her usual stretching, she started out along the track. Slowly, her worries dissolved. The patchy darkness didn't seem as threatening as her body traveled into it pace by pace.

As she cut through the thick mist, the moisture began to weigh her down. She knew she wasn't in the mood for this, and kept wiping at the droplets of water on her face. *Shit! Should've stayed home!* Taking deeper breaths, she tried to quicken her pace to complete her run as soon as possible.

As she ran, she tried to visualize the way Joey had explained running to her: *Think of making the distance in front of you shorter and the distance behind you longer. You won't get bored this way. You just have to set a goal in your mind.* She quietly laughed at his advice. Sometimes she just didn't understand him. Instead, she watched the dark outlines of the seagulls overhead. She couldn't remember seeing them this late in the evening before. They looked as though they were watching her, waiting for her to do something stupid so they would have a reason to cry out.

It was in the silence of the watching gulls and the darkness of the track that she first heard the running steps behind her. Looking over her shoulder, she saw a lone runner emerge out of the grimy blackness into the light of one of the old streetlamps. He was lit for a moment, the yellow light cast down painting him sickly, jaundiced, before he disappeared back into the darkness, only to reappear once again in the light of the next lamp, closer, faster.

She turned away from him. She couldn't stop her heart from matching the pounding pace of his steps. Holding her Mace ready, she stopped running, edging herself along the chain-link fence that surrounded the reservoir. A light breeze whiffed across the surface of the water, making her body shiver. His steps were getting louder, their pace quicker, blending into one sound. She found her chills suddenly replaced with a cold fear.

Loose bits of gravel crunched against each other, the noise building around her until it seemed to echo off the dark surface of the water. Her heart hammered against her chest. She couldn't take the sound of the runner's steps anymore. She turned, her eyes catching the movement of the runner just in time to see him fly by her without a word. From above, a gull's short cry made her jump. The gull's outburst sounded like *"jerk,"* and she had to suppress a nervous giggle.

Hearing the footsteps recede, she turned toward the sound again. This time it was to watch the runner disappear and reappear between light and dark as finally the darkness gave him cover.

"Oh shit," she nervously mumbled, a hand over her pounding heart. "Oh shit." She flopped against the fence, the metal mesh squeaking like a bed. She took a deep breath, and her heart began to slow. *A good scare's good for the cardiovascular system...oh shit!* She let out another nervous laugh at her own expense. It was more like a drawn out sigh of relief. She shook her head.

Feeling calmer now that she was alone again, she let go of her brief fears. Pushing off the fence, she gave her legs a stretch, buying some time. Straightening up, she looked down the track.

No one.

She started to run in place.

No one.

The track lay ahead of her.

Not even the sound of his steps.

She was alone again. All she had to do was make it from one island of light to the next. That's all.

"Jerk," she said out loud. *You're right, bird,* she thought, and resumed her run.

As she ran, she couldn't help comparing herself to the other runner. She envied his kick. He was obviously a dedicated runner and thought her behavior a little strange. *Jerk!* It *had* sounded like that. She looked up as she ran, wondering where that shit bird was anyway. The sky was empty.

Her body fell into a rhythm, and she stopped watching the sky for something she could no longer see. Instead, her eyes dropped down to watch her thigh muscles as they snapped taut, her weight traveling from leg to leg, each step bringing her closer to the end of her run. Pleased with how quickly the track was passing below her feet now, she started to feel better. She was thinking that, in fact, her legs looked pretty damn good.

Then she slammed into someone.

It felt as if she had hit a brick wall. The sudden impact jolted her backwards onto her ass, knocking the Mace canister from her hand. She found herself looking up at the runner in front of her. He stood just on the edge of the light that washed down from one of the old streetlamps, silent, still.

Fucking rude. I'm not the jerk here, she thought. Quickly her thoughts were replaced with a feeling that he seemed to be waiting and somehow he just didn't look *right.* His face seemed to be too soft to be on a body that carried him the way he ran—if that was him at all. It had the look of being incomplete, almost fetal. But that wasn't really it, she knew. There was something else she couldn't put her finger on. She reached for her Mace and started to get up. He still didn't move. She shook her head. *Just fucking rude!*

Straightening up, she started to apologize nonetheless. "I'm sorry, I didn't see you," she said, wiping away some of the wet dirt that stuck to her shorts. Suddenly, that foolishness turned into surprise and that surprise into fear as the runner quickly moved behind her, grabbing her around the neck and snapping her head back. She heard her neck bones crack against each other, the pain shooting through her like an electrical charge. But the pain also brought up a burst of anger, and her hand with the Mace flew up, pointing it over her shoulder. Pressing down on the trigger, a thin stream of liquid shot out and his grip on her loosened. Throwing her body against his, she felt him crash into the fence, and she broke free. Stepping away, she rubbed the back of her neck staring in disbelief. Her attacker lay against the fence, his hands over his eyes.

"What're you, fucking crazy?" she screeched, and kicked at him. *"Fucking bastard!"* And she swung her hand, slapping him across his face, knocking one of his hands away. She went to strike again, when he turned toward her. Her hand froze in midair, and she slowly took a step back.

His face had taken on a look different than what she had seen before. It was as though he had a reason for being now, as if she had given him a purpose. She could have sworn she saw a dark shadow glide across his face.

A flap of wings over her head. A sound, an echo, a cry. Steps behind her.

She twisted her head over her shoulder, almost crying out from the pain that stabbed at the bones in her neck. Her hand flew back up, her fingers digging in to her neck. The dark shadow blended back among the trees. Silence. Suddenly, the stillness was broken with a curse.

She quickly turned back. Her hand dropped to her side and her anger fled as the panic hit her. She heard him curse at her again. She backed away from him as his mouth was forming the words a third time. Pivoting on her feet, she started to run hearing him cry out, calling her a *"Motherfucking bitch!"* With those words, her panic was complete. She ran blindly along the track, her mind and body taking the path of least resistance. Hearing nothing but the pounding fear of her heart, she blocked out all sensations except the awareness of running as she tried to put as much distance as possible between her and her attacker.

With each fearful step, her body seemed heavier, losing all gracefulness as it slammed into the track. Spiking jolts of pain ran along her neck. Her mind registered nothing but the sound of her feet crushing into the gravel trying to develop a pace. As the sound of her rhythm finally broke through, it was taken over by the sound of other footsteps pushing aside the gravel at a frighteningly faster pace. Her running, her mind, never wandered from the dark path she was following. All that mattered to her now was the distance. And in her panic, she measured that distance with each step she took.

Willing her tired legs to stretch out faster, farther, she was violently snapped from those thoughts as a mental image of her body still running played ahead of her. She saw herself run from the light and into the sanctuary of the dark, safely disappearing. But instead of running now, she felt a slight floating sensation. She was weightless. *Strange.* And for a beat of her heart, the ground and sky were mixed, horizons twisted. A quick rhythmic contraction, and the ground slammed into her, knocking out what little breath her lungs held.

"*Motherfucking bitch! You're about to pay for that!*" The words were screamed above her.

Fighting for air, she tried to get up, but the kick caught her square in the face, shattering her capped teeth and breaking her nose. The pain was instant, overwhelming. Her lungs desperately searched for the air that was all around her, but she couldn't seem to draw a breath. As her body fought itself, she became dimly aware that she was being dragged off the graveled path and into the bushes by one arm. She tried getting up, but she couldn't get her legs underneath her. Suddenly, she felt her arm drop, and she lay there, her lungs still seeking a breath.

She clutched her face, blood pouring from her nose; his hands tearing at her shorts, ripping her T-shirt. The cold, wet grass and rocks bit into her soft flesh, making her squirm, the movement of her body sending spikes of pain throughout her face and head. The sharp awakening of her nerves forced her lungs to finally take in the air.

Her first breath was an explosion of pain as she tried to breathe through a swollen nose and mouth. As her breaths came back in labored efforts, the coppery taste of her own blood assaulted her first. Then she became aware of him. She felt herself being pushed back along the ground with each thrust. Reaching down, her bloody fingers came into contact with his hardness, confirming the fear that her mind in its confusion of pain didn't want to face. She started to push at the panting figure, but stopped when she felt the sharp edge of the metal along her throat.

"Yeah, that's my knife." She heard the voice drift sweetly out of him. "You fight and I'll hurt you more. It's very simple. You want it like that?" As he spoke, the thrusting stopped and she thought she felt him grow small, giving her hope that it was over.

Her hope was dashed as his own fears and doubts touched him and he quickly resumed his movements. He pressed the knife into the side of her throat, knowing the fear that it would produce. And that fear made it close...*so close*. He started to talk to her, keeping his mind aware of the power he had over this bitch, over this Godawful thing beneath him.

"Can you *feel* it?" he asked. "It's close, *oh... so... close.* Can you feel it all?" *Yes*, he thought, *it is very close.* He longed to finish. His eyes began to close, giving into the anticipated moment.

She tried to hide from the sound of his sickening voice and the way his body slapped against hers. She needed a place to escape to, to run to. Feeling the pressure of the knife, she forced her head against the wet ground, waiting for it to be over.

She winced; the skin on her face felt taut as if, with any sudden expression, it would burst apart. Hearing his breathing, his voice above her, she wished for any other sound, and strained to hear the seagulls to take herself away, but there was nothing. *Nothing but that voice.* It seemed fouler than the act itself.

"*It's close...you know. Can you...understand what that...means?*" The voice now sounded childish to her, the question almost silly. Carefully, she turned her head toward him, and he relieved some of the pressure of the knife. His face looked incomplete once again, even worse now that his eyes were almost closed. *Like a corpse*, she thought. She looked beyond him, tried to take her mind elsewhere again. It was then that she thought she saw another figure step out of the darkness behind him. She squirmed, trying to get a better look, and the rapist took that as meaning something else.

"Yeah...sure...that's it. It's close, isn't it?" She squirmed once again. "Oh so very...*close*," he whispered. She pushed up against him, trying to see that figure, that one hope.

"*Yeah...see?*" he asked, almost forgetting she was there. "*See...*" He thought about all the others. They always came to him at this moment, his moment. They came with *their* sharing. They came with *his* sharing. They were there with him now. He could see their faces. Hear their voices. Hear their cries. Their cries of never wanting him. They screeched through his mind crying out against him. *It isn't fair. It isn't right. It isn't my fault.* He buried his face in her neck, the knife touching his flesh, touching hers. They were close, so close. They screamed at him. But it wasn't his fault...he could feel his tears, feel theirs. He could see them. See them now. He spoke to them.

"*Seeee...Seeee...?*"

She felt the warm words against her neck, and indeed she did see the figure behind him. He was close, so close. He reached out a hand to her. Out of nowhere, her own hand appeared, her fingertips touching his. She felt the warmth of them. A warmth that tingled through her more than that of any lover she had ever had, ever known. Their fingertips pressed hard against each other. *Close. Oh, so close,* she thought. She stretched out her hand further.

Something caught her eye. *Shiny.* She saw the figure bring up his other hand, something in it. *Sharp. Close.* He was close. She saw the knife in his hand, saw her hope.

Kill him... she wanted to scream out. But he dropped his hand away from hers. The tips of her fingers suddenly felt icy cold as she watched him drop back into the shadows.

Kill him, please...please... "Kill him," she mouthed.

"*Kill him!*" She screamed as the shadow blended back into the trees.

"*For God's sake! Kill him!*" Gone.

As she cried out, her attacker's voice choked and his eyes squeezed tight. He suddenly pushed himself upright, his hand flashing across her throat as he exploded his foulness into her, matching the expulsion of her heated blood from her opened neck. The richness of it hit him in the face, on his chest, and dripped down onto his hardness warming him, turning her cold. Muscles jerked as the two bodies, caught in the midst of life and death, clawed at each other, emptying themselves, their wills drained. All thoughts of before, the pain and the pleasure, ebbed, leaving nothing. Brief movements, brief moments passed. The voices silent. The cries gone.

He fell back onto her, spent. They lay there; one body panting, filling its lungs with short hurried breaths of life, the other turning colder with its own blood gone, limbs giving off small lifeless twitches before its mind fell into a final false sleep.

Sitting up from her, blinked away the blood that dripped down his face. But before he lost the moment, his hand shot out, grabbing her breast. Slippery with blood, he pulled at the nipple. With a swift, practiced movement, he took his souvenir.

Without looking back down at her, he got up, fixed his running shorts, and placed his souvenir down inside the front of them. Closing his eyes, he could still feel her warmth. Walking back up to the track, he pocketed his knife as the mist finally turned into rain.

Placing a hand over his groin, he started to run slowly, the blood mixing with the rain, running in pink rivulets down his body. Picking up his pace, he looked down at his groin, squeezed it and started to laugh. Just as he raised his head, he slammed into someone.

Off-balance, he felt himself take a step backward. He tried to take another step, but *something* held him in place. He looked at the person. There was an instant of surprise and recognition. He tried to speak, but found he couldn't say anything. His body shivered. A combination of chills and warmth ran down the front of him. Dropping his head, he saw the hand and the hilt of the knife protruding from his gut. Pain suddenly exploded in him. The hilt was angled up, and he threw

both of his arms around his attacker, trying to ease the pain by
taking his weight off the knife.

"*That's it…can you feel it? Can you feel it all?*" He heard the
whisper in his ear as he felt himself being walked over toward
the bushes. He tried to walk up on his toes to ease the pain
and fear of the knife angled into his gut, but he slipped and
the knife pushed in a little deeper. He knew that he was dying.
So did his attacker.

"Oh no, no…not yet. You're not leaving me yet. We
have a long, long night ahead of us." He felt the heated
breath of the voice speak directly into his ear. "A long and
stormy night…and we're not even *close!*" The bushes swallowed them, giving some relief from the rain. "Here, I picked
this space out just for you. I even have some things for us
here. Let me help now."

He felt himself being laid down on the cold ground.
With a small twist, the knife was withdrawn, taking something of his insides with it. He cried out into the night, the
sound of his pain echoing in the dark. It was a sound that
he had never expected to hear leaving his own lips. Quickly,
a hand covered his mouth, muffling the cry as his own hands
tried to hold in what had been ripped from him.

"Shhhh, shhhh, it's night… you'll wake the dead! Hush
now!" He felt the weight of the body above him, the hand
firmer on his mouth. He kept still. It helped with the pain.

"There, that's better, isn't it…*Louis?* I'm right, aren't I?
It is, *Louis?* You know you've missed a few meetings. But
this isn't about that." Louis felt the weight over him shift
again. He had trouble breathing with the hand over his
mouth.

"Nothing to say? Bit of a shocker isn't it? The pain, I mean.
Hard to find the words for it, don't you think?" Louis looked
up at the dark figure of Stephen. Stephen took his hand away
from his mouth.

Working quickly, Stephen pressed a knee against the rapist's
stomach. Louis doubled up from the searing pain and tried to
push Stephen's knee away, his arms straining. Stephen smiled
at the reaction. With his own practiced motion, he slashed
deep across Louis' biceps, severing the muscles. Louis cried

out, but Stephen hit him with two swift and hard punches and he went limp. Taking his time now, he grabbed Louis' hands, wrapping a thick plastic tie around his wrists. Once done, he lightly slapped Louis's face.

"Louis...Louis, my man, are you with me?" Louis began to stir. Stephen pinched Louis' lower lip, pulling it. "Louis," he said, "this may hurt a little bit, but did you know they can do this with laser now?"

And then Louis felt the knife starting to do things again.

Lightning flashed, lighting up the sky, showing the gulls that still hung high above the waters. Thunder clapped down with a roar just as the lightning died, and the birds disappeared into the darkness again. The gulls, too late for the woman, broke out of their silence and cried against the rain that poured down on them. Somewhere on the dark earth below them, there were laughter and, finally, more screams. But the gulls didn't understand them.

Mr. Simon's Classroom

Hunched over, Mr. Simon paced.

The attic was a mosaic of peeling paint. With an array of skylights, it was well-lit, and Mr. Simon welcomed the light. During the hot summer months, the greenhouse effect would speed up the process of peeling. Mr. Simon didn't mind; he liked looking at the peeling paint. He liked the heat, too. Sometimes for hours he would watch the tiny peaks of paint cast their shadows across the wall as the sun gave way to the motion of the earth. The colors of the different layers of paint changed with the light, lending an illusion of movement, of life. At times he actually saw his room as a kind of chameleon going from color to color; a body that knowingly touched upon certain parts of the spectrum absorbing those colors like a sponge. And Mr. Simon knew a chameleon was life that used the light to expose its true properties.

Hunched over, Mr. Simon paced.

Chameleon or not, deep down, Mr. Simon also knew his room just reflected the remnants of the colors of his life. Much of the time, they were vague colors, reflecting vague thoughts. But he was working on that. He did understand that there was a symbiotic relationship of some sort within his four-walled world, between his light, his room, and his students. *Some sort.* So he kept careful watch over these elements.

The landscape he held domain over was one of desolation in miniature, an upheaval of painted sediments that gave witness, layer by layer, to the room's previous occupants. It was much like the layers of an onion. Much like the layers of one's personality. Much like the layers of skin, of flesh, down to the bones of one's body, into the very marrow of things. All could be exposed by the properties of the consuming light, one way or another. Mr. Simon knew that because of the light, he was insane. But for him, that was normal.

He stole a glance at the man seated in the room's only chair. Mr. Simon had found him as he was driving the highways that surrounded his affluent community, with its manicured lawns and polite people. The man had been standing by one of the entrance ramps, his thumb pointed into the flow of traffic. The sun was just going down, and Mr. Simon had been surprised to find one of his old students so close to home. He took that as a good omen. Usually, he had to drive well into the night and for some distance before he came upon any of them. Sometimes, he found no one at all.

At times, they were elusive and succeeded in hiding from him. Mr. Simon thought that this man might have tried to hide from him all of these years, but, there he was, big as life. And just like the rest of his students, this man couldn't hide forever. Mr. Simon turned away from the seated man.

Hunched over, he paced.

He tried to take a deep breath, but his body was wrapped tight in its shrunken skin leaving no room for air. He looked back at the man. His name escaped him, but that was all right. The man had grown to be quite good-looking, not that he had any *sexual* interest in him. That would have been disgusting and wrong. He had always been careful about that. But the man *was* good-looking. The years had been kind. Now, the warm glow of the sunset embraced him. Unfortunately, unlike a chameleon, the man absorbed nothing of this light.

Shame, Mr. Simon thought. This was some of the day's best light. Soft, quiet, with nothing burning—yet.

As the last of the sun's rays finally disappeared, Mr. Simon stopped pacing. He watched the bare bulb over his newly found student begin to burn. He had rigged the artificial light to a timer, set to come on when the sun disappeared for the night. With the rightful light gone, the man changed his color once again. The light from the bulb was weak, flawed, motionless. Yet the man seemed to absorb this false light, and by this act, murdered any life that he might have had a chance to show before. *It is wrong, all wrong*, Mr. Simon thought.

The man had been in the chair for two days now. And for two days, Mr. Simon had watched the light pass over him. But the light just hadn't been right. *Tomorrow...? Maybe.* If so, another flickering light would absorb the sitting man, changing him like a chameleon—just like he had changed.

Mr. Simon started to pace, but something stopped him. He remembered having conversations with a group of men about their victims being chance encounters. He couldn't see how that applied, though. His work was different now. He had chosen this man, like the others, for his chameleon-like quality. It was that quality that made the animal, made them, pretend to be something they weren't in order to survive. *Smart, very smart.* He admired that, but saw through it. Mr. Simon's job was to separate these creatures from the rest of the world, to keep them from blending back in, to collect them all once again. He was good at it, too. So far, he had reunited sixteen. But he knew he had been better at it, once, somewhere. He did remembered telling that group of men about it and politely listening to their stories. But that had been years ago.

Mr. Simon paced.

The ones he did bring back papered one wall, which he had sacrificed for them. One by one, face by face, picture by picture, they all ventured back into his classroom.

Mr. Simon briefly angled his head toward his latest find. The scarred skin of his body held his head downward. He turned away as he continued to pace the room.

Toe to heel—twenty-one.

Toe to heel—twenty-two.

Toe to heel—twenty-three.

Toe to—

The man was speaking to him, causing him to lose count. But that was okay. He could lose count. It didn't matter. The paces were always the same. His attic room was always the same. Unless, of course, he counted with his shoes on, and then the room was just a little smaller, yet the same. It would always be the same, no matter who toe-to-heeled it.

He came to one end of the room and stopped, facing the wall with the photographs on it. All of the faces stared back at him flat-faced. He touched them and found no form to them. *How quickly they lose their life,* Mr. Simon thought. He turned to the sitting man. He wanted to touch the man's face, but still the light wasn't right. He looked up at one of the skylights and saw a hint of a quarter moon staring down. *Tomorrow. Maybe tomorrow.* Mr. Simon let out a large sigh. The man was still speaking, demanding his attention.

"What was that?" he asked, walking over. The man's question didn't matter, he was just being polite. Leaving his room uncounted for the moment, he carefully sat on the floor. Mr. Simon touched the chair's leg, admiring it. He twisted his head up at the man. He didn't seem afraid. Which of the children had he been? Mr. Simon couldn't remember. But he had known the man as a child; he *was* sure of that. Otherwise, why would he be here?

"Why not let me go?" the man asked again. His voice was even and controlled.

"Sorry, what was that?" Mr. Simon asked, letting his hand drop from the chair leg. He wondered if the man's voice would remain so calm. He enjoyed testing his students' limits.

"*Please...*hasn't this gone on long enough?" The man was nude, but it seemed he no longer cared. His voice cracked for a moment, and he cleared it, continuing. "Now listen, you've taken good care of me. You've washed me, cleaned me, fed me. I know you mean me no harm, otherwise you wouldn't go through all of that trouble." The man had been sitting there, facing the wall with nothing but the photographs to stare at. He was fatigued, terrified, and he didn't want to wind up among the photos on that wall. From the neck down, all of the subjects of the photographs were burned. The only parts of their body that weren't burnt, besides their faces, were where the restraints had held them. But the most horrifying part of the photos was not the burnt bodies, but the faces. They conveyed the pain of burning in a way that the charred meat of their bodies could not.

"You've been no trouble at all," Mr. Simon said, "but school isn't out yet. Can't go. We can talk if you wish, though." He watched the seated man. He was beginning to have doubts; the man's voice didn't sound like any of the children's voices. Nor, in this light, did he look like any of the children he had taught. Suddenly, Mr. Simon smiled. *Chameleon,* he thought. *Sly. Very sly.*

"But I was never one of your *students*. I'm too *old*. Jesus! Can't you see that?" The voice wavered and cracked.

"What is your name again?" Mr. Simon asked the older seated man. He knew sometimes his memory failed him.

"My God! I've told you my name! *I've said my name a hundred fuckin' times!*" the man shouted. The photographs were becoming all too real to him now. Mr. Simon stared before he spoke.

"Well, first of all, I've told you my name. It's 'Mr. Simon,' just in case *you* don't remember. I can understand if you don't, it has been a number of years. Now, one other thing…in *my classroom*, no foul language. None, you understand? So, once again, your name, what is it?" Mr. Simon spoke with the voice of infinite patience and authority. So many names, so many faces. Didn't they understand all of the sacrifices he made for them? He couldn't understand why they didn't seem to appreciate him bringing them all together once again. *Selfish,* is all he could think.

The man sighed. "Robert, my name is *Robert*." It sounded almost like an apology. "I was just hitchhiking, that's all. That's all I was doing. Just looking for a ride." Dropping his head, Robert closed his eyes. He couldn't look at the photographs anymore.

"Robert," Mr. Simon spoke the name softly. "Yes, Robert, that was it…yes, yes. *Robert*." Mr. Simon barely mouthed the name as he laid his head down on the floor. From this angle, Robert's head eclipsed the bare bulb behind him. The skin around Mr. Simon's neck was drawn tight and unforgiving, not allowing him to look up.

With his head down now, his eyes came in line with the metal chair bolted to the floor. Mr. Simon noticed the paint on it was a little singed, peeling, like the paint on his walls. Nearby was the large basin that he used to wash down his students. Next to it was a good-sized knife. That wasn't his. He had found it when he went to burn Robert's clothes. He thought it was a little strange that one of his former students would carry such a weapon. Yet, in a way, the two items looked rather nice together. Made the room look *tidy*.

Yes, it was Robert. Mr. Simon reached out and tentatively touched Robert's foot. Robert kept his foot still, and Mr. Simon withdrew his hand. *Robert.* The name was familiar, and he felt better about his lapse of memory. Still, he had trouble marrying the adult face to that of the child. *Maybe 'Bobby' as a child?* He tried to get a better look at Robert, but Robert's head was down. *Nap?* Mr. Simon didn't think it was naptime yet, but he'd bend the rules for now and let him rest.

Feeling restless himself, Mr. Simon got up from the floor and walked behind Robert. Stretching up on his toes, he desperately tried to straighten his body enough to reach the bulb. Just barely touching it, he gave it a push. Robert's seated shadow began to run from one side of the room to the other like a baseball player caught in a squeeze play.

Feeling his tendons tighten, Mr. Simon came back down to his true size, inches shorter than he had been years ago. The fire had consumed his body and shrunk it, turning it in on itself like an overdone steak. Bent over, his arms hung from his body simian-like, with veins pumping hot blood beneath the burnt asphalt of his skin. On one arm, only two veins ran straight. They led to two empty knuckles where his middle fingers should have been. Either the fire, the explosion, or the doctors had taken them. He didn't know and no one said.

He watched Robert as the overhead light slowed, finally stopping. He still couldn't tell if Robert was sleeping or not. But if the light was right, he knew by this time tomorrow he would be photographing Robert, pinning his picture to the wall to join the rest of his class. Mr. Simon had been pleasantly surprised at how easy it had been to get his former students to drop by. *So many of them hitchhiking at night. So many eager.*

Usually, they were either hungry, thirsty, or just wanted to touch him in the dark. But none of this third group ever got that far; Mr. Simon knew his drugs. Over the years, his burnt body had required many different ones. He had done his homework. True, he had overdosed the first four or so with chloral hydrate, the old, faithful Mickey Finn. It had taken a little time to accurately judge his students' body weight and to calculate the effect of alcohol when combined with the drug.

The first two had died quickly. Still, he hadn't let them go to waste. He had taken his time on them, practiced their transformations as he peeled back the burning layers to expose the true self beneath. *Waste not, want not.* Always told his students that. The next two had lingered awhile. He was getting the hang of it. Eventually, he started using several different concentrations of the drug in the food and alcohol that he offered up. Robert had been a quick study, and Mr. Simon had brought him home in no time at all. Painfully, he started to pace again.

Toe to heel—one.

Toe to heel—two.

He had been a good teacher, he told himself, a discoverer of new minds. He might still be in a classroom, had he set the timer more accurately. Instead of waiting until sunset, the igniter had gone off in the middle of the day.

He had picked a clear day, knowing that the interplay of the light from the setting sun and the light from the burning building would be beautiful. Add the flashing lights of the fire trucks and the police cars, and the spectacle would have been dazzling. Mr. Simon sighed.

Toe to heel—nine.

Toe to heel—ten.

The school had been his third in as many years. He did have vague memories of other burning buildings, but they seemed to be from a different life, a different time. He had always been careful; he remembered that much. But his classroom had been in flames, and they were all around him. Something had gone wrong. He knew plans had to change; he had to play the hero. It was his only way out. How could anyone fault him for anything after that?

It was when he had just dropped the last of his students to waiting hands, that something else that was not in the plans exploded. Mr. Simon had been thrown against the window frame and collapsed to the floor. He remembered seeing the flames racing along his body. He managed to get up and was trying to keep the flames from spreading to his face when there was one more explosion. This one punched his body out of the window. When he hit the ground, the impact blew the flames out. Except not only were the flames gone, but also his clothing. He was nude and his skin was smoking, peeled back, revealing things he had never seen before. The flames had changed him. Changed him into something else.

Chameleon-like, he had absorbed the light, the heat, the flames. He had tried to rise up from the ground, a Phoenix in bloom, but his legs wouldn't work. There had been a jagged piece of bone sticking out of his blackened leg. It was picked clean and the light of the fire danced off it. For some reason, Mr. Simon had found that moving light beautiful. Slowly it had faded.

Toe to heel—twenty.

Toe to heel—twenty-one.

He had gone into the hospital a hero. It was two years later, when the public had moved on and no one remembered his name anymore that he had exited by a side door. He was four inches shorter, with much of his own skin gone. They had replaced what they could, but like Odysseus' bow, he stayed bent over, the strings of his body drawn tight. During his painful rehabilitation, he had had plenty of time to think about what had gone wrong, and had come up with nothing. He had his own doubts about the timer and the explosions that followed. He could make no sense of it. In the end, he had longed to be dead. Instead, he was alive, entombed in a body that had been baptized by flame.

It hadn't always been like that. He had a vague memory of collecting people that weren't his students. He thought he had been doing this for many years. From state to state, he found them. Two here, three there. They added up. Sometimes the wrong people would notice, and he would have to move on.

The arson was a recent development. The burning of the schools was now a part of his behavior that he didn't understand, but then again, he didn't need to understand...he just did it.

Toe to heel—twenty-nine.

Toe to heel—thirty.

Mr. Simon stopped pacing and made his way over to Robert. Reaching for the light again, he swung it. He loved the movement of the light across his favorite room. It was the room he spent most of his time in. The rest of the house was small, isolated, suited to his purposes. But he lived for this room, his room—Mr. Simon's classroom. Yet, disappointingly, not all of his students made it to his room. He'd had to let some of them go; he had to pretend that he didn't even know others. He would just give them a ride to wherever they were going, hoping to meet up with them some other time. Sometimes things just weren't exactly right.

Some of his students, he learned, had grown too big for him to handle. Since his metamorphosis, his body wasn't as strong as it had once been. Others wouldn't take the food or the drink he offered. Still others wouldn't even get in the car. There were a number of reasons, but he was persistent. He had a baker's dozen to go before his classroom was at its full attendance once again. Those that he had brought back had the opportunity to share his pain. Robert would make the seventeenth. Tomorrow he would be added to the wall, and then it would be back onto the streets looking for the rest of his class. He strove for perfect attendance.

"Robert...sleep well." He knew he should let him rest, dawn would bring a full day for him. He dimmed the light as he left, leaving Robert in the darkness he had grown to dislike so much.

"Should be a clear day tomorrow," Mr. Simon said. "I'm sure school will be out." And he bid Robert a goodnight. He left Robert in the darkness he had grown to dislike so much.

Robert heard him leave and raised his head. He didn't have to see the photographs on the wall to know the faces. Tomorrow would be his third day, and the faces in the photos seemed very much alive to him now.

Thinking of the sins that had brought him here, he started to weep.

Go To Sleep

Mr. Simon stirred from his dream as the needle pricked his skin. His burnt body tried to react, but the movement was lost like a fleeting thought.

"*Go to sleep, Mr. Simon. Go to sleep.*" The whispery voice was soothing. Mr. Simon continued to dream.

A Long Time

Robert was dead. Mr. Simon was now sitting where his student had been sitting earlier, and now, Robert was dead. He lay nude over the washbasin on the floor. Most of his blood was pooled in the washbasin, having apparently drained from the slit across his throat. Robert's knife was bloody, no longer tidy. Mr. Simon had no idea what time it was, but the sky was still starry. He did notice that some of the blood around Robert was beginning to cake. Also, Mr. Simon noticed that his mouth felt like dried cotton. He had been trying, without much success, to identify the drug used on him.

Mr. Simon felt the coolness of the night. He was as nude as Robert had been. The restraints that held him in the chair were tight but not uncomfortable. There was someone behind him. He knew he was in trouble, but the photos of his students kept his attention. It seemed he was about to join his class. Mr. Simon wished for the daylight.

"Could you do me a favor?" he asked the person behind him, as his eyes went from student to student, noting those in attendance.

"Depends on the favor."

He knew that voice. *Somewhere. Who?* "Could you swing the overhead light for me? It's so *still* in here."

He heard the tap of a fingernail on the light bulb. The shadows began to swing and loop around the room.

"Thank you," Mr. Simon said.

"No problem."

"May I question you about something?" he asked.

"Depends on the question."

He tried his restraints. *Nicely done.* He gave up. "Are you an ex-student of mine?" he asked, knowing the answer. The voice behind him triggered certain memories.

"No."

"I didn't think so."

"It's been a while," the voice said.

The man was trying to help him remember. Mr. Simon thought that was very considerate.

"Did we teach together, by any chance?" Mr. Simon asked. Still the wrong question, but on the right track.

"No."

"No?"

"No, before the schools."

Mr. Simon was quiet a moment. Something worked itself up from his depths. He almost laughed.

"Weren't we friends?" he said over his shoulder.

"Yes..."

"Good friends?"

"Yes."

"We hunted together, didn't we?"

"Yes."

"They got away, didn't they?"

"Yes."

"The Society, then?"

"You could say that."

"Yes, yes...The Society." Mr. Simon paused in his thoughts. "How is everyone?" he finally asked.

"Fine...for now."

Mr. Simon was silent for a moment. Sadly, he asked, "Am I so insane?"

"Yes."

"Is that why you're doing this? Am I that much of a threat to The Society?"

"No."

"No...Hmmmm. May I ask a question that's been puzzling me for a very long time?"

"Yes."

"Was the last burning my fault? I mean, did I make a mistake with the timer?"

"No."

"No...I see. And about the second and third explosions?"

"Not yours."

"Why?"

"I was young then."

"No, not *that*."

"Why what?"

"Why are you doing this now, Stephen?"

"Might say it's all in the stars."

A thin stream of fluid arced over his shoulder, landing along his thigh and on what was left of his groin. He had smelled the lighter fluid even before it was sprayed on him. *This is going to take a long time*, he thought.

He tried to twist his head to look over his shoulder, but the scar tissue and the restraints limited his movements. The only thing he could see as he twisted was the peeling paint on the walls. *Well, at least I'm in my classroom with my students*, he thought as he tried to look around again. It was no use. He just would have liked to see one more sunrise.

"Stephen?"

"Yes?"

"School is out?" he asked.

"*Forever*." Came the answer.

The match followed the same trajectory the stream of lighter fluid had taken. It took a few moments before the already burnt flesh ignited in its own juices.

As Mr. Simon screamed, a knife flashed in front of his face. Flickering light played across the photographs. His students stared out at him sharing the same expression on their faces while the paint on the chair began to blister and peel.

Mr. Simon, elementary school teacher, arsonist, serial killer, and one-time hero, would have his one last wish. Sunrise was two hours away.

Pandora's Box

The knife glided over the well-oiled whetstone in a lazy circular motion. The sound it made was like a distant whisper. Suddenly, there was another sound, a creak. The knife stopped and Stephen's eyes darted about. He placed one hand over the knife and stone, his other hand ready to grab the metal box. He shifted his body so he could listen better. Nothing— just the house's timbers complaining about the changing temperatures. Another creak, and the house settled like an old man easing into his favorite armchair. Still, Stephen waited. *Nothing.*

He began to relax, but only a little. There was much at stake, and now was not the time to get sloppy or careless. Stephen leaned forward and listened for a few more moments, just to make sure. Satisfied, he took a long-deep breath. Too many lives hung in the balance, and there was a lot of work to finish. The knife waited for him. He sat back in his chair, the knife starting to whisper over the stone again.

The cutting weapon took well to its sharpening, gliding smoothly across the stone like silk over satin. Honing its edge wasn't really necessary. Of late, it had been cutting into only soft tissue, not bone. But the metal held an *awareness* that very few would understand, much less attribute to it.

Stephen knew that there were certain angles at which the knife cut more efficiently. Certain temperatures affected its temperament. Certain parts of the body were ideal for it. A certain amount of blood was also important. Too much blood, and the movement of the blade could be impaired, interfering with the cut. The knife had to be allowed to cut on its own. That was its sole purpose. The tempered metal could not be ignored.

He let the knife slide over the stone at its own pace. When the friction began to build, he stopped. It was natural to do so. Wiping the blade down with a chamois, he brought it up to his ear. Carefully, just at the edge of the cutting surface, he flicked it with a fingernail, and it rang out like a tuning fork singing to him.

He had to laugh. It was amazing what James had done with this blade over the years. He had never asked where he had gotten the knife from, nor how many bodies it had left its *resonance* in. Had he asked, James would not have answered. The knife was as legendary within The Society as James was himself.

So, it had come as a hell of a shock when he had presented the knife to him. James had made no fuss over the presentation, but Stephen knew that the gesture had put him at odds with some of the others in The Society. He always felt that this had been James' purpose. In the back of his mind, he also felt that James had known this day was coming.

Stephen balanced the knife in his hand. If James had known, he wondered, had he given him the knife so that *he* could share vicariously in the killings? Or *was* it simply to put him at odds with the other predators? Stephen wasn't sure. All he did know was that James hadn't stayed alive all of these years by chance.

Stephen put the knife down and picked up the metal box. Brushing some of the dirt from its surface, he placed it on his lap. The box was no larger than a kid's lunchbox, and it bore one other similarity: everything inside was sealed in Ziploc bags. Reaching in to his pocket, he retrieved another baggie.

The box's hinges creaked as he opened it, letting out a slightly pungent odor. He dropped the baggie into the box with the other nine lower lips zip-locked tight. He had never been much of a collector, but this was different. This would be a message to James. He wanted it clear that there was one predator at work here. Stephen knew some of the bodies that were too close to home would never be found. Others, the local authorities might overlook, not making the connections. It didn't matter. His message wasn't for them. Stephen knew it wouldn't be long before James got wind of what was actually going on.

He had hoped to reduce The Society by fifteen members before the next meeting. After that, he had marked another ten for James' knife. Three he planned to do right after the meeting, when they would least expect it. If he kept to those numbers, that would bring his tally to more than half of them. *More than half.* He was amazed at how well it was going. It was easier than he had ever expected. In fact, it was their arrogance that helped him out. Many of the members thought they were untouchable. *They were the hunters.*

Stephen laughed. They were wrong. He shook the box. *Dead wrong.* But he had to work faster. His major problems for now were time and distance, but before long, James would overshadow all of that. Stephen ran his fingers over the Ziploc bags and the pieces of dead flesh they held. It was a dangerous gambit, but he had no fear. Still, he wondered if he was holding Pandora's box, and if so, what was he unleashing?

Checking his watch, he closed the box. Time to put it back. When he finished with the killings, those pieces of machine-pressed sheet metal would be the final entombment for the members of The Society. He would then bury the rotting flesh forever.

Stephen ran his finger over the cutting edge of the hunter's blade. A red line appeared, the tiniest trickle of blood. He watched it for a moment. Getting up, he brought his finger to his mouth, letting his tongue touch the blood; it quickly disappeared. He had to get a move on, the plane wouldn't wait for him. He would have to leave the knife behind because of airport security. No problem—he would just do it another way. Besides, a penknife would work just as well on the soft flesh. He had packed two extra Ziploc bags in his carry-on.

The Dream

The dream came and went, seemingly with a will of its own. Sometimes it would end as soon as it began, only to pick up at the point it had left off to continue its journey through the night. As it held onto the dreamer, it would change its details a little, like a storyteller tailoring his tale to the audience. In the whiteness of it, they were always there in one form or another.

"He forgives you." The pain was there...

Martinez's Fan

Lieutenant Martinez sat at his desk, beads of sweat along his brow gathering like storm clouds. The air-conditioning was down, and a fan swept across the small room fluttering pieces of paper that stuck out of the folders containing backlogged and dead-end cases. With each sweep, the loose papers waved, reminding Martinez of his failures. The heat was unbearable, and Martinez cursed at the inadequacy of the fan.

A single drop of sweat broke away from the others, landing on the papers in his hand. They were from his wife's lawyer. He really didn't believe she would follow through. He put the papers aside and picked up the crime scene photos, hoping to see anything he'd missed the first thousand times he'd inspected them. He slowly flipped them one by one.

Summer was half gone, and he was glad for it. The crime rate always soared during these hot months. The heat fueled too many tempers. Too many things were going on. Too many people were out and about. Especially too many people out jogging. He hated joggers. Fucking joggers were always finding bodies somewhere. Martinez swore that their primary purpose in life was to jog along a path and look underneath bushes just so they could come across a pale, lifeless foot. Even better if they could see themselves on the six o'clock news talking about the horror of it all. Babbling on about how they could never jog through this park again without seeing that poor girl in their minds.

Tough shit, then, Martinez thought, *don't jog. Get fat and have a fucking heart attack like the rest of us.* He was forty and about to be divorced. The proceedings had left him with a stack of bills and a lot of extra pounds. His daughter, his only baby, was in college, and he constantly worried about her. His career was stuck in its own midlife crisis, and he had another seven years before he could retire on a pension that would still probably leave him in a midlife financial crisis. He needed a break, something big. Something he could use now.

He'd thought he had an ace in the hole a number of years ago, but Christian had fucked that up for him. Now, this shit with his ex-wife. What irked him was that she hadn't left him for anyone. She'd just left him. She'd had enough.

He would have felt better if there'd been a reason. Another lover. She wanted to start skydiving. Float down the Amazon bare-ass naked for a year. Whatever. He would have gone for something, anything. Instead, it was nothing. She wanted her life exactly as it was, just without him. That's what hurt so much. The nothingness of it all. He'd been a good husband, a good father, a good cop. Yet, after all these "goods," not much was left to look back on. He had to make his move;

that was the plain and simple truth. And he needed to step up before he could step out. He had a feeling that somehow he had the solution in his hands now.

Martinez continued to shuffle through the crime scene photographs from the reservoir track in Central Park. He stopped at the girl. She was his daughter's age. Fucking joggers found her. *What in the hell was she doing out on a night like that by herself?* The question rang in him without an answer.

Martinez moved on, stopping at the rapist. A big problem faced him here—who got the guy that got her? It had certainly been convenient to have that piece of shit delivered, so to speak, to his doorstep, but he had a gut feeling that the person who had solved this one might turn out to be an even bigger problem.

The rapist's face in the photograph held his attention. It was smooth, childish looking, even with the lower lip cut away. The missing lip seemed out of place with what was done to the rest of the body. The question had been driving him nuts for the last two weeks. The placing of the girl's nipple where the rapist's lower lip had been just didn't play right either. *A statement?* Maybe the "hero" killer had known the guy? Had known the girl? *No, not the girl.* This wasn't a lover-type thing. It only made sense if the killer knew the rapist.

From the footprints that had survived the rain, it looked like the second killer had stood and watched as the rapist did his thing. There were no overlapping prints, no scuffle. Just one set, his. So he stood there, watched, waited. The muddy footprints found near the girl matched the ones around the dead rapist. No, the girl wasn't this killer's concern. She was just a by-product while he waited for the rapist to finish. Then he took his anger out on the rapist. No hero here, just another cold-blooded murderer. But there was something else, too. The question was how to play it.

Lieutenant Martinez put the photo down and started to pick at his face for scabs that were no longer there. It was an unconscious habit, making its appearance whenever he was bothered by something. It had begun in his youth when acne scarred him. He had kept his hands to his face for most of those years. The adolescent curse had kept him from being popular like so many of his other classmates. He hid behind his hands keeping his thoughts and his feelings to himself. Now, his mind worked on those bodies in the photos as his hands worked his face.

The lip, the nipple, was it all a distraction? Maybe. Keep everyone off the main track? He was sure he had a killer with a purpose here.

Something from the past nagged at him. He was about to address it when there was a knock at the door, and the haunting thought slipped away. "Shit," he murmured, turning the photographs face-down.

"Yeah?" Martinez called out. The door opened slightly and Nestor stuck his face in.

"Got something you might be interested in," he said, letting himself in carrying a thick folder. Sweat stuck his shirt to his body. He pulled at his sticky shirt, trying to get some air between the wet material and his skin.

Nestor had been working with Martinez ever since Christian had left the force. It had seemed like a good move at the time, although it was a bit strange. Martinez had requested him. Nestor questioned him about it, but all Martinez had said was, "You can take it or leave it."

Gigi had pushed him into taking the position. Nestor had never liked Martinez; thought he was an asshole. But the lieutenant was known for keeping things in the spotlight. The word was that this was a man on the move; a big prick, but if you watched your back, someone of value. That had been the word. Words change.

Somewhere, someone with more clout than Martinez had pulled the plug on his career, stopping him dead in his tracks. The inside information dried up and the piles of unsolved cases grew. The word was out. Martinez was on the infamous downward spiral. But by then, Nestor had settled in and life wasn't too bad. The workload from Martinez was a bitch and it kept him busy, but his paintings were going well and Gigi was the love of his life. All in all, Nestor was content. But now Gigi was once again prodding him to move on. She felt he was overworked and unappreciated. Nestor agreed, but something lately had been tugging at his attention, and he wasn't quite ready to put in for the transfer yet.

Nestor watched Martinez pick at his face. *Ain't nothing there*, he wanted to say, but kept it to the business at hand. He continued to pull at his shirt. "You remember my brother-in-law, that state trooper across the big river?"

Martinez leaned forward, trying to catch something of the breeze from the fan. "'Big river'? You mean the Hudson and you mean fucking Jersey? And, no, I don't remember your brother-in-law the state trooper."

Nestor gave a half-assed grin. "Yeah, well, they found these two bodies in a room out in Summit..."

"Summit?" Martinez asked.

"Yeah, in Jersey." Nestor gestured over his shoulder. "Anyway, there were these two bodies, with one strapped to a metal chair, burnt like he was just tossed out of hell."

Martinez didn't try to hide his annoyance. "Why the fuck am I supposed to be interested in Jersey's fucking problems?"

Nestor stepped in front of the fan to cool off, but before it could do anything, Martinez protested and motioned him away with his head. Grudgingly, Nestor moved over. "Yeah, well the guy in the chair, like I said, was burnt to shit except for his face, and—" Nestor hesitated, wondering if what he had in mind was too much of a jump. Martinez was looking impatient, restless in his chair. The lieutenant's impatience broke through.

"What's this, a fucking dramatic pause?" he said. "And...and *what,* Nestor?"

"The guy's lower lip was cut off." Martinez's hands froze in place. "And what's more," Nestor continued as Martinez placed his hands on top of the photographs, "they found this refrigerator in the house full of body parts, souvenirs, trophies, whatever you want to call them. A lot of parts from a lot of different people. I mean a lot!"

"They find the lip?" Martinez asked, having a feeling that they hadn't.

"No, no lip." Nestor thought it was interesting that Martinez should bring up a question about the lip. He filed the thought away and continued. "The burnt guy's name was Jeff Simon. Years ago, he was a teacher. Seems there was a fire in the school where he taught. He goes and saves some kids and winds up burnt pretty bad. That was the first time he was burned, but not the first time he *burned* something. Turns out there were two other fires, both at schools where he was teaching before. He would torch them and move on. Nobody put this together until—"

"Why'd your state trooper relative tell you this?"

Nestor shrugged his shoulders. He knew Martinez was sniffing around. "My sister and him were over for dinner and we were shooting the shit. That's it."

"Yeah?" Martinez touched his face for a brief moment before continuing. "You shoot the shit with the trooper guy about the goings on here?"

"No. We just shoot the shit, Lieutenant. Is that okay?"

"Sure." Martinez eased back in his chair.

Nestor knew Martinez loved to sidetrack people, trying to trip them up. It was a good technique, but Martinez wasn't very subtle about it. He wasn't subtle about very much.

"Also," Nestor said, finally picking up at where he had left off, "it seems Simon had a weird effect on the local population. People disappeared wherever he showed up in town. When he left, the population stabilized. Go figure. Anyway, he gets burnt in this one fire and his mom visits him every day in the hospital. Once he's out, he stays in his mom's house and lives off disability. But the thing is, as soon as he moved in the house, she moved out. Nobody has seen or heard from her since." Nestor paused a moment. Martinez's face was blank.

"So," Nestor continued, "the Summit police are digging up the cellar and yard, looking for Mom and a few others. Simon also had a little darkroom set up in the house; so far no photos or negatives of any kind. Looks like the darkroom was cleaned out. The two bodies were found in the attic. The chair Simon was in was bolted to the floor, facing one wall. On the wall, there were a lot of tiny holes, like from pushpins. I don't really know at this point what might have been up there. My money's on photos 'cause of the darkroom." Nestor paused. He was trying to draw Martinez out, but Martinez didn't seem to share his excitement. He still had that blank stare.

"Well, the second body on the floor was a Dale somebody, forget his last name. Anyway, he just got out of prison after doing a ten-year piece of time for armed robbery. He would hitchhike, rob the driver at gun or knifepoint, toss the driver, take the car. His throat was cut, but he also had the same restraint marks around his wrists, ankles and chest as Simon…so, he spent some time in that chair. The Jersey people figure he was up to his old tricks and he thumbed the wrong ride. No weapon so far. Both bodies were nude." Nestor paused again. He waited for some sort of comment from Martinez. Nothing again. Martinez just had that stone-cold, pockmarked face. *Okay, asshole.* Nestor pressed on.

"Now, do you remember a number of years back in Brooklyn with those dead kids?"

"Nestor." Martinez addressed him as if he were talking to someone who just didn't understand the meaning of life. "There have been many dead kids in Brooklyn. Any *particular* ones you have in mind?"

Nestor smiled. Martinez knew exactly what he was talking about, but he sat there, looking up at him. Nestor played along. "The seven dead kids in that apartment, with the other souvenirs."

"Oh yeah," Martinez said, doing a quick snap of his fingers and pointing at Nestor as if dredging up a long-forgotten memory. "No, wait, don't you mean the *eight* dead kids, counting the one little girl your maverick buddy killed? Yeah, I remember." Martinez nodded his head. "I remember it pretty well, in fact. That partner of yours fucked up a number of different things in a number of novel and interesting ways that day. Yeah, I remember." Martinez wondered who was the bigger psychopath, Christian or that big serial killer. It had been *his* tip that Christian was acting on. *His.* That piece of information was meant for him. Christian had claimed that Nestor hadn't known anything about it and that he misinformed him about the tip. Martinez knew Christian had covered for his partner. He eyed Nestor as he continued.

"I remember, for instance, that the psychopath's name was Isaac Richards, a big, fat recluse with a taste for children. He'd feed the cat he kept in the first floor apartment a little something extra now and then. Yeah...I seem to remember. And the connection between all of these wonderful stories and this walk down memory lane of yours?" Martinez knew Nestor had something here.

Nestor ignored the sarcasm, placing the file on Martinez's desk. He took a photograph out, turning it toward the pock-faced lieutenant. "Christian's shot took off most of his face, but you can see from the autopsy photo that there's a tattoo on the inside of the lower lip. Now, this may be a long shot, but I think they are all connected somehow."

Martinez glanced at the photo and looked up at Nestor. "Detective, you got personal problems I should know about?" Martinez sat back in his chair. For a moment, he'd thought Nestor was on to something. Now, he was just pissed. "Long shot? How fucking long do you think it is between here and Jersey?"

"Yeah...well...Lieutenant, just one more thing." Now Nestor stopped, pausing dramatically. He waited until Martinez was about to bitch. Martinez shifted in his chair and Nestor jumped back in.

"We got an ID on that dead rapist with the missing lower lip. A certain Mr. Louis Harms, with a room in his apartment full of body parts. No rap sheet, not so much as a parking ticket. Same deal on that burnt teacher—on the surface, he was clean, a real good guy. Except for the body parts, the missing people, the missing mom and the torching of schools. They're also looking at other places he might have dropped a match in. Besides those two guys, I did some checking across the country, and two other bodies came up with a lower lip missing. One also seems to be a bit of a collector of human flesh and model citizen to boot. Hailed from Falls Church, Virginia. Nothing so far on the other one. I think the locals screwed it up. That one was about fifty miles outside of Jacksonville, Florida. But I'm still waiting. All east coast so far—"

Something changed in the lieutenant. Nestor watched as Martinez's hand went back to work on his face. Something. Very slightly, but something. *So, you scar-faced motherfucker, what's biting at your ass?* Nestor wondered. Martinez's hands worked. *Fuck you, asshole.* Nestor was pleased. *Just fuck you.*

All of this was, in a way, for his ex-partner. Christian had made a mistake. There was no going back, but mistake or not, Christian had been a damn good cop. Martinez just wanted Christian out of the way, period. Nestor knew that, but he couldn't figure out why. He had always felt the lieutenant was afraid of Christian for some reason. He wondered what Christian knew that would have the lieutenant looking over his shoulder like this.

Something.

Nestor had hit a nerve, he was sure of it. Stepping in front of the fan, he quickly summed it up. "Four guys with missing lower lips. At least three out of the four like to have body parts hanging around the house. Another dead collector from years ago with a tattoo on his lower lip. A tattoo on the very same part of the anatomy that the others are missing. Plus the fact that with so many different body parts found, it almost seems like a swap meet. I think all of this shit is the tip of the iceberg. I think we have a club for members only here. And what's more, no one seems to have caught on yet."

Martinez dropped his hand and leaned forward, picking up the photograph, no longer taking notice of Nestor. In the photo, two rubber-gloved fingers held down the lip, showing the tattoo. It seemed that Nestor has been burning the midnight oil. *Still,* he thought, *he's no Christian.* Christian was ambitious *and* dangerous. Christian knew too much, but he had the good sense to keep most of it to himself. Nestor, on the other hand, was an open book. He knew Christian would never have come to him like this. Maybe it was time to unofficially team them back up a little. *Keep your friends close, but keep your enemies closer.* It looked like his investment in Nestor might pay off yet. Martinez looked back up at the sweaty detective.

"You still keep in contact with Christian?"

"Yeah," Nestor said a little suspiciously. "He's upstate. Living in a small town now."

"How quaint." Martinez's fingers started on the pocked contours of his face again. "You know, maybe you should review this old case with him—another walk down memory lane. See what you turn up." Martinez watched Nestor carefully. "A few days on the department," he added. "Just don't make a big deal about it for now."

"Sure, sounds good, a few days." Nestor wondered if Martinez wanted him to turn over his mother to him next.

Martinez tapped the file. "Also, keep working on this. See what else you can turn up. Just don't mention this around until we get something solid, got it?"

"Yeah, sure, I get it."

"Okay, two more things. One, other than those few days, you do this on your own time. We have cases to work. Two, nothing leaks to the papers. No 'anonymous sources,' no 'highly placed officials confirm' shit, okay? No sense in building headlines before we've got a handle on this thing."

"Yeah, I figured that all out." Nestor thought of the pleasure he would get cornering Martinez in the ring.

"Good, good." Martinez looked back at the photo of the tattoo again. He knew it was Japanese, and he had seen the photo before. *Keep them close.*

"What's the name of that little town?" he asked without looking up.

"Tranquillity, with two L's."

"Sounds nice and *peaceful*, with one *L*," he replied. He had known exactly where Christian was. "And this tattooed symbol translated means what...?" Martinez asked playing, dumb.

Nestor shrugged. "It could mean a few things. Linguistics says it's got a couple different meanings. It's kind of a freewheeling thing. A meeting, an association, a society, maybe a gathering. Not sure."

"Hmmm, how quaint again. Let me know if you can pinpoint it down from all of those choices." Martinez raised his head. "Your friend Christian, what does he know about this theory of yours?"

"Nothing."

"Good. Keep it that way. Just keep *me* fully informed. Not like your child-killing ex-partner exiled to some small shit-kicking town." Nestor was silent. "Anything else?" Martinez asked.

"Uh-huh, yeah, as a matter of fact. Just a little something." It was a long-awaited question that had gone unanswered. "That day in Brooklyn, after everything went down...how did you get there so fast, Lieutenant? I mean, you even beat the medics."

Martinez's hands stopped picking at his face, and he stared levelly at Nestor. "Piece of advice. Don't let the past fuck up your future. Stay in touch, Detective."

Nestor reached for the folder, but Martinez placed his hand over it.

"Leave it...you can pick it up later, after I leave."

Nestor pulled at his sweaty shirt. Walking over to the fan, he picked it up and placed it on a stack of files, farther from Martinez' desk.

"Better over here, not so much hot air." And turned on his heel and left.

Martinez sat motionless as the door closed. He turned back to the photo of the tattoo on the inside of Isaac's lip. Taking a deep breath, he reached for his Rolodex and flipped through the cards till he came to a number without a name. He dialed. A woman picked up. She didn't sound real.

"Yes," he said to the voice, "for Mr. Kellogg. Just tell him Victor Martinez. Yes, I'll wait for his call. Thank you." Martinez hung up the phone. His eyes wandered over his small office, but they weren't looking outward at all. It was only a moment before his phone rang.

"Hello? Yes, fine, and...oh, good, good. Yes, it's been awhile...Listen, I have something unusual here... Who?" Martinez looked at the folder. Again, his eyes weren't looking outward at all. "Diaz, Nestor Diaz..." he answered. "Yes, one of the two in Brooklyn...Yes, his partner was Christian...Yes, that old case. Well, some bodies were found with their lower lip missing and a photo of Isaac's lower lip turned up...Yes, the rumors. Yes, The Society...Oh, okay. Copies are no problem and anything you can do with the arrangement...sure, fine. I'll keep you updated...sure, okay, will do, James..." And the line went dead. Martinez held the phone in his hand for a moment before placing it back down. His feelings were mixed, but he had no choice.

The small fan turned and blew across the divorce papers and photos. They fluttered on his desk as if they had a life of their own. Leaning over, he placed his hand on them settling them down. A drop of sweat broke away from his brow hitting his hand.

"*Fuck.*" For the next few days, there would be no break from the heat. He looked over at the fan. Nestor had been right; it was better over there.

A Gathering Of Wolves

"*Pleeease...*"

The kitchen was hot, but Stacey knew it wasn't the heat from the kitchen that made her palms sweat. It wasn't the heat from the kitchen that ran that line of sweat down the middle of her back, either. It was fear. Her intuition had always been on the money. It wasn't failing now. She wiped her palms along her pants as she waited on her second platter of hors d'oeuvres. Four more platters to go after that one. *Four.* She didn't want to go back to that meeting room anymore. No, not *that* room with *those* people.

This was her sixth month at the RiverView Hotel. Overlooking the waterfront, it catered to the powerbrokers of Savannah. She was trying to work her way up the ladder in the Food and Beverage Department, but it was slow going. She was persistent, though, and knew she had to put in her time. In her present position, that involved carrying numerous trays to the "one hand drinking, one hand picking" crowd. Stacey had quickly lost count of the platters she had hefted up on one arm. Lost count of the number of phony smiles that by the end of the evening would turn her face into a sore rubber mask.

Lost count, that is, until tonight. This evening, she was very aware of each smile, each pleasant word. She was also aware of all of the other rubber masks in the room. No, she didn't want to go back in there with *those* people. If she couldn't get anyone else to cover, these four platters were going to be the longest in her career.

"*Pleeease,*" she said again.

Part of her told her that she was being silly. She was safe, she was fine. She just didn't *feel* safe or fine. She was frightened. Terribly frightened. She begged.

"*Pleeease*..."

Wiping her sweaty hands on her pants, she wished she could do something about the cold trickle running down her spine. Rosie was her only chance.

"Please, Rosie, just the last four trays. An hour at the most. You can keep all the tips."

Rosie had just come off covering another shift. Finishing her own eight-hour shift, she had been packing to go home when one of the other girls had called in late. Her asshole manager had looked in her direction, and she had known she was screwed. The girl had finally shown up, and now she just wanted to head home.

Up on one leg, she held onto Stacey for support while changing her shoes. No matter what Stacey said, Rosie knew she was out of there and heading straight for a bubble bath, with or without her boyfriend. Stacey was still pleading.

"Please? C'mon."

Rosie hated doing this to her friend. "Honey," she said, switching to her other leg, "I would love to help ya, hon, but I'm *dead*. I've been on since six this morning. Dead, I tell you. Absolutely dead!" But her friend would not give up.

"Rosie, there's just something about them that makes me afraid." Stacey touched her stomach. "They're—"

"What?" Rosie asked, finished with her other shoe. "What are they? Listen hon, your hormones are in an uproar, that's all. I'm *sorry*, babe, I've got to go!" Rosie did a quick spin on her toes and planted a good-bye kiss on Stacey's cheek. "I really do. Bye." With one more kiss on Stacey's other cheek, she was out of the kitchen in a flash.

Stacey watched the kitchen door swing closed. "Shit-shit-shit!" she said, stomping her feet.

"Hey, yo," one of the chefs called to her. "If you're finished clicking your heels together in my kitchen, *Dorothy*, your shrimp is up!"

Stacey walked over and grabbed the tray, the chef muttering something inaudible. Heading for the kitchen door, she called back over to him.

"Hey, yo…Fuck you, and y'little dog too." She was in no mood, no mood at all. She pushed against the kitchen door with her back, wishing she were somewhere else.

Going down the service hall, she held the tray of shrimp as far away from her as possible. Normally, she would have swiped one, especially big ones like these guys, but the smell was turning her stomach and she couldn't even bring herself to touch them.

She knew it had nothing to do with her morning sickness. None of this did. For two months it'd been kicking her ass, but she could handle it. But to her, these neatly arranged circles of crustaceans were laid out like…like…*tiny bodies? Shit yeah*, she thought, *tiny bodies. Tiny.* She knew she shouldn't be thinking like this, it wasn't right. But she didn't know what was wrong. She didn't know why she was afraid, she just was.

Picking up her steps, she hurried down the hall, wanting to get rid of these cold little jumbo shrimp bodies as soon as possible.

No arms, no legs, no heads, split open down the middle.

Her stomach churned.

As she came closer to the meeting room, she started to slow down. "Okay, okay," she whispered. "Just a bunch of guys in suits."

Coming to the door, she was about to push it with her free hand when someone suddenly opened it, startling her. It was like he was waiting. *No big thing,* she thought. Guys flirt. She wasn't exactly an eyesore, even at two months. And this wasn't exactly the first time the *"I'll-get-the-door-for-you"* hit had been tried. *No big thing,* she tried to tell herself. Still, she was freaked out.

"Come on in," he said. "Pretty good timing, don't you think?" She smiled. He was nice-looking, pleasant. Just a passing face in the crowd. Still…something. Not just him. All of them. Something about all of them…together. Individually, she wouldn't have given any of them a second thought. Grouped like this, it was a different matter. They stood in their tiny little circles, talking, whispering. *Conspiring.* They were like, like…*tiny little cold shrimp bodies.*

"Thank you, sir," she said. "Care for any shrimp?" Stacey asked as she stepped into the room. No one looked directly at her, but she felt every set of eyes in the room knew exactly where she was. She tilted the tray towards him, forcing her mouth into a smile that wavered. "Shrimp?" she asked again.

"No, thank you," he said, smiling. "I really don't eat that stuff. Special diet, you know. And the name is Douglas." He extended his hand to her. Stacey shrugged with the tray in hand. "Oh sure, sure. Work, I know," Douglas said. She smiled once again and moved deeper into the room.

Little odd bodies, little cold bodies.

The room was Stacey's favorite. It was small but plush. High-backed, overstuffed chairs upholstered in dark leather filled the room, their heads and armrests worn from countless bodies. Heavy curtains over the windows filtered out the nighttime activities of the waterfront. Medieval tapestries depicting the hunting of unicorns and their protective longhaired virgins covered the walls between them. The room conveyed richness and warmth. It was meant to settle a person, give them a feeling of intimacy with whomever they were meeting. Stacey had walked her platters countless times for other groups in this room. Sometimes it even worked its magic on her, and she would feel part of the group she was serving. Tonight, though, the room seemed smaller, more claustro-phobic…darker. The tapestries, normally her favorite things in the room, now seemed nothing more than the kidnappings and slaughter of rare beasts. She wanted no part of the feelings she got here. She took another small step into the room. Her stomach tightened. *Get a grip on yourself,* she thought. *It's just a gathering of guys in suits.*

Gathering.

She found it funny how she had got caught up in that word. This was more than a mere meeting; *it was a gathering.* Her heart began to race. *You're freaking yourself out,* she thought. She started to work her way around the twenty or so talking bodies, offering the food as she went.

"Pardon me…hors d'oeuvre?" The words came out automatically, the smile frozen on her face. Weaving herself among the small groups, she tried to make as little eye and body contact as possible.

A gathering of wolves.

They were all extremely polite, as if on their very best behavior. This wasn't how they normally behaved, her gut said. That was something quite different. Something beyond her wanting to know. Strip away their masks and she knew there would be teeth.

Long, sharp teeth.

She looked at the tray and the group of men. The food was not disappearing fast enough, and the eyes in the room were starting to break away from their feigned indifference, taking more notice of her. The masks were dropping away. The sweat continued to run down the middle of her back. *Screw this.* One more pass and she was out of there.

Intent on leaving, Stacey didn't notice the table until she turned and banged into it, almost dropping her tray. *That's gonna be a black and blue!* she told herself, rubbing her hip with her free hand.

She wondered when they had set it up. It hadn't been there during her first tray. She took a step away from it and saw a number of oddly shaped packages on it. For some reason, the packages didn't sit well with her.

Okay, that's it. Icing on the cake! Fuck the last pass, let the bastards starve! She was definitely out of there. She took another step back from the table, turned, and bumped into someone.

"Oh! I'm sorry, sir!" she said, as her thoughts were cut off in midstream, leaving just her fears. "I didn't see you there." It was Douglas again.

"Shrimp?" she asked, her smile still stamped on her face.

"Oh, no. Special diet. Thanks," he said.

Take the fucking things! her mind screamed.

"Remember...Stacey," he said, making a show of reading her name off her nametag.

Eat the fucking things! her cheeks hurt from smiling.

"Wouldn't be good for me."

Eat them and die! She took a small step away.

"Can I help...?" Douglas offered.

Get the fuck away! One more step back.

"No sir, I'm fine. Excuse me." She turned and was about to move away when someone touched her arm. It was a light touch, but she was very aware of it. It made her think of a ghost, a soul. She almost dropped her tray again, but caught herself in time.

"Sorry, didn't mean to startle you." He was a small man, not much taller than she was. Impeccably dressed, he had a smile that would have charmed the pants off anyone. Even without seeing Douglas move off, she knew this man was the leader.

Leader of the pack.

She wanted to chuckle, but couldn't find it in her. Her heart beat too quickly. It was a feeling she couldn't control. The only thing worse than her heart beating this fast was it stopping completely. But the strange thing was that she couldn't make up her mind. Was she frightened of him or not? Her heart raced on.

"My name is James." He reached out his hand to her, and she couldn't help but take it.

His touch was warm and comforting. She felt a bit calmer; the fluttering of her heart more like the nervousness of flirtation than terror. She was conscious of her sweaty palms, but he seemed to take no notice of them. If anything, he held on to her hand a moment longer then necessary, making the touch more intimate. Above his smile, his eyes held her. Finally, he released her hand as if he had just stolen something from her. She could have sworn that a little of her breath was drawn away with it. There was no other way she could describe it.

"If you don't mind, Stacey," he said, the words flowing from him never interrupting his smile, "just leave the tray. We'll call you when we need some more food. My associates here are not much for snacks. I hope that you find that agrees with you." He placed a fifty-dollar bill on her tray.

"I'll leave the tray, sir, but the money isn't—"

He held up a hand. "Stacey, please don't insult me. I know I'm putting you at an inconvenience. The money is my apology. No discussion here. Besides, I can tell you have a good heart. Okay, Stacey?"

"All right, sir. Shall I just leave the tray on the table?"

"That will be fine. And Stacey?"

"Yes sir?"

"Thank you...*oh so much.*" The smile seemed broader, more magical, if that were possible. It was ridiculous. He was old enough to be her father, and thirty seconds ago she had been terrified, but now she wanted the lips smiling that smile to kiss her. She thanked him again and tried in vain to return the smile with the same intensity. Feeling silly, she turned and set the tray on the end of the table, taking the fifty-dollar bill. Slipping it into her blouse pocket, she noticed that there were more shrimp missing than she had realized.

Out, she thought. *Don't press your luck. Just get out!* Turning, she saw James still smiling at her, but, differently. Something in her went into high gear.

"Oh, Stacey?" It still sounded sweet to her, but with a cutting edge.

"Yes?" She had an urge to touch him. It was like the idea of touching a dangerous caged animal just to see if you could get away with it. Except here, there were no bars. She wanted to move away, but instead she stepped a little closer. His voice was barely a whisper.

"Stay true to your nature," he said. "Love and protect that baby you're carrying. Here," he continued, a breath away, "for the baby." And slipped another fifty-dollar bill in her blouse pocket with his thumb and forefinger. His eyes held her in place as his two fingers gently massaged her nipple. Even through her bra, his touch brought it to an instant rock-hardness. Closing her eyes, she breathed in sharply. Her nipple felt even harder.

"Save that for the baby...hon." She heard, and her eyes suddenly shot open. James was licking his two fingers. Smiling, he slowly stepped aside.

There was a clear path to the door. None of the eyes in the room seemed to be watching, but she knew better. She made her exit, barely aware she was still smiling and nodding. Once on the other side of the door, she wanted to touch her breast. The dampness she felt around her nipple had to be sweat; it couldn't be anything else. Instead, she rubbed her palms on the sides of her pants. She fought back a sob, her heart wanting to explode once again. Shaken, she broke out in a run down the hall and flew through the kitchen doors.

"I'm going the fuck home and I don't give a Goddamn shit!"

The chef almost dropped the third platter he had ready for her. *"Hey—"* he started off, but Stacey cut him short.

"Don't say a fucking word!" she screamed, pointing an accusing finger. She wanted to strike out at someone, anyone. The chef stared, placing the tray down.

"Say, Stac?" he tried softly.

"Not a word," she whispered. "Not a *fucking word.*" Dropping her hand, she lightly touched her stomach. It was such a fear.

She took the two crisp bills from her blouse pocket and looked at them. With that money in hand, she felt like she *owed* him something. Something he had paid for but that she was unwilling to deliver up. She tore the money into bits and threw the pieces as far as she could before fleeing the kitchen. She felt lucky to have gotten away with her life and the life of her baby.

Such a fear.

The Society

Stephen watched as James stepped in and saved the waitress from Douglas. He was amused by Douglas' crude attempts with the hired help. He didn't think Douglas was going to make it in the long run. As a matter of fact, he *knew* Douglas was not going to make it. He had learned long ago that a number of their kind had a shelf life, an internal self-destruct mechanism of some sort. They waited, wanting to be caught before some internal clock or fantasy in their head ran out. Over the years, he had seen too many on that edge, and he knew Douglas was one of those about to topple over it. Stephen couldn't understand why James had brought such a stupid, dangerous creature into The Society, but he knew it would never do to question James—at least not to his face.

Stephen had been in The Society for ten years now, and that aging killer still amazed him. When James had finished toying with the waitress, Stephen watched him move from person to person, working the room like a politician on a campaign trail. James' size was deceptive. Stephen knew beneath that double-breasted suit beat a heart that fed a body with a single purpose. One that hardened his body, hardened that purpose.

Like a bird of prey, it was James' eyes that dictated his movements. They were sharp, black, unforgiving, almost an entity unto themselves. Seldom were they still. When James focused on someone, his smile drew the person in, but his eyes took the person apart. His aquiline appearance was further enhanced by the sweep of his hair. Straight, feather-like streaks of gray ran back through it as if the colorations of age could rise up on their own with a screech of his voice. James looked, acted, and seemed decades younger than his actual age. And, like the rest of The Society, he was out there. The hunt kept his senses sharp. He took in everything, his movements covered everything. Even so, no one in The Society knew exactly who James' victims were, much less what he did with them. To the outside world, James was a rumor at best; a ghost, a hint of a nightmare that no one could really believe existed in the flesh. His nature honed him and he never fought it. He was the quintessential predator and still the brightest star in the sky…for now.

Turning from James, Stephen took a sip of his Pepsi. It was warm and flavorless. He couldn't bring his mind to forge a taste. He took another sip, still not tasting anything. His mind was elsewhere, and thinking about James, he could taste everything. With the passing of the years, he had gained the experience and the maturity to survive the path he had started upon. The stars were still there waiting for him. He could feel his hands around them as he reached to pluck them from the sky. It was so easy.

The heavens he was now blazing through held several fewer celestial bodies. The lights he ripped from the dark of the night to place forever in the dark of the earth were his destiny. He was choosing the next one to be brought down, when he heard James clear his throat.

"Gentlemen, let us have your attention up here, if you please. Take your seats; the food and drinks will continue once we finish." James paused. "Or they may not." There was a smattering of laughter.

James looked around at his people as they seated themselves. Over the many years, he had selected them carefully for their talents. For the most part they were good. They learned and they stayed out of the spotlight, surviving. *Still*, he thought, scanning the faces, *too many are missing*. Someone was catching on.

"Thank you, gentlemen," he resumed. "As you know, I've been the head of The Society for many years now. And as you also know, The Society had been around many years before that. What it represents is as old as human nature itself, as old as *our* nature. Gentlemen, part of our nature, or any creature's nature, is the will to survive, and that endeavor involves The Society." He let his eyes drift over them. He knew who would survive and who would be eliminated. Previously, the choice had been his alone, but now someone was taking that choice out of his hands. This couldn't be allowed. *He* was The Society. But he hadn't maintained control all of these years by rushing blindly into things. James settled back to the business at hand.

"Tonight, we have two issues for consideration, both of which involve the survival of The Society. First is the matter of a new member." He put on his best disarming smile, surveying the members. *Too many missing,* he thought again. Twenty-three were present, and he knew that they too noticed the missing.

James knew over the years that a little thinning of the herd was normal, but the numbers had always been kept up. What faced him now was not natural. Thirteen were missing so far. "A Judas number," as his father would have called it.

From his experience, the authorities might pick up one or two on minor or unrelated charges not knowing what they actually had in their custody. But this wasn't the case. Others committed suicide, thus ending their careers. Again, not the case. And a few went dormant. Those, for the most part, surfaced again. It might take months, or years, but sooner or later, their driving impulses took over and they started to kill again.

Still not the case.

Now, he had to fish these waters in front of him. Either someone had lain dormant, or had simply planned and waited.

Of the two, the one who planned and waited was the more dangerous creature. He was about to bait the hook to find out.

His eyes settled on Douglas. Stretching out his hand toward him, he continued. "Douglas has paid his tribute to The Society and, as we all know, it was accepted by us. Which, of course," he added quickly, "accounts for the fact that he is still alive." He continued once the laughter died. "Douglas will share the northeast territory with Stephen." He glanced over at Stephen, and his smile deepened. "With the dense population, I'm sure they will find plenty of raw material to go around."

Stephen raised his Pepsi in a salute to Douglas, but Douglas' eyes were riveted on James. Slowly, Stephen lowered his drink as James started to speak again.

"Now, gentlemen, before we continue with our new member, I must go off on a bit of a tangent." The smile left his face and his voice hardened. All in the room knew an admonition was about to follow.

"A number of us, myself included, have a touch of wanderlust in our character as we go about our work. If one of us should cut across someone's territory, do not, I repeat, do *not* leave any surprises for fellow members in their backyards." He had their undivided attention. "This is not open to discussion. We cannot account for some of the lesser hunters that do not belong to us, but we can, out of respect, account for ourselves. Is that clearly understood?" There were murmurs of assent from around the room. "There are to be no mistakes about this." James' voice once again changed.

"Now, if you should come across one of the lesser hunters, feel free to do whatever you deem necessary. Although, keep in mind, knowing their style, they do make good cover." He gave them all a knowing look. "Good, now back to the subject of our territories and young Douglas." His face lightened up. "Since he will have to share his territory, it seems only *a propos* that Stephen be the recipient of Douglas' gift to The Society."

A round of applause broke out, and Stephen once again saluted with his drink that went unacknowledged. Before putting it down, he took another bittersweet sip from it, shooting Douglas a quick glance.

With a foolish grin plastered across his face, Douglas got up from his chair nodding to all around him. Package in hand, he walked over to Stephen handing him the gift. Taking it, Stephen stood and shook his hand.

"I will cherish this, Douglas." Stephen noticed some long red hairs sticking out of the package. *Sloppy,* he thought. He had an urge to crush Douglas where he stood, but smiled instead and sat back down, placing the gift on his lap. Stephen's fingers curled and dug into the leather of the armchair. Beneath one of his pinkies, the worn leather ripped. Douglas stood above him, beaming down.

"Yes, yes, I know you will," Douglas said. "She was a good one. I'll tell you the story later. You know, a little history on the gift." For the first time in years, Douglas felt good about himself. To be recognized for his talents in such company was an honor.

Stephen watched Douglas' face. "Thanks," he said. "I look forward to hearing about it." *A braggart. Dangerous,* Stephen thought, as he heard the other members applaud the traditional giving of the gift. He looked down at the package and knew it was the scalp of a woman. He really hated the obvious. James' voice brought him around again.

"Now with this gift, we give something in return to assure all that Douglas indeed belongs to us. We all know that with this marking, you and The Society are one even beyond your own death. This symbol of our allegiance to The Society and to each other dates back to the early sixteen hundreds. This mark of ours, this...tattoo, if I may use such a crude description of it, had its birth among a certain class of Samurai of that period. They were a Society within an already elite class." James paused, grinning. "Yes, history class again." His people laughed.

"It was during the *Sengoku-jida'* period, 'The Age of the Country at War,' that they came into existence. It was a time of fierce inter-clan fighting. Yet, out of these rival clans, certain samurai rose to attain positions of power by the sheer number of their kills. Within these circles, an acknowledgement of their ability and of their nature surfaced. But even with their prowess and the notoriety it garnered, few of these samurai could ensure their standing within the power struggles of those times. To enhance their longevity, The Society came into existence. To join was, and is, an honor." James began to walk around the room as he spoke.

"A certain number of kills was required of each member, and a souvenir of the last kill was presented as a token of their submission to The Society. If the applicant was accepted, the ideogram of The Society was tattooed over the new member's heart. If, however, he was deemed unworthy, he was beheaded on the spot. Maybe one in twenty were accepted." He paused a moment, looking around. Most of them were like children to him. Not in his affection towards them, because he had none, but in their understanding of their own nature. Most of them would have been beheaded the first day. Still, one worked with what one had. James strolled, continuing with the history lesson.

"Their power grew, but so did the fear of them. Eventually, some of the warring clans set aside their differences to attack The Society. One by one, the members were set upon by assassins in overwhelming numbers. Finally, the clans, thinking The Society had been eliminated, returned to warring among themselves. But a number of the members had escaped underground. The ideograms on their chests were burned off and the new members now had it tattooed on the inside of their lower lip. The Society had become a secret organization, and many of the assassins were in turn assassinated. And so, the hunt began." James stopped in front of one of the many tapestries. Behind him, men on horses with long spears were attacking the mythical beast, while a virgin was being carried off. James broke into a wide grin.

"Now, if we all pull on our lower lips, you can see that is exactly where we place our mark to this day." James watched carefully as they all laughed. *Children, all.* "Now...now..." he calmed them down, "The Society has survived in one form or another all of these years. But times have changed and so have we. We have learned and we have survived and we continue on." He looked around the room slowly. He started to shake his head.

"Gentlemen, a few erroneous numbers, official and unofficial, from our FBI boys." There were groans. James held up one hand. "Please, I don't make this stuff up, I just report it." Laughter. "Now, it has been estimated by them that our kind number from one to two hundred in the United States alone. Some insiders feel that that number is too low." There was more laughter. James held up his other hand. "Just reporting...now, others believe the number of us out there worldwide is closer to five thousand." James continued to shake his head. "My, how do these rumors start?" His voice became hard. *"They wish the number were so low!"* There was silence. James looked around. *Can they understand?* He started to breathe through his mouth as if he was nearing the end of a great race. *Can they?*

"Gentlemen," he continued rapidly, "we are *not* a figment of someone's imagination. We are quite real. We take their young, their old, their weak, their strong. We take husband, wife, brother, sister, relative, friend, and acquaintance." His voice grew heated, his eyes flashing. "Those that are alone, those that are surrounded. Protected, unprotected. The good, the evil...it does not matter. *We*...gentlemen...*We!* We take our prey as predators do. We do not go bump in the night—" James brought his hands up, a pastor blessing his flock. His breathing eased, his voice softened to a whisper. But his eyes still hunted.

"We, gentlemen, *are* the night. And it is the quality of that darkness that survives." He paused, the question still plaguing him. *Do they truly understand?* Slowly he continued.

"The *elite* of our kind is here within this room. *History* is in this room. *The Society* is in this room!" James smiled his smile as the members stood from their chairs, applauding. *Can they understand?* He wasn't questioning the outside world; they had no say in this. They never had. He listened to his people applauding themselves. *Can they? Do they?* There was no answer for now, he knew. He had a darker business to attend to.

"Once more, gentlemen, may I continue?" He motioned with his hands and they sat down quietly. "Our shared mark is a reminder of our commitment: to our true nature, to each other. And as to my own commitment to The Society and to young Douglas, I will *personally* take him under my wing." An uneasiness immediately settled over the room. *Good,* James thought. *Keep them all guessing—except for the one.* He knew that one way of getting to the top dog was by taking out one of its pups. And if there *was* a hunter in the pack, he had just thrown Douglas to him. James had another curve to throw.

"Unfortunately, gentlemen, we also have some other, more pressing matters at hand. I don't wish to take the wind out of young Douglas' sails, but we seem to have a predicament." James paused, forging concern. "You will have noticed that some of our kind are absent from our gathering." Stephen watched James with an even keener interest now.

"I will be collecting some information from my sources, and in six months' time there will be an emergency meeting." If the bait had been taken, James knew Douglas would not be showing his face at that meeting. James gave him even odds of surviving the remainder of the week.

"Gentlemen," he said, turning his thoughts back to tying up loose ends, "the reason for this unusual turn of events is that there seems to be a *predator* in our midst. Quite frankly, for the first time in generations, we are being hunted."

At first there was complete silence, and then an onslaught of questions from all over the room. James tried to speak over the noise.

"Gentlemen, please," he called out, holding up his hands. "In a few moments, I will tell you who I believe has fallen, but first...but first...Gentlemen, please! I'll have all the information at the next meeting. The host town where we will meet again...the town...Gentlemen! If you please!" The voices began to taper off. "The host town is called Tranquillity."

Can they understand? He had a feeling that they might never have a chance. "Tranquillity, New York," he said.

Stephen shifted ever so slightly in his chair

John Roberts And The Wolf - 1814

The town and surrounding lands that were to be known as Tranquillity had yet to be settled, much less named. The simple fact of it was that it wasn't meant to be a town. It wasn't meant to be anything. It was all a mistake. Just as it had been a mistake that in December of 1620, the Pilgrims had landed in Massachusetts. They had set sail for Virginia from Plymouth, England, but were blown off course. Running low on beer and with mutiny in the air, once they landed in the middle of a harsh New England winter, they simply stayed. Mistakes are made. A hundred and ninety-four years later, in August of 1814—right around the time the Redcoats were burning Washington—a simple mistake would cause the axle on Mr. Alexander Burns' wagon to break.

The water was cold, and Alexander Burns' feet were sinking in the mud. He was using a tree limb to help his family work their wagon out of the river. His wife, Sara, had taken the reins of the two horses, adding her weight to the effort. She was a tiny, determined woman with no weight to speak of other than her will. With the horses, this made little if any difference. Sara and Alexander's sons, Luke and Samuel, aged nine and twelve, had a far greater effect on the horses through liberal use of the whips. Yet, as much as the Burns' family tried, the simple facts were that the wagon was overloaded, the river bottom muddy, and the horses tired. Besides all of this, Alexander had overlooked a simple maintenance problem; during the hot summer months of their traveling, he had forgotten to keep the axle greased and it had dried out.

As two of the six other families that had already made it across the river were coming back to help them, Alexander pushed, his wife pulled, and his sons whipped. The wagon rocked forward. With his back straining, his feet digging themselves deeper into the mud, Alexander managed to push the wagon forward a few inches. It immediately dropped back. His makeshift lever snapped as the full weight of the wagon came down on it. Alexander barely got out of the way. A second later the rear axle splintered, scattering mud, water, and a few family belongings.

The first of the two wagons that had come to help stopped short of the river. John Roberts stood up in his wagon, surveying the landscape. The countryside was green with soft rolling hills.

Squinting as was his habit at sea, John Roberts noticed that some areas were a little overgrown with low shrubbery, but workable. A good treeline for lumber stood half a mile off. Better yet, they hadn't seen another farm in a day's travel, if not longer. That was good, there would be fewer questions asked.

John Roberts looked to his good friend Alexander and climbed down from his wagon. Patting his horses, he handed the reins to his eldest girl, Mary, who had been walking alongside. She had a crush on Samuel, who stopped whipping the horses and came over to give her a hand holding the reins. John Roberts saw that, but didn't mind much. He figured it was part of nature's way, nothing you could do about that. Besides, Samuel was a likeable boy, pleasant in his own manner. His own son, John, his eldest, was with the head wagon. John was his pride.

Walking into the river, John Roberts stopped next to his friend and smiled. Both men looked to be cut from the same cloth, as if they had shared the same womb, suckled at the same breast. Confined to the small hulls of ships, they were slight of build, as if the tiny, crowded spaces they had lived in had limited their growth. The salt of the seas and the winds that fed the sailing ships had weathered their faces, leaving a weariness on them beyond their age. A harsh life had ringed their eyes, and the cat-o-nine-tails had scarred both backs.

To John Roberts, it felt good being in water without the heaviness of salt to it. They had been following the river looking for a good ford for some time now. The river seemed to have a number of personalities, as did the seas of the world. In some places, it was shallow and calm, moving lazily, but too muddy for the weight they carried. Other places, it raced like the Devil, hell-bent on moving its waters through the pieces of earth it separated. Here, though, he could hear the water's breath flow about him without the cries of men. He smiled with a peacefulness he hadn't felt in years. The word "tranquil" came to his mind.

"Might be the place," he said to Alexander. The wagon could be fixed; both men understood that. John Roberts had been a ship's carpenter for most of his years at sea. But they also knew that they couldn't run forever. Both John Roberts and Alexander Burns were deserters from the American Navy. There was a chance that they might be hunted, but they would take it.

"Might be, at that," Alexander agreed.

John Roberts tried to look under the wagon, but the water was too high. Dropping his shoulder, he reached underneath the back end and along the splintered axle. What he didn't feel told him the story. He faulted his friend for nothing, not seeing any sense to it. Alexander knew what he had done. They had served on the same sailing ships too long now to try to stand above each other. Could be, he thought, that this was the Lord's way of telling them to stop, no more running. He straightened up, feeling the water push against his legs. This was some of the coldest water he had ever felt.

He looked up and down the river. It looked good. *Yes, it is about time to stop,* he thought. "Water seems plentiful," he said to Alexander. "Strong flow. Good for drinking, washing. I'm sure there's a table about somewhere we can sink our wells." He knew Alexander was tired. Neither one of them were made for running. "Good a place as any we've seen." All of the families knew winter was just a few months off. There was plenty to do before the air turned cold and the ground hard.

"Aye, and we have plenty of trees there," Alexander said, pointing. "It looks like I'm staying put, John Roberts." Alexander always called his friend by both names, but he wasn't the only one. Most of John Roberts' friends and acquaintances did the same. "The other families can vote their mind," Alexander added.

"We're stronger if we stay together," John Roberts said. He turned to the second wagon and told them to fetch the others before they got too far ahead.

The second wagon, a family named Petersons, would not make it past the second snowfall. Once the decision was made to stay, the seven families would spread out over the countryside, each house built within sight of another. The Petersons' place wound up a mile to the right of John Roberts', while Alexander took up the land off to the left. The rest of the families branched out from those three farms. John Roberts was right about the water table, and the following spring, all of the families sunk water wells except for one. After the first snowfall, the Petersons' middle child, Michael, came down with a fever, spreading it to the rest of the family. Inasmuch as they could, the other families helped, but they couldn't stop the sickness. In the end, they quarantined the Petersons in fear the fever would affect them. Two days after the second snow, John Roberts noticed there wasn't any smoke coming from the Petersons' chimney. Fighting his way through the high drifts, he found them all dead in one bed. Some of the bodies had teeth marks through the thick clothing, and one of the smaller children lay partially eaten. He found a wolf dead in the corner of the house without a mark on it. It had thrown up some of what it had eaten, and looked like it had died on the spot. He figured that the creature had choked to death, but wasn't sure. To play it safe, he burnt the house with the wolf and the Petersons in it. Came spring when the ground softened, the families gave the remains a proper Christian burial. John Roberts had taken the dead wolf as a bad omen, but said nothing about the animal to anyone.

Alexander waited until the Petersons' wagon was gone before he spoke to his friend. "I know as a Truth, John Roberts, that our strength be with our numbers. There be that chance that someone may come looking. Still, they'll vote their mind without me saying anything to the contrary to them." Alexander started to unload his wagon, calling his sons over. He turned back to his friend. "All I ask in our travels together is a strong back or two to help get my family's belongings up on a dry piece of land." Alexander started to retrieve the few items that had fallen into the river. John Roberts looked about.

"We'll unload your family first, Alexander," he said, "and mine second. We'll be staying here, by the looks of it. And by the grace of God, like I said, it seems as good a place as any." John Roberts let the cold waters run through his fingers. *"Tranquil,"* he said to no one in particular. "It looks to me as being tranquil."

John Roberts walked out of the river that he would be buried next to some twenty years later. Before his own death, four of his ten children, some yet unborn, would have died before the age of five. He would also never know what had happened to his eldest son, John. On the eve of John's eighteenth birthday, his father would send him for some supplies over to adjacent Menkerit county. Most of the supplies were needed for Beth, John Roberts' wife, who carried a child that would live well beyond its fifth year but die in his mid-years a slaver. Along with the supplies for the unborn child, a couple of pounds of nails and a new hammer were also needed. The younger John left with some chickens and hard coins of silver to barter with the few other families that were settling in the area. Younger John had a knack with people, and this made him well-liked. People always felt that with his good nature, they more than got a fair deal with him. Sometimes, trying too hard to be fair, people almost had to chase the younger John away with the promise that if they found anything wrong with the items of trade, they would come looking for him.

John Roberts watched that day as his son worked the wagon running parallel with the river. Calling out to him to be careful, he stood in the spot where he had helped Alexander that first day with his wagon. It was also the spot where he and Alexander killed that man.

Three days after his son should have returned, John Roberts went to that spot to wait. The baby was close, and he couldn't leave his wife, and the waiting tore at him. Alexander and the other families searched for his son, but John Roberts had it in his heart to do it himself. After the birth of the baby, he searched the surrounding lands in a five-day radius of travel. He found nothing of his son, wagon, or horse.

The only information that John Roberts came across was that he was last been seen in Menkerit county. It was in that county that John Roberts believed his son had fallen to foul play. Alexander could never tell him anything different, but John Roberts felt that this was his punishment for killing the bounty hunter. At the time, the bounty hunter gave him no other choice but to be the cause of his own death. All of the families agreed in the event of things that if ever a man warranted killing, this man did. Still, it never eased John Roberts' mind that he did the final killing and knew God had witnessed it. He began to curse the day he had left the sea. He also cursed God and Menkerit county for taking his son. In years to come, he would rain havoc on one, not being able to touch the other.

All of these events had been set in motion a year earlier. The heads of all seven families were mariners. Of the seven, Alexander and John Roberts were the only deserters. The two had served together under Commodore Perry upon his flagship, *Lawrence*. It was during the battle of Lake Erie, when Perry was credited with saying, "*We have met the enemy and they are ours*," that the two seamen became deserters. What they met in that battle, they didn't like. With the war against Great Britain, and to a lesser degree, France, going on since 1812 over the maritime rights of neutrals, none of the family heads were interested in the sea-going life anymore. British ships were impressing American seamen into their own navy, claiming that they were deserters from the British Navy or they were of English descent. War raged upon the high seas, and life for any American seaman was perilous at best.

The two deserters had made their way back to New England to collect their families looking to become farmers. John Roberts and Alexander felt that New England wasn't a safe place for them to hide, so they traveled down into New York with five other families, keeping away from the coastal regions. They were two and a half days into the state when Alexander's axle broke in the river.

Three years later, the bounty hunter William Reed, the man John Roberts would kill, came hunting for them.

The Killing Of Mr. William Reed

William Reed was a man once considered to be, for the most part, of good character. He was lean, with a quick wit that at times covered a short temper. Fate and hard times had pushed him into becoming something he wasn't, but he took well to becoming it. An ex-seaman, he hunted deserters, knowing what to look for. He knew his missing kind well, and there was no lack of work.

At times, the work was easy, his hunts made all the easier by those buying new goods for a new life. Mostly wagons, teams of horses, cooking pots, bolts of cloth and building and farming supplies were the first things he looked for. It was anything they could afford to escape with. Later he narrowed it down with questions asked, the answers remembered for a piece of silver or two. He was a hunter of living, breathing men, and he was not well liked for it. Yet the offer of money eased tongues and pointed fingers in the right direction. That, and pointing him away from themselves in order to keep their own dark secrets safe.

At one time he had been a ship's accountant, and he looked upon the men he hunted as "accounts outstanding." According to the records he kept, he had brought twenty-eight of these men back into the arms of the law. Eighteen men he had killed outright with one or more of the four flintlock pistols he carried. Three others, he had knifed. The balance of his accounts were hung. He watched every hanging.

With each man he killed, he took a small piece of scalp that he tied to the mane of his horse. As he spent long hours in the saddle, he would run his fingers over them, waiting for the next one. With those who were hung, times being what they were, a piece of silver handed over to the hangman would allow him another small patch of hair to be added to his horse's mane. With hungry, greedy men, it never took much.

It was a full moon when William's horse entered the cold river. Covering his flintlocks with the long oilskin coat he wore, he let his horse drink. He watched the light of the moon sparkle off the slow-moving waters. This was the time of the month he liked hunting his deserters the best. He never understood the feelings that had developed over the years, he just accepted them. He knew certain men had certain natures that were as fixed as the stars and moon overhead and he left it at that. If one knew how to read the sky, it was easy to navigate its darkness. The same held true with men.

William surveyed the area. He knew he was close. He always knew. That was a part of his nature he never thought about, either. Nature or not, finding these two had proved no problem so far. Night or day, months or years, seven seagoing families were easy to track over land. Now, word of mouth had the families within the next set of hills and doing quite well these years, except for one. It had been told to him that they didn't make it past the first snows. It was a shame, but his accounts weren't with them or the other honest families. It was time for the other two to pay up, bringing his accounts to thirty. The only problem William Reed had was that the two deserters were family men, and family men were the most dangerous. He knew he was taking a chance with two of them. One man, he could watch and safely travel with tied to a horse. But the idea of two did not sit well with him. He knew he would have to kill one, if not both.

He gave a single tug on the reins and the horse pulled its head up from drinking. Guiding the animal to the shore, William dismounted and took out four thick pieces of canvas from one of his saddlebags. Kneeling, he tapped the front leg of his horse, and it lifted up its leg. Wrapping the canvas around the hoof, he repeated the ritual three more times. He had done this many times before, and the animal seemed to know it was to walk lightly and silently. Still, he wanted to give his horse some time to get used to wearing them again. Next, William checked all four of his flintlocks. Satisfied, he remounted and gave his horse a kick, touching the mane and his collection of human hair. He had cleared two spaces for the patches of scalps he expected. Of the two, he planned on collecting John Roberts first. Alexander Burns would come after.

It was now a month past the autumnal equinox and beneath a Hunter's Moon, he gave the killings some thought. If any of the other families got involved, he would simply add them to his collection. With his fingers entangled in mane and hair, he rode silently, both man and animal like ghosts shining pale in the bright moonlight.

John Roberts' house and barn were dark. William rode first around the barn, scrutinizing the structure and surrounding land. Next, he acquainted himself with the house. Leaning forward on his horse, he noted the house was built strong, with no waste of good wood. Even in the moonlight, John Roberts' skills as a ship's carpenter showed. It was a large house that spoke of a large family; a house built with no plans of leaving it. That was a shame.

Reed studied the house a moment longer, then looked back over to the barn. He would set fire to the barn, and when John Roberts came out, he would kill him on the spot. He would do the same to the Burns' farm. Two more patches of hair for his collection. Pulling lightly on the reins, he started to make his way silently back over to the barn, when he heard the voice of John Roberts behind him. William dropped the reins and started to reach for one of his flintlocks.

"Keep your hands off those pistols you be carrying, Mr. Reed." John Roberts had watched William from the house. Both his and Alexander's families were hiding in the last farmhouse over the hill. They had heard of William Reed, heard that he chose to do his killings by cold moonlight. Talk had been that he had done a killing just twenty miles south three months ago. Both men had been waiting each month with the full moon for this hunter of men. John Roberts found the silence of the man and horse eerie.

"Mr. Reed, kindly place your hands down by your sides." Reed slowly did as he was told. John Roberts stayed behind him. "Thank you, Sir. Now, your kind is not needed in these parts. The questions you asked traveled quicker than you did, Sir. Proper people always know when bad times comes riding in on a horse." John Roberts paused. "By chance, could I persuade you to leave us be?"

"No, you cannot." William was firm.

"I hold a pistol to your back, Mr. Reed." The warning was clear enough. "I'm a fair enough man to tell you that." John Roberts cocked the flintlock. The sound was like a small bone breaking. "I'll ask again, Sir. Could I persuade you to leave us be?"

"Once again, John Roberts...No, you cannot. You are a deserter, John Roberts, and will be held in account for that!" Reed turned slowly in the saddle to face him. For some, it was hard enough to kill a man, but even harder when the man stared you down. William looked at John Roberts, wondering what he had here. He knew that he had underestimated the man.

John Roberts faced the man on the horse. He was not a killer, but right now, he was at war. He pulled the trigger, and the flintlock misfired with a small flash. William Reed never even moved.

"Well, Sir, we may add attempted murder to your crimes. Yet, I fear for you, that it will matter not." Reed pulled out one of his pistols, cocking it.

John Roberts moved quickly, flinging his pistol at the bounty hunter and leaping at him dragging him from his horse by his coat. Caught off-guard, Reed's pistol went off, the ball from the flintlock striking his horse behind the ear, shattering its skull. The animal toppled, pinning Reed's right leg, as John Roberts tumbled backwards.

Scrambling, John Roberts grabbed a rock and brought it down on the hunter's head. The blow was solid, but not solid enough. He was bringing the rock down a second time when he felt the knife pierce his side. Staggering back, he grabbed his side, letting the bloody rock fall.

As Reed fought to get out from under the weight of the dead horse, he managed to cock another pistol taking aim at him. With a flash of powder and smoke, he fired and the ball cut through the flesh along John Roberts' scalp. The deserter lay on his land, stunned from the shot.

Hazily, John Roberts looked around. His head throbbed as he watched a man struggle with a dead horse. *Wet. His head was wet with something.* He touched his head. *Shot...?* He knew he had to get up. Slowly, he stood. He looked back over at the other man. He was almost free. *Run!* his mind told him. *The river. Run!*

He had taken only a few steps when he heard the crack of another pistol. Nothing struck him, but the sound of it helped clear his mind. He knew he had to run for his life. Had to keep running to draw Reed away from Alexander's farm.

As he ran, he looked over his shoulder and saw that Reed had finally freed himself and was reloading the flintlocks. With most of the country being open space, John Roberts didn't like the odds. The river was his only hope.

Reaching it, he waded in, the icy water stabbing into him and exploding through his body into his head.

He stopped and looked back over his shoulder. The bounty hunter was nowhere in sight. He was hoping to lose William by hiding beneath one of the overhanging bushes further along the bank. The cold of the rushing water started him moving again. He ran on.

As he turned a bend in the river, a dark figure stepped out from a bush aiming a pistol at him.

Quickly, John Roberts turned to run, just in time to see Reed enter the river aiming his own pistol. The crack of the pistol behind him shattered the night and knocked Reed off his feet. Alexander had shot William a moment before he was about to fire into John Roberts' back.

Reed lay in the river, his flintlocks wet, the powder ruined. The ball from Alexander's pistol had caught Reed in the midsection, tearing away flesh and life. Reed clutched at his wound, his blood flowing away with the cold water. Alexander spoke first.

"I waited for this devil all these nights by the river. I fell asleep on watch, but the shots woke me." Alexander knew Reed was a dead man, had to be, but he no longer had the stomach for this. He could see John Roberts holding his side, his head dark with blood. "Are you hurt much?" he asked his friend.

"The wounds will heal," John Roberts kept his eye on Reed, "but I fear what has to be done may not heal itself proper. Can you finish him?" Still, Reed did not move.

"No, John Roberts, 'tis not in me."

Hearing this, William Reed went into a fit of laughter. "That's why you are deserters! You are weak and deserve to die!" he yelled, condemning them. Getting up slowly, he spat at them. His wound kept him doubled over, but he produced another short dagger from behind his back. He pointed it at them and started to walk down-river, away from them.

"Alexander, can you load another shot?" John Roberts asked calmly, walking slowly in Reed's footsteps.

"Aye, being done."

Walking carefully in the riverbed, John Roberts called after Reed's retreating body. "How does it feel, Mr. Reed, to be the hunted?" Reed was coming to the point where Alexander's wagon had stuck itself in the mud years ago.

Reed turned and answered. "John Roberts," he yelled, "you tell me—how does it feel to *hunt?*" He could go no further; the mud made it hard to walk in the river. He watched as John Roberts took the pistol from Alexander.

John Roberts looked at the man in front of him, feeling the heaviness of the pistol and the heaviness of what was about to be done.

"Mr. Reed, you are a devil!" he cried out, walking closer to him. He felt the mud sucking at his feet and stopped. He raised the pistol. Despite the pain, Reed straightened up his body.

"If I be the devil, then you be my God, John Roberts. It was men like you that made me what I am today." He spat at them again.

John Roberts held the pistol steady. "The only thing I will make out of you today, Mr. William Reed, is dead."

"You may indeed bring me to my end, John Roberts, but I was still cast and molded by the likes of you."

"If so, I stand here corrected then, Mr. William Reed," he retorted. John Roberts backed out of the mud, not wanting to share the same earth with the man. "You are neither a creature of the devil, nor of God. You have no purpose to serve but your own." He walked around to the side of Reed, cocking the pistol as he left the cold waters. "You, Sir, are a bastard son of two kingdoms." He stopped, aiming the pistol. "William Reed, you are an abomination, and have laid ruin the tranquility of my soul."

Reed laughed. "There be others, John Roberts," he warned. "There be others. If one was made, many were made. God, devil, or man, that is the way." And continued to laugh.

John Roberts pulled the trigger, and this time the pistol he held fired. For a moment, he felt a pleasure he had never experienced before.

They burned the body and belongings of William Reed along with his horse. The only thing they didn't burn was a strange journal they found packed away in a large saddlebag. John Roberts kept it, but he kept it hidden. He would get up before the rest of his family to study it by candlelight. Beneath that burning light, he would turn the many pages that held strange symbols and drawings surrounded by foreign writings. Yet there was much he could read, with many pages written in a language he knew. Of even those pages he couldn't read, there was something inside of him that understood them. He knew it for a book of killing, but he also knew it was more than that. It was a book of souls taken and of souls lost. It looked into the nature of man—a look that was a right only God should have. And because of that, the book gave him a sense of power that stood him above the rest. And for that, he knew it was Evil.

The journal was saved, and the burnt human remains of William Reed that had once written in it and had once taken so many lives were scattered. In the remaining years of his life, John Roberts would think back to that day, remembering the flames seemed unusually bright.

It was a year after John Roberts' death that the loosely knit community, not wanting to be part of Menkerit county, decided to give themselves a name. Alexander Burns remembered what his friend had said to William Reed before he killed him. In peaceful memory of his friend's soul, he named the town Tranquillity. The name suited people. It was rumored that it had something to do with the river, but beyond that, nothing else was said or known. Another rumor that went around, was that one of the original settlers, John Roberts, was a murderer. That he took on the soul of someone he killed and made many pay in Menkerit for his missing son. But very little was said of that. What was freely spoken about was the curse that many felt had settled in the area.

Tranquillity—Present Day, August

Christian stood above her, watching her sleep in the early morning light. She lay nude on her stomach. Her thick, wild, sandy blonde hair obscured the small pillow she loved to sleep with. Carefully sitting on the bed, he rested his hand lightly on her smooth back. The milky whiteness of her skin stood out in sharp contrast against the dark sheets. He ran his fingers over the tiny fine hairs that covered her lower back and legs. Over the creamy roundness of her ass, the hairs disappeared only to reappear elsewhere, darker, coarser, thicker. It was toward these hairs that his hand now traveled, touching, probing. She began to stir, so he pulled his hand away and watched as she settled back down into her slumber once again. It was good being home. He hated to be away from her for too long. He wanted to make love to her, slowly, carefully. He let his hand settle on her again. As he did, there was a banging noise overhead, followed by footsteps and someone yelling out, *"Hey!"* He knew exactly who it was.

"Oh, no. That's not Palmer, is it?" Katie mumbled into her pillow, not moving from her position. "Please, say it's too early for him. Besides, did you lose something down there?" she asked, wiggling her ass.

"You were awake?" Christian asked, feeling like he'd been caught with his hand in the cookie jar...so to speak.

"Of course I'm awake. I heard you come in. And what's with your little hand-puppet routine? Do you think I'm dead?" She continued to wiggle her ass, but with Palmer on the roof, that was about as far as it was going to go. Besides, Amy would be up soon anyway, especially when she heard "Unta Bart's" voice. Then there would be no stopping her. Their daughter was the only one in town that called Palmer by his first name. "Unta Bart" was her favorite playpal and, at four years old, she made good use of him. Sometimes with Palmer around, Amy forgot about her parents.

"Hey! Hey!" His voice carried down to them. "You kids forget about me up here? What's doing? Are ya naked down there? You're naked, right? You need a skylight up here, that's what! I can't see!" It sounded like he was doing a rain dance up there.

Christian kissed Katie's back. "A little romance tonight?" he whispered to her.

"Definitely," she whispered back, turning around. Her eyes traveled over his face as if she was seeing him for the first time. "It's been nice having you back these last few days. I know with Cecilia being sick and everything...well, it's just that I miss you too much. And Palmer's right," she said, throwing her arms around his neck, "a skylight *would* be nice. But let's get him off the roof first."

"Skylight?" Christian asked, watching a sly grin touch the corner of her mouth. "Skylight?" he asked again, wary of the cunning behind those mischievous green eyes of hers. Katie was silent. Slowly, the grin grew. *Her mouth was made for laughing,* he thought. Pulling herself up, she gave him a kiss and slipped out of bed to dress. *Skylight?* He knew he was screwed.

Christian watched his wife throw on a pair of sweatpants and search for a sweatshirt from a pile of clothing. He had a hard time believing how trim her body was at thirty-five, very soon to be thirty-six. She was a natural; good genetics and a fairly decent diet. It didn't take much to keep her fit; trying to keep up with their daughter was about all she needed.

Katie finally found a sweatshirt that had seen better days and pulled it over her head. But even in the baggy clothes, she made his heart beat fast. He knew he was a lucky man.

Palmer's steps were now directly overhead. *Must have the balance of a mountain goat,* Christian thought. "Hey, Palmer," he yelled up at the footsteps over his head, "why are you up there anyway? I thought you finished the roofing."

Palmer's voice echoed back down to him. "Nope, not done. A little measuring here and there before my shift. What's for breakfast?"

"Hey, if you fixed it right the first time, you wouldn't have to check anything," Christian yelled as Katie came over to him. She put a finger to his lips and began to unbutton his uniform.

"Sheriff," she said to him, "you're off duty, relax. Besides, do you two fools have to yell back and forth like that? Come play with Amy before Palmer gets to her." She opened his shirt and kissed the scars on his neck, touching his shoulders where the pellets from the shotgun blast of that maniac had hit him. She had always felt that that serial killer had wanted him and Nestor alive. She was sure he had been hoping to catch them both with the birdshot he had loaded. Other than that, she refused to think what his sick mind had had in store for them. Still, she knew they had been lucky to survive. But the vest he wore hadn't stopped everything. After the shooting, it had been her job to heal him.

It had been six years since the shooting, but she knew he still carried the death of that little girl on his conscience. He had been a different man since that tragedy. His "retirement" from the department hadn't helped, either. The whole thing had almost torn them apart, but they had stuck it out. And finding the position as sheriff up here was heaven-sent; out of the blue—and about as quiet. She knew, compared to what her husband had been used to, it was *very* quiet up here, but he never complained. She believed he could have been truly happy, had it not been for his sister Cecilia's illness. The cancer was eating away at her and doing the same to his heart. The trips to visit his sister were taking their toll on him, and Katie knew that she would have to be the healer once again. *Thank God for Palmer*, she thought. They were lucky to have him around.

Katie let her hands run over some of the lumpy scars. A number of the pellets were still lodged in, too close to blood vessels to be safely removed. Reaching up, Katie gave her husband a quick kiss on the lips. She wanted more but would wait for tonight. Palmer was yelling something down from the roof.

"See you downstairs," she said quietly. Angling her head toward the roof, she shouted, "Hey, Palmer! If you wake Amy up, I'm gonna throw your butt off the roof!" Palmer fell silent, and she smiled at Christian as she started out of the room. He had to laugh.

"You're a classy woman, Katie Lord," he called after her. Christian shook his head as he watched her go into Amy's room. He was amazed at her goodness and at a loss as to what to do for her birthday. No matter what he did, it wouldn't be enough. He would have to run down to the city and pick up something special for her. He just didn't know what.

"Hey, did she leave yet?" Palmer's voice came down cautiously. But before Christian could reply, his wife and daughter came out of Amy's room and sat down on the top of the stairs. His daughter was a mirror image of her mother, from the unruly blonde hair to the mischievous eyes and mouth. They both waved to him and started to bounce their bottoms from step to step giggling all the way down. Christian couldn't figure out which of them was more of a kid.

"Yeah Palmer, the two *children* left. You can yell again," he said, wondering if Palmer had a good idea for a gift.

"...know how many people in this town?" Palmer yelled, picking up where he had left off talking about his workmanship. It sounded like he was yelling over to Menkerit County. "If I fixed everything right the first time, how would I have work for my old age? Good God, Christian, use your head! Ya stupid or just a bad businessman?" Christian heard his footsteps starting to retreat from overhead. "Hey, nobody answered me...what's for breakfast?"

Unbuckling his gun belt, Christian yelled back. "Hey, you still there?"

"Somewhere. Why?"

He called up, a little softer. "Hey, what should I get Katie for her birthday? Any ideas?"

"Yeah," Palmer said, but didn't volunteer any more information.

"Ball buster," Christian mumbled. Louder, "Yeah? Yeah what? And speak up, but not too loud, I want it to be a surprise. That's the whole idea."

He barely heard Palmer's reply.

"What?"

"I said, a heart.*"

"A *heart?*"

"Yeah, one of those heart pendants," Palmer's voice drifted down. "One with diamonds and stuff. It's symbolic. You know, love, life, strength, and all of that other crap. But she won't be worried about all that other crap, she'll just love it." Christian thought it wasn't a bad idea and told Palmer so.

"Come on, you earned your meal," he said. "Now get off my roof and let's eat." Palmer's footsteps trailed off as he was yelling something back about stealing Christian's daughter and maybe his wife. Christian laughed, but it died as he turned and caught a glimpse of himself in the dresser mirror. There were so many scars—many running deeper than anyone knew. If he could have, he would have done things differently, but this was the way everything turned out. Sometimes you just didn't have the control you thought you had. He turned away from his reflection.

Emptying out his pockets, he took a small key and opened up a drawer placing his .357 revolver on top of a .45-caliber automatic. As he locked the drawer, he heard Katie screech and curse. A moment later, she yelled up to him from the bottom of the steps. He could hear the despair in her voice.

"Christian! There's another headless body down here! We have *got* to do something about this!"

Flea-Flea

Christian sat at the breakfast table and listened to his daughter screaming. It was too late to save her. He reached over and took his wife's hand, giving it a kiss. The screeches from his daughter were now traveling in his direction. Finally, he caught sight of her headlong flight back into the kitchen. He flinched as her head just missed the corner of the breakfast table, slamming into his thigh instead. Hugging his leg, she looked up at her father, screamed, and buried her face in his lap before looking back over her shoulder. She let out another screech as she saw Unta Bart crouched over, heading straight for her. She disappeared in a flash. Palmer ran by, grabbing a piece of toast off the table as he went.

"*Christian!* Kissing my hand will do you no good!" Katie reprimanded her husband. "These bodies are your responsibility!" Christian kissed her hand again. "*Stop* it!" she said, slapping the top of his head. "Listen, you have got to make him leave them outside! *Two* in the kitchen this week! *Two!*" Amy and Palmer made another pass through the kitchen. Christian grabbed the last piece of toast before Palmer could snatch it. Palmer mumbled something in passing.

"Christian?" Katie waited for an answer. He stared at her, trying to come up with a good one. Buying time, he looked around the kitchen. His eye fell on a cut section of a thick wooden beam that lay on top of the fireplace mantle. The culprit in question slept upon it. Christian shrugged.

The kitchen, like the rest of the house, had enough room for a dozen kids to run around in. The house itself had been built with horizontal space in mind. The rooms were long and low, giving an illusion of distance. An ex-sailor, which would account for the low ceilings, had built it; it was as if he were still living beneath the deck of a ship. As long as Christian kept his eyes level, the rooms never felt claustrophobic to him, but he always half-expected the sound of Ahab walking the deck above.

The house had two working fireplaces, one in the kitchen and the other in the living room. They gave off enough heat to warm the whole first floor of the house. He remembered when Katie had first walked into the house and spotted the two fireplaces. By the expression on her face, he knew the rest of the house could have been a burnt-out shell and it wouldn't have mattered. "It's beautiful," she said. "Of course, it'll need a little work, but I *love* it!"

Christian was a bit more reserved, knowing how "a little work" often turned into a *lot* of work, and even a lot more money. Still, he couldn't hold her back.

Besides the kitchen and the living room, there were five other rooms and a bathroom on the first floor. One was an office for Christian. Once it had been completed, he almost never set foot in it again, preferring to use the computer in their bedroom. Another room served as a sewing room that Katie never sewed in. There was a small guest bedroom off the kitchen. Next to the guest room was a "general room," which, in practice, was Katie's office. Here she worked on her illustrations for children's books. The last room was being held in reserve for when they had the second child that Katie hinted about.

Her enthusiasm and plans hadn't been confined to the first floor, either. She had opened up the attic, making it their bedroom. Her plans had also called for a second bathroom up there along with a room for Amy. Christian never disagreed with her over these plans feeling that the lower floors were confining. The attic roof had started out about twelve feet high, slanting down at a forty-degree angle to a height of six feet. Along this six-foot wall, a battery of windows faced out toward the backyard and the woods beyond. Christian always felt that climbing up to the openness of the attic from the lower rooms must have been like climbing up from the hull of a ship to an open deck. He could almost envision sails running down along it.

At one time, he knew the attic was used as a hayloft, but Christian wasn't sure if it was part of the original design or was added later by a different carpenter. Either way, making it their bedroom was an idea that Christian had jumped on. In his mind's eye, it was on open place to escape to, but knew there was no way he could do this work himself. All of this work had fallen to Palmer, the best carpenter in the county. Along with being handy with a hammer and saw, Palmer had also been acting sheriff for several years. He had been relieved when Christian came up to Tranquillity and took over the position. The previous sheriff, Adams, had retired rather unexpectedly leaving Palmer to fill the post. With Christian as sheriff now, he was a deputy again, giving him more time for his carpentry work. He had always preferred working with wood to settling domestic disputes and handing out parking tickets, and he was more than happy to take on Christian's home improvements.

It was during these renovations that he had exposed a beam with a verse from the Bible carved into it:

"And I looked, and behold, a pale horse:
and his name that sat on him was Death."
                                              -Revelation 6:8
                                              John Roberts

Once they had determined that it wasn't load bearing, Christian had Palmer cut that part of the beam away, and he placed it on the mantel over the kitchen fireplace. Katie had thought it was a little morbid and surrounded it with dried flower arrangements. Christian had pointed out that the dried flowers were dead and weren't any less morbid than the piece of wood. She just glared at him, and from then on he let her do her arrangements without any further questions.

Flea-Flea, their cat, stomach full, was asleep on the section of beam among the dried flowers, his paw hanging down, obscuring part of the verse. Christian came up with the best defense that he could for the headless bodies.

"Hon, he's a *cat*, he does cat things," Christian said. "Think of them as presents." He got that stare again. She wasn't buying it.

"Christian, he left one of his *presents* on the kitchen floor again. A baby rabbit this time. He ate the head and left the body!"

Christian continued trying. "It's his way of sharing the hunt. He's including us in his world, that's all. Look at him...doesn't he look cute?" Flea-Flea had been a black, mangy-looking bundle of fur and bones when Katie had found him on the porch over a year ago. He had lain there half-dead with two puncture wounds in his hindquarters and a long gash along the side of his right eye. Katie hadn't worried about the gash along his head, but the puncture wounds were infected, and his whole body was hot to the touch.

The local vet, Jim Knowles, had urged them to put him down, but Katie wouldn't hear anything of it, so the vet shot him up with antibiotics and wished her luck. For the next week, she rinsed out the wounds with hydrogen peroxide and fed him with a small spoon. He never put up a fight. He did, however, recover. It was less than a month before he'd left his first corpse on the porch where she had found him. He thanked her about twice a week, providing her with a wide variety of small woodland creatures for her delectation. His ritual of eating the head and leaving the body outside had been changing in the last few weeks. Expanding his territory, he was now leaving his thank-yous in the kitchen.

"Christian, I love Flea-Flea." *Flea* had been her cat's name when she'd been a child. When Christian had asked why she'd repeated the name, she had told him that it was her second cat. "I just don't want any more dead animals in the house. I—"

"He's a *cat*," Christian tried again. "A predator. That's his nature. He doesn't know anything different. He doesn't think he is doing anything wrong. If you were another cat, you'd be honored."

"Okay...I'm honored," she said wearily. "Let's just try to keep my honorary awards outside of the house. I would like to keep the kitchen a dead-animal-free zone. The only thing non-living in the kitchen is whatever we all decide to eat. Okay? Maybe Flea-Flea will get the idea."

Christian nodded. "We'll try. I'll start burying the bodies. I'll even get Flea-Flea to watch. That might work, okay?"

"Thanks, babe. It's just—I *stepped* on this one. Barefoot." They watched as Palmer continued his morning chase. Christian raised his eyebrows.

"Don't worry, hon," Katie said, getting up from the table, "when she's old enough, I'll tell her that you're really her daddy." She made a show of counting back on her fingers, and shrugged. "At least, I'm *pretty* sure you are," she deadpanned. Christian chucked a crust of toast at her and she ducked, giggling.

She was feeling better and he was glad. He was amazed at how buoyant her mood always was. She seldom stayed angry. Amy was the same. In fact, it seemed that the only characteristics she had inherited from him were his leanness and his stubbornness. If she had banged her head on the table before, she would have stopped and stared at it like it was the table's fault. She would then have walked off, and only when she was sure no one was watching would she have rubbed her head.

For the most part, she was an introverted child, preferring to express herself with her artwork. She would work side by side with her mother for hours, not making a sound, drawing or painting on anything she found. Lately, though, she seemed to be coming out of that internal world a little. She would try to explain parts of her drawings to him or to her mother. Christian knew, at least on his part, that even with her explanations, he couldn't make heads or tails of her artwork. Still, he encouraged her, though she seemed to need no encouragement.

There was another screech, and this time it was Amy chasing Palmer as he came slamming into one of the kitchen chairs, panting from his only morning exercise. Flea-Flea looked down at them from the old beam, yawned, and went back to sleep.

"Whew!" Palmer said as Amy sprinted by, expecting Unta Bart to continue the chase. Christian knew that Katie would grab her at the next go-round and sit her down for her breakfast. With Palmer at the table, Katie would have little trouble keeping her in her chair. Watching his deputy's heaving chest, Christian caught his eye.

"Where's your vest?" he asked, knowing Palmer hated wearing it. Palmer felt he was the best carpenter around and figured he was safe on those merits alone. Christian had heard the joking argument too many times.

"It...uh... doesn't match our uniforms," Palmer protested. This was a new one. Christian looked over at Katie, who just raised her eyebrows and looked back over at Palmer. Christian leaned forward on the kitchen table.

"Palmer," he said slowly, "our uniforms are *khaki*. The *vest* is khaki. You wear the khaki *vest* under your khaki *shirt*. The khaki vest will stop bullets, not the khaki shirt. If you *don't* start wearing the vest, I swear I'll shoot you myself." Christian sat back in his chair.

"Okay, but—"

Christian held up a hand. "Listen, the Murphy boys were acting up last night, and I almost arrested one. You know, what's his face...? One of the twins, that damn talkative one."

"Richard." Katie interjected absentmindedly, waiting to grab Amy.

"Yeah, that one. Thanks. So Palmer, wear the vest, that's an order." Palmer sighed as Amy ran by. Katie tried to grab her and just missed. Amy gave out another little squeal and kept going.

"Christian," Palmer argued, "*you* never wear a vest." He turned to Katie who was pouring some Cocoa Puffs into a bowl for Amy. "*Katie?*" Palmer was looking for support.

Katie stopped what she was doing and just held the box looking at the two of them. This was a sore subject with her, and Palmer realized his mistake too late. For his own protection, he slouched down in his chair.

"Palmer...Christian...you're *both* assholes. You both know how I feel about those vests. If Christian hadn't had his vest that day, he wouldn't be here." Katie stared at her husband. "*Amy* wouldn't be here, either." Christian looked abashed. "And furthermore, did you know I still have that shredded vest of yours? Just a little reminder to let me know how lucky I am that you're still here. You and Nestor going after a serial killer without backup. Assholes! I swear!" Katie was about to say more when the phone rang. She slammed the cereal box down and walked into the living room to answer the phone.

Christian stared at him, but Palmer had no intention of cutting him any slack. He knew he should be wearing a vest, but he also knew Christian should too. The Murphy boys were no joke. Sooner or later, there was going to be a serious clash. Still, he tried to keep it light.

"Hey, don't look at *me* that way! *You* brought it up."

"Palmer, she's right. Just wear it, okay?" Christian watched as Palmer's face took on a more solemn look. Palmer was a damn good cop. Christian had been lucky, first Nestor and now Palmer as partners. When he had come up to Tranquillity, he hadn't been too sure how things would work between them. He had entertained thoughts of firing Palmer, but only briefly. Christian had learned quickly that things worked differently in a small town than in the city.

Katie walked back into the kitchen with the cordless. "Phone," she said, smiling. Her mood had changed again. Christian reached for it, but Katie shook her head. "It's for Palmer."

Palmer looked at Katie and vigorously shook his head. The smile was widening on Katie's face as she nodded slowly. She handed him the phone. The voice on the other end of the line was loud enough to have been in the same room. *Rita Burns.* Christian hid a grin behind his hand as Palmer reluctantly took the phone.

"*Palmer! Palmer!* Where the *hell* are you?" Palmer held the phone away from his ear.

"Right here, Rita. I'm right here." Palmer's face dropped. "Yes, Rita, I know it's late…Yes, I know. Yes…I was just leaving…Yes, Rita. Yes, eating…Yes. Yes Rita, I have a home…" Palmer was getting reamed. There was no mistake about it. Rita Burns was Tranquillity.

Rita Burns

Rita enjoyed the human side of things. She hated technology. Technology hadn't delivered Tranquillity's mail for over forty years. Technology hadn't helped her get to know every house and every family within the town limits. And technology, she knew, wasn't worth a damn for keeping a small town together. You needed good old-fashioned *talk*, word of mouth, person-to-person. A "good day" in passing. A solid hand-shake. A steady, firm voice ringing out in church praising God. A "welcome" pie baked for a new person or family in town. What you saw with your own eyes and heard with your own ears made a small town what it was. And what you didn't hear yourself, you could hear from someone else. Everybody knew everybody's business, and everybody took care of each other. That was small town life. That's what kept people close. That's how you knew who was trouble, and who wasn't.

Sixty-eight, Rita had never stepped one foot outside of the town limits. She had never seen a reason to do so. She could trace her roots back to one of the original settlers, Alexander Burns, and was always happy to tell all about it. She had been married once, in her younger years, and given birth to a boy. A bad heart valve took him from her after only a year, but during his brief stay, Rita had cherished every day with him. After the baby died, Rita had divorced her husband, citing irreconcilable differences. The truth was, she was heartbroken and didn't know how to deal with it. She never blamed anyone for her troubles, and she listened to everyone else's. It wasn't long before she became the town's conscience. A year or so after her baby had died, Tranquillity's mayor *cum* postmaster had let it be known that he was ready to give up delivering the mail. He also let it be known that the job was Rita's to turn down. Hungry for some-thing to do, she had taken it and never looked back.

For the last forty years, Rita had watched the town and her mail route grow. Her post office was, as she saw it, the abso-lute center of town. Next to it was the sheriff's office, a small building with a two-man cell. On the other side was Sam's Market, where everybody did their food shopping. Bill Cross and his wife owned and ran the store. The original owner, Sam Greene, had died thirty years before, and at the time, Bill had been the store's manager. Since Sam had no family of his own, he had left the business to Bill. Bill Cross kept prices fair, but he was a cutthroat businessman nonetheless. Over the years, he had taken over the hardware store across the street from the market. After that, the movie house at the south end, next to the funeral home. He had tried to buy one of the only two garages in a ten-mile radius, the other one being in Menkerit.

He had come close, but the deal fell through. Bill didn't care that much. He had his fingers, if not his hands, in most every pie in town. Despite that, he was well-liked by the town's people—as long as his eye wasn't wandering over their property. For the most part, he was content, but from time to time he had that buying urge. Once, he'd made a run for mayor. Fortunately, the good folks of Tranquillity figured he had enough control over their lives, and he was soundly beaten. He took the loss gracefully. Truth be told, he'd never figured he had much of a chance, but it had been something to do.

Rita, on the other hand, felt the contest was a waste of good money and time for both sides—she knew Bill was destined to lose. Rita hated to waste anything, and she told Bill as much on more than one occasion and in front of more than one person. Bill was known to reply that, for such a thrifty woman, she sure wasted a lot of hot air. The rivalry seemed fierce, but it was essentially good-natured battle between two people who loved to do battle.

Except for the occasional flare-up between Rita and Bill, which, lately, was usually over why he was the only one in town who never received his mail on time, the town was pretty quiet. Quiet, that is, when the Murphy boys weren't running wild about the county. But little of this was seen on the surface or by any passersby. Tranquillity wasn't exactly a tourist trap. It was more of a place to drive through, stop for gas, stretch the legs, and grab a bite to eat. That's all. Its tree-lined streets were pleasant enough, and on a warm spring day with the breezes cutting across town, it felt like Anytown, USA.

Out-of-towners couldn't get lost in Tranquillity even if they tried. Most everything was on Main Street or one of its cross-streets. Anyone who did occasionally wander off Main ran into streets with local historical names like Burns, Roberts, and Petersons. Some of the other streets were named for reasons long forgotten: There were Wolf, John, and Beth. A bakery and shoe store were on Rose Street which was named because someone once remembered that there was a rose bush somewhere in the area. The two bars in town were on Oak and Spruce, although there never had been any oaks or spruces in the area. A diner covered a good part of Spring. Midtown, where the post office was, was considered downtown, no matter which direction you were coming from. The movie house was at the south end, the garage at the north end. On either side of Main, the town ran on for less than a quarter mile before thinning out. So as not to confuse the geographic layout, one side was called East End and the other, West End. Down through the East End, running parallel with Main Street, was Broadway, which was very narrow. The West End had Madison, equally as narrow.

Most of the land surrounding the town was farmlands. A river that most simply referred to as "The River" cut through these farms, meandering like a snake. A fair stretch of it paralleled the road that led to the highway out of town before it swung around, snapping like a whip to turn toward the back of Tranquillity's only church, in which Father Toland spoke his heavenly piece.

River and all, Tranquillity was a pleasant "drive-through town" that might deserve a comment or two in passing. "Anytown, USA" was its blessing, and also its curse. "Anytown"…at least on the surface. All things change.

As it stood now, the town was what it seemed. It was exactly the way Rita liked it. In all of her years delivering the mail, nothing much had changed for her. She went from house to house for those that couldn't come get their own mail at the post office. She couldn't think of a single family that hadn't had her in for dinner at one time or another over the years. She knew everyone almost better than they knew themselves. And if she didn't know them better, she would pretend to. She attended every wedding, christening, and funeral. She knew every paved and dirt road, along with just about every secret, dirty and otherwise.

So when she retired from the mail route, Palmer had suggested that she take over as dispatcher at the sheriff's office. It would, he figured, be a win-win situation. She could keep her finger on the pulse of the town and put her gift of gab to good use. He knew that if anyone got past her, it had to be an emergency. Palmer was right; since then, the town had never been so quiet. Even the feud between Rita and Bill had settled down to a staring match in passing.

Unfortunately for Bill Cross, Rita had also trained the new mail carrier, and he still didn't get his mail on time.

Christian had had a short-lived run-in with Rita when he became sheriff. He'd had the idea to change the protocol of their communications, making it more formal and business-like, less small town. He told Palmer about his idea and Palmer had just smiled and nodded. "Good Idea," Palmer'd commented, and said that he'd like to come along when Christian explained it to Rita. The two rode over to Rita's farm, Palmer grinning all the way out.

They'd parked in front of the immaculate house. Rita took pride in her home which had been handed down from generation to generation. Because of her age, Palmer did a fair share of the upkeep, usually the heaviest work. In exchange, she'd give him tips on how to improve his own work; she was the only one in the county that might have given him a run for his money in the carpentry business. He'd told her on numerous occasions that he was glad she couldn't get around as much as before, 'cause it would have killed all of his work on the side. Every time he told her that, she would show him a new "secret" for keeping an old house in shape. Several times, she had shown Palmer what he thought was the same finishing technique and he had reminded her that they had done that already. She'd ignored him and continued on with her lesson, adding a new touch or twist that would impress him. He'd stopped interrupting her after the third time.

Christian knocked at the door and Rita answered cradling a twelve-gauge Remington shotgun, a cigarette hanging from her mouth. Straight as an arrow and about as wide, she stood a bit taller than Christian. Her hair was dyed a bright red, in sharp contrast to her blue eyes. She claimed to have picked that color to cover her gray so that when she went hunting, her red hair kept her from being shot at. Some in town found that argument doubtful, mostly fearful of missing her with the first shot. When she smiled, which was seldom, her skin would wrinkle up like the bark on a tree. But she did smile a lot when Palmer was around. She had a soft spot for him.

"Going hunting, Rita?" Christian questioned as he let Palmer through the door first.

"All depends how long you boys keep me," she snapped back, eyeing Christian as he passed her. Her house was cozy, all throw rugs and polished hardwood. From what Palmer had told him, Christian knew all of the furniture was handmade.

"Come sit in the living room. I'll brew some tea." She wore an old pair of jeans and a wool shirt and had yet to put the shotgun down. There was a small table set up where she had been cleaning the weapon. Palmer was still grinning as Rita disappeared into the kitchen.

"What the hell are you grinning about?" Christian was looking around the living room while trying to keep an eye on Palmer and his grin. Even though he and Rita lived within sight of each other, this was only the second time he had been in Rita's house. It was now going on two months since he'd taken on the position of sheriff. He hadn't wanted to charge in and had decided to wait before initiating any real changes. He thought now was a good time.

"C'mon, Palmer, why that grin of yours?" he asked again.

"Nothing, just happy." Palmer sat down in a big easy chair, rubbing his hands along the smooth wood. "Just happy, that's all." Christian was about to say something when Rita came back in with a tray of tea and the shotgun tucked under her arm.

"Here," she said, handing the tray to Christian, "just grab it and find a seat so I can put the gun down." Christian took the tray and placed it on the coffee table between some magazines. Rita placed the twelve-gauge on the smaller table among the cleaning supplies, pointing it away from them. Christian sat on the sofa waiting. Rita glanced at him.

"Grab yourself a cup. I don't wait no tables round here. There's no sugar, but you got some pure honey in the smaller cup there next to your hand. Don't be shy, your hands ain't broken."

They both thanked her, and as Christian reached for the honey, Rita asked what she could do for them. Christian started to explain how he wanted to make the calls to them more professional. Halfway through, Rita went over to the smaller table, sat down, and started cleaning her shotgun again. Christian sipped his tea, not paying much attention to Rita as he spoke. Palmer kept quiet, watching her.

"Now, the reason for all of this—" Rita pumped the shotgun. Christian fell silent. He looked at her. Her look told him that he could stop right there. She started with a rapid verbal assault, not needing the weapon in her hands.

"Sheriff, I know you're from the Big Apple and everybody's a hotshot down there. I'm old. I don't waste my time here. God knows we don't have enough time to be wasting any. Now, about your plan. I know your voice, and you know mine, right? Don't bother to answer, we both know how it ends. So, if I call you or that grinning fool Palmer over there, it isn't a social call. If you haven't noticed yet, my social-calling days are over with. So now, if it isn't a social call, what is it? You can answer now." She had the shotgun across her lap.

"Police business?" Christian ventured.

"Right you are. So, let's put our heads together. I know your voice, you know mine. I know Palmer's, he knows mine. Both of you know each other's voices. So adding all of those voices of ours, I come up with three. You got the same number?"

"Er, yeah, yeah...three," Christian said.

"And do you ever hear anybody else on the police radio, other than us three?"

"Well, that is... er, no."

"Fine. So what's with the all the changes? It ain't broke, is it?"

"No, I guess not."

"Smart boy. Teatime's done." She got up, placing the gun on the floor. Christian put his tea down and stood up along with Palmer. Rita took Christian by the arm, walking him straight towards the door.

"Now, I know you're still new in the area, so if you get lost going to one of the heinous crimes we have around here every three hundred years or so, I'll direct you. Keep in mind, not once did the wrong piece of mail ever turn up in the wrong hands. I know my town." Rita's face wrinkled up briefly. "I *think* I can handle dispatching you two boys around, Sheriff. Now get your worried fanny out my door, I'm going hunting or to bed. Don't know which yet. Bye." Palmer scooted ahead just as Christian found his body being propelled out the front door. It slammed firmly shut behind them. Palmer turned to Christian.

"Kind of makes you feel like you were just strip-searched, minus the rubber glove."

Christian laughed. He knew when he was beaten.

Palmer

Katie slid some eggs sunny side-up onto Palmer's plate while he continued "yes-ing" Rita over the phone. He hadn't checked in on time, and she liked to know where her boys were. With one more "yes," he handed the phone back over to Katie.

"She strip-searched your butt, huh?" Katie giggled. It had been their in-joke since that day Christian had crossed over into Rita's territory.

Palmer laughed, starting in on his eggs. "Jeez, thanks for giving me up! That woman's relentless!"

"And speaking of being relentless," Christian jumped in, "you don't wear your vest, I'll tell Rita." Palmer looked up from his eggs, catching a little trickle of yoke down the side of his mouth with his crooked pinky.

"Hey, you wouldn't," he said in mock terror, licking the yoke off his finger. Both of his pinkies were curved inward, permanently bent. He jokingly referred to them as some genetic thing, but a hell of a help in holding a hammer.

Palmer had thinning hair that seemed to have stabilized in the last few years. A deep scar ran along his lower lip from a piece of a two-by-four that his circular saw had spit out his way. The flying wood had fractured his jaw and knocked out two of his front teeth. It had taken a number of trips down to New York City for a friend of his to make up a bridge for him. It took another few weeks for him to get used to it. In the meantime, Rita had berated him for standing in the wrong spot at the wrong time while cutting the wood the wrong way. Palmer knew she was just fussing over him in her own way. His lip had healed quickly, but he had grown very conscious of the scar that cut across it.

He had never married, and at the age of thirty-nine with no dates in recent memory, he seemed to be heading for permanent bachelorhood. He had had a girlfriend years ago. They had been with each other for over three years, and things had been great between them, until that one day he went to her apartment and found a large suitcase on the bed with a few of her belongings scattered around it. The smaller matching suitcase had been gone. A lipstick message across the bathroom mirror had simply said, "Sorry."

She had taken off about the same time that Sheriff Adams, Christian's predecessor, had found the headless body and the deer on the road. Man and animal both had been gutted, their intestines spread out along the dark pavement. There were rumors that the killer had left some sort of a message that Sheriff Adams never let anyone see. Adams took an early retirement soon afterward, leaving for parts unknown. The sheriff's sudden departure at the same time as the departure of Palmer's girlfriend left a lot of tongues wagging. It had also left Palmer as sheriff, at least for a time. He had done a good job, but his mind was elsewhere. A few years had passed, and one day, the town council had called him to a private meeting. There, he had met Christian for the first time.

Bob Dawson, the council head, had cleared his throat awkwardly and said, "Bart—" Palmer knew the use of his first name was a bad sign. "Bart, this is Christian Lord, he's up from New York City. He's an ex-city cop with a ton of medals from down there and he's here to fill the, er, open position of Sheriff." The other council members were silent.

Palmer had looked at them and then over at Christian.

"Glad to meet you, Officer Palmer." Christian offered his hand and Palmer took it. He had glanced back over to the council members; they were all sheep-eyed. He had turned back to the new sheriff.

"If it's all the same to you, uh, Sheriff, it's Palmer. Just plain Palmer." He let go of Christian's hand, not sure how to take this all.

"That's fine with me," Christian had said.

As the council filed out of the room, Dawson had turned to him and whispered, "Sorry, we had no choice...sorry." They had left, leaving him and Christian alone. Palmer had faced Christian again.

"Listen, Officer Palmer," the new sheriff had started, but Palmer angled his head as if he was listening to something else. Christian immediately corrected himself. "Sorry. Palmer. Let's have a seat, if you don't mind." Christian looked at his deputy. "I know when Sheriff Adams left some years ago, there were some things going on, personal and otherwise. I just wanted to take this time and explain how I got here. And out of respect to you, I also want to clear up anything that might come up in the future." Palmer could tell that Christian was uneasy.

"You might say I was forced into an early retirement from the NYPD. I made a bad call and it resulted in the death of a child." Christian stopped and touched his chest for a moment as if he were trying to find the words. Dropping his hand, he continued. "I was an embarrassment, a liability. Behind the scenes I was given a choice—either move on and they'd help set me up with another law enforcement job, or stay where I was and watch my career come to an abrupt end. I was just getting married, starting a new life, so here I am." Christian said nothing else. They looked at each other for a moment. Palmer finally got up to go.

"Thanks for telling me," he said as he left. That had been a little over five years ago. The issue of sheriff and the issue of the dead child had never come up between them again. It had only been a matter of weeks before Palmer was reaching over for the extra pieces of toast.

Amy's screeching was traveling towards them again. As she turned a corner, Katie stuck out her arm, scooped her up, and placed her in her chair in one swift movement. The expression on Amy's face was one of shock, then of disappointment that the chasing game was over. Katie put her Cocoa-Puffs in front of her, but Amy crossed her arms, waiting for Unta Bart to feed her. Palmer looked at Christian and grinned.

"Oh yeah, sure," Christian said. "Like I have a choice in this matter. Feed her, or she'll starve to death. Besides, you're already late for your shift."

Palmer chuckled, turning his attention to Amy, making noises with the food, which thrilled her to no end. "Hey, I almost forgot," he said, stopping his food sounds for the moment as Amy waited patiently. "Next few weeks, I'll be bouncing around with some carpentry jobs. One or two will be out of the county. I might need a day or two for those. Could use the extra cash."

Christian nodded. "Won't be a problem. Everything should be quiet. I'm just a little concerned about the Murphy boys. Like I said, last night they were a little disorderly. They seem to be entering one of their periods. They start anything, I'm gonna throw 'em in the lockup, no questions asked. I want you to do the same. Other than that, let's just coordinate our days; I'll be going back and forth to see my sister."

Katie came over and gave Christian a kiss on top of his head, putting his breakfast down. Her sister-in-law had been fighting the disease for a number of years now, and she wasn't doing well. Christian had been running himself ragged traveling back and forth the last few months, and Katie dreaded the next few weeks. Christian had to decide whether he was going to put her in the Sisters of Calvary for the Terminally Ill, or continue with the home hospice care. If he decided on Calvary, she knew that would be the first step to Christian's finally facing the prospect of his sister's death. Unbeknownst to Christian, Katie and Cecilia had been writing and calling back and forth for some time. Katie knew Cecilia had already accepted her fate. Right now, she was hoping Palmer wouldn't say anything. She tried to change the subject.

"Hey, babe," Katie said as she started to massage his shoulders, "last night, I made a pot of stew for you. It's in the fridge. You can pick on it whenever you get hungry. Okay?" The words were just out of her mouth when Palmer popped the question.

"So, how's your sister doing?" Katie shot Palmer a look, but he caught on too late. She reached over and gave him a little slap in the head.

"Heeey!" Palmer looked wounded.

"Katie, it's okay." Christian reached up and gave her hand a squeeze. "The chemo was a waste of time and not worth the pain for her now," he said. "It's really taking too much out of her. Honestly, Palmer...I don't know what's worse, the disease or the cure." Christian dropped his hand from Katie and picked at his food. "Anyway," he continued, changing the subject himself, "don't forget that hunting season is just around the corner and we'll have our hands full." Reaching up, he squeezed Katie's hand again.

Palmer nodded, a spoonful of cereal heading towards Amy. She began to giggle. "Yeah, you're right. I almost forgot," he said. "God, all the nuts will be up here. I hate weekend killers."

And he went back to the strange food-sounds as Amy broke out into laughter that only a child could produce.

Palmer's Secret

Rita was racing down Main street as if she actually had somewhere to go. It was an early morning routine of hers to make her presence known in the town and keep a vigilant eye and ear out for any new gossip she might have missed during the hours of the night. Rita knew that people woke up to more problems than what they went to bed with and she needed to keep abreast of it all.

As she took her long strides through the tree-lined streets, she locked eyes with each passing face, voicing a greeting, careful to detect any hesitation in voice or manner. Her smile-less face and red hair flashed at them like a warning in the morning light. Old Rita's radar was pinging away after a good night's sleep.

Today, though, she had caught no one off-guard. It seemed that the night had been quiet, and there was no news to be had—as hard as it was to believe. She glanced over her shoulder at Palmer. He was her best bet for now.

"Palmer! I know you, boy," she said, letting her words fall behind her, keeping her pace strong. "You've been up to something for a couple of months now. Too many trips out of town." Rita eyeballed a fellow senior citizen in work overalls. They nodded to each other. His eyes didn't waver. Nothing. *Hell!*

Palmer nodded and winked at the older man, the relief that he had passed Rita's scrutiny evident upon his face. "Rita—" he began, but was cut short as Rita suddenly stopped in front of his patrol car. He ran into her and she spun around, poking him in the chest.

"*Palmer!*"

"Sorry, I was just trying to keep—"

"Palmer, the only thing you're trying to keep is the wool over my eyes! I know there's a secret somewhere!" She scoured his face, her own wrinkling up with suspicion. "What's this I hear about work over in Menkerit? You been spending some time running about there, or so you say." She paused, waiting for him to make a mistake.

Palmer looked a little uneasy. "Just some wraparound sun porches for a couple of houses. No big deal." He started to search his pockets for the keys to the patrol car. Rita knew he was looking for a way out, but she wasn't quite finished with him yet.

"When do you propose to do this work?"

"Next two, three weeks or so. No real rush." Finding the keys, he looked as relieved as the older gentleman from before. Rita eyed the keys in hand.

"Two, three weeks? Palmer, what's got your interest?"

"Nothing, Rita, it's work and nothing else. You know me." Palmer took a tentative step toward the car. His escape looked promising.

"Okay, you say so." She knew she wasn't getting anywhere, but she also knew something was there. Just a matter of time, she thought. She looked down the street toward the sheriff's office. There was a stack of old traffic summonses she wanted to go over. The summonses were handed out for minor parking infractions, but seldom paid. For the most part, it was just a slap on the wrist. Her face wrinkled up again in a slight smile. If she remembered correctly, Bill had some unpaid parking tickets. She would bypass the public slap on the wrist and go straight for his wallet. That might just make her whole day. She turned back to Palmer.

"Palmer, don't you go missing, there's work to be done around here."

He had opened the car door, and leaving it ajar, he strode back over to her. Putting a hand on each of her cheeks, he gave her a kiss on her forehead. Her face became a mass of wrinkles with a smile cutting across it.

"Palmer! You damn fool! You get in that car and drive around and do something!" Palmer chuckled at Rita as she fluttered her hand, shooing him off. She spun on her heel and headed toward the sheriff's office, embarrassed, but pleased.

Palmer watched her as she ducked into the small building, slamming the door after her. He had to shake his head—she was one hell of a character. As he turned to go, a number of people suddenly seemed to have appeared out of nowhere. They strolled, unhurried, down the street, smiling and nodding to him. It was almost as if they knew the coast was clear. Nodding back, he got into the patrol car and started it up. He sat there a moment before pulling out a photo of a woman from his shirt pocket. Running a crooked pinky over it, he started to hum.

The photo, taken from a distance, was of an attractive blonde. Caught off-guard, her face was bright, full of life. It brought a smile to his face. No one knew about this one, and he was going to keep it that way.

He flicked the photo with his finger and slipped it back into his pocket. Pulling the car out of the space, he drove down Main street humming and waving to people. He turned left on Wolf and headed out of Tranquillity, humming all the way. It was a catchy tune.

The Bait—Three Weeks Later

Douglas' clock radio went off at 4:45 a.m. He was an early riser, a leftover from his bedwetting days when his parents would wake him and hurry him off to the bathroom. Reaching over, he hit the radio, silencing the jovial voice of the weatherman. Turning back to Joanna, his wife of eight years, he lightly patted her on the ass, a small but important ritual he performed each morning before getting out of bed. Pulling back the covers, he swung his feet around, feeling the pressure in his bladder. He sat on the edge of the bed, holding it in until the clock read 5:05 then he hurried off to the bathroom, flipping on the lights. Once the door was closed, he stood watching another, smaller clock. Waiting motionless until 5:15, he rushed over to the bowl, a sigh of relief escaping his mouth as he peed. Finished, he washed his hands for five minutes, again watching the clock for the correct time.

Time and timing. The numbers were very important. The numbers told you when you could do things. When you had to do things. Some more so than others. Control. Self-control. He knew...

Finally completed, he allowed himself to relax as he brushed his teeth. This ritual was a little more elaborate than patting his wife on the ass. It was also a little more important to him. It was part of a deeply rooted system of punishment and reward. And there were other rituals deeply rooted within him where the punishment and rewards were far greater.

Cupping his hands under the running faucet, he rinsed his mouth with cold water. Stripping out of his pajamas, he jumped into the shower and waited a moment until the hot water kicked in. Later, while his wife continued to sleep, he would skip breakfast in order to get to the bank early and catch up on the work that the manager had piled on his desk. But before the bank, he would take a slight detour to watch the house of number eight and wait until she left for work. She was also an early riser, and he wondered if she shared his problem. He had been observing her, trying to get her schedule down for a week. He was fairly confident that he knew her routine now. He was wrong.

This morning, he would miss her altogether, getting him to the bank in a foul mood. Once there, he would try to settle in before his co-workers showed up. He would spend most of the morning pushing papers around, wondering what had happened to number eight, when a phone call from his wife would interrupt, urging him to come home. Taking an early lunch hour, he would rush home. On the way out of the bank, he would let Robin, the bank secretary, know just in case anyone should need him. No one did; no one would; no one cared. By 5:05 that afternoon, Douglas would be dead. He had gone about his morning routine not knowing it was his last day. His wife knew it, though.

The last month or so had been interesting for Douglas. He felt honored that James had handpicked him for The Society. He'd had no idea that such an organization even existed, but they had already known everything about him. James seemed to understand him, and that acceptance had even soothed his anger somewhat.

But that had been weeks ago, and the pressure within him was building again. The Society couldn't provide the kind of recognition he was ultimately seeking. It wasn't enough to be known to a few dozen men. He wanted the world to know of his suffering, his anger.

After his sixth victim, he was finding it all a little too easy— and the police just weren't getting the idea. So he made sure his seventh kill was a case study. About the only thing he hadn't done was walk into the police station and butcher the woman in front of the desk sergeant. Still, even with number seven under his belt, they hadn't caught on. He couldn't understand what was wrong. Were they too stupid, or was he too clever?

The only thing he knew for sure was that the pressure had been building for years. He didn't know exactly what the pressure was, but he knew it was there. It was like a separate being that spoke to him without words. He knew of *it*, and it knew of *him*. Master and slave. Body and shadow. He was just incapable of distinguishing which was which. And anyway, it didn't matter anymore.

The pressure had finally come into existence eight months ago. It had actually been a great relief. It required one victim a month—a nice, easy pace. That became his cycle, *its* cycle. One problem was, he wanted a little more. The other problem lay with the police now. They had only put three of his kills together so far. Three! He had to laugh. But James knew. James had known right away. And when he'd seen James, it was as if the unknown entity within him had come to life.

The man that would take him under his wing had shown up one day at his front door, dressed in a tailored gray wool suit. It was a Saturday, and his wife was on one of her endless shopping sprees, which he could ill afford. James stood there, smiled, and held up a folder, opening it to show him newspaper clippings. *Clippings of his victims.* One by one James held them up, in the exact order in which they were killed. Douglas had thought that maybe the man was a cop, and the idea of being caught, of finally receiving his due recognition, his reward and punishment, excited him. Somehow, James had known of his excitement.

"Do what you must, and when your mind is clear, we'll talk," he'd said, and walked away.

Douglas closed the door and gone upstairs with an excitement he'd only felt after a kill. He'd locked himself in the bathroom and masturbated for five minutes, watching the small clock. He'd then washed his hands for another five minutes and went back downstairs to wait.

Half an hour later, Douglas saw the small man with the sharp features a few houses away, waiting, standing perfectly still. Douglas knew he would have to go down to him, and he didn't like that at all. It felt like an act of submission. Douglas decided to wait it out by his house, but the man just stood there without moving. Douglas looked at his watch. He felt the pressure building around his bladder. Finally, he gave up and joined the man on the sidewalk. They strolled through the neighborhood like two gentlemen of leisure. Looking at his watch again, five minutes had passed with neither one of them saying anything. Douglas spoke up.

"You a cop?"

"No."

"Reporter?"

"No."

"Then who—"

"James. You may call me James. That's all you need to know for now."

"I suppose you know—"

"How's your wife, Joanna?" James asked, catching Douglas off guard. His voice was playful, almost mocking.

"Fine," Douglas said. He avoided looking at him. The man next to him didn't seem like the type that you should watch too long. Still, he felt strangely drawn to him.

"Fine?" James parroted. "No, I don't think so. Joanna's not fine," he said. "She isn't happy with you, is she?" The mocking tone was gone. There was an edge now.

"No, she isn't," Douglas confessed. He didn't know why but felt compelled to nonetheless.

A group of small children ran out of a yard, almost bumping into them. James sidestepped them and watched as they ran off. Douglas took the chance to steal a glance at him. James seemed to stalk the youngsters with his eyes, giving a little laugh when they disappeared around a corner. The two men continued on.

His euphoria at being discovered was ebbing. Douglas felt like he didn't exist next to this man. Starting to feel a little restless, he almost missed the question, it was asked in such a low voice.

"We're missing a little something from this folder of ours, aren't we?"

Douglas knew the piercing eyes were on him. "Missing what?" he asked.

James stopped. "Missing your first intended kill," he said. "That's what." Douglas faced him. The little man's eyes bored into him. He spoke quietly.

"Let me tell you something, Douglas. In the beginning, you worked out of your rage. Rage at being passed over in your middle management position. A position overseen by a degrading manager who is years younger than you. A position you're stuck in because you're passed over by every attractive woman that your boss fancies. A position in a small and insignificant hole-in-the-wall bank that draws more from you than you draw from your meager pay stub." James' eyes flashed around his surroundings, checking. He zeroed back on Douglas.

"And speaking of more, your wife always wants more. But you find that you can't accommodate her, either in bed or by the dollar. As a matter of fact, I would say you still have a problem with nocturnal enuresis. Sometimes you leave your wife's bed, stand there in the bathroom, and wet yourself as punishment for your inadequacy. This usually happens during your cooling-off period between kills, and is compounded by your frequent masturbation. Sometimes you may even try to make love with your cold, uncaring wife during this time and hold off on your masturbation. Those attempts may last a few days at best, but you prefer your fantasies and masturbation, which gratify you more when the added pressure of trying to please your wife is eliminated." James smiled at him, cocking his head to one side. "How are we doing so far?"

"*Who the fuck are you?*" Douglas wanted to grab him by the throat, but was afraid to do so. Something told him it would be a grave mistake to lay so much as a finger on him. Besides, James seemed to have a window into his very soul. His question went unanswered as the little man turned from him and continued walking. Douglas found himself automatically following.

"Now, if I may continue," James said. "You would be shocked at the amount of official records that pile up without people knowing. Discovering someone's life story is simply a matter of knowing where to look. In your case, a matter of digging up things like the psychiatric reports of what you did as a youth to those animals." James was silent for a moment as they walked. To the passing eye, they were two men strolling, nothing more. James smiled, his voice pleasant.

"I would say it started with some stray cats, finally working up to your mother's favorite. So when you buried your mother's cat in the back yard with just its head above ground and then proceeded to mow the lawn…know what that tells me? " James didn't wait for an answer. "Tells me, Douglas, that with your current *projects* underway, I know you are working up to certain *things*. But quite honestly, you need guidance. You're making too many waves. People drown in rough waters, Douglas. You're thirty-four now, and you've been very, very lucky so far. It's good to be lucky, but luck always runs out. Skill and knowing your true self and the nature of what you are going after is what keeps one ahead of all the rest. That is the key." James turned to face Douglas. "Is Mother still healthy?" he asked.

"My mother is *fine* and she'll *stay* fine," Douglas blurted out, caught off guard by his own answer.

"Oh, I'm sure of that," James toyed.

Douglas tried to ignore the comment, but something nagged at him. He also tried to ignore that. "So, how did you find me?" he asked, trying to get away from those haunting thoughts.

"Oh, on paper, on computer, on experience…doctors, lawyers, Indian chiefs. You weren't difficult to track." James smiled. "Sometimes requests. There are trails everywhere if one knows what to look for, who to listen to, who to tap into. With you, the radius wasn't small. But the women were all good-looking white-collar professionals. All about the same age as your wife, if I remember correctly. With a little cross-referencing and with *connections* I've made over the years, it's just a matter of *B* following *A* before you get to *C*." James glanced over as they walked. "Something like your first kill will more or less determine the balance of your kills. Things finally surface with your first one. It's like a creature breaking through its shell, escaping from its incubating prison." James was silent for a moment. There was a heaviness to the silence. James didn't let it linger.

"Let's say it's the little touches of creativity that most can't help. That's where the trail lies, the common thread that knits all of your kills together. It's there, and you can't hide it. Like fingerprints, if you wish." James leaned in a little closer. "Your first attempt failed. That enraged you, and you knew you had to try again." Douglas wanted to pull away but held his ground.

"You looked at your co-workers, your wife, your mother, and knew in your mind what you could do to them…and that's where most people stop. For you, however, that wasn't real enough, and some of your fantasies weren't real enough for you, either. You finally brought yourself to the point of acting on your urges, joining them together. You wanted something in your life that you could control from beginning to end. *Maybe just this once,* you think…this one time to prove your self-worth. But the woman who should have been your first victim got away. Why? Because you couldn't do it. You weren't ready. I would hazard a guess, in fact, that you *let* her go. So you return to your tiny, meaningless life, only now you're even *more* of a failure. Time passes and nothing changes for you, but things build in your head. So you try again. Your second attempt is a success. In fact, I daresay you went a little overboard. You overcompensated for your failure the first time around. You took out the rage of your failure on this victim, and the result was extremely… brutal. Very, *very* careless." James paused, and

Douglas could feel his eyes, cold and uncaring as a scalpel, dissecting him.

"On another level, your second kill was a curiosity. The first *real* kill, to see if you were *man* enough to do it again. So, *B* follows *A,* and down the line. Yet the sad part, Douglas, is that there's no acknowledgement of your deeds. You vent, but nobody takes notice. So then, you *think* you leave a calling card, a style. But the style was always there, you just had to look for it. But in your mind, you make it more obvious, to try and get their attention. A waste, a very dangerous waste of time. But let us finish, then, by saying that I heard your cry for help."

Douglas hadn't noticed that they had stopped walking. They were back in front of his house again. His mind was a jumble of questions.

"Before, you said that sometimes you get requests. What did you mean?" Douglas asked.

"Well, well, young Douglas, you do pay attention." James flashed his smile.

"So?"

"Well, sometimes I do a little behind-the-scenes work. Like an angel on the shoulder, I whisper the right information in the right ear, for the right price. The locals get the credit and I increase my retirement portfolio. In your case, the local police asked me to profile this bothersome person that continues to elude them." James' smile broadened. "Yes, they knew of you. And sometimes the killer is caught, sometimes not. Sometimes he just disappears. Oh, but sometimes he goes on, and on, and on." Douglas was quiet. James had a very disarming smile.

"You know the old saying," James said with a conspiratorial smile, "'takes a thief to catch a thief.' What better way to meet one's acquaintances, one's peers? Don't you think?"

Douglas was quiet for a moment, then asked, "So you're what, a shrink? An informant? What?"

"Douglas, I am many things. I gather and disseminate information. The sheepskins on the wall just make my information all the more believable and expensive."

Douglas wasn't sure what to think. He wanted fearful cops. Front page headlines. Men in bulletproof vests charging in. He wanted the world to end with a bang, not a whimper.

"Disseminate?" He was disappointed.

"Douglas, it's a big world. There still may be a surprise or two left out there for you."

Douglas looked around. It was a beautiful day. "What do you want from me?" he finally asked.

"You might say I'm also a collector of a sort. There is a society, and we would like you to join. We can use a man with your...talents." James' smiled reached all the way to his eyes. Douglas thought that for the first time, it was truly warm.

Long before his wife got in on the action, Douglas was a dead man.

The Blonde

Joanna looked out of her bedroom window. She held the phone away from her ear. Every time she had tried to defend herself, she was interrupted by the angry voice of her husband. She simply gave up. *No matter.* Finally, the receiver at the other end slammed home, making her jump as the line went dead. Her shoulders dropped, and she sighed. Turning from the window, she tossed the phone onto the bed, and her eyes brightened. Her part was done.

"Okay, Douglas is on his way. It'll take him about forty-five minutes from the bank. He was really, *really* pissed when I told him the basement was flooded." Joanna had been afraid that the story would come out sounding practiced, like a lie, and that Douglas would know. But her deception had flowed out easily, and he had been none the wiser.

Impatiently, she shifted her weight to one leg. For what she wanted out of life, she didn't have any other choice. She had come this far, and she didn't want this fucked up.

"Are you sure you can do this?" Joanna watched him standing silent in the doorway. It seemed as though he was ignoring her. She didn't like that at all, and stomped her foot. "*Stephen,* are you sure you can do this?"

"Oh, I can do this." His reply was confident and soothing.

She was relieved. She needed to believe him, wanting to get out of this loveless and mostly penniless marriage. He had come along at just the right moment. It was as if he had been sent directly to her. In the last two weeks, they had met only four times, but he seemed to understand her in ways that no one ever had. He understood that she needed out of this life to get one of her own. What impressed her most was that he even refused to be her lover until Douglas was out of the picture. This made her want him more, but she had an even greater desire for the money her dead husband would bring. She went over to the dresser and started to fill a large bag with her jewelry. She hesitated and turned back to Stephen.

"What if something goes wrong?" She thought about the plan they had worked out together. It was a simple break-in. She knew her husband wouldn't tell anyone at the bank that she had called. He wouldn't want anyone to think he was doing personal errands on bank time, so she knew he would take an early lunch, making up some spineless excuse. She would be gone before he got home. Her husband would walk in on a burglary in progress, struggle with the "thief," and be killed. It was simple. She had herself covered no matter what, but still, she worried.

"Stephen...?" She needed reassurance again.

"Nothing will go wrong," Stephen said as he walked over to her. He began to stroke her long blonde hair. "Everything will be fine," he cooed, the strands easily slipping through his fingers.

"Yes, but anything can happen," she worried out loud dropping the last handful of jewelry into the bag. She looked at her watch, wanting to get going. Stephen continued to stroke her hair.

"Yes, you're right," he said, "anything can happen, but only two things *will* happen now."

She was a little confused. "Two? What two?"

He caressed her hair once more, softly pulling at the long blonde strands. It was very fine hair. He dropped his hand away.

"Well, Joanna, one of the two things is about to happen," he said.

She watched him walk over to the windows, pulling the curtains shut, plunging the room into shadows. He now seemed to blend with the shadows. A slight break in the curtains cast a little light on an object in his hand. It was shiny. Joanna kept staring at it. It looked sharp. She was a little confused once again, and then she caught on.

It was very sharp.

Under His Wing

Douglas fumbled with the house key, almost dropping it. "Dumb bitch!" he cursed. "Floods the fucking basement." He jammed the key at the lock, finally getting it in. Rushing into the house, he called his wife's name. There was no answer.

"Shit," he mouthed, and headed for the basement door. Flipping the wall switch on, he opened it and made his way down the stairs. Everything looked fine. There didn't seem to be any problem with the pipes. The only thing he saw out of place was a big pile of laundry in the corner next to the washing machine. That was unusual for Joanna, but other than that, he didn't understand any of this. Damn it, she knew how it was at the bank. This foolishness of hers could get him fired! He wondered if she was looking for an excuse to leave him.

Going back upstairs, he called out to her again as he checked out the kitchen and the other rooms on the first floor. Nothing. He was bewildered. What was this crap? Her car was still out front, so where the hell was she?

As he walked back into the kitchen to check the faucets for any problems, he saw the bottle of Pepsi on the kitchen counter. Douglas stopped. He could have sworn that it hadn't been there before. Picking it up, he noticed it felt warm. *But neither of us drink soda.* As he stood looking around the kitchen, when he heard some ot the floorboards creak from upstairs. He turned his head to the sounds.

With the soda in hand, he walked to the bottom of the stairs. Douglas paused. *Something wrong...*and he slowly started up the steps.

Coming to the top of the landing, he turned, stopping dead in his tracks, just opposite the bathroom. Their bedroom was at the end of the hall, and the door was closed. Joanna *never* closed doors. But there was *something* else. Douglas felt his hands suddenly go cold and clammy. As a matter of fact, there were two *somethings.*

Nailed to the bedroom door was the red-haired scalp that he had presented to Stephen weeks ago. Next to it neatly hung, was a long patch of carefully combed blonde hair…his wife's color, bloody scalp and all. It was at that moment that he looked down at the bottle of Pepsi and understood. He knew his wife was dead on the other side of the door.

Fear turned his legs to rubber. Spinning around, he felt them giving out, but he managed to take two steps before Stephen stepped out of the bathroom.

"Ahhh, thanks, I'll take that," Stephen said, snatching the soda from Douglas. He smiled and winked at Douglas suddenly pushing him over the railing. Douglas landed hard on the uncarpeted stairs. There were a dull thump and a sharp crack as his ribs and shoulder gave out.

Douglas lay there, taking shallow breaths. The left side of his chest was on fire. Stephen walked down the stairs holding an old police nightstick and sat right above him on the steps. He laid the nightstick across his lap and opened the Pepsi with a gloved hand. The soda hissed as the carbonation escaped.

"Bit thirsty," Stephen said, taking a sip. Recapping the soda, he put it down. "Found the nightstick down in your basement, Douglas. There was some dried blood on it. Not a lot, but it doesn't take much to verify DNA these days. Sloppy, my friend, very sloppy. Good way to get caught, don't you think? But then again, I get the feeling you're looking for some attention…*am I right?*" Stephen picked up the nightstick and began to work it through the air with a practiced hand.

"Is that the way you were as a little boy, always craving attention? Maybe mommy just didn't give you enough?" He started to smack the club against the palm of his hand. It made a dull thumping sound against the leather glove.

"*You gonna…kill me?*" Douglas' voice was on the edge of hysteria.

"Ah…Douglas, Douglas. Always about me, me, me, isn't it? It's that greedy little need for attention. Did you wet yourself just to get attention so your mommy would wash and touch you? No? Yes? Don't fucking know? *Huh?* Is that little boy in you still harboring all of those little-boy problems?" Stephen paused leaning in. "I noticed you didn't ask anything about your lovely wife, Joanna."

"*I know she's dead! You fuck!*" Douglas screamed up at him. The effort drove a white-hot spike into his lung with each word.

"Oh, come on now! You really don't care, we both know that! Hell, if it hadn't been for her, *you* wouldn't be in this situation now, would you? Actually, all of those women drove you to this, didn't they? It's all their fault, isn't it?"

"*You killed her!*" he screamed again.

Stephen rolled his eyes, mocking. "Oh, *Jesus!* It was just a matter of time before you got around to doing her, and maybe your mother, too! Just give me a break!"

"*Leave my...mother...out of this!*" The pain was making it difficult to speak.

"Sorry...touchy. Well, let's stick with your wife, then. You know, she wanted me to kill you for your insurance money. Couldn't do that, Douglas, I have certain principles. She deserved to die. Can't argue that, can you? Besides, at first she wasn't part of the plan. I hadn't expected to run into her at all. But she just kind of worked her way in. She had certain ideas about you."

In truth, Douglas didn't care about Joanna. The pain was taking its toll on him. "What are you...going to do?"

"Back to *me, me, me* again, I see. Well, Douglas, I'll probably do what we do best. No, let me correct that. What *I* do best." Stephen started to hum. He stood and excused himself as he stepped over Douglas, walking down a few steps. Leaning against the wall, Stephen fell silent but the club continued to beat against his gloved hand. Douglas looked up at him, trying to get past the pain, trying to think of a way out.

"James...James will know about this!" he finally said. "I'm his *favorite!*" His voice started to pitch higher. "You're a dead man if you do...anything else...*a fucking dead man!*" Douglas screeched from the pain and his fear. Stephen looked at him.

"Oh, that's right. Under his wing, and all that. Well, you're right. James *will* be pissed." Stephen was quiet a moment. The club stopped its beating against his hand. "But, you know what? I've decided to let you live—" The nightstick suddenly whistled through the air, shattering Douglas' kneecap. Douglas wailed. The second blow caught him across the jaw, cutting short his cry. "For the next few hours or so, that is," Stephen added.

Tossing the nightstick aside, he reached out and grabbed Douglas' ankle, dragging him down the rest of the stairs. Raw nerves ground against bone fragments. Douglas was still screaming, though not as loudly.

"Hey, hey, plenty of time for that later." Stephen let go of Douglas' ankle and, reaching up, grabbed his hair, yanking his head to the side. Blood ran down from Douglas' mouth, and he grew quiet as Stephen brought his face close.

"You're nothing more than a *pathetic murderer*. That's all you are," Stephen hissed. "*A murderer!* Nothing more." And he spit in his face.

Stephen twisted Douglas' head. "Say, your lip is a little swollen. We'll have to see what we can do about it. But first, you know, we should do something about your hair." His grip tightened.

The knife slid from behind Stephen's back. The fine metal whispered its presence.

Like his wife before, Douglas found the knife to be sharp.

Very, very sharp.

Moth

In the end, it was just as Douglas had feared; he never received the recognition he deserved. As it was, when his stripped and broken body was found in the basement, if it weren't for his fingerprints, they would have been hard-pressed to identify him. Dental records would have done little good. At first, some speculated that he had walked in on a burglary, or that his wife had had him done in for the insurance money. But neither theory accounted for the brutality of the murder. Time passed, and no claim was ever made for the money. His wife seemed to have disappeared without a trace. Some even remarked to the police that she might have taken off with another lover. She seemed to them to have been that type of a woman, although in truth, they admitted, they really didn't know her all that well.

Most did agree that, dead or alive, Douglas had never been very popular around town. There was something about him that made people uneasy. His violent passing stirred a little sympathy, but not much. Interest was rekindled when certain bank figures came to light. It seemed that some of the figures had been doctored, and that actual bank funds were a little less than they should have been. In time it turned out to be another one of Douglas' hidden rituals.

The speculation on the exact amount of missing money ranged from a few hundred dollars into the millions. The FDIC covered the bank's losses, and those in the know knew the actual figure to be half a million dollars to the penny. The bank managed to keep their findings quiet and, for the most part, out of the news. The money was never recovered, and the town's attention returned to Douglas' wife and a possible drug connection. He might have stolen it, the theory went, but she had killed him for it...or the Columbians had.

Douglas went, for the most part, unappreciated and unknown, no notoriety beyond that granted to any other small-time white-collar thief that went in a little over his head and reaped his just reward.

But, he didn't go totally unappreciated. In the end, James knew and appreciated the sacrifice Douglas had made that day for The Society. The bait, after all, had been taken.

James sat in his car down the road from Douglas' house and watched as Stephen left late that night. He had known when he'd first met Stephen that he was a rarity, a true gift of nature like himself. He'd had high hopes for Stephen; they shared a common flame.

"Moth," he whispered as Stephen walked down the street, a man without a care in the world. James put his 9mm underneath a newspaper on the passenger seat. Starting his car, he pulled out slowly and followed him for a moment.

As he drove past, Stephen suddenly stopped in the middle of the street and looked up at the stars. Continuing on, James watched his rearview mirror and saw Stephen switch his gaze to his car. Turning left at the next corner, he lost sight of Stephen.

James drove into the night beneath the twinkling of the stars, knowing he was going to have to pay Stephen a visit. But first, there were a number of other matters to attend to.

The Dream

The dream came and went seemingly with a free will of its own. Sometimes it would end as soon as it began, only to pick up at the point it had left off to continue its journey through the night. As it held onto the dreamer, it would change its details a little, like a storyteller tailoring his tale to the audience. In the whiteness of it, they were always there in one form or another. Within his dream, he knew he fought the demons that were his. He watched as they entered. The voice washed over them.

"He forgives you." The pain was there...

He saw Christian enter the brightly lit apartment. Christian had his gun out and everything around him was white. The glaring whiteness hurt his head and seemed to burn into the hidden regions of his mind. Still, he watched.

Out of the whiteness, a half-dozen decomposed bodies of young children materialized. They were paired off in various sexual positions, their faces all turned away. He watched as Christian stood there and knew that that was the spot from which Isaac viewed his trophies. That one spot was safe for Isaac. From there, he didn't have to see their young faces and could relive his acts without facing his victims again, facing the guilt of his deeds.

The expression on Christian's face changed as he looked down on the white floor. Drops of bright red blood scattered toward the children. The droplets started to move. In the whiteness of the room, he heard the heavy breathing, the cry of relief. More scattered blood appeared on the floor. Not blood. Not from that spot. No, not blood at all. That was where Isaac masturbated.

He could tell Christian felt contaminated. He watched Him carefully step around the droplets on the floor, bumping into another child as he did. Christian spun, stepping back from the small body. The child was mummified, its arms outstretched like a crucifixion. Small pieces of paper covered its entire body and face. Christian stepped closer to the child, bumping into something else. He looked down, a worn prayer bench at his feet. Christian dropped to his knees and made the sign of the cross with his gun, slowly lowering his head. The dreamer heard him speak.

"Forgive me Father, for I have sinned..."

A child's voice echoed in the whiteness of the room. "Take a piece of paper. Read it, place it on your tongue."

The dreamer came out of his hiding place with his gun in hand as Christian raised his head looking up at the crucified child. Tiny bits of paper fluttered where the mouth should have been.

"Take a piece of paper." The young voice was angelic.

Christian's hand reached up, hesitating.

"Take a piece of fucking paper!" the voice boomed at Christian, no longer young. The voice ricocheted painfully inside his skull.

The dreamer slipped back into his hiding place, holding his head. The pain was unbearable. He watched Christian reach out and take a slip of paper from over the child's heart. The spot began to bleed. All of the other children moved, moaning unpleasantly. The child's voice filled the room, cleansing him.

"He forgives you." The pain disappeared.

Cecilia

Christian had curled up, tucking himself into the old leather armchair. He smiled and shifted his body, trying to get the circulation back in his limbs. The living room was covered with Amy's artwork, a one-woman show of paintings, pencil drawings, and crayon renditions of a world that was chaotic to a casual observer. Amy's private four-year-old universe was full of visions she alone was privileged to see. The artwork, like the artist, was uninhibited. There were no rules, no boundaries to stay within other than the edges of the paper. Even those were ignored at times during her creative process, the paint or crayon easily running over onto the table or the floor sharing the artist's stroke. Within this colorful world of Amy's, Christian's sister Cecilia lay on the couch dying.

"I like to dream," her voice distant, relaxed. For years, uninhibited cells had refused to stay within any boundaries of their own. It was a chaotic rampage that changed the canvas of her body. Like Amy's work, the cancer was unfocused and egalitarian. It had begun in her liver, but now spread throughout her body, reaching its tendrils into most of her major organs.

Christian looked around the room at the swirls of color on all of the pieces of paper. Each one was an explosion of life. His eyes settled back on his sister, wishing Amy's paints could do the same for her. When he had first arrived, he had found his sister asleep on the couch, and he had sat watching her. As she had slept, her body had twitched as if she was trying to shake off a dream or the disease. He had thrown a blanket over her, and this seemed to calm her down. Now, she sat up on the couch, her legs tucked underneath her, the blanket hardly disturbed by her thin, ravaged body. On the end table was a small stack of Amy's artwork. Cecilia reached over and placed her hand on it as Christian slowly stretched, his flesh tingling with the welcome flow of blood.

"When I dream," she said, "everything is there, but not everything. You know what I mean?" Cecilia's voice was clear now, just a little drawn out. Christian knew she was coming out of the painless world of her dreams, falling back into her wasted body. The transition between the two worlds didn't take long. Her face tightened. The pain had waited patiently for her to waken. Sometimes when he came to visit and caught her sleeping, he wished for her sake that she could stay in that other world. But today looked like it could be a good day. Conditioned to the pain, she seemed to make the transition well, and her face relaxed. He smiled.

"In there, I'm whole again," she said with a wistful smile. "You daydreaming now?" she asked.

Christian's own smile faltered a little. He had checked out Sisters of Calvary a week before. She needed 'round-the-clock help that only a hospice like Calvary could offer. Once he admitted her to Calvary, though, he could no longer deny the inevitable.

All of the patients there were terminally ill; the hospice was dedicated to easing the suffering of its people. The rooms were large, private, and well lit, with oversized picture windows. Visiting hours were twenty four hours a day, and the patients could eat anything that they wished. It was a place of caring, but not a place of hope. He knew the decision was soon going to be out of his hands. The doctors had told him that she had two months, tops.

Getting up from the chair, he walked over to her as she rolled her head to one side. Freckles spotted her face and arms. The bandanna that she wore had slipped aside while she slept, showing her normally long red hair was short and patchy in spots from the effects of the chemo treatments. In the beginning, she had taken to wearing wigs, but she didn't bother anymore. Her skin had become paper-thin. Two flesh-colored Band-Aids stood out on her arm, the brightest spots of color on her. She had just turned forty. Christian sat down on the couch and straightened the bandanna.

"Came over to baby-sit until your day nurse shows up," Christian said. "I didn't expect to fall into a coma," he laughed halfheartedly.

Even with what she was going through, Christian thought, she was still beautiful. She had been fighting the disease for five years now. Before that, she'd had a series of ongoing battles with her late husband, Jimmy, that had originated in a bottle and ended, as often as not, with a nightcap of his fists against her flesh. It ended when he was found stabbed to death late one night in an alley behind a bar. The killer was never found. Cecilia had fallen ill soon after that.

"Well, next time wake me," she said. "I'll be sleeping long enough soon." Cecilia knew her brother would never wake her up. He'd rather sit in the chair and wait until she woke up, thinking he was doing her a favor. She licked her lips. The chemo was killing her, the disease was killing her, and sleep was stealing what life she had left. "Just wake me next time, okay?" she said.

Christian nodded, adjusting the blanket around her feet. "Sure; I'll wake you with a kiss."

"Good. These drawings for me?" she asked, picking them up from the end table.

"Yeah. I don't know what the hell Amy's drawing half the time." Christian took one from her and started to twist it in different directions. Cecilia snatched it back from him.

"C'mon, give me that. She's only four." She started to twist it. It wasn't making sense to her either; then she saw it. Her face lit up. "It's Flea-Flea." She showed it to him right side-up. Christian just stared.

"But he's not black, he's green."

"Trust me, it's Flea-Flea."

"Okay, if you say so. I'm lost."

"Christian, her inner vision will clear. Four, remember? C'mon, let's eat, and then you hit the road and get back to your family."

"All right, but I get to cook."

"Fine by me. Just help me up. The old bones ain't like they used to be." Cecilia placed Amy's drawing back on the end table. She started to bunch the blanket up.

"Here, I'll do that." Christian stood and took the blanket, folding it.

"Since when did you get neat?"

"Katie, she folds everything. My underwear has creases in them." Christian chuckled as he placed the blanket on the couch. "Ready Freddy?"

"Uh-huh, but easy." Cecilia swung her legs around and slowly unfolded them. "Ohhhh...too long in that position." She stopped. "Give me a second," she said. Christian was quiet, letting her work at her own pace. She looked up at him and gave a knowing look. "I know, lost a few more pounds." There was guilt in her voice, as if she had done it by choice.

"That's nothing. You just got to knock that marathon training off," he tried.

"Yeah." Cecilia nodded to him and reached up. "Ready."

He leaned over, and she placed her hands on his shoulders. Carefully, he cupped her elbows and they braced against each other. He lifted her effortlessly as she pushed down with her elbows. Standing, they looked at each other.

"Speaking of running—"

"Don't."

She ignored him. "Time's running out."

"Stop it," he said, his voice sharper than he intended.

"No. You can't keep going back and forth like this." Cecilia rested her head against his shoulder. "Christian, it's just time," she whispered. "That's all. Not that bad." She turned her face and kissed him on the cheek. "Now, feed me and get home to your family. It's a long ride and you can't keep taking this much time off."

"Don't have to worry. The town's quiet," he said. "They like it better when I'm not around. They think of me as an outsider. It's Rita and Palmer who actually run that place. Well, mostly Rita." He laughed. "Come on, into the kitchen and I'll give you the latest dirt on everyone as I whip up a meal." Arms around each other, they headed toward the kitchen.

"You know," Cecilia started, "you owe me a dance one of these days."

"Sure, how 'bout a little swing?"

"You're an ass."

"I know."

Say Hello

Gigi was due in seven months, and for the next five, Nestor knew he could still call this room his study. At least, that's what he hoped. Lately, though, baby *things* had been popping up in the corners of the room or stashed away in the closet. One evening, he found rolls of wallpaper with dancing hippos next to his heavy punching bag. He put them away in the closet and started to work out on the bag. Two nights later, it was an unassembled changing station. That was also closet-bound before he attacked the bag. The following night, more stuff.

He left it where it was.

Gigi was definitely "nesting." He had noticed the change in his wife and the little changes all through the house. He teased her about it, but for the most part, he let her be. He couldn't really complain. He was guilty of expanding out of his study and taking up residence in the living room with his paintings. It was the room with the best light, and Gigi understood.

His paintings were his escape from the sometimes harsh reality of being a cop, and her nesting was her escape from the fears of childbirth. Gigi wasn't much for big or sudden changes in her life. She had to be eased into them. It was one thing to try to get pregnant, another to actually *be* pregnant. Nestor hoped the remaining seven months would be long enough, since she didn't have much of a choice now.

Everything in his wife's life had a certain pace. Their courtship had been long and drawn out, though she eventually admitted to Nestor that she had fallen in love with him within the first few weeks. Still, it took her another two years to agree to marry him—with her turning down the first proposal in a Mexican restaurant. The second proposal went better, and two years later, they actually tied the knot.

The house was another big jump from the apartment they had rented in the Throggs Neck section of the Bronx. Nestor worked on her slowly, with nice, leisurely drives up to Westchester County and out to Long Island, always commenting on the houses. His pretense for these weekend outings was that he was looking for new material to paint. On their fourth weekend of searching, she had turned to him and said, "Just pick a damn house. Make sure I can get to work and we can stop all of this driving around." He finally picked a house on the Island with easy access to the trains and highways leading into the city.

With the repairs and closing, it had been almost a year before they moved in, which was enough time for Gigi to get used to the idea. Her nesting now was a pretty good sign that she was accepting the idea of motherhood. This was reinforced by the amount of ground he was losing in his study. He didn't mind. He knew the baby would be the biggest change in her life. He had the feeling that she had decided to get pregnant more for him than anything else, though they never brought this up.

Nestor thought he heard her coming up the stairs. *Probably something else to go in the study.* He glanced at the computer screen. Just the usual names in the chat room, and he shifted his attention to the map above the computer.

So far, Gigi had kept all of the baby stuff away from his work area. There, he had his computer, books on serial killers, printouts, and a large map of the U.S. on the wall. The map, with its different-colored pushpins and multicolored states, gave this part of the room the feel of a miniature war room. Right now, he sat alternating his gaze from the computer screen to the map on the wall. He couldn't decide which bothered him more, the map or the chat room. One was reality; the other…he wasn't quite sure.

Like misplaced state capitals, Nestor had black, white, red, and green pushpins stuck across the country, with a few trailing into Mexico and Canada. So far there were a total of ten black pins, representing confirmed lipless bodies. Four white pins were possible lipless bodies. He was sure he was missing some, and equally sure of more to come. But combined, the black and white pins didn't bother Nestor as much as the other two colors. The red and green pins that surrounded the others were frightening. Red meant a confirmed victim, and green, a possible victim.

He had already run out of the red and green pins several times, and there were well over two hundred of them on the map. Now, he was adding a fifth color. He held a handful of yellow pushpins for people missing and unidentified bodies found. A few of them found their way onto the map. Sitting all the way back in his chair, Nestor tossed the rest of the yellow pushpins on top of a stack of faxes and printouts.

The large stack of papers contained his missing-person and unidentified body reports, and he knew that what was in those papers wasn't even the tip of the iceberg.

He played with some of the pins as he thought. As near as he could figure, the blacks and whites had been dying in the last six months, but they'd been killing for years. How long? How many victims? He wouldn't even venture a guess. With the lines and groupings of the reds and greens, the country seemed to be cut up, as if territories had been staked out. He was tired. He just wasn't up to adding any more pushpin bodies to the map tonight. Giving up, he turned around in time to see Gigi drop a throw rug she was carrying next to the punching bag.

"More nesting stuff?"

"Oh, stop it, you!" She hadn't even started to show yet. She was a fit woman. Just under five feet six inches, she still maintained the poise of her classical dance days. Nestor remembered that when Christian had met her, he had been taken by her looks, and rightly so. Her flawless olive skin bespoke her Spanish and Mexican heritage. Her face was exotically beautiful, accentuated by blue eyes and jet-black hair.

Gigi gave Christian a slap on the head whenever he referred to them as "Beauty and *that* beast." But Nestor knew Christian was right. It had been a twist of fate when the bike messenger swerved, missed him, and sideswiped her car. Nestor had been in a rush to get to the precinct, and was crossing against the light when it happened. The bike messenger cursed and kept going, leaving a long scratch on her car. Pulling over to the side, she'd gotten out to inspect the damage. Nestor went over to her and identified himself as a police officer, then he started to babble. He had never been so nervous. She finally cut him short and asked if he was trying to ask her out. Nestor barely got the word "yes" out, and they met the next day for coffee. That started it all.

Nestor put his arm around her waist and rested his hand on her belly. He didn't want to think what he would do without her.

"Baby rug?" he asked as she looked over the material on his desk and gave a quick glance at the computer screen. Her eyes settled on the yellow pins.

"You're adding another color to the map?" She didn't bother to hide the concern in her voice about the changes.

"It's nothing. Just trying to make some sense out of this, that's all."

"Still eavesdropping on that chat room." It wasn't a question, it was an accusation. "Those people aren't well."

"Just keeping an eye out." Nestor looked over at the screen. He was in a chat room for people interested in serial killers. There was some straight talk about serial killers, past and present. A few in the chat room used more emoticons than words. These, Nestor put in the same category as the apocalyptic criers and the ones he thought of as the "Helter-Skelters." For the most part, it was gibberish, armchair detectives and nut jobs. It probably wouldn't lead to anything.

"Martinez is using you." It was a relentless topic with her, and she was never one to hold back her opinion. "He's never going to change. I don't like him and I don't trust him." She had her idiosyncrasies, but she was straightforward, and the cop in him loved her for that.

"Gigi, I know what he's up to," he said, looking back up at her. "I know how he is. I'm doing this for myself. I—"

"You'd be better off painting. A few more pieces and you'll have enough for a show. Isn't that what you really want?" She leaned over and picked up a few of the yellow pins, looking at the map.

"Gigi, I'm a cop, I like all the pieces of the puzzle to fit."

"Okay," she said, tossing the pushpins back down, "I'm not going to argue. Anyway, Christian should be over soon and dinner's not ready." She patted his shoulder, starting to leave.

"Oh, by the way," she stopped at the door, "the floor is too hard for your tender flat feet; the rug is for you...thank you very much."

"I was kidding...and my feet aren't flat!" Nestor began, but Gigi had disappeared down the stairs already. "They just hug the ground closer, that's all," he called after her, eliciting an entirely unladylike snort of laughter from down the stairs. He looked back at the map and went about his work, thumbing through some reports.

Gigi had been right about both his painting and Martinez. He knew Martinez had his own agenda that he wasn't privy to. Then again, he wasn't feeding Martinez much of the information he had gathered so far, either. Just enough to keep him off his back. Nestor also knew that he was getting more territorial. And territoriality was exactly what he ran into when he tried to get information from other cops.

Some law enforcement agencies were extremely protective about sharing facts from any of their ongoing cases. Or, for that matter, any cases at all. And getting any real information from outside of the country was like pulling teeth. Anything unusual showed up in the newspapers first. Following up on it was an experience.

He had found the FBI to be the most tight-lipped and tight-assed of all the agencies he'd had to deal with. What's more, their information, once he actually got some, hadn't been anywhere near good enough to justify their elitist attitude. Once, a field agent had come by after his first phone call to them and tried to grill him without giving anything back to him. The agent even had the nerve to request copies of any data he might have gathered. Nestor claimed that his curiosity about the serial killers was just a side thing, like his paintings. By the time Nestor was into his second half-hour on the merits of oils vs. acrylics, the agent was grabbing his coat.

Inside or outside the country, his fellow officers seemed to be as territorial as his killers. *His killers.* The thought made him chuckle. He was beginning to think of all of those pushpins as *his.* At times, it was easy to forget that they represented actual people who had laughed and cried, had dreams, families, friends. It was easier to think of them as numbers, especially if he never saw the bodies. In general, he tried not to put a living face to the information. But sometimes, he couldn't escape it. That's when he found himself at the punching bag wondering who was more indifferent: the killers or the police. They seemed to be sides of the same coin imprinted from the victim.

Putting down the reports, he started to toy with the pins again. It took a certain type of cop to work with this shit, and he wasn't sure he was that type of cop. At one point, Nestor had felt like giving up. He had the impression that whoever was taking out these killers was something of a hero to his fellow police officers across the country. "Let sleeping dogs lie," he was once told over the phone, followed by a sharp click. The lack of cooperation was unbelievable at times. It was little wonder that some of these predators had gotten away with so much over the years.

Lately, he'd come across some reports mentioning an unknown predator referred to simply as *Him.* The first was from Lincoln, Nebraska. A number of miles out of town there, four male bodies had been found mutilated, their hearts missing. The bodies were all located within a mile of each other. That had been in 1959. In 1968, four more bodies popped up within a mile of each other in the foothills surrounding Denver. Again, the hearts were cut out. In 1977, *He* surfaced again. The modus operandi had been the same. But this time around, there were only three bodies found. All were in the Santa Ana Hills near El Toro, California.

In '86, *He* seemed to double back to Lincoln, Nebraska. Four new bodies showed up in the same places where the first four had been found. This time around though, the hearts weren't missing. They were found where they belonged, except that they had been placed back into the chest cavities upside down. Each heart had had a bite taken out of it. These had been blamed on a copycat killer who'd read an old newspaper report from 1959. Nestor didn't buy into that theory. They had been *His*.

It seemed to Nestor that this one liked open spaces and nine-year intervals. He didn't know if these two factors were unintentional or a conscious act. With this bit of history, he had looked for some unsolved murders in rural areas, but concentrated on the foothills around Denver once again.

He didn't have to look far. He came across a report from 1995 of a human heart found in a glass jar where one of the bodies had been found twenty-seven years before. Just the single heart. It had been fresh, and part of it had been missing; looking like someone had bitten into it. Nestor felt that all of these bodies, along with the heart, were meant to be found. Calling cards. A little "Hello" from the darker side. But to date, that was it on *Him*.

He had never found anything between these years. What would his total body count be today? How many more red pushpins were missing from the map? How many more bodies were out there missing their hearts? Was this really his timing? Or again, just a big "hello", saying "I'm still here." And if not, whatever happened to *Him?*

Nestor shook his head. Most serial killers were males from their mid-twenties to late thirties. They were generally white. Many were married with children. Their intelligence level was usually average or above, and they tended to kill strangers of the same race as themselves. Some monsters were roaming the highways and byways of the country with an immense amount of freedom to kill. A number were stationary killers... *homebodies*. These lured their prey into their web. Then there were the seekers that worked from a home base and left their victims where they had finished with them. Others dumped their prey, keeping their own "backyard" clean.

Nestor was sure that there were those out there who combined all types of behaviors. And what the pins on the map told him was that they didn't stop. He knew it was true that serial killers had a "cooling off" period between victims, unlike mass murderers, who would kill four or more victims in a single location at one time. His killers were also different from spree killers, who committed murders in two or more locations with connecting events. No, the serial killers always came back to their killing. It was a need, a part of the psyche fueled by fantasies that festered and fermented over the years, categorized by multiple victims, usually three or more. His map showed the cream of the crop. What really made up these monsters? What demented world did they stroll through? He didn't know, but he felt numbers were the true culprit. It was all a matter of numbers. There were about six billion free wills walking the earth now. Six billion possible combinations of genetics. Six billion combinations of parenting, environment, dreams, drives, and goals. Six billion, and more on the way. It was a no-win situation.

Nestor scanned the pushpins for the thousandth time, looking for a pattern. He could make nothing of it. It was more like a shotgun effect, his map riddled with death.

If there was a society of killers out there, he wondered if there could be some sort of a rift among its members? Two black "killer pins" were placed in areas where no one else was missing or killed as far as he could make out. Just a black pin standing out in the open. A "victim" caught and slaughtered lipless. Someone running scared? Someone not expecting to be killed? He wasn't sure. There were so many unknown variables.

One thing he was certain of; there wasn't only one hunter hunting the others at work out there. Two black pins had been killed almost back-to-back, time-wise, in widely separated parts of the country. No one man could move that quickly. But other than the possibility of two or more hunting, he still wasn't sure what to think. His instincts pushed him toward the infighting theory. Still, he was at a loss.

The sound of the downstairs doorbell broke him away from his thoughts. He knew it was Christian; he usually swung by on his way home from visiting his sister. Earlier, on the phone, Christian had invited him and Gigi up for a long weekend, maybe sneaking in a day of hunting with Palmer. He could use some time away from everything, and *fuck* Martinez and his schemes.

He looked up at the map again. Ever since that day in Isaac's apartment, he and Christian hadn't spoken about serial killers. Even with the stuff he was working on now, Nestor knew he wouldn't bring anything up to Christian. The death of the little girl had taken a heavy toll on his friend, and he wasn't about to open that wound again. Christian had more than paid his dues. *Fuck Martinez. Let sleeping dogs lie.* Sometimes not a bad piece of advice.

He was about to sign off from the chat room when Gigi called up to him. Spinning around in his chair, he yelled down that he'd be right there. He turned back to the computer, leaned back in his chair and stared. In the chat room box was a name he had never seen before, "Hymn101." He waited and watched the screen, but "Hymn101" never spoke. Nestor placed his fingers on the keys, but did nothing. *This is stupid!* But he never took his fingers from the keys.

"Nestor!" Gigi called again. *Could Hymn be...?* Nestor wondered. He shook his head. *This is really fucking stupid!* Gigi called once more and he could hear the impatience in her voice.

"Okay!" he yelled back. As he began to sign off, "Hymn101" came alive online.

Hymn101—Aren't you going to say HELLO?

The line appeared just before he heard the familiar "Good-Bye." Gone. Hymn101 was gone. Was he?

Nestor looked at his computer. He was sure it meant nothing. He was probably making a mountain out of a molehill. Being paranoid. An asshole, that's all. But the cop in him kept him paranoid. Taking a final look at the map, he thought he had a right to be paranoid.

Getting up, he gave his punching bag a slap, missing his days in the ring. Going down the stairs, he saw Christian at the bottom. His friend had a big ol' shit-eating grin plastered all over his face.

"Hey! How's my favorite PR?" Christian asked him.

Unfortunately for Christian, Gigi had been walking right behind him. "He's *not* Puerto Rican!" she said, slapping him in the head.

"Ouch!" Christian flinched, hunching his shoulders. "Gigi! I could get brain damage!" He paused until he judged it safe to continue. "Besides, we *both* know he's Puerto Rican!" She spun on her heel and smacked him again. "*Hey!* That was the same spot!"

"That's my sweetheart!" Nestor said, smiling as he walked down the stairs. "Sic him, Gigi, sic him!" The two friends embraced.

LOL

Nestor was back up in his study, his hands hesitating on the keys. Gigi was fast asleep. She had outdone herself with dinner, making Christian's favorite dish of pasta shells stuffed with ricotta and fresh spinach. Christian worked on the salad as Nestor tended to the two bottles of wine he had brought along. Their dinner conversation revolved around Gigi's pregnancy, Nestor's paintings, and a little Martinez, Katie, and Amy.

As they neared the bottom of the second wine bottle, nostalgia drifted in. Gigi had held herself to half a glass of wine, pleading her delicate condition, and growing more bored than tired, she gave them both a hug and a kiss goodnight. Before she wandered off to bed, Christian again extended his invitation. Gigi said she thought it was a great idea, and gave him a little extra squeeze. After she was gone, the two old friends sat around the living room finishing off the second bottle, reminiscing.

Between stories, Christian spoke of his sister and the growing problems with the Murphy boys up in Tranquillity. Nestor talked about his paintings and the idea of being a father. He said nothing of the map and its deadly pins. Finally, though, Christian had to start on the long drive back to Tranquillity.

Nestor's hands rested on the keys. He wondered if he was getting in over his head. He knew Gigi would rather he put this time into his paintings, but this was different. His paintings were something he could easily control. When he put the brush to the canvas, he decided on everything from start to finish. What started here in his study was a different matter. He felt that, with or without his choice, he was being painted into a picture. He just wondered whose hand was holding the brush. His fingers finally started in at the keys.

Surfing over to a search engine, he typed in "profiles of serial killers." The site returned 868,688 web pages, over 16,000 more than when he had first logged on a month before. He refined his search, and the engine returned 18,367 web sites. Scrolling down the first page, he passed "Psychos R Us," "Serial Homicide Case of the Day," "Serial Killers Anonymous," and "Criminal Profiling—Serial Killer Info Site." He even scrolled past "Serial Sonnets," the exploits of serial killers put to the tunes of popular songs. In mid-page he came upon "Serial Killer Hit List" and double-clicked it.

The site downloaded a laughing skull welcoming the visitor. Nestor clicked directly to the "hit list." Pedro Alonso Lopez appeared on the screen, the "Monster of the Andes." Pedro was on top of the list, credited with over three hundred kills covering Peru, Colombia, and Ecuador. Nestor read how, in 1980, a flash flood had uncovered some of his female victims. The page went on to explain that Pedro later led authorities to over fifty gravesites.

He moved further down the page, stopping at H. H. Holmes. Holmes was hanged in 1896, but only after his body count tallied over two hundred. He had killed most of the lodgers in his mansion. Next on the list was Gilles de Rais, an ally of Joan of Arc. Gilles had enjoyed killing young boys. He had confessed to the murder of a hundred and forty youths. On October 26, 1440, he was burned and hanged.

The list went on. Dr. Harold Shipman, a London family practitioner, one hundred and sixteen, plus or minus. An Indian bandit known as Veerappan was credited with one hundred kills, and was still at large. Pee Wee Gaskins, with a hundred or more kills, had been electrocuted in 1991. Nikolai Dzhurmongaliev, who had served many of his female victims to his dinner guests in the Russian republic of Kyargyzstan, was described as having the mentality of a lone wolf. Bruno Ludke, a German deliveryman, murdered eighty women from 1928 to 1943. Nazi officials caught him and shipped him to a hospital in Vienna, where they conducted experiments on him; he was later executed by lethal injection. Andrei Chikatilo, the Soviet Hannibal Lecter, had had a ten year reign of murder, amassing over fifty victims. Jane Toppan, born in 1854, had died in a state asylum at the age of 84 with a confession of thirty-one kills. Many believed her body count was closer to a hundred.

Nestor stopped.

The "Hit List" continued for twenty pages. He wondered how much of the iceberg was hidden beneath the surface. These were known, documented cases. How many were unknown? What was really out there?

Exiting the site, he went back to the home page. It was getting close to midnight; a few more minutes, and he'd call it quits. He decided to check in at the chat room first.

There were fifteen people there. A number of them were familiar names: "EvilBeing666," "FeverCine," "Jumpshot9," "TooSassy4U," "GrimRip001." Nestor's name, "Ed.Hopper2," was tame compared to many of them. He was boxed between "TooSassy4U" and another name he wasn't familiar with, "44MagDum." Nestor watched the conversation go back and forth, not joining in.

Nothing was really going on. There was some small talk about the true identity of Jack the Ripper, the parole of Charles Manson, Jeffrey Dahmer and the killing of gays, and the difference between serial killers and mass murderers. A brief discussion flared up about whether Gary Leon Ridgway was the Green River Killer, until TooSassy4U chimed in, flirting, after being ignored. The other discussions dwindled, and TooSassy4 took center stage. Nestor's gut reaction was that TooSassy4U was not all "she" made herself out to be. No one seemed to care.

Nestor checked his watch again; close to midnight. He was off in the morning, but had a ton of things to do around the house. He was preparing to sign off when Hymn101 signed on.

Hymn101—Hello again.

TooSassy4U—hello.

Hymn101—Not you, Sassy.

TooSassy4U—excuse me.

EvilBeing666—hi! long time.

Hymn101—Nor you, 666.

Hymn101—I said...Hello.

Nestor was silent, but his fingers were on the keys again. What was Hymn101? Biblical? No, he thought. But something nagged at him. He waited it out.

Hymn101—Playing hard to get? So shall I. In five seconds, I will sign off and never sign back on. 1...2...3...

Nestor took a chance and started typing.

Ed.Hopper2—Hello.

Hymn101—Nice of you to remember your manners. Shall we have a private moment together?

Nestor's instant message screen came up. Hymn101 was on it.

Hymn101—There, isn't that better? Now, do you come here often?

Ed.Hopper2—I pass by once in a while.

Hymn101—That's not true. You're a bit of a voyeur, but I'm sure you think you have your reasons. It's all quite interesting though, isn't it?

Nestor paused. *I'm sure you think you have your reasons...*What was that supposed to mean? He continued to type.

Ed.Hopper2—What's interesting?

Hymn101—Why, the real ones of course.

Ed.Hopper2—What real ones?

Hymn101—The true predators. The ones true to their Nature. Very, very rare breed indeed. Very few in number.

Ed.Hopper2—How few?

Hymn101—A lot fewer then there were a few months ago. Don't you think?

Nestor took his fingers from the keys and shot a tentative glance up to the map.

Hymn101—Thinking? Don't take too much time, I get bored easily.

Nestor went back to the keys.

Ed.Hopper2—How do I know—

Another message popped up from Hymn101 before Nestor could finish his question.

Hymn101—Ah, did you see that? It's midnight, the witching hour, the changing of the day that happens only at night. It's a new day, Ed.Hopper2.

Nestor looked at his watch. He tried to reply.

Ed.Hopper2—How do—

Again, he was interrupted.

Hymn101—How did it feel to kill him?

Ed.Hopper2—Kill who?

Hymn101—Don't be coy.

Ed.Hopper2—Kill who?

Hymn101—My friend in Brooklyn, Isaac. You put six .38 slugs into him. Remember, *Nestor*?

He stared at his name. It was as if a hand had reached into his chest and begun to squeeze his heart. *Police report or newspaper clippings.* That had to be it. He knew his and Christian's names were all over the papers. *Son of a bitch!* But how did this guy know...? Another message appeared.

Hymn101—1...2...3...4...

Ed.Hopper2—Don't know what you're talking about.

Hymn101—How did it feel?

Ed.Hopper2—Don't know what you're talking about.

Hymn101—Fine...1...2...3...

Nestor gave in.

Ed.Hopper2—Felt nothing. He was an animal.

Hymn101—Yes, Nestor, but he was my animal. But, in a sense, you and Christian saved me some trouble. He was no longer an asset to us. He had grown too unstable. It happens. Power corrupts. I had been planning to put him out of his misery very soon. Can't have too many crazies running around killing people, now can we?

Nestor was rattled, but he didn't want to give Hymn101 the satisfaction of knowing it. He knew he was being zeroed in on, and tried to keep his responses strictly in line with the questions from Hymn101, hoping to learn something. He wasn't looking to get baited, he was looking to bait.

Ed.Hopper2—How was he yours? What do you mean by "us"?

Hymn101—You tell me, Nestor. What do you think, or better yet, wish to think?

Nestor paused. The only thing he thought was that this could turn out to be a roller-coaster ride from hell. He started to type again.

Ed.Hopper2—What's your name?

Hymn101—Never mind my name. It is what I am that should give you food for thought, not what I am called.

Nestor knew he was being sidetracked, fucked with.

Ed.Hopper2—You're wasting my time. You can be traced.

Hymn101—Traced...? I don't even own a computer. This particular model belongs to another associate. He would love it if I were to take it and leave right now, but I just don't have the heart to leave yet.

Nestor had had enough.

Ed.Hopper2—Who are you?

Hymn101—Why, Nestor my lad, that's easy! I'm like room 101...your worst fear.

Nestor took notice of the reference to the room in *1984,* and wanted to slap himself in the head. That was easy enough! He took a shot in the dark.

Ed.Hopper2—Are you Him?

Hymn101—If you should hear, "Ah, ha, ha, ha, stayin' alive, stayin' alive..."

Ed.Hopper2—Are you Him? 1...2...3...

Hymn101—Now you're counting? Cute, real cute...and yes, I am Him.

Nestor felt that squeeze around his heart again. He pushed on.

Ed.Hopper2—The last I heard of you was in 1986. How long have you been around?

Hymn101—A minor correction. You heard of me last in 1995. The heart, the glass jar...didn't want the bugs to get to it. It was in the reports you received. As to your question, I've been around a long time. Longer than you can imagine.

The cold stab of fear was there. *It was in the reports you received.* Who was this guy? Who was feeding him? Nestor's hands felt clammy as he typed.

Ed.Hopper2—Thought you were dead. Been busy?

Hymn101—Oh, not dead at all. Busy? Yes, very much so. One day maybe you'll read my Journal and see how busy.

Ed.Hopper2—Why do you keep a journal? Isn't it incriminating?

Hymn101—We have always kept the Journal. It is what we pass on. Now, as for its being incriminating, if you never knew about me, how would you know about a Journal?

Nestor noticed that there was that reference to a *we*, an *us*. Hymn101 also said the Journal was passed on. Passed on to whom? He typed again.

Ed.Hopper2—Now I know about the Journal.

Hymn101—What, Nestor, do you actually know? Come, be honest.

Beneath it all, Nestor knew what he was reading now amounted to practically nothing, just hints of things. Someone well informed, typing, telling stories. He decided to take another chance.

Ed.Hopper2—I know about the society.

Hymn101—You know nothing.

Ed.Hopper2—I know.

Hymn101—No Nestor, you know nothing. I am The Society!

Those last four words hit a nerve. " How..." he started to type, but Hymn101 popped back on the screen before he could finish.

Hymn101—Now, why don't you give your lovely wife, Gigi, a kiss for me. Sweet dreams.

Nestor furiously started to type, watching the last message from Hymn101 appear on the screen. He hit Send, but Hymn101 had already disappeared from the screen. Nestor's hand froze in place and his anger swelled at the mention of his wife. He had just had his buttons pushed. *No, not pushed, slammed.* He sat there. His fears weren't answered, they were just being realized.

He moved his cursor over to Print and heard Gigi come into the room as the printer hummed across the paper. He turned to her. She stood against the doorframe in a long nightshirt, her hair all ruffled to one side. She yawned and scratched the side of her head. It was the first time he had really seen her as being pregnant, being vulnerable.

"Nestor," her voice was sleepy, "it's late, come to bed."

"Okay, in a minute," he said, and watched her amble back off to the bedroom. The printer started to beep. Turning around, he saw a red light flashing on his printer. It was low on ink. He looked at the last message.

Hymn101—**LOL**.
Laughing Out Loud.
He looked at his watch. It was a few minutes past midnight, the start of a brand new day.

A Black Pin

James' rubber-gloved fingers worked quickly, fluidly. Even the fresh blood on the keys didn't slow them down. His last message to Nestor glided across the screen.

"LOL."

He sent the message. It raced along the telephone lines and was delivered in less than a heartbeat. He thought the technology was interesting, but not as interesting as facing the one you wanted the message to get across to. He knew Nestor wasn't getting the whole message yet. Depending on how this played out, he might get it in time. James turned the computer off. *Nice technology, but just not the same.*

Snapping the thin rubber gloves from his hands, he placed them in a small bag, getting out a fresh pair. Flexing his fingers, he felt the slightest twinge of what could be the early stages of arthritis. Ignoring it, he slipped his hands into the gloves and swung around in the chair.

The room was large and heavily paneled, with books covering a good portion of it. The spaces between the volumes held the heads and skins of exotic wild animals. A staircase ran up to a smaller library that housed an extensive collection of rare books spotted with the heads of less exotic creatures. It was a collection he would have to go over later. A taut rope hung down from the staircase.

James sat there admiring the expressions of the animals, forever frozen in time. It amazed him how a taxidermist could remove the stamp of death from their faces and replace it with the dignity that the animal had possessed in life. The process did not work as well on people. People could only maintain a certain dignity up to and before death. Once death slipped its fingers over its intended victim, James knew the dead human animal fell short of its living grace. He had learned a long time ago that death did not come equally to all of God's creatures.

James' hand absentmindedly ran over the two sharp spikes and the heavy hammer that lay next to the keyboard. With that, his mind was brought back to the project at hand.

Picking up the spikes and the hammer, he flexed his fingers around them and found the sensations from before had disappeared from his joints. Getting up from the chair, he walked across the room with his instruments in hand.

James' slow-moving image was reflected in twenty pairs of glass eyes that enhanced the illusion of life over death. One other set of eyes, not made of glass, also reflected James' movement following him through the room.

"Sorry...I had to use your computer." James placed a hand on one of the two spikes sticking out of the wall. Each spike had been driven through a foot. The rope from above held the weight of the body, cutting into the flesh but keeping the spikes from ripping out.

Extremely weak from his wounds, the man still had no problem crying out as James added his weight to the spike. The man had been hanging upside down for nearly two hours, nailed to the wall between the heads of a cape buffalo and a zebra. James grabbed the other ankle just beneath the spike and shook it. The man cried out.

"These are not Stephen's rights...understand?" James dropped one of the spikes, and with the other, went back to his work.

The screams and the pounding of the hammer competed with each other. With newfound energy, the man flailed about, but it was short-lived. James was Death, and unlike the other creatures upon the wall, there would be no dignity to the remains he would leave behind.

The Dream

...the demons that were his. He watched as they entered. The voice washed over them.

"He forgives you." The pain was there...

Nestor *was moving in behind Christian and off to the side. The children were there. They turned their heads, but looked past Christian and stared directly at him. He turned his face away, retreating into his hiding place. Hearing them moan, he turned back to see Christian kneeling in front of the crucified child with a blank piece of paper in his hand. Christian began to place it in his mouth, when suddenly Christian's name was called. He saw Christian quickly stand, his gun pointing, the piece of paper turning to blood in his hand. Nestor was pointing with his gun and yelling. The dead children all turned their heads to watch. Some continued to moan, while others whispered among themselves.*

"*Where?*" Christian *cried out.*

"*Your left! Your left!*" Nestor *was panicky. Christian swung his gun around. A door opened. Isaac. He was large, grotesque. He dangled a child in front of him by an arm. A silk robe with a dragon covered his body.*

The child's head hung lifeless to one side. Isaac's free hand was hidden behind him. Nestor yelled, but his voice was too loud and Christian didn't seem to understand him. Christian tried to yell over Nestor's voice, but the whiteness absorbed everything. Christian tried again, his voice suddenly booming.

"*Drop the kid, Isaac...Let's see the other hand...!*" The dead children all turned their heads to watch, falling silent.*

Isaac *swung the child back and forth like a pendulum. The dragon's face peeked out from behind the child and smiled. Suddenly leaning over, Isaac held the child still. He whispered in the child's ear. The child brought its head up, eyes opened wide, and looked beyond Christian. Its voice whispered in the whiteness of the room, traveling directly to him.*

"*He remembers you.*"

Gun in hand, Stephen stepped out of his hiding place...

Fade To White

The white light enveloped Christian. A moment later, the crack of thunder rode over him. He sat up quickly in the squad car as the rain poured down. Another series of thunderclaps rolled across him, pulling him further from sleep. When the rain had started, he had decided to wait out the weather. Calling Rita over the radio, he had informed her that he was pulling over next to the river, where the outcropping of rocks was. *Do you know where*—he had tried to say, but had never gotten past, *"Do*—*"* when her voice came back quick and snippy.

"Sheriff, you mean where the sandbar extends about fifteen feet into the river and where Amy loves to fish from?" He had just been given a scolding about questioning the Queen of Tranquillity. Before he could sheepishly agree, she had wished him a pleasant nap and "Yeah-ed" him to death about his intention to stay awake. Her *"Over"* was short and to the point.

With Palmer gone, the fatigue of the last couple of days had taken its toll on him. He had been trying to see his sister every other day for sometime. The drives were long, almost three hours each way. But even with everything else, he had gotten Katie's birthday present out of the way. He couldn't wait to give it to her. He just had to figure out how. Yawning, he rubbed his face.

He had been thinking of his sister when the drowsiness crept up on him. Awake now, he felt better, and stretched as the lightning lit up the sky, bathing him again in its whiteness. The thunder followed, masking the sound of the first shot shattering the light atop of the patrol car. The second shot, with its own crack of thunder, blew what was left of the light off the roof. Before that sound had died, Christian was down, gun out, on the front seat, pushing the passenger door open. Scrambling out, he slid face down into the mud, almost tumbling over the embankment and into the river. He heard their laughter before the sound of a car took them away.

Spinning around in the mud, he lay on his back as the rain beat down on him. Breathing heavily, he got up slowly, looking at the shattered lights. *Stupid bastards!* He'd just had his fill with the Murphy boys. Holstering his gun, he got back into the squad car soaking wet. Starting it up, he headed towards the Murphys' house, taking the longest route possible. He needed to cool down a bit, but there was a darkness about him that he knew he wouldn't be able to shake off completely.

Another bolt of lightning zigzagged across the sky, the whiteness of it fading as the night quickly reclaimed its domain.

The Murphy Boys

The Murphy boys were Tranquillity's local terrors, and the township was blessed with four of them. The twins were the hardest to keep in check. At nineteen, Daniel and Richard were kept in line to some degree by Brian who was twenty. He in turn toed the line behind Kevin, the oldest at twenty-one.

Their consecutive births had been a labor, not of love, but of necessity. Their father had wanted cheap, long-term labor for the farm, and produced them as such. He would have had more if it weren't for the fact that after the twins, who pleased him because of his minimal effort, his wife, Mary, had had her tubes tied without his knowledge. For the next year, he gave her his best shot, night after night, with none of the expected results. She slowly convinced her husband that he might be at fault, sowing seeds of doubt within him about his manhood. But being the practical man that he was, he had done a little checking. Finding himself not at fault, he then turned on his misguiding wife. By the time the boys were four, five, and six, she had been hospitalized twice for "farm accidents." There were other accidents between those hospital stays that weren't as bad. With those, she could stay home and mend herself.

It wasn't until her sons started having accidents as well that a fatal accident finally occurred. His body was found impaled upon a pitchfork in the barn. He had apparently fallen from the loft, with one of the prongs piercing his heart. There were no witnesses, and Sheriff Adams found no one at fault. With small towns living by rumors as well as truths, rumor had it that the angle of the pitchfork was a little wrong. Tongues also wagged about the distance from the top of the hayloft to the chalked outline of the body—minus the rendition of the protruding pitchfork. Those that whispered with heads close over a morning coffee figured he had had to take a running start. A running start off the loft holding the pitchfork against his chest, doing a swan dive down on it—without snapping or cracking the wooden handle, of course. Most found it—questionable.

So the tongues wagged, spreading various versions of his flying start into the afterlife—but then again, maybe he had just slipped. Few tongues talked about that possibility, but it was usually said during a lull in the conversation.

The owners of said wagging tongues knew that the senior Murphy hadn't been much of a man, and all were in agreement that it was surprising he had lived this long, accident or not. Rumor also had it that Sheriff Adams had a bit of a liking for the now-widowed Mary, and an accident *was* an accident. No one at fault. Case closed. Small town talk. Rumors.

With the untimely demise of her husband, Mrs. Murphy's farm fell into disarray. The boys were not inclined to keep up the chores that their father had pressed upon them, and Mary was neither able nor willing to pick up their slack, having no great love of the farming life, either.

Fortunately, her husband had been a great believer in life insurance, and Mary sold off much of the land, adding to the family's newfound wealth. At first, mother and sons lacked little, if anything at all, except for a strong male figure to guide the boys. Other then Sheriff Adams, who had more of an interest in their mother than in them, the boys were left to fend for themselves, and grew up accordingly.

Over the years, they came to consider the county, and especially the town, their own, figuring that their "family" ties with the local law gave them a free hand. Their pull with the law lasted until Sheriff Adams found the deer and the headless body just outside of the town limits. Along with the rumors of the flying/diving/tripping pitchfork accident and the now-confirmed rumors of his infatuation with the widowed Mary, there were still the rumors that Adams had found a message of some sort near the bodies that he failed to disclose. Shortly afterward, true or not, Sheriff Adams had pulled up stakes and headed out of town.

By the time of Sheriff Adams departure, most of the money was gone, leaving Mary with no one to turn to but her sons. And without Sheriff Adams' protective umbrella, the boys began to accumulate strikes against themselves. For the most part, at ages fourteen, fifteen, and sixteen, the strikes were mostly an annoyance of their presence. It was just that since there were four of them, it seemed all the worse.

But a pattern emerged, and people couldn't ignore it forever. The trouble started in earnest when the boys got the idea that acting-sheriff Palmer was taking up with their mother. In actuality, nothing could have been further from the truth; he was heartbroken over the disappearance of his girlfriend and was merely trying to keep things as peaceful as possible. The boys didn't see it that way. They figured he'd woo her and break her heart, just like Adams. They were determined to do something about it.

It happened one fine, hot August day. Palmer had come by to check up on the boys and was talking with Mary, when she had gone inside to start dinner. The boys took the heat of the day as a sign, and tried their collective hand at murder. They asked Palmer if he'd like a Pepsi. The heat being what it was, he told them that would be nice. They laced the soda with half a bottle of aspirin. The soda was a little too cold, and stir as they would, the aspirin wouldn't dissolve. Finally losing patience, they decided to take their chances, and served it to him. He looked at it and asked what the white crap was floating around in his drink.

"Aspirin," Richard answered. The younger of the twins by a minute, Richard was incapable of lying. This was not due to an honest streak; rather, it was because lying took a certain amount of creativity, a certain skill. He was lacking in both respects. "It was a lot of aspirin," he added.

"Aspirin? What are you kids, nuts? Trying to get me sick?" Palmer looked at the four of them and shook his head. "Aspirin. Next time boys, try a little rum and not so much ice!"

He left quite alive. The three brothers turned on Richard.

They were capable of murder, they just didn't have the means yet. That night, they gave Richard a beating that kept him out of school for most of the week. Their mother, seeing perhaps an echo of her husband in her sons, started to keep her distance from them.

Christian's first meeting with the Murphys occurred a month after he became Sheriff. There had been a rash of petty break-ins. On Palmer's advice, he knew exactly where to go.

The boys had some of the stolen goods in the basement of the house. But, with Palmer's prompting, and given the boys history and unhappy childhood, Christian just kept them locked up in the two-man cell overnight before releasing them to the custody of their mother. After that, they learned fast. As the years passed, they kept their mischief, for the most part, out of the county.

It wasn't until their mother decided she had had enough of this world that their outlook really changed. Whatever her reasons were, she supposedly took them to the grave with her. But once again, rumor mixed in and mixed up the truth. With the boys running off somewhere causing trouble for someone, Palmer had swung by to check up on Mary. It was rumored that he found her slumped over a letter confessing to the murder of her abusing husband. Some said that death took her in mid-sentence as she wrote about her sons. But no letter was ever found.

Another rumor that made its way over hot coffee cups was that she had waited until Kevin had turned twenty-one before she killed herself, hoping that in her absence, he would take some responsibility for the younger boys. As it turned out, Kevin did take control, but like his father, only to suit his means.

When it came out that one of the drugs she had taken had been aspirin, the boys took to beating Richard again. They knew that, in reality, he had had nothing to do with her death. It was just their way of coping with their grief.

After that, the boys really began to turn mean, but they still had the good sense not to shit where they ate. They kept most of the trouble over in Menkerit County. Assaults, B and E's, auto theft, missing livestock, the fingers all pointed to the Murphys. They had become cagey, almost smart, not giving Christian and Palmer or the Menkerit cops anything solid. But Christian knew it was only a matter of time before they made a stupid mistake—a crack he could get his fingers in. After that, he knew they would crumble. As it was, there was hopeful talk about town that sooner or later their paths would indeed cross his. When that happened, the town hoped Palmer wouldn't be there to save their four asses.

The rain came down as Christian drove slowly along the back roads. Lightning flashed briefly, joining Heaven and Earth together. The time was at hand.

Fade To Black

Christian parked the cruiser down the road from the boys' house. Reaching over, he pulled the shotgun from its vertical mount next to the radio. The rain pelted him as he got out of the cruiser, but he took his time walking up to the house. As he approached it, he heard an angry voice over the pounding of the rain. It sounded like Kevin. He went to the front steps and looked into the living room window in time to see Kevin slap one of the twins and then the other, knocking the second one down. Christian heard his name.

"That Sheriff Lord ain't no fuckin' jerk-off here, ass'oles." Another slap caught the other twin off guard and sent him flying against the wall. Once the shock wore off, he took a small step towards his older brother. Kevin just straightened up, and the younger brother backed down. *Daniel?* Christian wasn't sure. He never could tell them apart. Brian, the middle brother, stood next to Kevin during all of this, silent but nervous.

"Why you gotta brin' shit down on us?" Kevin said, looking at the twin who was still against the wall.

Christian had heard and seen enough. Turning from the window, he went to the front door. Taking a deep breath, he kicked it in, catching Kevin in mid-sentence. He moved quickly. The oldest Murphy froze as he found the barrel of a shotgun just under his chin. But Kevin kept calm as he found his voice.

"Well, well, Mr. Sheriff, why don't you jus' come in outta th—" The butt of the shotgun caught Kevin across the bridge of his nose, dropping him to his knees. He put his hand to his face. Blood trickled between his fingers as he cursed.

Brian made the mistake of moving. The wooden stock of the shotgun flashed a second time, catching Brian in his shoulder and dropping him in his tracks. Before the twins could move, Christian swung the shotgun at the them, and they threw their hands up protectively around their heads.

The sound of the shotgun pumping a round in the chamber made both of their bodies jump simultaneously as if they still shared the womb.

Swinging the gun up, Christian's first blast blew a hole in the ceiling. In rapid secession, the next three blasts took out the windows in the living room. Rain began to blow in around them. Christian looked at the boys. None of them moved.

"Control them, Kevin," Christian warned, and wheeled, leaving without saying another word.

The wind and the rain banged the broken door against its hinges. Kevin got up, letting the blood flow from his broken nose. He screamed over his shoulder for his brothers to cover the windows. None of them moved. Suddenly he turned and yanked Daniel out of the chair and then grabbed Brian from the floor, screaming about the rain coming in. As the brothers ran to get something to fix the windows with, Kevin turned back to the door.

"Motherfucker's jus' fucked with the wron' one here," he said wiping the blood from his nose with his sleeve. It continued to flow. "Have a feelin' this ain't over with." He watched the door being batted back and forth by the wind and rain. "Ain't over yet. Jus' beginnin'. I can feel it." Kevin walked over to the door, looking out into the darkness.

"*Ain't over ya motherfucker!*" he cried as tiny drops of blood flew from his mouth. "*Ya cocksucker! It ain't!*" he screamed, bringing his hand back up to his nose just as lightning lit the sky once again.

In that instant of brilliance, Kevin saw Christian standing fifteen yards away, the shotgun leveled directly at him. The lightning died with a crack, and Christian faded into the black of the night.

Katie's Idea

Katie had been working on sketches for a new children's book when the noise of the storm woke Amy up. Curled in her mother's arms, it took a half-hour of stories for her to fall back to sleep. Putting Amy back into her bed, Katie had come downstairs, resuming her work, but it was no good. Her thoughts kept going to Palmer and all of the plans ahead. She knew it was just a matter of breaking it all to Christian.

Hearing her husband pull in behind the house, she had officially declared the work a lost cause for the evening and headed for the kitchen to greet him.

Christian always preferred to park the patrol car behind the house, using the back entrance to the kitchen for his comings and goings. He claimed it was less of a mess for her this way. The truth was that he really didn't want the front of the house to scream, "*Sheriff lives here!*" even though everyone in the county knew. But when she saw him come through the door drenched and muddy, she was glad he was tramping the mess through the kitchen instead of the living room. She gave him a quizzical look and asked if he was okay. A "yeah" was all she got, along with a quick kiss on the cheek as he headed for the bedroom stairs.

"That's *it? 'Yeah?'* " Her hands shot up into the air as she watched the wet trail he was leaving behind him. "Hey, buster! The shoes!"

"Sorry, hon," he said, turning around and unlacing his shoes. "Just got bit by a tree. I need to shower and warm up. Can you make me some tea?" She watched him disappear upstairs, leaving her completely confused.

"A *tree?* You…? Hey, wait… the socks!" She yelled up after him, coming to the bottom of the stairs. She wasn't afraid of waking Amy; it had been a long day, and she knew she was out cold.

"No," he called down, "I didn't get bitten, the patrol car did. Here's the socks!" She caught the flying wet socks in time to keep them from hitting her in the face.

"*Car?*" she mumbled, walking to the back door, dropping the socks in the sink as she went. Outside, the rain was still coming down, but not quite as hard as before. She had no problem making out the damage to the patrol car. "Jeez, what the hell happened?" A moment later, she heard the shower running.

Christian was sitting up in bed when Katie came in, carrying the tea. He smiled at her as she set it down on the night table.

"Well...*how was your night?*" she asked, sitting next to him. Katie made herself a little more comfortable on the bed. Her husband looked a lot better cleaned up. "Careful, it's hot," she warned him about the tea. "Okay, sooooo...?"

"Aw, it was nothing—" Christian started to say as he took a sip of the tea. He winced.

"Told you it was hot, dummy. Now tell me." She took the cup from him blowing on it.

"I was just driving down by the river, and the storm snapped a branch off smashing the lights pretty good. So I dragged it off the side of the road to get rid of it, and like an ass, I slipped down the bank. All in a day's work." He ventured another smile at her. He didn't like lying to her, but he didn't want her to worry about the Murphys, especially with Palmer out of town. Besides, the Murphys needed a first-hand lesson from him, and they had no one to bitch to. They had been lucky with him tonight and they knew it. Katie handed his tea back to him.

"Oh, okay. Here, try the tea now," she said. He took a sip. No complaints. "For a moment," she continued, "I thought it might have been the Murphys."

"No, haven't heard anything from them. How's Amy?" he asked, looking to change the subject quickly.

Katie rolled her eyes, laughing. "My God! She was a terror today. She ran herself into the ground. I think she's on drugs," Katie said, laughing. "But the storm shook her up a little. We had to cuddle. She's really out now."

"Good," he said. "I gave her a quick check when I got out of the shower. She had the covers pulled over her head. I had to unwrap her like a mummy."

Scooting closer, Katie started to caress the back of his neck. "Christian, if that branch was heavy enough to do that to the lights, what would have happened if it had hit the windshield?"

"That's easy," he said, dropping his head so she could rub it better. "I'd be getting the windshield fixed instead of the lights."

"Christian!" she said, shaking his neck, "C'mon, you're skirting the issue!"

"That's good," he said, straightening his neck. "Fine massage until you tried to break my neck! And no, I'm not trying to skirt the issue. 'Cause there isn't an issue. Just a freak accident. No one got hurt except the lights."

"Okay, okay." She gave in. "Your neck is really tight. No whiplash?"

"Naw, everything's fine. Just a little more stressful with all of the running around."

Katie knew he was right. The added strain of Palmer being out of town for two days didn't help much, either. She was glad that he was due back tomorrow. Christian had just come back from visiting his sister when Palmer had had to leave. *One coming, one going.* Now, her husband just needed a little downtime before he relaxed and opened up. It had taken her some time to get used to that. She considered it a quirk in his personality, since she was completely the opposite.

Katie continued to work the tension out of his neck. She had something on her mind about Palmer, and wondered if this was the time to bring it up. He seemed to be relaxing. *Sure, why not,* she thought. Leaving his neck alone, she rested her head against his shoulder and took the tea from him, sipping it.

"How's my tea?" he inquired.

"Who's on Dave tonight?" she asked, pretending to ignore him. She took another quick sip before handing the tea back to him.

"Stupid human tricks. Wanna watch?" he asked.

"Sure, but Christian, there's something that's been bothering me lately about your missing deputy." She put out a hand and he handed the tea back to her. "Haven't you noticed anything different about him?" She sipped.

"No, why?"

"Well, it's strange with these trips out of town. I spoke to Lucy—you know, Sam's wife?"

"Seen her around."

"Okay, good, now here's the problem. Palmer's out of town doing some carpentry work, right?"

"Yeah, so far I'm with you."

"Okay, fine. So how can he do his carpentry work when he lent most of his tools to Sam so Sam could finish his back porch?"

He turned to her, frowning. "Maybe it's a small job, or maybe there're tools on the site. I don't know. I never question what he does."

"I know you don't, but it's been bothering me. You know how I am when I get that knot in my stomach."

"Believe me, I know. Can I have my tea back now?"

"Here, not much left. But okay, I'm serious now. I think I know what he's been up to."

"Okay, Dave is coming on soon. You have my undivided attention for about a minute. Shoot."

"Fine, good, okay here's what I think...Ready?"

Christian looked at what little tea was left and made a face at her. "Could you possibly drag this out a little longer?" I would like—"

"Okay, I think Palmer has a girlfriend!" She blurted out. Christian stared at her for a moment.

"Fine, I'm happy for him," he said. "Can we watch Dave now?"

"That's it...? 'Fine...I'm happy for him? Can we watch Dave now?' "

"Yeah, that's it, Dave's on." He put his nearly empty cup down on the bed and reached for the remote.

"Wait," she started, placing her hand on his. "If he has a girlfriend, shouldn't he at least have us meet her or say something? I mean, we *are* his best friends." She was truly puzzled and slightly hurt.

"Hon, if you're right," he said soothingly, "he'll say something when he's ready. Maybe he's just uncomfortable because of that old girlfriend of his. You know he doesn't say much about her. Besides, when I leave town, does that mean I have a girlfriend?"

"No, of course not. Nobody would put up with you."

Christian looked at her with feigned indignation. "Whoa, hold it there. I'm *way* less annoying than Palmer."

"You know what I mean. You're married to a wonderful woman, have a wonderful daughter, a wonderful house that needs a wonderful skylight and besides all of that, you're about to renew your wedding vows to show me how wonderful you truly are!" She thought she worked all of that together quite well. When he looked at her blankly, she gave him a quick kiss on the lips. "Dave's on," she said.

He was visibly thrown. "Wait a minute, 'wonderful, wonderful, blah, blah, blah...skylight, blah, blah, blah...*wedding vows?* You're kidding, right?"

"No, hon, I'm serious." She tried not to whine, but it was close. "We've been married over five years now and it's been great being married to me, hasn't it?" She took the teacup from the bed and put it on the night table. "I just thought it would be nice to renew our vows, that's all."

"Is this going to be a simple 'I do,' 'You do,' 'We both do,' type of thing or should I be fearful of something else?"

"Almost...kind of...in the church...with Father Toland." She climbed on top of him. "With our friends and family." She slipped off her top. "I think you should be scared shitless. What do you think? And besides, it's my birthday tomorrow and I found your gift!" She reached under the pillow, pulling out a small box. "Can I open it now?" Katie's eyes sparkled like Amy's. Both loved getting presents.

"Er, excuse me. Where did you get that?"

"It wasn't my fault!"

"Where?"

"I went to get something out of the glove compartment in the car and found it. Wasn't my fault, like I said." Christian closed his eyes. She was right. Actually, it was a good thing she'd found it. With all of the running around, he'd forgotten he'd left it in the car.

"Okay, but still—"

"Can I open it?"

"It's not—"

"Can I open it?" It was a no-win situation. Christian sighed.

"Go ahead, happy birth—" Katie didn't wait for the rest of the good wishes as she ripped into the wrapping paper and box. Opening it, she gasped.

"Oh, Christian, it's beautiful!" she exclaimed. "Here, put it on me." She handed him the diamond heart pendant. He opened the clasp and put it around her neck. As he did so, she rubbed her breasts against him. He grinned at her, shaking his head.

"Okay, loose woman, here." He straightened it, laying it flat between her breasts. Katie looked down.

"Not too bad between my tits, huh?"

"No, I can actually say, not too bad!"

"*Thank you,*" she said quietly, leaning over giving him a kiss.

"You're welcome," he mumbled against her lips.

"So, what about our vows?" Katie mumbled back accentuating her question with a little shake of her breasts. Leaning back, she knew she had him.

"I think the skylight should go off-center a bit, right over there." He pointed over her bare shoulder. She slapped his hand down.

"Christian!"

"Okay, okay. Because it's *almost* your birthday...we'll do a skylight...and our vows. How's that?"

"You see how wonderful you can be! Now, just one more thing, me or Dave?" She leaned back over, kissing him long and hard. As she pulled back from the kiss, Christian started to caress her breasts.

"Well," he said, "I've had you before, so we'll go with Dave." She kissed him again as he hit the remote. Letterman's voice snapped in with the picture. He was introducing the first stupid human trick. Drawing back, Katie looked at him, an eyebrow cocked.

"Still Dave," he said, and she kissed him again. She slowly broke away and gave his lip a playful little bite.

"*Okay*...can I call you Dave?" he asked.

"Sure, you can call me anything," she said, as she reached for the remote.

"Oh, wait! Before we turn off Dave, just one thing." He held her by her shoulders. "Don't play detective or anything with Palmer. You know how you get yourself into trouble."

"Well, do you think he'll bring her?"

"Where, to our second wedding? Hon, are you nuts? You don't even know if there is a woman. I hate to break the news to you, but he could be working!"

"For what? Tell me, for what? What does he spend his money on? Not food, we feed him! No, no way. Something tells me that he's up to something else. It's a woman thing. That's why we have them and you guys don't."

"Yeah, well, get your woman thing over here. Dave's stupid human is doing his thing."

"Say good-night to Dave," she said, picking up the remote with one hand and reaching for him with the other.

"Wait, wait. The guy's shooting milk out of the corners of his eyes."

"Say good-night to Dave."

"It looks weird!"

"Weird? I'll show you weird." She hit the remote just as the stupid human trick played in slow motion.

Blood Patterns

They seemed harmless enough. They had picked her up an hour ago, and she was still sitting around in her bra and panties. She didn't care, as long as they were paying for her time.

Miami hadn't turned out as she had expected. She had hoped to find herself a retired sugar daddy to keep her going, but all she'd got so far was busted—twice. Now she was low on cash, and any trick she could turn was a real help.

She asked if it were okay if she turned on the TV. Nobody said anything, so she put on Letterman. She was commenting on how weird this guy must be to shoot milk out of his eyes, when she turned around toward them.

The blow to her head killed her instantly. The one who wielded the hammer had been in The Society for six years. This was his twenty-fourth kill as a member, but it still felt fresh. He could feel all of the switches click into place like clockwork. That's what he loved about it, everything in its order.

One switch in his head shut off, and another clicked on.

When he was in the killing mood, he never saw what he killed as a person, as human. It was as if he was out of his body, viewing the events from a great distance. He had once rationalized it as being a bomber pilot of a sort. The pilot knew that by dropping his bombs, he was killing people on the ground. But they were so distant, they were just targets. But he knew that it wasn't all that simple. He knew there were more switches in his head, more relays. His hand tightened around the hammer. Some blood trickled down.

Another relay clicked.

Here was this thing, a thing that had been walking and talking a moment before, now at his feet in another form. All twenty years or so of its existence brought to an end. Now, the silence. Always the silence. Bombs falling. Silent explosions setting off other chain reactions. That was the beauty of it. Everything leading up to the finality of it all.

Switches.

He looked down at it. It had been a good, quick kill. He looked at the splatter pattern of the blood from the blow.

One more switch in the relay was hit.

He took pride in his blood patterns. They were always a good indication of the strength of the impact. He had an excellent assortment of his own photographs showing his talent. He knew for a fact that other photographs by police photographers were shown to law enforcement agencies. His reputation was growing. The angle, the impact, the force, all important teaching tools.

He would say he was glad he could help in a way with the education of these wannabe cops, but he was way beyond them all at this point. The Society had seen to that. It was the blood in that pattern that aroused him now.

Switch.

A sexual compulsion to see the thing's blood. *Haematodipsia* was the word he knew for that particular compulsion. Sometimes, he would get beyond that and continue with his ritual, making it to the final switch. The term *Necrofetishism* was the last switch in his relay. If achieved, he would go to work on it while it was still supple.

His hands tingled around the hammer. He knew the final relay was going to be made tonight. His fingers touched the blood on the hammer, rubbing the smooth liquid along the weapon. It took his breath away. He felt his own blood surge elsewhere. He began to close his eyes to savor the ecstasy of it.

There was a slight noise behind him. His eyes opened quickly. He had almost forgotten himself. This was the first time he had killed anything in someone else's presence. *Too much excitement.* Sometimes the sequence of switches was beyond his control. He relaxed. Since *He* was there, why not finally have a picture taken of himself with his latest? It would be a hell of a trophy photo. *Why not?* He found the thought intriguing, even exciting.

The very last switch.

"Nice shot," James said.

The killer turned, smiling. He almost had time to reply before the blow from the hammer caught him squarely in the head, just like the hooker. But the blood splatter pattern that hit the walls was well beyond what he had ever accomplished. Had he lived long enough, he would have wept at its beauty.

Switch.

James had his own switches. In a little while, both bodies would have towels covering their heads. Since the hooker was not his kill, he would simply dispose of it. But the chest of his kill would be cut into, the heart partially eaten and placed back in the cavity upside down. The body would then be prepared for its journey. Sometimes James kept the heart. Sometimes he buried it with the body. It all depended on his appetite. James had been doing it that way for over fifty years.

Chosin Reservoir, North Korea—November 1950

It was two days since the last attack. The Marines were stretched out along the western slope of the reservoir. They were cold, hungry, and low on supplies. Most had rags wrapped around their hands and feet to keep them from freezing any further. Long, slit trenches dug along the frozen earth were their homes. From the trenches, they looked out over the quarter mile of the Strip before it sloped back up into more hills. Enemy hills. This piece of "no man's land" was a killing zone; a chunk of real estate sliced from the surface of the moon. No soldier in his right mind would want to cross it. The Chinese had attempted it four times so far. Some of the Marines respected them for it. Most thought they were just plain fucking nuts.

The battered strip of land that separated the two warring armies wasn't the reason for the lull in the fighting. It was the crippling cold. For two days now, the bitter weather had worked its killing upon both Chinese and American. But finally, the crippling cold had broken, freeing the soldiers to kill each other once again.

The Red Chinese "Volunteers" swarmed down, entering the Strip at a full run. From their hilly stronghold they came, blasting their horns, trying to rattle the nerves of their enemy. Some ran with their weapons still frozen from the extreme cold. They died, singly and in groups, as the guns of the Seventh Marine regiment opened fire. As they fell, the frozen earth refused to take in their blood, and it froze, adding a second layer of red ice. Still, over the frozen blood of their dying comrades, the Chinese came, their weapons finally beginning to fire, finding their mark.

Keeping cover in the trenches, a number of the Marines didn't bother to fire at the incoming communist troops, waiting instead for the air strike that had been called in. With their backs against the icy earth, they watched the sky as the four Marine Corsairs flew in low. Once over the Strip, the Corsairs released their napalm on the advancing enemy. As the mixture of napthenic and palmitic acids ignited ground and human alike, the Marines that had held their fire stood up like prairie dogs popping out of the earth. They faced the Strip, enjoying the blast not for its killing effect, but for the heat it produced. As the wall of rushing heat washed across them, eyes closed to the warming touch and breaths were held against the stench of the thick gasoline mixture and burning flesh. As the Corsairs tipped their wings in a farewell victory gesture, the Marines slipped back down into the hard earth, waiting for the next attack.

One young Marine had taken in the heat along with some of the others, but unlike them, he didn't sink back down into the protective earth. Still standing, he fired a clip from his carbine at the few survivors closest to him. One of the Red soldiers he hit fell over onto the burning napalm that covered the ground. The enemy's body began to twitch as the flames fed on him. The Marine waited a moment longer, watching the body burn. Suddenly, leaving the safety of the trench, he ran out to the dying man, grabbing him by the ankle. As he dragged the burning body back, enemy sniper fire began to kick up the earth around him. A few of his fellow Marines returned fire. Making it to the top of the trench, the young Marine jumped in, pulling the still-burning body down with him. One of the other battle-weary Marines stopped firing and came over to him.

"James, wha' the fuck was tha' 'bout?" the Marine asked, slapping his hands together, trying to keep the circulation going. Four of his fingers were frostbitten.

"I'm cold, Sal," James said, doubling the body over so it would burn better.

"Is he dead?" Sal asked prodding the Red Chinese soldier with the tip of his carbine.

James squatted, warming his hands near the flames. "How the fuck should I know?" he said.

Sal watched, continuing to slap his hands together, feeling uneasy. "Hey, are you goin' fuckin' nuts?" he asked.

James looked up at him, tilting his head closer to the heat that came off the burning body. "No...no...look around, Sal, *this* is nuts." The cold had taken almost as many casualties as the Chinese. "For this," James said quietly, "I'm extremely sane."

In a few moments, the slapping sound stopped. Sal, who called Hoboken his home and had never experienced cold like this before, stood next to James, his hands over the enemy's body. Within a few minutes, there were a number of soldiers warming themselves around the body. Nobody said a word.

James

He was born James Felton Kellogg, the middle child of three. He had grown up on the outskirts of Johnstown, Pennsylvania, where, on May 31, 1889, the South Fork Dam had broken. Johnstown, settled in a deep narrow valley, had found itself in the path of a wall of water half a mile wide and seventy-five feet high. The unfortunate collapse of the dam had taken the lives of 2,209 people. In 1933, on the 44th anniversary of the flood, James took his first breath. Named for his father, his mother, Janet, insisted on Felton for his middle name. Felton was her maiden name, and she didn't want the name to totally die out. James Senior had no argument against it, so James was baptized into the Christian faith with given, maiden, and family name. With his birth, he became the younger brother to his sister, Margaret. Two and a half years later, he became the older brother to his newborn sister, Katherine.

His father, a religious man, had insights from time to time as to the workings of the mind of God. For the most part, he kept these understandings to himself, not burdening his family with details of the Creator's thoughts. But as young James grew, he learned to understand the timing of these insights. After a revelation, his father would take him hunting in the surrounding hills. There, as the senior James contemplated the hidden meanings of God's messages, he taught his son to hunt. Over time, as the younger James contemplated the hidden meanings of his own messages, he taught himself not to hunt, but to kill. He understood the difference well. And the difference he understood would set him a world apart.

As the years passed, the younger James became a voracious reader. He had few if any real friends. Schoolmates and teachers both disliked him, although never for any explicable reason. People just handled him like they were handling a very sharp knife. He found his friends in the words he read on the printed page. He would take these printed and bound friends out to the wooded foothills with him. Sometimes gone for days on end, he split his time between the books and hunting.

For him, the books had a certain life, a thought process of their own. But it was the hunting that he saw as a real entity, a true life force in itself. He saw it as a chance meeting of two beings that might simply start off as a fresh track, a broken branch, a slight noise. Up to that point, both the animal and he were unknown to each other. After it, there was a hint of the existence of another living form, another creature. To come upon that creature, to see it, to make it aware of *his* existence, to become a part of *its* existence, to let it know the hunt was about to begin: that was where the excitement lay. Sometimes if the animal didn't take to the game, he would wound it, never in a vital spot. Just enough torn flesh to get the idea across, forcing its survival instincts to take over. This would give it purpose where none had existed before. In turn, he would hunt it with his own newfound purpose. He had never lost an animal.

Once, at the age of thirteen, he had come across a lost hunter. For half a day, he watched him. Sometimes he stalked him up close. Sometimes he followed him through the scope of his rifle. Making slight noises, he controlled the hunter. At first, the hunter came toward these sounds, calling out, hoping they signified help. James would then move behind the hunter, leading him in a new direction. After awhile, the hunter re-acted fearfully to these unknown sounds, quickly learning that someone or something was fucking with him. He began to flee the sounds at a pace that soon exhausted him. Animal or man, James found the reaction to be the same, although the animals had better instincts. The hunt, or the evasion of the hunt, was part of the animal's nature. Man, on the other hand, wasn't use to being hunted, and it didn't take much to turn the tables on the hunter.

It was, James knew, a matter of control. That control, simply put, was based on fear. A fear that was put into the heart of the hunted. A fear that pumped the heart, sending the heated blood throughout the body. A fear that turned the blood-filled body to flight. With this fearful flight, rea-son exited.

It was all so simple, just a matter of getting to the heart of things. But most men couldn't comprehend the idea. It was no longer part of human nature. Men were always looking for *reasons* for things, especially for things beyond their control. As far as James was concerned, that was the problem. Without a reason, Man was just a frightened animal lacking the proper instincts to survive. The man in his sights now was such a creature. James knew it—he created it. But unlike the other Creator, his creation only took a day. James smiled down on his Adam, but he wasn't about to rest.

He stopped counting how many times the hunter had cried out, *"Who's there?"* But before sunset of that day, he had made up his mind to answer that question. That night, as the ex-hausted hunter slept, he sat next to him and watched him through the night. By morning light, the hunter was on the move, and James carefully led him to a clearing between two ridges. There, a small farmhouse stood. James stopped his hunt and watched the hunter work himself down along the ridge to the farmhouse. As the relieved hunter knocked on the screen door, he sighted in on him. The screen door opened, and James now had his witness. He shot the hunter through the temple from quarter mile away. There was no reason for it other than that James had come to grips with his true nature. Two years later, he came back to the farmhouse. The family of four that lived there disappeared, making the local headlines.

The following year, his father had another revelation, one more inward light that clearly showed the way of God's will to him. His father, after all those introspective hunting trips, had joined the Society of Friends, more commonly known as the Quakers. The irony was not lost to James in later years. In a sense, one Society drove him to the other. As his father embraced Quakerism, he began to share his insights with his family, which quickly evolved into preaching. The preaching emphasized the beliefs of the Quakers that human goodness existed. That something of God exists in everyone. They also recognized the presence of human evil.

James disagreed. There was nothing of God in him, nor was there anything of evil in him. He was merely himself. Nothing more, nothing less.

Though his father tried to bring his family deeper into his faith, a man unknown to James would change all of that. He came not in the form of a Christ, but in the form of North Korean leader, Kim Il Sung. Sung, watching the growing opposition to South Korea's president, Syngman Rhee, believed he would be welcomed by the South reuniting the two Koreas. On June 25, 1950, the North Korean armies crossed into South Korea. To Sung's surprise, the North Korean armies were not given the open-armed reception he'd hoped for. James Felton Kellogg, just shy of his seventeenth year and with a forged birth certificate in hand, left his family to push the communists back over the 38th parallel.

A few months later, as James sighted in on that single communist soldier in the frozen foothills of the Chosin Reservoir, the bodies of the missing family were all found within a mile of their farmhouse. A hunter found the first body in a shallow grave beneath a tree while taking his lunch. Heavy rains had washed away the top layer of earth that had barely covered it. It was almost as if the killer had wished the body to be found. It wasn't long before the rest of the family was unearthed. It was determined that all four had had their hearts cut out at the time of their death.

The hearts were never found.

Extremely Sane

The Chinese were back, this time in force. It was late afternoon as the sun swept across the black and white landscape like an avalanche. The light held no warmth, casting long shadows from the bugle-charging enemy. Clad in winter camouflage, they were preceded by mortar rounds, pounding a path, tearing up the ground like geysers suddenly springing from the earth. As the defending Marines' own barrage of mortars kicked in, a covering cloud of dusty earth filled the air, dimming the light of the winter sun even further.

In a rapid procession, the enemy mortar rounds worked their way up the side of the rugged hill, ripping out large chunks of it. Finding the range along the trenches, the explosions began mixing bodies and frozen ground together, blowing the Marines into the earth or out of it. As the Chinese troops closed the distance, the mortar fire lifted and the sound of automatic and small-arms fire replaced the booming concussion of the projectiles. The fighting intensified as the Marines fired down with their carbines while the Chinese fired up with their burp guns. The crackling sound of the battle was uninterrupted as the allies from a war just five years prior unloaded their magazine clips into each other as fast as they could load them.

As the distance lessened, the main weapons of choice became grenades, the battle turning into a throwing match of exploding shrapnel. Death rained in hot pieces of metal tearing through flesh in both directions.

At the start of the battle, James had sniped at the Chinese soldiers. With each slight movement of his finger, a distant body dropped. He never waited to confirm his kill. He didn't have to. Before the recoil had settled, his eyes were picking his next target. As the battle flowed toward him, he calmly cut a path down the center of it with his rifle. The Marines dug in with him took some comfort from his calm. As the mortar barrage lifted, he directed lines of fire as the Chinese continued to close the distance. They died by the numbers, but their numbers also drove them on.

One of the trenches on James' left was overrun, and he and his men were now in danger of being outflanked. He grabbed two other Marines, and they took all the grenades they could carry and ran for the enemy-occupied trench, lobbing the grenades as they went. The explosions kept the heads of the Chinese down as three grenades finally landed in the trench. Two Red soldiers almost made it out before they exploded, the shrapnel shredding their winter camouflage, peppering it red. They fell back into the trenches as two more grenades landed on top of them.

James and the other two Marines jumped into the trench as the bullets of Chinese burp guns erupted into the hard ground around them. The Chinese troops were still making progress up the hillside. Pinned down by the automatic fire, the Marines tossed the remaining grenades over the top of the trench. They were rewarded with explosions and screams.

As James was about to sneak a look over the top, a Chinese soldier jumped into the trench, almost landing on top of him. The enemy soldier didn't carry any weapons, and the terror of the battle was evident upon his face.

For a moment, everyone stared at each other. James turned to the frightened soldier and simply said, "Get out." The soldier looked from James to the other Marines in confusion.

"Get out!" James yelled again as he grabbed the soldier, pushing him up and over the side of the trench. A burst of gunfire from below caught the frightened soldier in the throat and he fell back, mortally wounded. James looked down on him.

"Hey, don't look at me like that," he yelled at the soldier. "They're *your* fucking friends, not mine!" Grabbing a burp gun from one of the other dead Chinese, he stuck it over the top of the trench and started to spray across the area. The other two Marines followed his lead. As they emptied the clips, James grabbed the closest dead soldier and stuck his helmet on the dead man's head. No bullets whizzed by when he propped the body up over the top of the trench, so James carefully looked over the dead soldier's shoulder. He was greeted with the sight of the Chinese finally retreating down the hill. He let the dead body go. The battle seemed over for now.

As the other two Marines lit up cigarettes, James happened to look toward the sky. He spotted four specks heading for the Strip, growing larger. They were coming in low and fast. A moment later, the retreating Chinese looked up and saw them, stopping dead in their tracks.

"Jesus fucking Christ!" James said as the Marine Corsairs with their loads of napalm became plainly visible. The Chinese knew exactly what was about to happen, and they turned their retreat around, charging back up toward the relative safety of the Marines. At first, most ran without firing their weapons, only wanting to close the distance between themselves and the dug-in Americans. They knew the closer they were to the Marines, the safer they were from the warplanes coming in overhead. At this point, a bullet was preferable to the thick burning gasoline gel that they feared so much.

The Chinese came on with a new determination as the retreat turned into an attack of desperation. As they ran, they began to open fire, at the same time looking for cover from the inferno that was about to be released on them from the heavens above. The Marines unleashed everything they had at the frantic troops. The Corsairs, coming as close as they dared to the entrenched Marines, let go of their napalm tanks, smothering the ground with flame. Against this backdrop of scorching death, white-clad Chinese, like Satan's angels springing out of the flames of Hell, ran into the guns of the Marines. In less than a minute's time, it was all over. Not one of the Chinese on the field survived.

James stood upon the dead bodies of the Chinese they had killed in the trench. Surveying the scene, he thought it looked good. He knew the mortar attacks would resume and something would have to be done about that. But that would be later, at his leisure. Right now, he needed a little walk.

Against the protests of the other two Marines, James climbed out of the trench and went for a stroll down the hill.

No, he thought as he walked through the scorched earth and the burnt blackened dead. *For this, I'm extremely sane.* And he started to whistle, looking forward to the coming of the night.

Evening

James' breath seemed to freeze in the night air as he held the body against him. At seventeen, he was smaller than most of the Marines he served with. He was barely large enough to have made it into the Corps.

Once, a fellow Marine had made the mistake of commenting about his size. The Marine never saw where the knife came from. The tip of the blade was just *there*, a fraction of an inch from his right eyeball. Every time he had blinked, he could feel his eyelashes touching the point of the knife. James kept him up on the balls of his feet for ten minutes like that without saying a word. Finally letting him down, James had stepped back, smiled and winked at him. The issue of height or size never came up again.

James found himself attached to the Seventh Marines, but in reality he wasn't attached to anything or anyone. He went to war not to serve his country, but to serve himself, to put himself to the test. By the third encounter with the Red Chinese, it was no longer a test. He had left frozen corpses up and down the line. It was all too easy. He knew, no matter what, that he was going to make it out alive. His destiny was elsewhere. This war, *his* private war as he saw it, was merely a means to sharpen his skills. He couldn't care less who made it off this hill. He just hated the damn cold.

The body he held in front of him was just as small and looked just as young as he was. Mortar rounds had started to rain down on their position just as he had reached the enemy hills. Now, there were two less mortar teams. As the body shuddered, he held it close, trying to feel the heat of the soul as it rushed out. But in this cold, he could feel nothing from the heavily dressed soldier.

He had slit the first Chinese soldier's throat from behind just as he was handing a mortar round to his companion. James' razor-sharp hunting knife had easily cut into the soldier's neck. He had no time to enjoy the first kill, though, as the second soldier turned out to be a bit of a struggle. Even though the soldier was covered in thick, cumbersome clothing, he moved quickly. Unfortunately for the Chinese soldier, he was a fraction of a second slower than James. That was all the time James needed. The knife quickly punched up into the man's throat and through his cheek. The soldier's hands clutched at the exposed tip of the blade. James jerked the weapon out, twisting it, severing the carotid artery. Without a sound, the body shuddered. With both enemy soldiers dead, James knew there was very little time.

Working quickly, he cut the front of the soldier's quilted jacket open. Plunging the knife into the chest cavity, he had the heart out in less than thirty seconds. It steamed in the cold air as if there was a soul leaving its mortal remains. As the last of the body heat drifted away in a cloud, he took a bite of the heart and placed it back upside down in the mangled chest cavity. He quickly repeated the ritual on the other soldier. Just as he finished, he heard a nervous voice from the third mortar team call out in the night. The panic in the voice carried clearly over the distance.

James had known that it wouldn't be long before the other mortar team would get jittery in the silence, missing the thumping sound of the rounds flying out of this position. He chewed as he listened. The other team stopped firing, and there was a minute or so of silence before one of the Chinese soldiers started to call over to him. James knew it was a diversion. He had heard the slight noises as one of the enemy soldiers tried to sneak up on him. James kept still and waited. Finally spitting out the meat, he started to crawl along the frozen earth to meet the Chinese soldier bellying his way over to his own death.

In the cold of the night, there was a brief scuffle as one more of the enemy had his chest exposed to the starry night. As the other soldier continued to call out, James crawled toward the voice, gift in hand.

When the object landed in front of him, the Chinese soldier scrambled to get away, thinking it was a grenade. When it didn't go off, he slipped back to his position, carefully picking it up. The blood on the heart was already frozen. Fearful, the soldier dropped it and turned in the small foxhole, bumping into James.

"Evening," James said.

That soldier wasn't quick enough either. No more mortar rounds flew that night.

The Demon And The Corpsman

James stood in the trench and watched as Sal, loaded down with weapons, walked away. Going past a number of wounded, he turned, looking over his shoulder.

"Sure y'don't want some eats? Ain't no sense goin' out on empty. Getcha anythin'?"

"Nope, fine here, Sal. Thanks." James said as Sal nodded and continued walking past men wrapped in rags, bandages and pain.

A gray dawn had broken on the "Demon Line" that lay in front of the trench that James called home. It was the third night he had crawled out and torn at the hearts of the enemy, adding to their fear. Fighting now raged at the extreme flanks, but the activity of the Chinese troops in front of them was at a minimum. During the last two days, the Chinese had made only halfhearted probes. None seemed to want to come in contact with the "Demon."

James reached inside of his parka, took out a piece of meaty muscle and put it into his mouth. Chewing it slowly, he looked around. *It is all going to shit here,* he thought. Along the flanks of the Marines, word had gotten out about the "haven" section, and they had poured in. James had a feeling that things were about to collapse.

He watched the medics running from one wounded soldier to the next, keeping the small vials of penicillin thawed in their mouths. James shook his head. Too many wounded. He lowered his head, trying to protect his face against the cold. One of the medics nudged him with his boot.

"Hey, could use some help," he said, handing some vials of penicillin to James.

Looking at the small, clear vials, James chewed slowly. "What am I supposed to do with these?" he asked.

"Follow me. Jus' put 'em in your mouth to thaw. I gotta give these guys a shot." The corpsman started off, placing vials in his mouth.

James stood there. "They're all as good as dead," he yelled after the corpsman. "You know that, they know that."

The corpsman stopped and turned around. Walking back, he took the vials out of his mouth. "Hey, listen, I ain't lookin' for no medical opinion here, jus' some help. Got that, fella?" The corpsman looked the small Marine up and down. "Jus' put the fuckin' things in y'mouth and follow me. That's all I want, 'kay?"

"Put them up your ass," James said dropping the vials. Two shattered. The medic stared at the broken vials, looked over to the wounded and back at James. He was expressionless as he drew a .45 caliber pistol from his parka. Cocking it, he pointed it at James' midsection.

"Listen Marine, I won't kill ya. But I *will* put a bullet in y'gut, cut y'open, and use the heat of y'fuckin' body to thaw these things." He took a step closer to James. "Got that? Now pick 'em the *fuck* up...and so help me God, y'break one more, I'll kill y'right where y'fuckin' drop it."

James looked at him and at the pistol. He spit out the meat and picked up the remaining vials, putting them in his mouth. The corpsman looked at the piece of meat on the frozen ground, slipping the .45 back into his parka.

"Where the hell'd y'get the meat?" he asked, the disagreement apparently over. James said nothing, just pointing out toward the enemy-occupied hills. The medic's expression didn't change. He had seen too much already. He didn't care what kind of man was in front of him now as long as the vials didn't freeze. Still, he hesitated a moment and eyed the Marine in a different light. *Don't give a shit. Jus' so long as the demon keeps those fuckin' Chinks on their side of the Strip.* The cries of the wounded drew his attention and he nodded. "C'mon," he said, and they moved on to the dying and the dead.

Matt's Friend—Present Day

The single rose. That's what drew Susan's eye to him. He had been sitting in the corner of the bar, alternating between taking measured sips of beer and glancing at those who walked in. It was a slow night, and he had more sips than glances.

Susan smiled. Usually, the more alcohol in their system, the easier her job. The only problem, as far as she was concerned, was that after twenty minutes of sipping and glancing, he had yet to look in her direction even once. He checked his watch. That was a good sign, she thought. Getting restless... maybe stood up? A good chance. She would give him another five minutes and then go over and say something. She had nothing to lose. At the worst, a no-thank-you. She supposed he *could* be an undercover cop, but she doubted it. He was too good-looking to be a cop. Maybe, if he felt dejected enough, he would want to party with her. *Yeah*, another five minutes and she would make her move.

As she waited, the door to the bar opened and the handsome man's face suddenly became all smiles. He handed the single rose to another man, following it with a kiss and an embrace. As they hugged, she could hear one of them commenting on how the weather was starting to change already and how it was near impossible to get a cab at this hour in Manhattan. She rolled her eyes and shifted her weight in her chair angling it back towards her drink.

"Don't you just *hate* that?" A drink was placed down next to hers, almost touching it. She shifted her weight once again and looked its owner up and down. Mid-thirties, neatly dressed, a little gut, wedding band, manicure. Businessman? A quick in-and-out? She liked what she saw, but wondered why she hadn't seen him before. *Maybe he had been in one of the booths.* Didn't really matter; she could handle him. She gave him a big smile.

"*You* don't have any roses for someone else, do you?" she asked. He laughed, and she found it infectious, joining in.

"No, no, I don't think so," he said. "But I *would* like to buy you a drink. Maybe share a little of your company...if you don't mind, that is?"

She looked him over once again, wanting to get down to it. "The drink is cheap. My company isn't."

"No doubt," he said, and gestured for the bartender, sliding a few twenties onto the bar.

She glanced over toward the corner of the bar where the two boys in love were adjusting their scarves, making for the door. The sound of glasses clinking brought her back to her current company. He stood next to her with his drink up in the air.

"I'm Matt," he said. "Cheers."

She smiled, reaching across to touch the rim of his glass with her finger. "Cheers. I'm Susan." She dipped her finger into his drink and then placed it in his mouth. With eyes half closed, he started to suck on her finger. The glimmer of the diamond pinky ring caught her eye. *Could still be a good night,* she thought. And the way he was going at it, maybe a little kinky shit tonight too—all extra of course. Maybe not a quick in-and-out after all. Whatever it'd be, she'd have this one wrapped around her finger in no time.

She pulled her finger back a little, and he followed it, taking a small step toward her. *Yeah, he passes,* she thought. *He'll be jumping through hoops by the end of the night.* She moved to make sure there was eye contact when he finally decided to let her finger go.

When he opened his eyes, he winked at her and took her finger, running it over his lips, smiling. The slamming of the bar door brought his eyes over her shoulder. The mood in him changed instantly—no more playtime.

Shit! She tried to control her anger, wondering who had ruined this for her. She turned to see another man standing halfway down the bar. Looking back at Matt, he looked like she didn't exist. *Figures,* she thought. *Maybe a threesome?* But from what she saw of the third wheel and the expression on Matt's face, she was dreaming—this was strictly business.

"Excuse me, be back in a moment," Matt said as he slipped past her and up to his... friend? She had her doubts.

Matt's back blocked her view and she couldn't make out much of the new guy. Their heads were close together and they appeared to be speaking softly to each other. When the whispers died, her best hope so far for a profitable evening turned around and came back to her. Grabbing his coat, he simply said, "I'll be back in five." She raised her glass to him and nodded, not expecting to see him again. The bartender walked over, setting down two more drinks and taking one of the twenties.

Susan sighed. "This sucks," and watched the two men leave. Turning back to her fresh drink, she eyeballed the money that was left on the bar.

Time Bomb

"You have me come all the way to this fucking filthy city and keep me waiting in that bar for hours!" Matt complained as they walked down an alley a few blocks from the bar. "It's getting piss-ass cold out here, and I'm not used to this damn weather. Besides, my drink and change is next to that low-class, big-assed bitch!"

"I know, I know. I'm sorry. I had trouble traveling." Stephen shot Matt a look. In the darkness, Matt didn't catch it.

"Yeah, trouble. Why the contact like this? You're a bit out of your territory, aren't you? God, it fucking *stinks* out here." Matt looked around.

"I know. But like I said, it's safer this way. Listen," Stephen said as they stopped, "we have a problem. James was right...he knows. We *are* being hunted. Killed off." Matt looked at Stephen as if he were crazy. Stephen's expression said otherwise. Suddenly, he felt shaky. He took a pack of cigarettes from his coat and lit one. Inhaling, he held the smoke a moment before letting it out. When he did, it seemed to take all of the oxygen from his lungs. The smoke suddenly smelled as foul as the alleyway.

"Who?" Matt asked. "You said you knew!" The words barely got out.

Stephen's reply was matter-of-fact. "Yes, I know for sure."

"Who, then?" Matt's cigarette hung loose in his hand, forgotten.

"There are two hunters."

"The fuck you mean, *two?*"

"You might say it's a competition. Who can be top dog, the most kills, Final Jeopardy round. You know what I mean?"

"What in the fuck are you talking about? *Final Jeopardy?* Is this a fucking game to you? Just tell me! You know or not?"

"Yes, I know...I know them both."

"Fucking *Christ!* Who?" Matt screeched, flinging his cigarette away. "Who the *fuck* are they?"

"One is...*James.*" Matt's demeanor changed. Stephen saw the fear rise to the surface of the man. It was almost a physical sensation.

"Stephen...you gotta be wrong!" Matt's voice combined doubt and dread.

"No, I'm not wrong. I know." The alleyway was dimly lit with a few beaten up garbage cans laying about. Judging by the stench of urine, it seemed to be a popular stopover for drunks who couldn't make it to the next bar in time, or just didn't care. Stephen stepped a little closer as Matt spoke.

"James...? Why?" Confusion was laced in Matt's voice, his mind desperately searching for a reason. "James is *everything.* He *is* The Society. Why would he do this? You gotta be fucking nuts!"

Coming closer still, Stephen put his hand around the back of Matt's neck. "Matt, you have to understand," Stephen spoke softly, "he's been challenged. It wasn't supposed to be like this. It wasn't part of his plan, but things change. That's why he's been around for so long, he adapts. That's the beauty of him. That's the lesson learned."

Matt started to shake his head. "Stephen, I don't know what you're talking about. Lessons learned? What is all this shit?"

Stephen brought his other hand up to Matt's face and held him gently, child-like. "You really don't get it, do you? You really, really don't know?" He started to laugh. His laughter annoyed Matt, and Matt pushed his hands away exploding.

"No, you're right! I don't get it. And this whole fucking thing is funny to you? What if you're fucking *next*, huh? You gonna laugh then?"

Stephen took a small step back. "In all honesty Matt, I'm pretty sure I'm not next in line."

"Oh no? So, you fucking tell me, who the fuck would be crazy enough to bump heads with him?"

"That's easy Matt. It's me." Stephen took another step back. "But I do believe he's coming after you next and I'm going to let him have you." It was a cool night, not that cold, but he was pleased at the way Matt shivered. Stephen smiled and turned, walking away.

He had no fear of this killer. Matt was a strangler, no weapons, and just women. *No balls.* But that might change. As he reached the mouth of the alley, he stopped, half-turning.

"Might as well finish off your hooker friend back there. You don't have much time." And he walked out of the alley, knowing a time bomb had just been set.

Hopefully, it would go off in James' face.

Slipping

Matt was back home and out of that godforsaken city, but it did no good. The fear had taken hold, its roots running deep. He felt like an animal snared in a wire trap that either had to gnaw off its own leg or die. He had been in his apartment waiting for James for just over a week. The snare was growing tighter.

His fear reflected in everything he did. He had lost weight and sleep, and his will to survive was not based on his determination, but his fear. He was filthy, afraid to take a bath or shower in fear that the running water would cover some warning sound. He wouldn't play the radio or TV either, for the same reason. To pass his time, he read his father's Bible. It showed him how weak he was. He slowly began realizing that his father had been right all those years. He had always been weak. He had thought that he had shown his strength by killing, but now he was coming to understand that he was just frightened of everything in his life. His father had known it all along.

Matt had thought of running, but he was too afraid of being caught out in the open by James. His hope was that he could reason with him and tell him how Stephen had come to warn him. He knew, given the chance, he could also explain how he was doing God's work with these hookers. Actually, he was doing work that God seemed afraid of doing Himself. Surely, James would see beyond all of this?

Taking his father's Bible in hand, he lay down on his bed, drawing the sheets around him. Under the covers he touched the .22 automatic he slept with. It wasn't a good feeling, the gun. He was afraid of them. But he needed it. Even though James was old, he doubted he could physically take James. It wasn't long before fatigue began to take him.

With one hand on the Bible and the other on the weapon, he slept.

Movement on the bed woke his body and shook his soul. In the dark, he could tell that the window was open and the curtains were fluttering toward him. For a brief second, he felt relief. *It was just the window.* He felt the movement on the bed again. *I never opened the window.* He was afraid to move, but slowly his hand searched for his gun. It was gone. When he heard James' voice, he stopped searching.

"Go ahead, turn on your night light, but don't touch anything else. I can see."

Sitting up slowly, Matt reached for the lamp and clicked it on. James sat on the edge of the bed, with the Bible lying between them. A knife lay on top of the Holy Book and the .22 was on the bed beside it.

"What were you looking for? The Word or the weapon?" James asked, indicating the gun with a nod of his head. Picking it up, he tossed it closer to Matt. Matt didn't move. James placed the point of the knife on top of the Bible and spun it. The tip of the blade worked itself into the cover of the book.

"I see you found God. It would have been better if you had found me first." James looked at Matt. He stopped spinning the knife, laying it down next to him. Picking up the Bible, he opened it and started to flip through its pages. Matt's eyes strayed to the gun. James looked up from the Bible and simply said, "Don't," and continued to turn the pages.

With that knife next to James, Matt knew he didn't have a chance to get to the gun. He needed time. Perhaps he could reason with James. His mouth felt awfully dry. James addressed him.

"Matt, did you know I have a favorite quote?" he asked softly. Stopping at a page, he held the Bible up a little. "Ah, here it is...and what a coincidence. It's from Matthew, chapter 6, verse 21: 'Where your treasure is, there will your heart be also.'" James closed the Bible and set it back down on the bed.

"*Listen*—" Matt started, but James interrupted him.

"James, you can call me James."

"James...James, I swear I have no idea what is going on here—"

"Oh yes, you do," he interrupted Matt again. "You know quite well. Stephen tried to set you against me, didn't he?"

The little man started to spin the knife again. Matt wished he wouldn't do that, but said nothing. He knew the combination was deadly. *Time, needed time.*

"James, he was talking about the two of you killing the rest of us in some sort of competition or something like that. He wasn't making any sense."

"Oh, it makes sense if you think about it. But you wouldn't give things like that too much thought, would you, Matt?"

"James, please, I would never go against you," Matt pleaded, leaning forward as he spoke. The patriarch of The Society cocked his head to one side, and Matt leaned back. "I don't know how you could think that about me," Matt continued. "You brought me into The Society. All those years, like a father to me—"

James stopped spinning the knife. "You *were* waiting for me, weren't you?" he accused.

"No, I swear, I—" Matt saw the flash of the knife, but felt nothing until the blood started to drip down his cheek. James went back to spinning the knife.

"Don't touch it, it's just a little nick. And don't...don't *insult* me again with your lies. We understand each other?" The blood started to drip onto the sheets. "From this point on,"

James continued, "just either answer 'yes' or 'no.' Nothing else. Understand?"

"Yes...but—"

"Shhhh...say nothing." The knife stopped spinning again, a warning. "Nothing but what the question requires, understand?"

"Yes."

"Very good. Now, were you planning on using this deadly weapon against me?" James nodded toward the gun. "And pray for me afterwards while continuing on your quest to rid the world of these ill-painted women?" Matt looked around for an answer, a way out, and found nothing. He turned back to James.

"Yes," came his reluctant answer. Despite his dry mouth, he was beginning to sweat.

"Stephen's a bright one. Much smarter than you. He's been planning this for a long time, don't you think?"

"Yes."

"Well then, we seem to have a problem of loyalty here. He's playing us against each other. Smart, but unfair. Did you know that he was hoping that you would do his dirty work for him? Or at the least, slow me down. Did you know that?"

"No," Matt answered. The knife flashed and he knew he had another nick on his face, but this one he felt right away. *"Yes, yes, I knew,"* he answered quickly, this time bringing his hand up to his face.

James nodded. "Now, back to the matter at hand..." He moved quickly and Matt suddenly found the point of the knife against his throat. "Here's the plan—" James had started to say, but before he could continue, Matt grabbed for the blade of the knife. James simply pulled the knife through his fingers like he was wiping it dry with a kitchen towel. He gave it an extra little flick.

The knife cut deep, almost severing two of Matt's fingers. Muffling his anguish, Matt threw himself back against the headboard, his skull striking with a resounding crack. He grabbed his fingers as blood began to run down his hands.

"Why, Matt!" James feigned surprise. "Do you know how many people over the years have grabbed for the knife?"

Matt held his injured fingers, the blood pooling in his cupped hands. The pain pulsed with every heartbeat. *Time, needed time,* Matt thought.

James read the animal fear in Matt's eyes. Now, they were getting down to basics. This pleased him. "Matt," he said in a soothing voice as if nothing had happened, "what's your favorite passage from the Good Book? Anything you want to hear—"

Matt's movements were quick. The pooled blood in his hands caught James in the eyes. Slashing out blindly, James tried to keep Matt at bay while his free hand frantically wiped the blood away. But Matt was going for something else. Grabbing the gun, he rushed the shot, hitting James in the upper arm. The bullet tore through James' bicep. But before Matt could get off another round, the gun jammed. Frantically, he tried to clear the chamber. Quickly looking up, he saw James' eyes staring out from the dripping blood. The knife whistled through the air. A thin red line appeared along Matt's neck and Matt's face went blank with the realization of what had just happened. It was only a heartbeat before the thin red line opened up and Matt toppled from the bed as the blood from his carotid artery spurted out, staining the sheets.

James was on him in a flash, smiling his smile. He complimented Matt. "It was a good try, kid."

Matt lay dying. But death wasn't quick enough, and he felt the point of the knife enter his chest.

James sat in a small chair looking over at the body.

That shouldn't have happened. I must be slipping.

His arm throbbed. It was a clean wound; the bullet had missed the bone.

Slipping.

It bothered James. He had stopped the bleeding an hour ago. Still, he sat there and thought about it. The bullet had entered the exact spot where another bullet had torn into him in his youth. This was only the second time in his life that he had faced his own mortality.

Kill Me

James followed the corpsman, listening to the sounds of the fighting from the flanks. It was heavy and getting closer. *Not good.* He was handing the thawed vials over to the medic when the first few mortars slammed high above their position. Right on the heels of the explosions, the cracking reports of small-arms fire echoed across the Strip.

The assault was moving fast. The Chinese had apparently overcome their fear and were throwing themselves against the Demon Line. In the fury of the developing battle, Marines from both flanks were running in, carrying wounded comrades and as much ammunition as possible. Those that weren't burdened down were firing and throwing grenades over their shoulders as they ran, trying to keep the advancing enemy troops at bay.

Explosions large and small shook the ground and ripped at flesh. Between the explosions, the bugles of the Chinese rang, mingled in with the angry cries and warnings of the Marines. The new mortar teams were finding their range, and the Marines were being pinched in from both sides and blown apart up the middle. All hell was raining down.

James had just taken the last vial out of his mouth when a bullet ripped into his arm. The impact spun him around, knocking him into the corpsman. They hit the ground just as a burst of gunfire ripped through the air above their heads, catching two Marines that were running for cover. Both men fell dead on top of them. Pushing them off, the corpsman grabbed James' arm, palpating it.

"Bullet went through," he yelled, looking around frantically. "Don't think it hit bone, jus' muscle." A mortar exploded nearby, showering them with hard frozen dirt. "*Shit!*" The corpsman cursed, grabbing the .45 from his parka and holding onto his helmet. "Not much I can do for ya—*Ah, fuck!*"

James saw the expression on the corpsman's face change as he swung his .45 around. The pistol boomed out twice, hitting two Chinese soldiers. James grabbed a carbine from one of the dead Marines as three more Chinese came over the trench, firing at them. The corpsman was hit once. He managed to get off another round before he was hit again and lay still. James shot the two lead soldiers and they dropped. The third soldier ran toward him, firing wildly. James returned fire, wounding him, but he kept coming. Then he was on James, screaming, swinging his weapon like a club.

James blocked the first blow with his carbine, but the soldier swung again, managing to knock the rifle out of his hands. Kicking out, James caught the soldier off-balance, toppling him backwards. The .45 lay in the corpsman's outstretched hand, and James grabbed for it just as the soldier jumped back on top of him, screaming, trying to dig his fingers into his eyes. James fought off his clawing hands, putting the muzzle of the .45 against the side of the soldier's ribcage. With a feral grin, James pulled the trigger twice in rapid succession.

The impact threw the soldier off and to the side of him. Getting up quickly, James saw more Chinese soldiers coming over the trenches, firing at the remaining Marines. By now, most of the Marines were cornered, holed up in small pockets, firing into the oncoming communists. Those Marines that had been caught out in the open had been cut down.

It was time to leave.

Twenty yards away, a rocky ridge ran above him and he saw three Marines running along it, trying to make it to safety. If he could make it to the top of that ridge and skirt along it himself, he would have a better chance at survival. With a quick look around, his mind was made up.

Ignoring his wounded arm, he grabbed a bandolier of ammo from another dead Marine, along with a fresh clip for the .45. As he was loading it, someone grabbed his ankle. He spun, about to fire, and the hand of the corpsman went up to protect his face.

"Wait!" the medic cried out, his voice hoarse. "Wait. Kill me, or help me." James saw that the corpsman was hit in the leg and what looked like a gut shot.

"Doesn't matter," James said looking up toward the ridge and safety. "You're dead either way." He went to move away, but the corpsman held onto his ankle.

"*Kill me, or help me*," he said once again, coughing up blood.

James looked quickly at the ridge and without hesitation, turned back to the wounded man, putting the .45 to the side of his head just as a Chinese soldier ran by, loaded down with ammo. He looked surprised to see an American with a pistol against the head of another American. James looked into the eyes of the enemy soldier, smiled, and pulled the trigger.

Shocked, the Chinese soldier stopped in his tracks. James just watched him with the smoking muzzle against the remains of the corpsman's head, the smile still on his face.

"Demon," the soldier whispered. "Demon," he said again, and started to run. James shot him. Without wasting any more time, he started to move up toward the high ridge, the din of the one-sided battle echoing around him. He figured he had five minutes, tops, before the Chinese finished their mop-up.

As he climbed toward the ridge, he saw one of the Marines that had made his way up just moments before, come running back down. There was gunfire coming from behind him as he sprinted. As the Marine ran, James saw two grenades arch over the soldier's head. One grenade hit the ground in the path of the Marine, exploding but missing the running soldier, not even slowing him down. The second grenade bounced off a rock and headed straight towards him.

James hugged the frozen rocks and buried his face as the grenade exploded. The concussion tore him from his handhold, knocking him back down toward his dead comrades. Hitting hard, he tried to get up, but his legs slipped out from under him. Dazed, the sounds of the battle echoed within him; a cacophony of cries, curses, warnings, death. *A weapon!* His mind screamed, adding to the deadly choirs. His hand reached out, his fingers touching a carbine. The sounds cleared, separating themselves as his hand gripped the weapon. He turned to kill. There was a fleeting glimpse of the rifle butt just before it cracked into the side of his head.

The Answer

James didn't move.

Dead. He needed to play dead.

There were Chinese voices all around him. The explosions and firefights were over and he felt rough hands going through his pockets. The searching hands tore at his parka, finding the partially eaten heart. Immediately there was an outcry and then silence. The silence was broken by a single voice carrying a sharp note of fear in it.

James didn't move.

But he knew the owner of the voice was on the verge of some sort of action. It came quickly. The slap across his face snapped his head to one side. Still, he didn't move. He was slapped again, this time harder. The voice was now a shriek of rage, and James heard the bolt of a burp gun fly home with more excited yells. Someone kicked his bloodied arm and his eyes flew open from the pain. The Chinese soldier's hand stopped in midair, poised to strike him again.

"No need for that," he said, "I'm awake now." The soldier ignored him, and the blow whipped his head to the side, splitting his lip. James slowly turned back to his captors, using the extra time to look around as much as he could. Between the feet of the soldiers that surrounded him, he saw a small number of wounded Marines under guard not too far away. Other than that, the dead from both sides were being carried away. The Chinese bodies were taken out of the trenches, while the American bodies were being piled up at the far end of the trench. With a torn American flag near them, a Chinese military film crew was photographing the carnage, recording their side's victory. James didn't really care. His only concern now was how to get the hell out of this alive.

Bringing his head around, he looked up at the faces of his captors. For all he'd heard about the stony-faced Asians, they didn't seem all that impassive to him.

They were men, and all men had fears.

One of them dropped the half-eaten heart in his lap. James had something to work with. He smiled up at them, not even looking at it.

"Are you the Demon?" the one that had been slapping him asked in excellent English. "Are you the Demon?" The soldier raised his hand one more time. James held his stare and saw the hesitation in the eyes and hand. It was pure fear.

"What's the matter, Chinaman," James said, "you don't like my take-out?" Watching the soldiers' eyes, James picked up the heart and took a bite out of it. A few of the enemy cried out. Pleased with their reactions, he began to laugh.

As he did, the first incoming round screeched high over-head, slamming into the ridge above them. Icy rocks showered down. The Chinese soldiers around James scattered for cover. *Here comes the cavalry,* James thought. The only enemy soldier that stayed close to him was the one that had asked him if he was the Demon.

"*Are you the Demon?*" he now screamed down at him again. "*Are you?*"

James stopped laughing. He started to answer, but three mortar rounds hit the ridge in rapid succession, cutting his answer short, quaking the ground with a resonance of its own.

One more round smacked into the ridge, and the communist soldier was knocked to the ground. Curling up, he tried to make himself small, crying out in English.

James took a second bite out of the heart, and tossing it aside, grabbed a nearby helmet. Crawling over to the quiv-ering soldier, James was as indifferent as the incoming shells.

"*Hey,*" he screamed in the soldier's ear, spitting the meat into his face. "*I have an answer for your question.*" His grip tight-ened on the helmet.

As the rounds fell indiscriminately on their position, James beat the head of the Chinese soldier with each deafening explosion. His fourth blow crushed in the man's skull as the world exploded in bursts of hard earth and soft flesh. The high explosives rained in.

James paused his beating of the dead soldier as the thun-derous earth fell back from the sky, covering him and his deed. For a brief instant, he feared for his own mortality. And like the man he had just killed, he curled up, trying to expose as little of himself as possible. His body tight, his muscles shaking, he thought he heard an explosion. The sound swept through him as if he could breathe it in, and suddenly, he was flying through the air, searing pieces of metal riding along with him, burning, spinning. The explo-sions, the fighting, the dying, all became a streaking, screeching blur. For the second time in the battle, every-thing went black.

Bore's Job

"Private...Private! Private Kellogg! Are you awake?" It was a woman's voice, but James ignored it. He had been awake for the past couple of hours, trying to listen to what was going on. When the pain had first awakened him, he had seen the IV snaking down into his arm. He had tried to move and felt the restraint of the handcuff attached to the railing on the bed. There was a curtain around him, but he could hear the other wounded in the rest of the ward. This was not good. His wounds were suddenly the least of his worries.

"Private Kellogg?" the woman said; the sound of the bed railing squeaking as it was being lowered. He felt the warmth of her hand as she shook him lightly. "James, can you hear me?" At the mention of his name, he heard someone clear his throat. She stopped shaking him and he thought she turned away from him.

"Excuse me, sir," she said, a note of irritation in her voice. "Sometimes we get a better response when we use their first names." The same warm hand now tried to open one of his eyes.

"James...?"

Turning his head towards her, he opened his eyes and saw the hand of the nurse suddenly pull back. She hesitated a moment and then broke into a smile. She was plain-looking, but the smile was pleasant. Two officers stood next to her. One was a Naval officer and the other a Marine Corps officer. Both carried thick folders and neither was smiling.

"Private," the nurse said, reaching for his wrist, "do you need anything for the pain?" She was timing his pulse with her watch, no longer looking at him. James said nothing, rattling the handcuff along the metal of the bed. Looking back at him, she looked grieved.

"I'm sorry, I had nothing—" she started, but was interrupted by the Naval officer as he stepped forward, opening the folder he carried.

"Private Kellogg, I am Captain Nelson, and you are under arrest for—" he stopped, looking over some papers in the folder and then back up, "for the murder of Naval Corpsman Alan Cullum during a battle at the Chosin Reservoir in the Republic of North Korea. This is your counsel, Lt. Borsilli, and he will be handling your case. Is there anything you wish to say?"

"Excuse me," Lt. Borsilli said, "I would advise my client not to say—" James rattled the handcuff against the metal railing till Lt. Borsilli fell silent.

"Funny, Captain," James said finding his voice hoarse, alien, "I don't remember seeing you there when the commies overran us. I must have just missed you. I'm sure you have some fine stories to share of your heroic deeds." He smiled a chilly smile.

Nelson flushed, and he addressed the nurse. "May we leave Private Kellogg with his counsel?" He pulled back the curtain, letting the nurse exit first.

The captain turned and stared at James a moment before turning to Lt. Borsilli, giving him a quick nod of the head. He pulled the curtain shut before Lt. Borsilli could give him a courtesy salute. The lieutenant turned back to James.

"Never did like those Naval lawyer types," he said, dropping the folder on the bed and holding out his hand for a handshake. James just rattled his wrist again. "Oh yeah, sorry. You seem to be attached to the bed. Well, in private, I'm usually called 'Bore.' Heard you guys had a hell of a time up there." Bore sat down on the side of the bed, waiting. James was silent, trying to find out who knew what.

"Yes, well," Bore continued through the silence, "not too many survivors with the Chinese over-running the positions and the counter-attack. Big mess actually, but enough survived to put you cuffed to that bed. It, er, seems that there were two witnesses to the murder of Cullum." Bore reached over and opened the folder producing three documents. One was in English and another one in Chinese with what James assumed was a translation.

"This," he said holding up the one in English, "was from a wounded Marine, Private Salvador Colibri, who *thinks* he saw you shoot the medic. But in the heat of battle, not everything is what it seems to be. Besides, Private Colibri succumbed to his wounds shortly after his statement." He looked at James for any sort of reaction. James was silent. Bore shook his head and continued.

"But he also goes on to state how you were helping with the wounded and how you had a hand in lessening the mortar attacks. That part is good for our case. Tell me James, any of this sound familiar?"

James took a deep breath before answering. "Yeah," he said. "You might say I took the heart out of their attacks."

Bore looked at him, cleared his throat, and leaned forward. "Listen, there's been some unofficial talk…rumors, really, of patrols coming across Chinese laid out in rows with their hearts missing or cut out and put back upside-down with a bite out of them. One Army patrol led by Cpl. Jimmy Bo…" Bore paused watching James to see if the name rang a bell. The only reaction he got was a shrug. "Most called him 'Jimbo.'" Bore tried again. Nothing.

"Okay," he continued, "well, he's the only one that filed an official report of coming across enemy bodies like those. Now, these bodies might be good for psych warfare, but not the kind of news the people back home want to read about the guys here. So do us both a favor, leave the word '*heart*' out of any of your statements, okay?" Without waiting for a reply, Bore sat back and continued.

"Well, we could have gotten away with just this from Private Colibri," he waved the first paper and then dropped it. Picking up the other document in Chinese, he held it up in front of James.

"Like I said, a lot of things happen in a battle. But it's the statement by a certain Li Wu Cho that's gonna make my job really hard. You shot him, which was good since *he* was the enemy, but you didn't kill him. He has decided to switch sides. Good PR for us, bad PR for you. He claims he actually saw you shoot Cullum in the head." Turning to the English translation, Bore flipped a page and quoted, "'The Demon stared straight into my soul and killed the helpless wounded American by shooting him in the head.'" Bore dropped the document and was silent.

"You should have been there," was all James said to Bore.

"Well, I wasn't and now I'm trying to save as much of your life as I can." Bore stood up shaking his head. He took a breath. James saw a look in Lt. Borsilli's eyes that he couldn't mask.

"Listen, whatever you did, you did. I'm sure you saved a lot of lives in the long run of things. But we're getting pressure from on high to produce some scapegoats, and your ass happens to be at the top of the list at the moment. It'd be bad PR to shoot you, so you're going to prison, no matter what James, and that's the truth. My argument is going to be that you guys were being overrun—"

"We were overrun."

"…like I said, you guys were being overrun and this was a mercy killing. Now, if that flies it's a matter of how long you're gonna spend behind bars."

"How many years am I looking at?" The restraint of the handcuffs began to take on a different reality.

"Worst case? Twenty. What I hope for, ten-to-twelve. Those are the numbers. Actually, it's gonna depend on how the war's going." Bore stood up. Looking at James, he knew that the animal on the bed in front of him should be shot. Instead, the war had its ups and downs and James was sentenced to ten years in Leavenworth Federal Prison. Against Bore's personal beliefs, he did his job well.

Wolves, Sheep, Strings—Present Day

Ed.Hopper2—When did you start to kill?

It was Saturday, and Gigi was out shopping for more infant items to push him out of his study. He had been in the process of replying to e-mail from a police department in a small community out in Oregon that was missing two local hunters when an IM screen from Hymn101 popped up. The information he was trying to track down out west was turning out to be a dead end, since he wasn't a relative of the missing hunters and the local police felt they could handle their own problems. Besides, hunters made mistakes and that was the cruel fact of it. Basically, he had been given a polite fuck-off, but he had wanted to keep trying.

That was before Hymn101 sidetracked him. He would get back to Oregon later.

Nestor looked at the time on his screen. Twenty minutes had gone by and he still wasn't learning much from Hymn101. But he had a feeling that *Him* had something to say.

Hymn101—You're being redundant.

Ed.Hopper2—When?

Hymn101—It's all in the Journal.

Ed.Hopper2—What else is in the Journal?

Hymn101—Insight. All about what separates the wolves from the sheep.

Ed.Hopper2—What separates the wolves from the sheep?

Hymn101—Numbers, teeth, and intent.

Okay, Nestor thought, *I'll give you that.*

Ed.Hopper2—Can I see the Journal?

Hymn101—You would have to see me first. I don't think you want that. Besides, none of this is in your Nature.

Ed.Hopper2—What do you mean?

Hymn101—Exactly what I said.

He wasn't getting anywhere. He decided to push a little.

Ed.Hopper2—Tired of playing games. I think you are full of shit. Just one of those bored computer geeks with no life. You just spend enough time online and get yourself a little following of other bored wannabes. I'm signing off.

The reply was instant.

Hymn101—Before the war.

So, Nestor thought, *he has something he wants to say.*

Ed.Hopper2—Which war?

Hymn101—Do the math.

Nestor eased off.

Ed.Hopper2—Where before the war?

Hymn101—Wise not too push me too hard. You were getting a bit rude before.

Ed.Hopper2—Where before the war?

Hymn101—Home.

Ed.Hopper2—Where's home?

Hymn101—Home is where the heart is.

Ed.Hopper2—Funny.

Hymn101—Sorry Nestor, must run. Will be back momentarily. Why don't you hang around? We can chat some more.

Nestor sat back in his chair as Hymn101 signed off. He knew he'd be back. Hymn101 was leading up to something. Nestor started to print out the instant messages that he had so far.

The printer hummed and he looked up at the map with all of the pushpins. The yellows were now in place. It was getting colorful and more deadly. Nestor had a feeling that during this little break of theirs, another pin was being added. He wondered where. His screen came alive again.

Hymn101—Why, hello again, Nestor. Glad you waited for me. Any new questions? Any new doubts?

Nestor's fingers worked the keys. But by the time he went offline, he was no closer to understanding where Hymn101 was taking him. He was still being fucked with, being pushed in some way. He reread the printout and dropped it on his desk. Looking back up at the map with the pins, he did have some new doubts. He couldn't figure out who was pulling the strings or who they were attached to.

What really bothered him was not knowing how many strings ran to him. He might have to bring in Martinez sooner than he had anticipated, just for insurance sake. Nestor fingered the printout. He was being played, and he didn't like it. Nestor looked at the last message on the printout:

Hymn101—Say hi to my good friend Palmer. Until we meet, Nestor.

Looking at the words, they seemed unreal. *Palmer?* What did Palmer have to do with any of this?

The message didn't make sense. Nestor looked at his watch. Reaching for the phone, he dialed Christian. *Palmer—what the fuck this got to do with—*Katie picked up and said hello.

"Hi Katie; Nestor." He could hear Amy in the background.

"Oh! Hi, Nestor! Hold on a sec, okay?" She sounded frazzled. He could hear her telling Amy to be careful with the paints around Flea-Flea. She came back on the line.

"Sorry Nestor, Christian is visiting Cecilia and I don't know who makes a bigger mess, the cat or my daughter." Katie began to laugh. "How's Gigi?"

"She's good, thanks. Slowly pushing me out of my sanctuary, but I still love her."

"You'd better!"

"I saw Cecilia the other day. I think you guys made the right decision. She seems more comfortable at Calvary."

"I know. You're right, but it was still hard on Christian putting her in—*Amy!*"

"Bad time?" Nestor asked over Katie's voice as she admonished Amy, the cat, and the paints all at once.

She came back. "Sorry. When the baby is born, make sure it's not an artist, okay?"

Nestor laughed. "Okay. Listen, sounds like you're a little busy. Just want to know if Christian is swinging by?"

"No, he didn't say anything about it."

"Well, can you tell him to give me a call? It's kind of important. And before you ask, nothing to worry about."

"Okay Nestor. I'm sorry. It's a madhouse here today. I'll let christian know, and tell Gigi I'll give her a call, 'kay?"

"You're too good for that guy."

"I know," Katie replied, laughing, "I'll be sure to tell him you said so, though. Bye."

"Bye." As Nestor hung up, he heard his wife pull into the driveway. He was wondering how Christian was going to take all of this, when Gigi called up to him from the car. He put the printout away and turned off the computer. He didn't want her to come across any of this stuff.

Getting up from his chair, he stretched and looked around his room. She called again. It was about to get a little smaller, he feared.

Katie had cleaned up the paints that Flea-Flea and Amy, working as a team, had knocked over and smeared. When she finished, she put Amy in for a long-needed nap and placed Nestor's message on top of the dresser in the bedroom. Back downstairs, she let Flea-Flea out to do his hunting and started to work on her illustrations again.

By the time Katie was halfway through a new illustration, Amy woke and looked around. Coming out of her room, she found the message for her father. It was on a large piece of paper and there was a lot of white space. She ran back to her room with the paper and drew a cat that looked remarkably like a rabbit. She was getting better.

Sisters of Calvary

A Styrofoam head with a red wig sat on the table next to the bed. Christian noticed that someone had drawn a rather good likeness of his sister on it. He had a feeling Nestor had paid a visit, but Nestor's touch of color wasn't the only artwork in the room. Amy's colorful world covered most of the hospital room.

Cecilia sighed as she licked her lips. They were dry and cracked. Christian took a small jar of Vaseline from the bed table. Taking a dab, he rubbed it on her lips as gently as he could. Slowly, Cecilia reached up and took his hand, helping him rub the Vaseline along her lips. She smiled, getting a little on her teeth.

"The air mattress is good, thanks." Cecilia remarked as she kissed his fingertips, bringing them down from her face a little. "And thanks for the Vaseline, too; I needed that."

Christian watched as his sister's eyes followed the length of his fingers to his hand and up along his arm to his face. It took a moment or two for her to focus on him this close. There was still a strong spark of life in her eyes, though. He felt her squeeze his hand.

"I just asked for the mattress, no big thing, " he said, smiling at her. "Easier on your body?"

"Yeah," she said, taking a deep breath. "Softer. Keeps the ol' bones from poking through my thin old skin. They don't have to rotate me as much, either, and I can sleep better."

"Good. How're you feeling now?" *Maybe two weeks left,* Christian thought. His mind fled from the idea.

"Okay, but wake me next time you come in. The hour doesn't matter. Don't like to sleep too much." Her words were beginning to draw out even more. "Can I have a sip of water with a straw?"

"Sure. Crushed ice?"

"Uh-huh. The cold is good." Christian checked the plastic ice bucket and only came up with some tepid water.

"How's the 'copping' business doing?" she asked, sounding a little tired. "Shoot any bad guys?"

"Copping is good, and no real bad guys," he said, picking up the ice bucket and bringing it to the bathroom. Emptying it, he came out and told her that he would be right back. He was just going to run down to the nurse's station for some ice.

"Hey, wait," she cried out. "Don't go. Come back here." Christian did as he was told. "Just press the button here," she said pointing to a long, white cord pinned to the side of her bed. "I have room service now. Not too shabby."

"No, not too shabby at all," he agreed, putting the bucket back down on the table and pressing the call button.

"See," she said, "that's better. Here, just help me up in bed a little." She reached out. He was surprised how light she was.

"How's that?" He adjusted her hospital gown.

"That's good. How's Katie and Amy? Any more artwork for my gallery?"

"Yeah, two more. I think they're cats, not sure."

"Good. How's Palmer doing?"

"Palmer's fine." Christian sat back down on the bed. "Still messing up the house. I think him and Katie have a skylight project going on."

"Both good guys. Palmer called the other day to say hi. It was a bad day for me, so I didn't stay too long on the phone. But I think he understood."

"Yeah, he's a sweetheart. Has Nestor…?" Christian pointed over to the Styrofoam head.

"Came by with Gigi. He's the one who drew the face on my wig holder. He's pretty good, you know. He should work more on his art. *Hey!* You know Gigi looks pretty good pregnant.

"Yeah, but they couldn't have done it without my advice!" His sister laughed. Taking Christian's hand, she asked if he was happy.

"Yeah, Katie and Amy are the best things that ever happened to me." He looked at his sister and was silent a moment. The tears were welling in his eyes. "Cecilia…" he started, but couldn't finish and dropped his head.

"Hey." She shook his hand back and forth. "Don't make me slap you like a redheaded stepchild." She worked her fingers in between his and squeezed as hard as she could. "I got the easy part in this deal. You got the hard part. You've got to keep going…look," she took her hand from his and put it under his chin, lifting it, "I'm doing it." She wiped the tears from his eyes. "Hey, behave, room service is here." The nurse at the door hesitated a moment and then came in, placing the ice water on the table next to the wig.

"See, she even knows when I want ice. Not too shabby."

The nurse broke into a smile. "Well, well missy, are you finally awake now? That poor brother of yours been glued to that one chair for a good part of the day!" The nurse started to cluck her tongue at Cecilia as she checked the IV and then her pulse. Christian went to move out of her way, but the nurse told him to stay put. She was a good-sized woman, but moved with a fluidity that conveyed a sense of confidence. Her dark skin was a sharp contrast to the white of her uniform. She continued teasing Cecilia.

"My, my, that poor man all twisted and such in that chair," she said, winking at Christian.

"The dope didn't want to wake me," Cecilia complained as Christian poured some water for her. He held the cup and straw near her mouth and wrapped both of her hands around his taking a sip from the straw. Her eyes shut tight for a moment and she ran her tongue over her teeth.

"Whew!" she said, "that's cold!" The nurse started to straighten out the bed, looking over at Christian.

"Hmmm…dope, she called you? Why, you don't look like any sort of a *dope* to me! Now you see how she talks about you! Why, Cecilia," she wagged her finger at her, "I should steal him away!"

"Nope…" Cecilia said taking another sip. "Can't steal him." Christian started to put the cup down, but his sister held on tight to his hands, bringing the straw back to her mouth.

"What do you mean, I can't steal him? You give me *one* good reason!"

"Can't steal him," she said, letting the straw drop away from her mouth, "he's my dance partner." The staff liked to keep the patients moving as much as possible. The nurse looked over at Christian and raised an eyebrow.

"Oh? Is that so? I don't believe it till I see it!"

"She's telling the truth." Christian chimed in, picking up on the cue. "Sometimes I even get to lead. Here, watch…feel up to it?" Christian got up from the bed, holding out his arms.

"Oh…sure," Cecilia said and he leaned over, helping her out of the bed. Christian let her do most of the maneuvering, not wanting to move her the wrong way or too suddenly.

"Here," he said, "just watch the IV." And she slowly stood up. Christian felt her grip on his arms and was amazed at the strength still there.

"Oh God. It feels so good to stand." She sighed and started to hum a slow tune as they danced in a small circle.

"Well, well," the nurse said, nodding, "I guess you're right. Ain't no way I'm stealing that man away from you!" She left the room, laughing.

"She seems like a good person," Christian said. He let his sister lead.

"Yeah, she's wonderful." Cecilia put her head down on his shoulder as they danced. He moved very slowly.

"Tired?" he asked.

"No, not really. Just feels good to stand and move around a little…you know."

"I know."

"Did you get Katie something for her birthday?"

"Yep. I got her a diamond heart pendent."

"Nice. She's a good woman. You're lucky."

"I know. Things are great. It's good dancing with you, you know that?"

"Thanks. Christian?" She let out a long sigh, making her head more comfortable on his shoulder as they moved.

"Yeah?"

"Sometimes when I dream, it's not all that good."

"Oh?"

"No," she said softly, her thin body settling against him. "Sometimes it's about Jimmy and how he died. Strange dream." And she started to hum the slow tune again.

One Of Them Is Dead

Christian toweled off. He had come upstairs exhausted, going straight into the bathroom. The shower had felt good, the hot water seeping into his body, relaxing it. When he had finally finished, the bathroom was steamy and his skin warm to the touch. Stepping out into the bedroom, a chilly draft hit him. Fall was beginning to make its presence known, but the room still seemed a little too cool. Wrapping the towel around his waist, he heard Katie and Amy come in downstairs. She called up to him, but he said nothing.

It was a late Sunday afternoon, and he had stayed through the night with his sister. She had had a rough night, but by daybreak she had finally fallen asleep. The nurses told Christian that she always fought the urge to sleep. "A waste of good time," she kept telling them. Christian hadn't pressed the issue, and they had talked through the night about their childhood, family, and friends until she had given in to her exhaustion. The nurses had assured him that she would be fine. He had left, leaving a note and the drawings. It had been a long drive back, and he was physically and emotionally drained. She didn't have much time. The most he could do at this point was to make her as comfortable as possible. He would have to go back down either tomorrow or the day after. Everything was close. So much was about to change.

Katie called up once again, interrupting his thoughts. Tightening the towel around his waist, he yelled back down to her, but the ladies of the house were screeching and laughing so much that he doubted either one could hear him. It sounded like they were heading for the stairs. Suddenly, an ice-cold shiver ran through him. He looked up at the ceiling.

He was about to yell for Katie again when the two of them toppled together at the head of the stairs. Amy broke away from her mother and headed straight for him. As usual, his daughter slammed into him, bounced off his legs, and slammed into him again. Grabbing his legs, she pretended to be scared. Katie sat at the top of the stairs taking a breather.

"Shhhh," Christian said to Amy, rubbing her back. "Settle down a little." Katie gave him a wave hello. Reaching down, he picked up his daughter and pointed at the bedroom ceiling.

"Amy," he asked in a very soft voice, "can you tell Daddy what is wrong with Daddy's ceiling?" The ceiling had a four-foot-square hole in it that was covered from the outside with a piece of tarp. Amy looked up, arched her back and pointed.

"Unta Bart...I has to do it."

"Have to do what, hon?"

"I has to fix it wit Unta Bart."

"Yes, hon, you and Uncle Bart have to fix it, okay?"

"Ho-tay."

"Thank you, Amy." Christian turned his attention back to his wife. "My dear?" he questioned. Katie gave him another wave from the steps followed by a smile. Christian raised his eyebrows. *"Dear?"*

"Dear...dear?" Amy mimicked her father's voice as she continued to point up toward the ceiling.

Katie got up from the stairs, walked over and put her arms around the two of them.

"You said we could do the skylight, right? So, we're doing the skylight." She gave Amy a kiss on the top of her head and smiled at her husband.

"Yeah, but not with winter coming on. You know how fast Palmer works."

Katie shook her head. "No, no, listen. He promised there wouldn't be a speck of snow drifting down on us. As a matter of fact," she said, gripping the top of his towel, "I think he ran out over to Menkerit to pick up the skylight he ordered. We can get romantic under the stars."

"Hon, it's *Sunday*. What store is open in Menkerit?"

She looked at her husband, knowing what was on his mind. "I don't know. Maybe it's from one of his jobs. You know how he works in mysterious ways. How's Cecilia doing today?"

Christian handed Amy over to Katie. Amy continued to point up at the ceiling.

"I may go back out tomorrow, or more likely, day after," he said, walking toward the bathroom to finish dressing. His sister's pending death was not a popular subject with him, and Katie knew not to push too hard with it.

"Would you like some company? I would love to see her again, and I'm sure she'd like to see Amy."

"Maybe, we'll see," Christian said as he disappeared into the bathroom. Katie decided to give him a little more time to himself.

"Okay," she called after him, "you decide." Katie tickled her daughter in the ribs and Amy laughed, dropping her arm. "Yeah, I thought so, you little devil. Okay, that's enough for now, be good." Putting her down, she let Amy run over to the bed and climb up on it. Amy was about to start to jump when Katie just shook her head no. She plopped down on her bottom.

"Good girl, Amy," Katie said, giving her daughter a thumbs-up. Amy returned the gesture, but used the wrong digit. Katie laughed.

"Is this what you teach my child?" Christian was leaning against the bathroom door dressed in jeans and T-shirt, toweling off his hair.

"Come over here so I can dry your hair," she said, toning her laughter down to a giggle.

"Er, she still has that finger up and it looks like it's in my direction now," Christian replied, walking over to the bed.

"Just ignore her. She'll forget it, and we'll skip the 'thumbs-up' as part of her ongoing education for now." Katie walked over to the bed and sat down. "Here," she said, patting the bed, "next to me." Christian sat down handing her the towel and bowed his head. Katie went to work on it vigorously. Amy still maintained her single-digit response.

"When's Palmer getting back, and when did he start this?" Christian asked from beneath the towel.

"Early this morning, before Amy and I went fishing down at the river. When we got back, Palmer was gone. He really should have been back already. This was supposed to be a surprise...a finished surprise. I think his hand slowed him up a little," she added as an afterthought.

"Hand? What did Palmer do to his hand?"

"I don't know, he got it caught or whacked it with something. He hurt it on the roof somehow. Really didn't say much. Looked nasty though, kind of swollen."

"Okay, whatever, he's a big boy." He turned to his daughter. "Amy, did you and mommy catch any fish?" Christian reached across and gently put her outstretched hand down, curling her finger back into her hand. "Don't do that, hon," he said quietly. "Any fish?" he asked again.

"*One!*" Amy shot up a finger. Christian was glad she chose the correct one.

"What did you do with the fish, Amy?"

"Put 'im *back!*"

"It was a small—" Katie started to add as the phone rang. "I'll get that," she said, taking the towel with her. "Oh, that reminds me. Nestor called yesterday. I left you a note." She picked up the phone. "Hello?"

Christian listened with half an ear while Amy told him how big her fish was. His daughter was talking up a storm. If there was one thing she liked as much as putting her inner world down on paper with paints and crayon, it was fishing. With her fishing pole in hand, she would stand, calm, at the river's edge, watching the passing waters. But she never drew a picture of herself fishing. Christian wondered if that was due to the time the river had almost taken her. He wasn't sure. As he "Yeahed" Amy, Christian noticed a change in Katie's voice. He looked over. Katie was nodding and looking worried.

"Okay, hold on." She handed the cordless phone over to Christian. "It's Rita," she said.

"Hello." He wasn't able to make out what Rita was saying. "Hold it, hold it. Connection is bad." He walked toward the stairs. Static fed back as the low battery indicator came on. He tried again.

"Yeah, Rita."

"Christian," her voice sounded shaky around the static, "I didn't know if you were back or not, but I figured I'd take the chance. It's the Murphy boys...one of them is dead," she blurted out.

"Christ! Which one?" The static crackled over the answer of which Murphy no longer walked God's earth. He tried to ask again when Rita's voice broke in.

"...not far from their place. Palmer's down there now. He's at their house waiting for you...*Christian?*" Her voice came in clear momentarily.

"Yeah?" The static was building again; he was losing her.

"There's something else—"

"What?"

"They're claiming you did it. They said you beat him to death." There was a burst of interference that swallowed Rita's voice as the phone went dead.

Tell-Tale Heart

Stupid.

Christian stood up, stretching his legs. He didn't need to gather much evidence to figure out what had happened. It was just that he couldn't believe how stupid they were. He rubbed the side of his knee joints, looking around.

Rita had caught up with Palmer over the radio while he was somewhere in Menkerit. He knew she must have given him hell for being over there again. Christian still thought it was strange that he would be over there on a Sunday. Whatever the case, he was glad Palmer had the Murphys contained.

He had finished taking pictures of the body and the surrounding area. The field was open and lightly wooded, the leaves turning for the season. For the most part, the area was isolated from the roads. He hadn't found any tire tracks, and figured they'd carried the body the last part of the distance. With the number of fallen leaves on it, they'd probably set him up during the night so they wouldn't be seen. He knew the area had been picked so they could have time with the body, but it wasn't so isolated that the body wouldn't be found.

As it turned out, finding the body was easy. An "anonymous" phone call to Rita gave the location. *Anonymous. Stupid!* Guilt and remorse had put their brother here, and guilt and remorse had made the phone call. He squatted back down.

Richard sat against the tree, his clothes neatly arranged. He sat there dead in a pair of jeans, a white cotton shirt and a light jacket. His sneakers were new, and one lace was untied. His jacket was zipped up three-quarters against the cold. There was a fresh grease stain along one sleeve; Christian thought it could have happened while they transported the body. The back of their pickup came to mind. The cord that bound Richard's wrists was lightly tied, not cutting into the swollen flesh, and there were no ligature marks. That made the binding postmortem.

Nor were there any signs of a struggle in the immediate area. No torn-up earth. No blood. There wasn't even any blood on the clothes Richard wore. Christian lifted Richard's hand, checking under his fingernails. They were clean and freshly cut, nothing underneath them. Leaning in closer, he smelled Richard's hair. Soap. Ivory soap.

From the condition of the body, Richard had been dead no more than ten hours. Rigor mortis was just beginning to set in, and that gave him a timeframe. Christian brushed some of the leaves off and straightened up.

He was sure his brothers had killed him in a burst of anger. Afterward, they wouldn't have known what to do. The body would have lain around, staring them in the face until they were forced to do something about it. Once they'd made up their minds, they would have worked on their story. They couldn't just bury him. People would start getting suspicious if one of them just took off on his own. They simply weren't left with too many options. So, they must have decided to pass it off as a murder. Best idea they could come up with. *Stupid,* he thought again.

Richard had been killed elsewhere, washed, dressed, and brought here. *Laid out, more like,* Christian thought. The Murphy boys had beaten their youngest brother to death and mourned out of guilt for what they did to him. Beneath this tree, they had tried to make it up to him. Even his hair was combed.

Christian looked at his watch. He was running out of time. With Palmer at the Murphys', he knew they wouldn't be going anywhere, especially since they were trying to pin this murder on him. Chances were, Richard had been killed in their house. Problem was, they'd have had plenty of time to do a thorough job cleaning up any mess—Kevin would make sure of that. But the major mistake they had made *was* in cleaning up the body. Not too many murderers did that. Another mistake was trying to blame the murder on him. *Stupid, just plain stupid.*

He had had Rita call over to Menkerit County for the coroner, Joe Richardson. She was to meet him in town and bring him over to pick up the body for an autopsy. Christian really wasn't concerned about Richardson's opinion or professionalism. Richardson couldn't find the cause of death if the victim came straight from Jack the Ripper. But it was procedure.

He checked his watch again, anxious to get over to the Murphys'. The best time to strike was now, while the Murphy boys were still uneasy with the "discovery" of their brother's body. He was sure that they were beginning to have doubts whether their story would hold up. He needed to get over there to reinforce those doubts.

On the way to the body, Christian had instructed Palmer over the radio not to say anything to the Murphys and to keep them all in the same room. He wanted them in plain sight of each other with as little communication between them as possible. Christian needed to keep each boy in his own world, within his own doubts. He knew Kevin would try to keep the other two brothers in line with the story. But Christian had no intention of dealing with Kevin at all. He'd go to Brian or Daniel, whichever one seemed more nervous. He doubted they ever read Poe's "Tell-Tale Heart." Guilt could do strange things to a mind, and he was hoping that would help nail them.

He knew word would get around town that the Murphys were claiming he'd had a hand in this. He didn't care. Nobody would believe it. Besides, it might give them a false sense of security. Mistakes had already been made, and he was sure more were to come. Those boys had been dumb, really dumb. He was disappointed in a way.

Hearing Rita's voice, he stood back up and waved her over. Her bright red hair gave the surrounding foliage a run for its money. Richardson was trying to keep up with Rita as she marched through the field towards him and the body of Richard Murphy. Christian looked back down at the corpse.

From the looks of Richard, the brothers had used their hands. *Mistake? Maybe.* He had doubts about a few things, though. Reaching over, he unzipped the jacket and opened the freshly washed cotton shirt. Richard's chest was discolored around the heart. The sternum and the surrounding ribs gave way when he touched them.

Christian stood up, hearing Joe Richardson huff and puff, bitching about Rita's pace across the field. She told him to shut the hell up. Seeing Richard, Rita stopped short. She shook her head.

"Christian, that boy might well have been a royal pain in the ass, but this ain't right. Known these boys since they were born to Mary and tha' no good husband. This was a family affair. Bound to have happened." Richardson came up behind Rita, cherry-faced. He put his hand on her shoulder to catch his breath. She shrugged him off. "Bound to have happened," she reaffirmed.

"Maybe," Christian said. "Maybe."

Richardson wheezed as Christian knelt back down and touched Richard's chest again.

Pig's Eye

"*You killed my fuckin' brother!*" Kevin shot out of his chair as Christian opened the door. Palmer quickly stepped between them.

Christian had left Rita and Joe with Richard's body. He'd told them that he'd be back as soon as possible with Palmer to help. Rita had assured him that she and Richardson could handle bagging up the boy, but Christian didn't want anything touched yet, at least not by Joe Richardson.

"Sit the fuck down," Christian warned Kevin.

"You *killed* 'im!"

"Sit!" he warned again. Palmer put a hand against Kevin. Christian noticed that Palmer's knuckles were bruised.

"Can't tell me wha' to do in my own house!" Kevin spat back.

Christian took a step toward Kevin. "Let me break the news to you. Your brother is dead. He didn't beat himself to death. That makes this a murder investigation, so I'll tell *you* what to do any-fucking-where I want. Now, sit the fuck down." Christian needed to let the other two Murphys know that their older brother was not in control of the situation. Any confidence they had in him had to be eroded.

Kevin was trying to hold his ground, and looked Christian over slowly before he spoke. "Mind if I get a beer then, Sheriff? Your boy here won't let us leave the room 'less we gotta piss."

Palmer spoke up. *"Sit down...now,"* he said, poking Kevin in the chest. Kevin just glanced in his direction.

"Jus' a dog and its master," he mumbled, but settled back down in his chair. Palmer took a step back.

Christian looked over at the two younger Murphys. Both were sitting on opposite ends of a dilapidated couch. Brian avoided his look, while Daniel locked eyes with him. For a brief instant, there was a flicker of regret in them. Daniel turned away.

Christian knew Kevin was watching the whole scene. He was positive Daniel was the weak link in this chain of misfits. He waited to see whether Kevin would act. If the older brother spoke first, it would be a distraction to take the pressure off his brother. He didn't have to wait long.

"Hey, c'mon, Sheriff, mind if I get tha' beer in my own house now?" Kevin had gotten up, stepping between Christian and Daniel. Christian smiled, deciding to switch gears.

"No, actually I don't mind."

The elder Murphy hesitated a moment before turning to Daniel behind him. "Hey, go get the beer." Daniel got up, looking relieved until Christian spoke.

"Daniel, would you mind getting me one? Rough few days, I'm beat...you know?" Daniel looked to his older brother and Kevin nodded. Kevin quickly turned on Christian.

"Think ya funny, right? *I'm beat!* Ain't got nothin' here. We didn't *do* Richard." Daniel came back into the room with two beers. Palmer spoke up.

"Oh, no thanks. I'm invisible. I'm not thirsty or anything. But, hey, thanks for asking."

"Sorry," Daniel said as he handed one of the beers to Kevin. "Palmer, wan' me to get you one?" he asked turning to him, his hand outstretched toward Christian with the other beer. His knuckles were swollen.

Palmer shook his head. "No, that's okay. I'll take some of—"

Christian suddenly grabbed Daniel's hand. Pain shot across his face as he yanked his hand back, dropping the beer. Rubbing his hand, he quickly sat back down. Christian moved in.

"So, Daniel, what can you tell me?" Christian edged in closer. "No, no, sorry…what do you *want* to tell me?" Daniel looked to Brian, desperate for any help, but his brother was staring resolutely at his hands in his lap. Kevin answered.

"Want to tell?" Kevin was up again. Christian had expected as much. "Here's wha' we'll *want to tell!* We'll tell you was the one tha' did Richard like tha'. We'll tell tha' in a court of law. Ain't nothin' gonna stop us. How's tha',Sheriff?"

"Yeah, Kevin, you do that." Christian spoke staring down at Daniel. "You know Kevin, you're right. I killed your brother. I beat him to death. What's more, I cleaned him up afterwards. Just hate messy bodies, don't you?" Christian squatted down next to Daniel. Kevin found himself blocked by Palmer.

"What do you think, Daniel?" Christian's voice was just above a whisper. "Think I beat Richard to death, bathed him, cut his fingernails, combed his hair? Maybe even put on his Sunday best?" Christian paused. Suddenly, he grabbed Daniel's hand again, squeezing. Daniel cried out in pain and Christian let him go.

"Hey…!" Kevin yelled, but didn't move.

"Farming accident?" Christian asked, the sarcasm thick. Daniel turned away protecting his hand. "Come on, Daniel. Get it off your chest. You can tell me." Christian looked over at Brian briefly and leaned in closer to Daniel. *"You know who Cain was, Daniel?"* he whispered.

Daniel whipped around. *"I ain't no Cain!"* he cried out.

Kevin was quick to push past Palmer. Christian stood up, facing him. Kevin spoke in a calm even voice.

"No law against hurtin' a hand now, Mr. Christian Lord." Kevin slipped between him and his brother. "Do wha' you gotta do. Same will happen here. Always been tha' way, always will." He took a small step closer, looking Christian in the eyes. "Besides, I've known. I've seen ya eyes. I know ya black heart. Ain't no lilywhite, Sheriff."

Christian eyes didn't waver from Kevin. "Daniel," Christian called over Kevin's shoulder, "thanks for the beer. Might as well pick it up with your good hand." Daniel didn't move. Christian had turned to go when Kevin grabbed him by the arm.

"Don't think you get way with murderin' Richard. I known ya wife and tha' little girl too. I seen 'em 'round—" The punch caught Kevin in the side of the mouth, knocking him to his knees. The other two brothers started to move, and Palmer put his hand on his gun.

Kevin waved his hand up. "Hold it, boys," he warned, spitting some blood onto his hand and wiping it on his pants. He looked up at Christian.

"Tha's twice you come into my house and disrespect me." He spat again, this time on the floor. "Won't be no third."

"No," Christian said, "don't expect so. We'll be talking. Don't leave the county."

As he and Palmer reached the door, Christian stopped and turned back. Kevin was already on his feet, watching them. Christian ignored him.

"Daniel," he said, "how long did it take to wash the blood off your hands?" Not waiting for an answer, Christian closed the door behind him. As they walked down the dirt road, Palmer cleared his throat.

"Well," he said, "that should go down well in court." Christian was silent as they came to the Murphys' pickup truck. There was a slick of grease between two of the ribs of the truck bed. Christian remembered the grease stain on Richard's jacket. He turned back toward the house.

The house was on a slight hill, with a dense coverage of woods around three-quarters of it. Between the house and the trees, there was an open space of about twenty yards. Christian didn't like any of this. That open space was not a good place to get caught in. What's more, he still had some doubts about the Murphys. Lost in his thoughts, he was pulled back by Palmer.

"What did he mean when he said that was twice you disrespected him?" Palmer asked.

Christian just shook his head. "No idea."

"Christian…?"

"Yeah?"

"Think we have something to take to court?"

"Court, Palmer?" Christian thoughts stopped short. "I have a feeling they'll never make it to court." Palmer said nothing as he got into his car. Christian called over to him.

"How's your hand?"

Palmer held it up, turning it in the air. "Oh, this old thing? Fine, just as long as I don't have to use it."

"How'd you do it?" Christian asked opening the door to his car.

Palmer laughed. "That roof of yours. It's nothing, just add it to the bill. Meet you over at the tree." Palmer hesitated. "Say—"

"Yeah?"

"When you gonna fix the lights on your car?"

"Not."

"No?"

"No."

"Why?"

"Just going to switch cars with you."

"Pig's eye," Palmer said.

"Say, Palmer, when you going to finish the skylight?"

"Not."

"Not?"

"Nope. Just gonna switch houses."

Christian chuckled. Palmer slipped into his patrol car and Christian watched him drive away. Turning back to the house, he saw Kevin standing on his porch. Kevin spat once.

"Pig's eye." Christian whispered. "Fucking pig's eye." And got in his car to tend to the younger Murphy. By the time he got back there, Rita and Joe Richardson were talking with Palmer, while Richard Murphy sat against the tree staring over the fields with his dead eyes, looking neater than he had ever looked before.

A Different Tune

Flea-Flea had just had his ass kicked.

Amy was upstairs, taking a late afternoon nap on their bed. Katie had just finished reading "The Butterfly Seeds" by Mary Watson with her. It was Amy's favorite naptime book; she liked hearing about the little boy Jake and his grandpa's butterfly seeds. Katie had rubbed her back as she read, making believe her hands were butterfly wings. It wasn't long before Amy was out like a light. Watching her sleep, Katie had smoothed a few wild strands of hair away from her face. Covering her with a small blanket, she had come downstairs thinking about a hot cup of tea and a book while she waited for Christian to come back from the Murphys. She had never cared much for the boys, but still felt bad at the death of one of them. It didn't bother her that they were claiming that her husband was responsible. Rita knew he had been at the hospital with his sister, and if Rita knew, chances were good that the whole town knew. Besides, she was sure the town would bet on the fact that they had killed one of their own.

How could you kill a person, Katie wondered, *much less a family member?* Years ago, Christian had pointed out to her that most murders were committed by family members or acquaintances. She had listened to what he said, but it was all still beyond her.

When the kettle began to whistle, she thought she heard Flea-Flea at the door. *Oh God,* she thought, *not another thank-you.*

She opened it, expecting the worst. But instead of a headless animal, Flea-Flea sat there with one of his ears torn in half. He meowed forlornly. She picked him up and felt the dampness on his fur. Taking her hand away, it was covered with blood.

"Oh, Flea-Flea! What in the hell did you run into?" she asked, walking inside with him. Grabbing a dish towel, she put it on the kitchen table, laying the cat upon it. He stretched out and didn't move.

Katie went to work on his bloody fur first. Finding a flap of torn skin near his belly, she ran into the bathroom to get the hydrogen peroxide. Hurrying back, she worried about the cat's reaction. When she lightly placed her hand on his shoulder, it felt like he was purring with her touch.

"Sorry," she said, and quickly poured as much of the peroxide as she could over the wound. All Flea-Flea did was lift his head. That really worried her.

Gently patting him down with some damp paper towels, she cleaned as much of the blood off as possible. Having a closer look, she decided there wasn't too much else she could do. His ear however, was another matter. The ear itself wasn't a life-or-death injury, it just made him look all the more ragged.

As she dabbed some peroxide onto his ear, Christian and Palmer came through the back door. She looked up at them, a helpless expression on her face.

Grabbing a chair, Christian pulled it over to Katie and the cat. "Well," he said, taking Flea-Flea's head in his hands. "Looks like he lost." He noticed the bloody paper towels and she told him about the torn piece of skin, saying she didn't think it was all that bad. Unbuckling his gun belt, Christian placed it on the table.

"What am I going to do about his ear?" Katie asked sounding lost. Palmer took off his own gun belt, placing it next to Christian's. He peeked at Flea-Flea's ear.

"Best to run him over to Doc Knowles," Palmer said. "Maybe three or four stitches will take care of it." He knew better than to crack any jokes. Katie might bitch about the cat, but it was *her* cat. "Got to watch out for rabies, though," he added.

Katie looked at him as if he had just given Flea-Flea the kiss of death. "Rabies?" she said.

Palmer backpeddled a little. "No, well, just a precaution. Flea-Flea's fine—I'm sure."

Katie let out a sigh. "You're right, but—" She suddenly stopped and turned from the cat. "I'm sorry. What happened with the Murphy boys? Is one really dead?"

"Yeah," Christian said. "Richard."

"That's a pity," she said. "I know they weren't the best-loved around here, but to lose a family member—" Katie caught herself again and shot a guilty look at Christian. Christian just smiled. "Who did it?" she asked weakly, going back to cleaning the cat's ear. Flea-Flea wasn't moving.

"Not sure," Christian answered. "Richardson won't help much. He's not opening his mouth prematurely, trying to be professional. Doesn't matter, he's an ass and doesn't have a clue. Anyway, he may still be determining whether Richard is, in fact, dead." Christian looked a little closer at the cat. He seemed to be thinking out loud. "I think it was all three...I'm not sure. Not sure about a few things. We'll see."

"Why?" Katie looked up from the cat. "Why? I don't understand."

"Understand what, Katie?" Christian asked.

"Why they would kill their own brother."

"I don't know, hon. It's just in them. Palmer knows them better'n I do." Katie turned to Palmer as he sat down at the other end of the table near the guns.

"Don't know," Palmer said, fingering the worn leather holster with his injured hand. Both holsters had .357s in them. "They've always been of one mind, as best as I can describe it. I guess they got caught up with one another. A little mob madness." Leaving the holster alone, he dropped his hand to his lap.

"But, but...why their own brother?" Katie looked more flustered. Christian jumped in.

"Like Palmer said, hon, they got caught up in the act. In this case, beating their brother. The act takes on a life of its own. Consumes them. The haze clears, but the damage is done."

Katie was shaking her head. "I just don't—" She looked down at Flea-Flea. His eyes were closed, and his tongue hung from the corner of his mouth.

"*Oh shit!*" Katie jumped. "*He's fucking dead!*" Her hands flew to her face. Christian leaned forward in his chair and poked the cat. Flea-Flea's head shot up. The cat yawned, stretched, and went back to sleep.

"Son of a *bitch!*" she screamed. "That's it, his ass is going to the vet! I hope Knowles rams a thermometer up it." Christian and Palmer started to laugh.

"Yeah, sure...yuk it up." Katie carefully picked up Flea-Flea, wrapping the towel around his body. "I'm outta here."

"Want me to go with you?" Christian asked, still laughing.

"No! I don't need you two morons. Besides, Amy's asleep upstairs. Let her rest. Palmer, you got that?"

"Yes, ma'am."

"Palmer...I'm serious."

"I know, I know. I'll be good." Palmer was grinning.

Christian watched her as she walked towards the back door with the cat. "You sure you'll be okay?" He needed to talk with Palmer, but he wanted to make sure she was going to be fine driving with Flea-Flea first. The cat was wrapped like an

Egyptian mummy, just his head sticking out of the towel. Katie cradled him like a baby.

"I'll be okay," she said. "I'm just afraid to see what this cat will be dragging in next time to thank me." She stopped at the door. "Oh, there's coffee on the stove from this morning." She went out.

The two cops were quiet as Katie's noisy Honda started up in the back yard. *Needs a new muffler soon,* Christian thought. That would be another trip down to the city he knew. The garage in town carried little more than make-shift parts, and everything else was a special order. The only other garage was in Menkerit, and they weren't any better. He had resigned himself to driving around with the shot-up lights on his patrol car for the time being, but Katie wouldn't put up with the muffler for long. The sound slowly died in the distance, and Christian turned back to the problem at hand.

"What do you think?" he asked his deputy.

"The cat?"

"No, you ass...the Murphys."

"Oh...I'm sure we're gonna have to arrest them sooner or later. I'll get a search warrant going." Palmer looked a little out of it. It worried Christian.

"Can you do this if we have to?"

"Can do," Palmer replied. "It's just I've known them since they were kids." Palmer got up to get a cup of coffee. "This whole thing caught me off guard."

"The problem," Christian said, "is that they feed off each other. If somebody had split them up years ago, it would have been a different story—hey, grab me a cup of coffee too, while you're at it."

"Okay." Palmer was restless. "Flea-Flea looks like shit," he said. He wanted to stay away from the subject as long as possible, but knew Christian was like a dog with a bone and would jump back to it.

"Flea-Flea's a cat," Christian said. "He's out there and this is what happens. He's not really a house cat. Katie worries about him when he's out, just won't admit to it."

Palmer agreed. "She's a good woman," he said. "Has a good heart."

"Yeah, she's not too bad at all," Christian said as Palmer carefully slid the coffee over. Sitting opposite his boss, Palmer waited for him to resume the subject of the Murphys. He didn't have to wait too long.

"If we have to get them, Kevin will act first." Christian picked up his cup. "Take him down, I'm sure the other two will fall in line, but they stay together, they'll fight. We have to separate them." Christian took a sip, making a face. He put the cup back down. "I need to get to Daniel first: I think he feels the guiltiest." He didn't want to go over this back in town. The office was probably overrun with people wanting to know what had happened. Rita was back there, and he knew she could handle it.

"Well." Palmer leaned back in the chair, "Kevin won't let them out of his sight now, especially Daniel."

"What do you think?" Christian asked, knowing the answer. He just wanted Palmer to get used to the possibility. He had to get his mind set a certain way. Cornered, the Murphys could be deadly, and Christian didn't want to get caught out in the open with his pants down between the Murphys and a uncertain deputy.

"They'll fight," Palmer answered with conviction. "Don't like the approach to the house. Too open."

"Yeah, saw that too." He was glad Palmer was thinking ahead. "Got to draw them out."

Christian fingered his cup of coffee. "What about the woods?" he asked.

Palmer shook his head. "No, don't think they'd fight from there."

"Yeah? What about a crossfire? If I was Kevin, I'd put my two brothers in the woods and I'd stay in the house. Keep our attention that way. It'd be a bad situation for us."

Palmer thought for a moment. "No," he shook his head again. "Kevin knows he couldn't depend on those two like that. He needs to have them in sight to control them."

"Okay," Christian said. *Maybe Palmer can do this,* he thought, but he had another issue he was worried about. "The town would love to get rid of them, but if it turns ugly, I'm not sure how much backing we'll get in the end." The two men looked at each other. Christian smiled and started to whistle the theme song from *High Noon*.

Palmer laughed. "Not too sure that's the right movie, Christian. Might be more like *Shootout at the O.K. Corral*. We're the Earps and they're the Clantons." Palmer paused. "Oh man, this sucks. I've got a ton of carpentry work to do!"

Christian looked at his watch. He was getting tired. "Well, nothing has happened yet." Taking a sip of coffee, he put the cup back down, pushing it away. "Still makes coffee like a Korean deli…" he said softly. He realized he was wishing Nestor were here for this instead of Palmer.

Palmer's brows furrowed. "What?" he asked, not sure what Christian had said about a deli.

"Oh nothing, just thinking out loud." He was quiet a moment. "Ever been shot at, Palmer?" he asked.

"No."

"Well, if we go, wear your vest. I'm just worried about everyone *staying alive* on this one."

Palmer nodded. "Yeah, well, that's a whole new song." Palmer smiled and took a sip of coffee. "Your wife sure makes a mean pot of coffee." And smiled again, taking another sip. Not wanting to jinx them, he didn't sing the song. He rubbed his sore hand instead.

The Dream

…as they entered. The voice washed over them.

"He forgives you." The pain was there…

Stephen saw Isaac suddenly drop the child, swinging up a sawed-off shotgun. Stephen took aim just as Christian fired his .45. Half of Isaac's face disappeared, but not before the shotgun snapped back in his hands.

Stephen lowered his gun and watched as the buckshot blast hit Christian. At first nothing happened. Stephen waited. The child Isaac was holding tried to crawl away. Slowly, red spots appeared on Christian. Christian looked amazed and brought his hand up to touch them. Suddenly, he was thrown backwards from the blast, landing against the crucified child. Stephen felt his own gun going off. Nestor screamed, firing his pistol at Isaac. A window shattered and Isaac disappeared. The dead children moaned, whispered, turned their heads back and forth to each other.

Nestor cried out.

"Christian!"

Christian was on the floor next to the child Isaac had held. The child was still. Blood from Christian and the child mixed together. Christian reached over and kissed the child on the lips. Whispered.

"I didn't mean to kill you."

All of the dead children sighed and turned their faces away.

"He forgives you," a young voice whispered.

Nestor cried out again.

"Christian!"

Stephen pointed his gun at Nestor. Nestor didn't see him, and Stephen pulled the trigger.

"You were dreaming. Same dream?" she asked.

"Yes. Did I say anything?"

"No, nothing this time."

"Go back to sleep, then."

Elements

Christian blinked.

It was two days since Flea-Flea had come back from the vet with five small stitches in his ear and a bandage wrapped around his midsection, and the same two days since Richard had been found against the tree. Flea-Flea kept indoors, sleeping most of the time. Christian and Palmer, armed with a search warrant, had found nothing incriminating in the Murphys' house other than some Ivory soap in the bathroom. Kevin had kept his mouth shut, and Daniel had avoided any contact with Christian as they searched the house. Meanwhile, the weather had been turning foul. A bitterness of the elements hung in the air, waiting for the right combination before it could come into play. It was all there, all for the waiting. Then the weather finally broke.

At first, everyone stood outside watching the clouds roll in. The first few drops were heavy, hitting with a distinct splat upon the cars in the driveway. As the clouds built, pushing each other across the sky, the space between the raindrops lessened until there was a solid wall of falling water. There was no angry thunder above, just the thunderous sound of the rain beating down against everything. The downpour finally drove everyone in from the porch.

Christian looked up at the bedroom ceiling just in time for a drop of rain to hit him in the eye.

"Katie?" Christian asked, turning to his wife as another drop of rain hit him in the head. "Where's Palmer?" He heard Gigi and Nestor start to laugh. Amy was running around trying to catch the rain in a small pot. One more drop splattered down on him, then suddenly developed into a stream of water. Katie had the good sense not to laugh.

"He's on his way over. I think," she said, her voice very controlled. She was about to lose it. "Rita was trying to reach him," she quickly blurted out. Christian grabbed her and pulled her beneath the opening for the skylight. She squealed as the rainwater hit her. "*Christian!*"

"This was your idea," he said. "Now, *you* stay here. *I'm* gonna go adjust that tarp. When you are no longer getting drenched, yell. Okay?" She started to giggle. "Nestor," he turned to his friend, "she moves, shoot her."

"Okay, no problem—*Ouch! Gigi!*" Nestor complained as his wife poked him in the head. They had driven up, planning to relax and stay the night. Nestor had looked forward to seeing his friend, but unfortunately the trip wasn't all pleasure. He found it unusual that Christian hadn't gotten back to him. He needed to talk to him about the e-mails and Palmer. He just had to find the appropriate time. Gigi poked him in the head again.

"'Shoot her?'" she said. "You're listening to that dopey friend of yours? *And you!*" She took a swipe at Christian. "You have *the nerve* to say, 'Shoot her!' Come here, Katie." Gigi put a protective arm around her, guiding her away while Amy continued running around trying to catch the raindrops.

Christian threw up his hands. "Okay, okay...I take it back," he said. "Everyone can yell when the leaks stop."

Katie reached down, grabbing Amy as she went by. "Christian, don't," she said. "Just wait for Palmer." Amy squirmed in her arms. "Here, hon," she said putting her daughter back down. "Stand here and catch the rain."

"Ho-tay!" Amy said as she went to catch another drop from the tarp.

"No, no...here, Amy." Katie held on to her before she could sprint off.

"Ho-tay." Amy laughed as she caught the water in the pot. Katie turned back to Christian.

"Why don't you wait till Palmer gets here? I really don't want you up on that roof."

"Listen, by the time he gets here, we'll have a foot of water. It's just getting worse."

"Hon, *please*, you're not good at heights."

Christian looked up at the ceiling shaking his head. "It'll only take a minute. The ladder's up already," he said turning away. "Come on, Nestor." Both men started down the bedroom stairs. "You girls give a yell when I have it right." He called back up.

"God!" Katie yelled after them as they disappeared. "You guys are *thick!*"

Gigi kept a hand on Amy's shoulder. "A few more pots?" she asked.

Katie nodded agreement.

"I think your husband was right," Gigi said. "It's getting worse." She ruffled Amy's hair as Amy giggled with each new raindrop that splashed up.

Nestor held the ladder as Christian climbed up to the roof. Pulling the hood of his jacket over his head, he called up a warning to his friend. "Hey! It's going to be slippery. Watch it, old man."

"Yeah, thanks, pal," Christian yelled down as he tentatively placed a foot on the roof. Hunched over, he brought up his other foot as his fingers grabbed between the shingles.

Nestor shielded his eyes from the rain. "You all right?" he asked. "You should've taken a flashlight!" He watched Christian work himself towards the flapping tarp that the wind had pulled free from the bricks Palmer had used to hold it down.

"Yeah thanks. A light would have been good," Christian yelled back. "Anyway, I'm almost there." Nestor didn't think that Christian sounded that confident and stepped back a little further from the ladder, trying to get a better view of what he was doing.

In the dark, the tarp seemed to blend in with the roof, but he could just make out Christian grabbing an end of it as he adjusted a brick. Nestor watched as he took a few more careful steps, repositioning the bricks as he went.

As Christian neared the top of the opening, Palmer drove up in the driveway, lighting up Nestor and the front of the house. Turning around, Nestor waved as Palmer got out of the squad car raising his hands toward the sky.

"Don't you know it's raining?" he called over. Nestor pointed at the roof, directing Palmer's attention to Christian.

"Hey!" he yelled, "be careful!" And Christian turned his head to the sound of Palmer's voice, losing his footing. The tarp gave under Christian's weight and he disappeared through the roof. A second later, Nestor and Palmer heard Katie scream.

Katie and Gigi managed to break Amy away from catching the raindrops and were just beginning to read to her on the bed when Christian came crashing through the tarp. He landed on one of the pots meant to catch the leaks, twisting his ankle. If it hadn't been for the three bricks that followed him down, he would have gotten off easy. Two of the three bricks hit him. One caught him just above his brow, opening up a deep cut. The second brick caught him on the side of the head, knocking him cold. The third one missed completely.

Katie cried out as she ran over to Christian. Amy, seeing her father on the floor, started to get upset when Gigi hurried her off to her room. She called over to Katie as they went, but Katie just waved her on as she lifted Christian's head.

The blood from his forehead ran down along his face, and Katie carefully wiped it away with her hand exposing a large gash. She ran into the bathroom to get a towel and her hydrogen peroxide. While she quickly rummaged, Nestor and Palmer, taking the stairs in leaps, rushed into the bedroom.

As Katie came out of the bathroom with towel and medicine in hand, Nestor knelt over Christian while Palmer looked up at the roof, scratching his head.

"Palmer!" Katie yelled at him.

"Hey! Hey!" He said backing away from Katie as she stormed toward him. "He'll be okay! He'll be *okay!"*

"He'll be *okay?"* Katie said, stopping next to her husband. "He's out cold on the fucking *floor,* Palmer!" she screamed.

Nestor intervened, reaching up and taking the towel and peroxide from her hands.

"Katie, Katie…he'll be fine," he said. "He just got clocked in the head." Nestor started to wipe the blood from Christian's face. He looked back up at her. "Just get me another towel for the peroxide, so I can pour some on it, okay?" He didn't need it, he just wanted to keep her busy.

"He's okay?" she asked nervously.

Nestor saw the lump on the side of Christian's head. As he felt it gently, Christian began to stir. "No more damage than a good right hook," Nestor said grinning. *"The towel?"*

"Oh, okay—*Palmer!"* Katie yelled after him as he headed toward the stairs.

"I'm gonna go up and fix the tarp before the whole house floods," he said making a fast exit down the stairs.

As Katie went to get another towel, Nestor kept wiping at the blood that had flowed down Christian's face and into his mouth. Concerned that he might have bit his tongue, he worked slowly wiping the blood away from the inside of his mouth. Nestor suddenly paused. Using a clean corner of the towel, he touched it to the inside of Christian's lower lip; the woven fibers of the towel sucking in the blood.

Beneath the red of it, the black ink of the tattoo showed through. It was identical to the one in the photograph on Isaac's lower lip.

The Society.

He took the towel away, slowly placing his ex-partner's head down. Kneeling back, he squeezed his eyes shut. He felt as if someone had just hit him in the chest with a sledgehammer.

Coming out of the bathroom, Katie saw Nestor's face and stopped short.

"Nestor?" her voice fearful.

The whole world seemed wrong to Nestor now. For a moment, he had trouble breathing. Out of habit, he touched the .38 he carried in his waistband.

"He's fine," he finally said. "Just like a little knockout punch. I used to get them all the time." He tried to laugh, but it didn't even come close. Christian opened his eyes.

"I'mmm...fine," he said; words slurred. His movements were clumsy as he sat up, first touching his head and then his mouth. Katie ran over taking his hand away from his face, keeping him still.

"I'mmm...fine... fine," he protested, but sat there a moment before moving again.

Concerned, Katie looked at her husband, a touch of blood at the corner of his mouth. And Nestor, for the first time in his life, looked upon his friend with fear.

Martinez's Idea

"Christian, we have to talk."

Christian looked across at Nestor. They sat in the kitchen with the remains of the late dinner between them. The rain had stopped right after Palmer fixed the tarp on the roof. During dinner as Amy stood on a chair helping to hold the ice on her father's head, Rita had radioed in that there'd been a fender-bender in town. Palmer cut his dinner short to take the call. Shortly after dessert, the girls called it a night, leaving Nestor and Christian to hang out over a couple of Coronas. Christian looked bruised, but other than the bloody gauze above his brow, he was fine.

"Christian, we have to talk."

The words rang in Christian's ears. He hadn't wanted it to come down to this. Nestor was like a brother to him. *Fucking Martinez,* he thought. He watched as Nestor took his .38 and placed it on top of the kitchen table. It was within

Nestor's reach, but not his. Christian looked at the weapon and back at Nestor.

"It's digging in to my side," Nestor said without conviction. "We have to talk—"

"I know, I know."

Flea-Flea was asleep on top of the beam with the carved quote from the Bible. During dinner, everyone had sat around warming themselves by the fire that was now slowly dying. It was by the heat of such a fire that John Roberts had first put his knife to the beam. After he carved the quote, he cut open his palm, letting his blood fill the wounds in the wood. He had started to kill after that.

"Christian, the tattoo. Tell me about it," Nestor said. It wasn't a request.

"Yes, the tattoo." The fire crackled, consuming the last of the wood. "It's not what you think."

"Christian, man, I don't know *what* to think." Nestor sipped his beer. Next to his bottle were a number of e-mail printouts. He slid them across to his ex-partner. Christian had yet to touch his beer.

"What's this?" Christian asked looking at the papers.

"It's from my new e-mail buddy, Hymn101. Nestor watched for any sign of recognition from Christian. There was nothing. "He claims to be the guy running the society." Still nothing on Christian's face.

"Mind if I read it?"

"I want you to."

Christian quickly read the pages, placing them face down as he did. He looked up at Nestor momentarily as he started on the last page.

Hymn101—Home is where the heart is.

E.Hopper2—Funny.

Hymn101—Sorry, Nestor, must run. Will be back momentarily. Why don't you hang around? We can chat some more.

Hymn101—Why hello again, Nestor. Glad you waited for me. Any new questions? Any new doubts?

Ed.Hopper2—What's this about?

Hymn101—Suppose you tell me. You seem to be looking for me. Are you sure you want to open that can of worms?

Ed.Hopper2—Yes.

Hymn101—I understand you have a new family member on the way. I would think your first concern would be that. Life is so fragile. Especially a new life. Have you heard its little heart beat yet?

Ed.Hopper2—Your head games won't work here.

Hymn101—Oh, I assure you, it is no game I play here. But, shall we play on or end it? If you sign off, you will never hear from me again. The ball is in play. Your choice, dear Nestor.

Ed.Hopper2—I'm in this to the end.

Hymn101—Too bad, I was beginning to like you. I'm almost finished with my work here. I'm afraid our paths are destined to cross. A pity. Your child, if he or she lives that is, will know nothing of you. Do you fear that?

Ed.Hopper2—Your game is not working.

Hymn101—Oh, but it is. It is. All is in play. Next time you're up in Tranquillity, say hi to your ex-partner. And one other thing.

Ed.Hopper2—What?

Hymn101—Say hi to my good friend Palmer. Until we meet, Nestor.

Christian looked up at his friend, letting the last sheet of paper with "LOL" across it drop on the kitchen table. It was the previous lines that held his attention. Christian touched his lip. Taking his hand away, he spoke to Nestor.

"Listen, this is between us, okay?"

"Who am I gonna tell?"

Christian started to grin. "You going to shoot me?" he said, nodding towards the gun.

"No. Sorry." Nestor felt a little foolish. He put his hand on the gun, hesitated a moment, and suddenly slid it over to Christian. Christian caught it in his hand and smiled at his friend.

"Thanks."

"*Nada*," Nestor said. He watched Christian's fingers start to tap the gun as if contemplating some sort of action.

"First of all," Christian started, his fingers finally stopping, "I don't know what to make out of the IM Logs. Just a crazy. It's easy being something you're not over the Net."

"Yeah, but why would he say something about Palmer?"

"Really don't know. This is a small town. It's easy to find out who is who. Maybe he *is* playing a head game with you. I don't know. But I'll tell you what, you have enough on your plate with Gigi and all. Let him fade away. Chances are he's a freaking nutcase."

"Not sure about him being a nutcase. He knows too much."

"Like what?" Christian asked.

"The Society. How did he know about the Society?"

Christian laughed. "Nestor, he's a palm reader, that's all." Christian shuffled through the printouts. "Here," he said showing Nestor a sheet. "You said, 'I know about the society.' You brought it up and he just picked up on it. Good palm reader. That's all you have."

Nestor looked at it, his face doubtful. "Didn't really notice—"

"That's okay," Christian chimed in, "that's why you have me around." He started to toy with the gun. "Listen, what you do, that's up to you. I'm just giving you my view on the situation. I think this 'Hymn' guy is off the wall, but you never know. He could turn out to be bad business all the way around. If you need to focus in on something, focus in on what you know." Christian suddenly looked uneasy. "Now, about the tattoo—" He took a long breath and let it out. The fire flickered and died. Flea-Flea twitched in his sleep. Taking hold of the .38, Christian looked at it. "You still holding your gun hand up too high?" he asked.

Nestor laughed. "Yeah."

Christian put the gun down on the table and slid it back to Nestor. Nestor palmed it. It looked small in his hands, too small to actually kill someone. He kept his hand on it, looking at his friend. A drop of blood worked its way out from under the gauze and trickled down the side of Christian's brow. Nestor watched it, saying nothing.

Christian leaned forward. "Listen, the tattoo was Martinez's idea. He was working on this contact he had who knew about these serial killers." By the time Christian finished the story, the line of blood on his brow was caked black.

Both men sat there in silence as Flea-Flea suddenly twitched and lifted his head, looking around as if waking from a dream. He stretched and went back to sleep.

At Play

On the ride back down to the city, Gigi commented on Nestor's silence. He played it off as a late night, an early morning, and not wanting to go back to work. He said nothing to his wife about the talk with Christian or the discussion about Martinez.

Martinez, that fucking cocksucker.

Nestor kept his eyes on the road, but his foot got a little heavier on the gas pedal.

Motherfucker wanted us dead?

The car picked up a little more speed. Gigi looked over at him.

"Nestor, you're speeding. Slow down," she said cautiously. He glanced at the needle and dropped the car back a little.

"Sorry."

"You know how these State Troopers are, they love to catch city cops."

"Yeah, I know. Honor among thieves," he said, changing lanes.

"Nestor, you okay?" Gigi asked.

He smiled at her. "Sure, fine," he lied. He didn't know how he was going to deal with Martinez. Nor did he know how he was going to handle Hymn101. He was also suspicious of Palmer's frequent trips out of town. But those were suspicions that Hymn101 had planted. And then there was all that information that Christian had kept from him these years about what he and Martinez had been up to. It was all a little too much.

In Nestor's mind, some things were right, but many things were still wrong. He was being pulled in so many different directions that he wasn't sure where the knockout punch was coming from. The only thing he was certain of was that there was one coming. *Enough,* he thought, but things continued to haunt him.

He glanced over at Gigi as he drove. Placing his hand on her stomach, he rubbed it, feeling the slight roundness that harbored their growing child. What Hymn101 had said ate away at him, but he couldn't let it stand in the way. Something was at play here, he just wasn't sure what.

He felt Gigi put both of her hands on his. He didn't have to look to know she was smiling.

Slipping Away

"How's your head?" Katie asked.

Amy was playing in the kitchen with Flea-Flea. Earlier, she had been playing "doc-ter," not wanting to leave Christian's side. She was fascinated with the cut on her father's forehead and kept lifting the gauze to look at it. The hands of a four-year old being what they are, sometimes she would accidentally hit it with her finger, making it bleed again. Finally, Christian took the bandage off. This way, she could look at it whenever she wanted. She immediately started to make new bandages in the kitchen and test them out on Flea-Flea.

"Head's okay," Christian said. He was laying down on the couch in the living room, dozing off and on in front of the TV. Katie had come over to him to see how he was doing and sat next to him. It was about two hours since Nestor and Gigi had left, and Christian was worried. His friend was getting too close to things. He knew Martinez could prove to be a problem to all of them if any of this got out.

Christian was drained. He could feel the heaviness inside of him. Bringing his hand up to his forehead, he prodded it. The skin around the wound felt hard. Katie reached over and took his hand away.

"Leave it, you'll make it bleed. Are you going to see Cecilia today?" She was hoping since his fall yesterday that he would stay home.

"Don't know." He was really feeling tired. "I called the hospital before."

"Oh, I didn't know." Katie was looking at the gash. "How is she?" she asked.

"She was sleeping. One of the nurses said she'd had a rough night, but she was resting okay now."

"Maybe that's what you should do, hon. Taking two shots to that brain of yours is not good," she laughed, turning his head. She poked softly around the edges. "I should have taken you for stitches."

"Stitches? Where?" Christian looked up at her. "Knowles the vet?"

"No silly, over to Menkerit County. To what's-his-face…Richardson."

"He's a freaking coroner!"

"He's a regular doctor too! You just deal with him when there's a body around. Live people *do* go to him."

"Richardson's an ass. I wouldn't let him touch me even if I was dead." Christian started to yawn. "Aw, you and Amy are doing a fine job. A little scratch here and there adds character to the face."

"Sure," she said, touching his close-cropped hair, "like your face needs any more character. Just do me a favor, 'kay?"

"What?"

"Don't drag in any thank-yous. Okay?" She ran the palm of her hand over his hair.

Christian stretched, wrapping his arms around himself. "Good, I don't have to kill anyone today. Too tired anyway."

"Go take a nap. I want to see what Amy is doing to that poor cat. She's much too quiet in there. I'll wake you for dinner." She leaned over, kissing him on the cheek.

"Okay," he managed to say as she got up. He was slipping away when he heard, *"Amy! You can't do that to a cat!"*

Sleep took him.

Isaac's Apartment

The dream came and went, seemingly sporting a will of its own. Sometimes it would end as soon as it began, only to pick up at the point it had left off to continue its journey through the night. As it held onto the dreamer, its details would vary a little, in the way that a commonly known story might take on characteristics of its narrator, emphasizing certain points but still sticking to the general scheme of things. In the whiteness of it, they were always there in one form or another. Within his dream, he knew he fought his demons. He watched as they entered. The voice washed over him.

"He forgives you." The pain was there...

"See them?"

"Yeah."

"I saw six, maybe seven...one on a cross. Isaac?"

Nestor was a little shaken. "No, no fat man, just them and the black door. I'll cover the door." His fingers readjusted themselves over his weapon. It was a nervous habit.

"You okay with this?" Christian asked warily.

"Yeah, I'm okay now. Let's do it." His hands were calm. He quickly made the sign of the cross.

"For who?" Christian enquired. Nestor didn't say.

Christian reached across, pushing the door. It swung smoothly in. Light poured out, blanketing the rest of the hall. Nestor counted down again, and on three, with guns pointing, both cops moved into the bright light of the apartment.

The apartment was immense and white, everything white. The pureness of it diffused the edges of floor, walls, and ceiling, blending into one smooth continuous surface. White curtains covered the windows. Banks of lights in the ceiling washed down on angles, eliminating any shadows. Only two things marred its purity. The first was the flat black door off to the left, a hole ripped into that blinding brightness. The second were the children.

"I have the door," Nestor whispered, noticing that there wasn't a doorknob. *Must be a slider,* he thought. He kept his distance. Christian stood just on the edge of his peripheral vision, next to the children.

Spaced out to the right of the door, the children were nude, young, asexual. Different lengths of wigs gave the only hint to their gender. They were paired off and placed in various sexual positions, forming points of a triangle, their faces turned outward. In the center of the triangle, a seventh child, mummified, stood upright, arms outstretched like a crucifix. Small pieces of blank paper covered the entire body. A worn wooden

prayer bench was at its feet. Christian went over to the crucified child, calling out to Nestor as he did so.

"We okay over there?"

Nestor's eyes and gun didn't waver from the flat black door.
"We're good," he responded.

Christian nodded to himself and took a pen out of his
pocket. With its point, he leaned toward the face of the child
and lifted one of the pieces of paper. On the back of the
paper in a scribbled script he read upside down, "He forgives
you." From over the heart, Christian lifted another piece of
paper. The same. He repeated the procedure four more times.
They all read the same.

Nestor called over, his voice edgy. "What'd you get?"

"Paper...says, 'He forgives you.'"

For a moment, Nestor was distracted from the black door
as he turned his head toward his partner.

"'He forgives you?' What kind of—*Shit!*" From the corner
of his eye, Nestor saw the black door begin to move. *"Christian, your left, your left!"* he cried.

Christian spun with his .45, but two of the children's bodies blocked his vision, and he couldn't see what Nestor was
warning him about. Moving quickly around the crucified child,
he saw Isaac in the black of the doorway.

Isaac was massive, grotesque. His head barely cleared the
top of the doorway. A long robe decorated with a dragon covered his entire body. In front of him, he dangled a child by one
arm. The child was nude, and its head hung to one side, shaven.
Tape covered the genital area, masking its sex and the bright
lights of the room drained any color from its skin. Isaac began
to swing the child back and forth. The movement caused the
head of the dragon to peek out from behind the child. Isaac's
free hand was hidden in the folds of his robe.

"Isaac," Christian's voice was calm, "drop the kid and let's
see the other hand." Christian aimed his .45 at the dragon's
eye that appeared between the arcs of the child's body. The
stitched red eye rested in the center of Isaac's chest. "Nestor?"
he called.

Nestor held his .38 with both hands. "I can pop our fat
friend here right between the fucking eyes. Say when." Nestor's

voice was as calm as Christian's. Christian knew Nestor was lying. Isaac was swinging the child so that neither of them had a clean shot. He needed to buy some time so they could position themselves better.

Isaac stepped away from the black doorway, moving toward the covered windows. Nestor held his position off to Isaac's right. Christian lowered his gun a little, wanting to keep Isaac's attention. He slowly worked his way to Isaac's left and his hidden hand.

"Come on Isaac, you can do this. Drop the kid...show me the hand." Isaac continued to move away from Christian toward the windows. Finally he stopped.

"Nestor?" Christian asked.

"No...not yet." Now Nestor began to move further to Isaac's right, hoping to divide the huge man's attention. Isaac didn't seem to notice or care. He kept his attention on Christian.

"Isaac," Christian warned, "you're a dead man in about five seconds. It doesn't have to happen this way. The kid. Put the kid down." Christian brought his pistol back up. The red eye of the dragon seemed to wink, daring him. It was a stalemate.

"Last cha—" Christian suddenly sensed movement within the darkness of the door. He began to shift his gun, but Isaac suddenly held the child still. Whatever moved in the gloom was gone. Christian spun back to Isaac. The red dragon's eye stared out at him. The giant serial killer leaned over and whispered into the child's ear. The child raised its head toward Christian, its eyes fluttering open. The despair in its voice was evident.

"We were warned." The child coughed out the words, its voice raspy. "But...he remembers you."

There was movement in the blackened doorway again. Gun in hand, Stephen stepped through. Catching sight of him, Christian started to turn, but Isaac dropped the child and swung up a sawed-off shotgun from the folds of his robe. Christian had no time to deal with Stephen and spun back, firing, just as Isaac's shotgun went off. The blast threw Christian back, his hand clenching on his .45. A second shot rang out from him, going low. Nestor cried out.

"Christian!"

Isaac stood on shaky legs. The .45 slug had torn through half of his face, shattering the window behind him. He raised his shotgun again as Nestor fired, emptying his .38 into him. The serial killer stumbled back against the window. What was left of his face registered surprise as the window gave, tumbling him out and onto the street below.

Christian had crawled to the child, his hand touching its shoulder. Much of his clothing was peppered red, spreading along the floor, mixing with the child's. He kissed the dead child.

"I didn't mean to—" he whispered as Nestor called his name again, turning him over. Christian looked up at his partner, the bright lights burning into him. He knew Stephen was in the darkness and pointed toward the black doorway.

"What? What?" Nestor asked, looking over his shoulder into the blackness Isaac had come from. He didn't see anything. "What?" he asked one last time.

The white lights proved to be too much for Christian. He heard the sirens in the distance and closed his eyes.

Last Dance

"Christian? Hon? It's the hospital. You awake?"

Christian's eyes focused on Katie. She was holding the phone towards him. He blinked a few times, looking up at her.

"I'm awake...hospital?" He was a little confused, and also suddenly a little frightened. "Hospital?" Coming around, he reached for the phone. There was blood on his hand.

Katie had tears in her eyes as she leaned over and wiped the trickle of blood away from his forehead.

Christian was quiet on the drive down. At first, he didn't want her to come with him, but she insisted. They had tried to reach Palmer to see if he could baby sit Amy, but there was no answer at his home. They checked with Rita who told them that Palmer was supposed to be somewhere in Menkerit County working on a carpentry job. She said she would try his cell phone and get back to them.

Katie was bundling up Amy for the drive when the phone rang. Rita informed them that either his cell phone was off or he was out of range. Christian had to cut her short as she started to bitch about Palmer and his recent disappearances. Halfheartedly, Rita offered to baby-sit. By the time Christian had finished thanking her, Katie was downstairs with Amy ready to go. Rita promised to keep trying to reach Palmer and get him back to town, assuring Christian all would be well and wishing him the best with his sister.

Amy sat in the backseat of the car carrying her new "docter" kit. She quietly prepared her bandages and worked them into her mother's hair. It was a three-hour drive with the noisy muffler. Christian drove all but the last hour.

Katie waited outside the room with Amy. Every now and then, as she looked in, Amy would point at her drawings all over the room.

Katie put Amy down and looked in one more time. Christian had a piece of ice in his hand and was rubbing it along his sister's lips. His sister tried to suck on it, but the effort seemed too much for her, and she pushed his hand away. Her face was gaunt, and Katie couldn't tell if the folds in the hospital gown covered flesh or just empty space. The nurses had removed the IVs, trying to make her as comfortable as possible in the final stages.

Katie let the door to the room slip close and went back to policing Amy. She wanted to leave Cecilia and Christian to their privacy. There wasn't much time left.

"You've really been...good to me, Christian." Cecilia spoke slowly, licking her lips. She reached out a thin arm, touching his face. The effort was monumental, and her hand shook. "I've had enough," she said, dropping her hand.

"I know." Christian watched her face, still holding the ice in his hand.

"I had the nurse call," she said.

"I'm glad you did. I was afraid I wasn't going to make it in time."

"Ohhhh, I knew you would, brother." She tried to move in the bed, but gave up. "I know I had you scared, but I fooled you...still here. I could always fool you...you could never fool me, though."

"Naw, you were always too smart for me. "

"No...not smart, just knew...*ice?*"

"Sure." He brought the ice back up to her lips. Most of the melting water ran down her chin, and she pulled on his shirtsleeve to take the ice away. Tossing the ice cube in the wastepaper basket, he shook the water from his hand and went to wipe her chin.

"Oh, leave it...not important."

"Okay." He rested his hand on her arm. It felt like tissue paper over bones.

"Katie said...you talked her into..renewing your vows." She grinned at him. Her breathing was uneven.

"Oh yeah. That was me."

"Five years with her...a good beginning...not too shabby...anniversary, two weeks?"

"We'll see—"

Cecilia touched him lightly. "I know, I know...but..Katie deserves this." There was a knock at the door and a nurse peeked in, waved and closed the door. Cecilia smiled. "She's the one...who called you."

"Oh," Christian said.

Cecilia saw that uneasy look in his eyes. She wanted to rest, but she continued. "Listen, no matter...what, you go to church...with Katie. Means a lot."

"I know, I will."

"Good, good...Christian?"

"Yeah?"

Cecilia closed her eyes for a moment, and Christian felt his heart falter. She opened them slowly. She gave a little laugh.

"Ha... scared you... huh?"

"A little."

"Sometimes...sometimes...I feel it. You know? It's like waiting for a...yawn. You can feel it...you don't know why...but you can feel it coming on...you know?" Cecilia brought a hand up to her face and touched her eyes for a moment as if she was trying to remember something or close them herself in death. She dropped her hand. "Ohhh...I feel like yawning, Christian..."

"Don't..." He saw the glassy look in her eyes.

"No...not yet...Iwon't," she said. She tried to move. "Help me out of bed...Please?"

"Are you sure?"

"Please?"

"Okay. Here, put your arms over my shoulders."

"Okay."

"Good, now watch your legs. I'll swing them to the side."

"Okay."

"You're doing fine."

"I know..."

"Okay, I have you now, your feet are on the floor...Ready?"

"Not sure. My feet touching?"

"Yep."

"Don't feel them."

"Floor's warm, that's all."

"Warm? Think so?"

"Like toast."

"Oh." She wiggled her toes.

Christian stopped. "Want to go back to bed?"

"No...*No*..." He felt her arms tighten around him. "No..." she said once more. "I'm okay...I can feel them...Ready..."

Christian nodded. "On three...one...two..." And she said three as he stood her up. She weighed nothing, no more than a breath of air.

"Ohhhh, this feels...good..." The words weren't spoken, they were exhaled.

"Doing good, kid."

"Yeah...good...kid..." She sounded sleepy. "Dance me around...okay? Slow."

"Okay, here we go." Christian held her, ignoring what the disease had made out of her body. She spoke as he moved her about in a small circle.

"Good...feels good." Christian felt her head nod to the side. Her arms twitched as if she was slipping into a deep slumber.

"Christian..." Her arms suddenly tightened around him.
"Yes, hon?" his voice choked.
"Tired...I feel a...yawn coming..."

Katie had been watching. She heard Cecilia's whisper, saw her
legs give out. Christian, holding her up, buried his face in her
neck. Katie closed the door.

Sweet, Sweet, Tender Uncle

"Candy?"

Her name was Karen, but everyone in the group called her
Candy. She detested the name. An uncle had given it to her.
She was fourteen when the name stuck, seventeen when the
uncle finally died. She had hoped his death would bring some
peace, but he had destroyed any real chance of peace for her
starting at the age of twelve. Before his death, he swore that
he would always be by her side, no matter what. In a way, he
kept his word.

Every time she heard the name, hatred welled up. The hatred fed her, nourished her, and so she kept the name.

At first, right after her father died, she found her uncle's
words comforting. He had told her that he would take care of
her, help her to grow into a beautiful woman. He had talked
about the pride her father would feel if he were still alive to
see her. How it was now his job to keep the filthy little scum
that lived in the neighborhood from destroying her beauty. He
had gone on to warn her that, as she grew older, fewer and
fewer men would want her, but that he would always be there
for her as her father would have wanted.

These talks first started when he would walk with her to
school. Then, at bedtime. Then, in the middle of the night. At
first, she would wake up, not to his touch, but to his voice.
Then, there was very little talking, just touching.

And then other things. Quiet things, private things.
Things that she couldn't talk about to her mother. Things
that couldn't be said to her friends. Things that she couldn't
say to herself. Things that couldn't even be said in the dark.
Just things.

Sometimes he would wake her three or four times in a single night. Those nights, after the second visit, she would sit up in fear. She would wait in the dark, not wanting to go back to sleep. Not wanting to be awakened again by another visit. Her fear grew and, after a while, she would wake up to the sound of his voice or the touch of his hands to find him not there. He had gotten not only into her body, but also into her head. Day or night, the nightmare was always there.

It was just after her seventeenth birthday that she woke to such a nightmare. His voice was there, but he wasn't. This time, though, she still heard him, even awake, his voice carrying from down the hall.

He had moved into the small house to help her mother tidy up the loose ends from the death of his brother. Her uncle was never one for working much and knew a good thing when he came across it. Needing help around the house, her mother let him stay on while she worked as a waitress in a futile effort to catch up with the mounting bills.

The free room and board were hard for her nocturnal uncle to pass up. The young Karen was even harder to pass up. As time went on, her mother stopped needing her brother-in-law around, but by then, her mother was used to having the company of a man around the house again. The fact that he looked a lot like his deceased brother and that he took to wearing his clothes didn't hurt much, either. But he wasn't her father.

Karen was fully awake now, and what she heard weren't his usual gasping and groping sounds. Her mother was working the graveyard shift and wouldn't be home until daylight. Karen had expected a visit from him, but was at a loss as to what to do now. She didn't want her uncle to think that she was coming to him, but the sounds just weren't right.

Quietly, she slipped out of bed. Pulling her nightgown around her, she walked down the hall and peeked into his room. In the darkness she could hear uneven breathing, but couldn't see anything else. She turned on the light.

The bed was empty, and her heart skipped a beat as she expected him to jump out at her. Then she heard moans coming from the other side of the bed. She walked carefully around the bed.

He was lying on the floor, holding his chest. He saw her and tried to call out between painful breaths.

"Candy." It sounded like someone was choking him.

Breath.

"Heart."

Breath.

"Doc."

Breath.

"Hurry."

Breath.

Suddenly his head whipped back from the pain, his back arching up. He cried out.

Candy felt the smile on her face. She hadn't had one there in a long time. She touched it as she crawled onto his bed. It felt nice. She looked down on her uncle. Swinging her bare legs over the side, she put her feet on his chest.

"Uncle, would you like to come to my room with me?" she asked, working her toes down to his groin. "Would you?" She started to work them back up his stomach and towards his chest again. "Uncle, can you hear me?" Candy asked, rubbing his chest with her toes. He tried to push her feet away, but he was too weak to do anything.

"Please…" he gasped. *"Don't…"*

"Please… Don't…" she mimicked. "I said those words to you a lot, didn't I?" She started to unbutton her nightgown. "But it never worked. You didn't stop, did you? And I was always your sweet Candy, wasn't I, Uncle?" She let her nightgown drop from her shoulders onto the bed. Lifting her feet off her uncle's chest, she slipped her panties off and dropped them on his face.

"This is what you want from me, Uncle…isn't it?" As she spoke, she climbed off the bed and onto him, straddling him with her bare legs. Balling up her underwear, she forced it into his mouth. He tried to fight her off, but the pain in his chest was too great.

"Take me like you always do and I'll call a doctor for you." She ran her hands across his shoulders. He began to gag and tried to remove the underwear from his mouth. Candy just slapped at his hand, pinning it under her knee.

"Don't you know how to treat me anymore?" she taunted him. "Don't you *want* me anymore?" She tapped his chest with a fist.

"Uncle, are you ignoring me? You never did before." She rapped his sternum. It gave a dull thump.

"Sweet, sweet, tender Uncle, do you remember?" This time, she really hit him. He gasped through the material, the tears running down his face.

"Do you remember the first time? I do." She hit him harder. He gave a muffled gasp and she hit him again. "I remember." *Thump.* "I was just twelve." *Thump.* "Twelve." *Thump.* "That's right... I was just..." *Thump.* "Twelve—"

He lay still. She stopped, hands clenched. Slowly she reached over and took her underwear out of his mouth. He gasped.

"Candy," he said weakly.

"Yes," she hissed, "that's my name, Uncle." Her hands formed fists again.

Thump. Thump. Thump.

Her punches rained down, building into a frenzy. It wasn't long before he lay still again. She hadn't noticed. Suddenly, her body tightened and her head flew back, her nails biting deep as she grabbed at his soft flesh. Raking them across, she left long bloody trails as she experienced her first orgasm.

That had been twenty years ago. In all the groups, over the years, she'd given her name as Candy. She never explained why.

"Candy...?"

Sometimes she couldn't help when her mind wandered back. She remembered how her mother had come home that morning and found her nude on top of her dead uncle, her hands swollen from beating him in the chest.

Her mother thought she had tried to seduce her uncle, and that he had died in the process. She never learned of the years of abuse. Nor did any of it ever came out in therapy, either. For the most part, no one learned anything. Karen would sit silently through the sessions, waiting out her time. After the failed sessions, the frustrated therapist suggested institutionalizing her, since she wasn't responding. Obviously the problem was beyond the help being offered. Labeled with major depression verging on suicidal, she was institutional- ized for just over a year. There, she was abused by two other patients.

Both patients died before she was released.

Once out, she was required to attend private therapy sessions, but she never felt secure talking on a one-to-one basis. It was determined that she needed the group dynam- ics to maintain herself. Over the years, she progressed to larger groups, finding comfort in numbers. The groups them- selves had a constant flux of people. The dynamics and personality of the group, even though guided by the thera- pist, changed with the flow of clients. Some people stayed, some people just *disappeared*. Seldom did she stay in a group longer than a year—she was always on the move from city to city.

"Candy? Would you like to add something to the discussion?"

She finally heard the question, the voice impatient. Candy looked at the therapist, who was silently taking notes, and the rest of the members of the group, who waited patiently. She didn't feel like herself. She just needed something of the fa- miliar. She didn't intend to stay in this group long, just long enough to get her bearings.

"No, I don't think so," Candy answered. Her eyes settled on Bobby, one of the male clients. It was his turn to lead the group. They had been secretly dating for the past month. She'd have to get her bearings and end it soon. She needed to move on, to put distance between her and the things happening around her.

Her world was changing. The people she usually kept in contact with seemed to have fallen off the face of the earth, and that frightened her more than anything else. She knew these people didn't disappear that easily.

"Are you sure?" Bobby asked. She knew he was always trying to take over the group, to show his dominance over the others, but more to impress her. She was polite and patient towards him in this respect.

Of all of the women in the group, she was the most attrac- tive. This always garnered her plenty of attention from the male patients. The attention made Bobby jealous. He had told her that it cheapened her, and in that sense, it lessened his own standing.

During the sessions, he usually either ignored her completely or attacked her. It all depended on how much attention she was receiving. Bobby reminded her of her uncle in a way.

"No, not today, thank you," she said to him. She knew he would pose the question a third time. When he did, she wouldn't answer. Instead, she would silently shake her head and drop her eyes slightly. He would read this as submission, and would be appeased. She would then flash him a coy smile. He would respond in like and move on to bother someone else. She knew it was time to lessen the group by one. She would bare her teeth later.

The therapist allowed a few more rounds of dialogue before he regained control of the group, encapsulating the session. He touched briefly upon everybody in the group, and was finished in a few minutes.

"Okay, ladies and gentlemen, that's about it for the evening. I see good progress here. Now, since our next scheduled get-together would fall on Halloween, we will have a break from each other and meet the following week." He looked around, making mental notes of who looked happy and who looked disappointed. Then he smiled his best disarming smile. "Next meeting, everybody bring a different psychosis." The group laughed. "Night-all," he said.

"Goodnight, Mr. Kellogg," one said.

"Take care of your arm, no more hurting yourself," another voiced.

"See you. Good 'Trick-or-Treat' to you." Down the line, his clients bade him good night. As they filed out, Candy walked over to James and quietly waited near him.

"Coming, Candy?" Bobby asked, wanting the last word with Mr. Kellogg. He knew she called him by his first name after session, and that bothered him. Bobby didn't think it was appropriate, and would have to speak to her about it. "Well?" he said, a little testily.

"I'll be downstairs in a minute or two." She knew this would piss him off.

"I'm not going to wait long—"

"In that case," she said, "I'll meet you later." Smiling, she turned her back on him.

"Goodnight, Mr. Kellogg," Bobby said curtly, not knowing what else he could do.

"Goodnight, Bobby. And thanks for taking over the session—you did a wonderful job." James knew he would take that as a blessing. He got one more "goodnight" from Bobby before the door slammed.

James looked into Candy's eyes and smiled. Of all his people, he had protected and guided her the most. She was one of the more unique members of The Society. A rare find. If James had been capable of caring for anyone or anything, she would have been the closest thing.

"Karen"—he was the only one to call her by her real name—"you must keep them happy. Keeping them happy keeps them off-guard."

"I know, James." She hesitated, looking at him.

"What is it, Karen?"

"How many are missing? I've tried to reach some of the others."

"Karen, you know we are a wandering lot at times." James' voice was reassuring, but did little to assuage her fears.

"I know, but—"

"Yes," he answered for her, "an unfortunate wind is blowing our way." He knew her fears. "But we will ride it out."

Karen wasn't satisfied. "What's really going on? What's happening to The Society?" She reached out to touch him on his arm, but drew her hand back slowly instead. The Society had been her home all of these years. James had been the source of her strength. She knew she would have ended her own life a long time ago if not for him.

"Don't worry, Karen. It will be over soon." His voice was soothing, but she still couldn't shake the feeling of dread.

"I'm scared," she finally said, touching him lightly. He took her hand from his arm and kissed it gently. Her eyes wandered over his face. "Nothing is going to happen to me, is it?" she asked.

"No, nothing," he assured her, smiling his smile. "Now run along and play. Bobby is waiting. Enjoy." He started to walk her to the door. "Besides, I'm running late for the gym. Go." James leaned across and gave her a kiss on the forehead.

"Whatever it is, James, make it end. Swiftly, please." Karen kissed him lightly on the lips and left.

Doc And The Yuppie

James jumped rope as if he were floating. The rope arced over him and barely touched the floor beneath his feet, humming around him. His arm had healed quickly, and except for a little twinge every now and then, he had no trouble with it. He had a little less than a minute to go when Tony, his trainer, came over.

"Hey Doc, 'bout ready?" James nodded, speeding up the rope for the last thirty seconds. It disappeared around him.

"Nice, Doc, always nice. Smooth," Tony spoke, not having to raise his voice above the spinning rope. He had been training boxers, wannabes, and weekend warriors all over the country for forty years now. Never had he seen the likes of this one. He never knew Doc's age and had never asked in the twenty years or so that he had known him; it was none of his business. He just wished he had had Doc when he was a youngster. But he had a feeling that about the time Doc was a youngster, he wasn't even a twinkle in his own father's eye.

The only thing he knew for certain about Doc was that he liked open spaces, at least in the ring. Liked to keep his fights dead center. That said something about a man. He also knew that Doc was a gentleman. He really liked Doc. Tony smiled to himself. Although he called him Doc, he never really knew what he did for a living.

"Nice, Doc, smooth." Tony watched the spinning rope. He never fooled himself with any illusions about his own boxing days. He had been good in his day, but the gyms were full of *good* fighters even then. *Great* was something else. He had never been great, never had a chance. The sport, and maybe a bit of life, had beaten any chance at greatness out of him. At the age of twenty, with a kid about to be born, he had "retired." It broke his heart. But it wasn't because of the kid, just too many hits around the eyes. Skin was too thin. A real bleeder.

First, second round, all hell would open up around his eyes, and he had to fight through the blood. He just couldn't see, couldn't fight. He was doomed to love the sport, but it never loved him back. A one-sided passion, but it was his passion.

The rope came to a stop, but he swore he could still hear the music of it spinning. *Damnedest thing.*

"Nice, Doc, always nice. Smooth." He always finished the warm-up with that comment. "Ready, Doc?"

"Yes. I need to work some kinks out," he said, handing the rope over to Tony as they walked toward the ring. The sounds of gloves against bags were only overridden by the voices of trainers urging their fighters to greater savagery.

"Good, Doc. But wha's with da' sweatshirt?"

"Chill in the old bones, that's all."

"Yep, yep, known da' feelin', Doc, known da' feelin'. How's da' hands doin'?" he asked.

"Not too bad, Tony."

"Tha's good, tha's good," Tony said, nodding as they came to the side of the ring. "Hands an' y'heart, tha's y'life, Doc. Y'life." Tony's voice went wistful. "Always connected, always. Y'hands do wha' y'heart says. Y'know da' ring, Doc. Y'know da' truth 'bout it. All da' same. Tha' there roped in square, jus' like life. Sometime y'against da' ropes, times y'on da' canvas. Times y'hear da' crowd." Tony was feeling a little embarrassed about his talk, but he couldn't stop himself. "Y'know, Doc," he heard his voice continuing on, "y'might hear da' crowd, but they don't hear ya. Too busy yellin', screamin' at ya. They jus' don't hear ya, Doc." He finally made himself stop. Doc was quiet, and Tony was glad for it. Tony smiled to himself. *Doc's a real smart man. Knows when not to say nothin'.*

"Wha' say we wrap 'em hands a little extra today?" Tony offered. "Got y'self a young-blood," he warned.

"Fine, Tony. You're the boss." James stretched his hands out, hands that had taken hundreds of lives. The nails were thick and a little long, but well manicured. The fingers were solid, the joints not noticeably swollen. James' palms were more leathery than normal skin. They were hands that possessed anything they held.

Tony took them, turning them back and forth like a mother inspecting a child's hands before dinner. He saw nothing of this. *Shame,* he thought, feeling the strength of the sinews beneath the aging skin. *With these hands, coulda been a champion. One of a kind.* He took the wrappings from over his shoulder and shook his head.

"Sure thing, Doc. One of a kind." Tony realized he was speaking out loud. He was having one of those days. He looked up at James and met his smile as he wrapped his hands. Tony heard the voice of Doc's sparring partner traveling through the gym, and worked quickly, expertly. Finished, Tony held up his hands for James to punch against.

"How they feelin' to ya?"

"Great job, Tony."

"Good. Now listen up," he said eyeing the kid as he climbed into the ring. The kid started to bounce around on his toes. "This here's not a bad kid, jus' a little yuppie-type punk. Y'know wha' I mean Doc? A little hothead. Comes on strong. Only guy I could find free in da' gym now. A little strong, Doc, a little strong."

James nodded. "I'll watch it. Thanks," he said as he slipped on his headgear. Tony picked up Doc's gloves, and James slid his hands into them. Tony quickly laced them up.

"Done," he announced. "Open." Tony put in James' mouthpiece. James bit down, securing it in place, and climbed into the ring.

As James entered, the kid looked shocked, then disgusted as their eyes met. James smiled, showing him the red rubber of the mouthpiece. The kid stopped moving and stared at the older man. Taking out his own mouthpiece, he tossed it aside with gloves outstretched as if he was about to be crucified. He made like he was addressing a packed house.

"What's this? What's up with the old guy? I'm warming up on granddads now?"

Tony walked around to the side of the ring. "Hey now, ya give him respect," he called out to the kid. "Ya call 'im *Mr.* Kellogg, or *Doc.* Ya hear me?" James turned his back, no longer smiling.

"Sorry, Doc. Sorry," Tony mouthed.

"Yeah, sure," the kid called back. "He'll need a doc in a minute or two." The young fighter turned his back and started to bounce on his toes again.

Tony shook his head as he addressed James. "Listen up, like I said, a little hothead. Full of 'imself, y'know. Piss and vinegar, just piss and vinegar. Nothin' more." Tony shot a quick look across the ring. Nonchalantly, he went on. "Drops 'is shoulder on 'is jabs, leaves 'imself open. A man with a good hook could nab 'im. Da' kid ain't careful 'bout it. Have to point it out to 'im one day." Tapping James on the head, he said, "Ya ready."

James turned around and watched his opponent's back. As the buzzer sounded, the kid whipped around, coming straight out of the corner at him. By the time James made it a third of the way out across the ring, the kid was poking at him with light jabs. He was looking to bully the him. James avoided them easily.

"Don't be afraid, Doc, old man. I'll take it easy on you," the kid said taunting. He started to dance around even more, putting a little power behind the punches now. James continued to avoid the blows.

"Hey, old man, am I going too fast for you?" He came in with a flurry of jabs. James dropped back, hit the ropes, and slipped to the side. The jabs hit thin air. James didn't waste any time.

The hook caught the young fighter square in the jaw, popping his eyes open in surprise. He suddenly found himself dropping on the ropes where he had expected his opponent to be. The older boxer, not waiting, bounced back a few steps away from him. He knew the boy would lose it and lunge at him. The young boxer sprang off the ropes, and, as he did, James hit him with a straight left jab, followed by a hard right hook. The short combination landed him back on the ropes.

The kid looked over at James and ran his tongue over his teeth. He thought he tasted a bit of blood. Tony was silent on the outskirts of the ring.

"Slick, old man. Real slick," the kid said, getting up slowly from the ropes. James moved back to the center of the ring. Tony broke his silence, cautioning James to keep moving, but James waited for his opponent instead.

The kid came out with his hands at his sides, raising them slowly as he came closer. He wasn't bouncing as much as before. This was serious now.

Jabbing, he worked on his distance, trying to see what Doc would go for. James waited, giving away as little as possible.

James knew the kid would step in quickly with a hard combination and drop back, trying to draw him out. He would be counting on his speed to counterpunch. Watching his opponent's face, James saw his eyes widen and his nostrils flare before the attack, giving himself away. The combination was hard and quick just as he had expected.

The kid led with a body jab, followed by two hooks. James dropped back as the second hook made some contact with his shoulder. James winced and favored the shoulder, dropping his hands and leaving the side of his head open. The kid took the bait and came back at him, switching up the combination. Both hooks missed this time, and as the kid jabbed to the body, he dropped his shoulder, leaving his head wide open again just as Tony predicted.

James took the body shot with a grunt and came back with two hard hooks from his good side, followed with an uppercut, putting his body weight into it. The kid's head snapped back, and he sat down hard on his ass with a cracked front tooth.

James looked down at him silently and turned his back, leaving the ring. Tony nodded his approval as he slipped James' headgear off and started to unlace his gloves.

"Nice, Doc. Nice. Glad y'left da' ring." Tony was beaming. "Chill in da' old bones seem to be okay?" he asked as he removed the gloves.

"I guess so. I had some doubts about some things, but now my—" A cup of water hit him in the back of the head. He kept his back turned.

"That's it for you, you old shit? You just gonna walk away?" the kid said climbing out of the ring.

Short-term anger, James thought. He knew it well. He waited before turning around, giving the kid a chance to think about the situation.

"Well, old man?" The kid was on cue. James noticed that his voice wasn't pitched quite so high anymore. *Hothead, but he's got some doubts now.*

"That's all you got?" The kid had worked himself into a corner, and he couldn't get out without losing face. Tony began to say something, but James placed a hand on his arm, silencing him. Turning slowly, James tossed aside the other glove, still not looking at the kid. The sounds of the gym died around them.

"You were just lucky!" the kid hissed. James locked eyes with him and moved in quickly. The kid saw something in James' eyes. Something that scared him, something that he couldn't comprehend. He stepped back.

"*Boy*," James said, his voice low and almost conversational, "you haven't been on this earth long enough to *fuck* with me. And, were it not for a previous engagement, I would simply rip your heart out." Stepping closer, James whispered. "Say one more thing to me boy, just one more thing, and you may yet meet me out of the ring...but on my terms." And James winked at him, smiling. The smile never reached his eyes. Taking a step back from the kid, he heard Tony's nervous voice.

"C'mon, Doc. It's wha' I told ya." James walked away, leaving the kid standing there. Noises filled the gym again.

"Tell y'wha', Doc," an unsettled Tony said as they walked toward the locker room, "Y'even had me scared there a minute, yes sir!" He had seen the look in Doc's eyes. "Still got tha' class. A guy like y'Doc, all class. But it's over now, y'know, over." Tony's heart raced with a newfound fear as they got to the locker room entrance.

"No, not over yet," James said. "One more to go." Tony didn't understand, but Doc was beginning to feel like himself again.

Time For One More

Bobby still lay beneath her. They were on the floor and she was straddling him, the only position she would do it in.

He had been dead for two hours now. The poison had taken its time as he made love to her. Toward the end, it had raced through his body like his passion had done earlier, and she took over, bringing herself to a climax. Now she waited. It was Candy that had done the killing all of these years, but it was Karen who had been thinking of her uncle now. All of those times under his filthy hands, his filthy voice telling her how pretty she was.

The thoughts were playing through her head when she sensed *Him* behind her. The knife sliced through the air, piercing her sternum. It had been so swift she didn't even have time to blink. She knew she was killed. In her final few seconds of consciousness, she felt arms around her. It amazed her. There was no pain, and she thought she felt a kiss.

C.S. Bacon

James took Karen with him. It was a long trip, but he had everything prepared for her. When he finally arrived, he took his time and buried her deep. It was a secret place with four other, older graves on the side of the hill. James finished patting down the fresh earth and stood facing the small valley. Rubbing his hands, he grew conscious of the growing pain in the joints of his fingers.

No, not slipping, he thought. *Just nature running its course in another direction.* He opened and closed his hands. *Pity.* He'd have liked to continue to add to the other graves down there, but things were taking more and more time.

James looked over his valley. It had been so many years since a single entry from the Journal had caught his attention. Unknown to him, that page would send him on a ten-year odyssey before he finally turned this valley into his personal burial ground.

That single page was a curiosity that simply read "Haven," with the signature "C.S. Bacon" just below it. It had taken James a number of those ten years to find out that C.S. Bacon stood for Charles Stratford Bacon, long believed to be gone. It was several more years before he stumbled across the old man and the entrance to the valley.

"You come for me?" the old man had asked. He was gnarled, each breath a sigh. James had found the man sitting in an old leather armchair in front of his small, run-down shack. His clothes were as weathered as his skin.

"No," James had replied, feeling he had stepped back in time. "I was told that if anyone might know about Haven, you would."

"Not for me?" the old man asked again. He kept one hand hidden in the side of the torn leather cushion.

"No, not for you," James reassured. The old man's hidden hand produced a hand-rolled cigarette and match.

"Who told you I might know?" The question was meant to be casual. It wasn't. James was silent. "I see," the old man said, placing the cigarette in his mouth next to a deep brown sore that had carved itself into the soft tissue of his lip. With his nail, he flicked the head of the match.

"Got this sore here from smoking too much," the old man said, lighting the cigarette. He inhaled deeply. "Still got time for one more," he added, exhaling.

"You have a name?" James asked, wondering what else was hidden in that torn cushion.

"No...not for you." The old man inhaled and exhaled again, expelling a little less of the smoke from his lungs than he took in. "You have that look about you," he said through the misty smoke, inhaling and exhaling once more. Taking the cigarette from his mouth, he pointed with it.

"Haven, in there." He placed the slow-burning tobacco next to the open sore on his lip. The woods were thick where he indicated.

"No roads?" James asked.

"In there." The old man repeated. Inhaled. Exhaled.

James walked back over to his car and grabbed a backpack out of the trunk. Shouldering his gear, he went back to the old man.

"Any problem with leaving my car over there?" James asked. The old man was quiet in his smoking, saying nothing. Inhaling. Exhaling. James turned and left, disappearing into the dense woods. It took him a full day on foot to find Haven.

James had expected a town, a backwoods community, something. From what he could tell, though, there had never been
one. Instead, there were one hundred and thirty-eight graves
nestled between the rolling hills. The graves themselves had
no markers. Most were just slight depressions in the land. There
had been no effort to conceal them; the isolation of the surrounding hills did that for them. James settled in and spent
two days in Haven.

Of the dozen graves he had dug up, not one held any
sort of a coffin. In most of the graves, the skeletal remains
were nothing more than a jumble of bones. James had
counted the number of skulls he found in each gravesite to
get an idea of the correct body count. Of the twelve graves,
three had four skulls in them, along with enough bones to
make up the matching bodies, give or take. Six other graves
harbored three bodies each in the rich earth. The balance
of the graves held a single individual. All of the remains
were of adults. The clothing had either been stripped before burial or had rotted away along with the flesh of the
bodies. Of the thirty-three bodies he exhumed, none had
been wearing a wedding band or any sort of jewelry. Even
more intriguing was the fact that not one of the skulls had
any of its teeth, nor did he find any loose teeth in the exca-
vated earth.

What he did find was that most of the jawbones had
tiny fractures around the tooth sockets, and the fractures
had not healed. He knew that meant that the teeth had been
taken forcibly either just before death, or right after. A hundred and thirty-eight graves. James had a gut feeling that
there were many more yet to be discovered.

Once James had replaced the remains, he had made
his way back to the old man's shack and his car. The old
leather chair was empty and stood sentinel facing out toward the hidden valley. James didn't have to look to know
that the old man was gone. Going inside the shack, he
found buckets filled with teeth. Whatever possessions the
old man had other than the chair, he had taken them with
him. Back outside, James sat in the old chair, finding it
very comfortable. He slid his hand in the torn cushion,

bringing out a hand rolled cigarette and a match. He lit the cigarette and exhaled.

"Bacon," he said, and watched the light shift across the hills.

It took him another two years to buy the land. Once he took possession, James burned the shack, along with the leather chair. Two years later, he found old man Bacon again, still smoking. They had an interesting conversation.

James looked down on Karen's grave, wiping the dark earth from his hands. He flexed his fingers.

"Time for one more," he said, and walked away. Like the members of his family that surrounded her on the side of the hill, he left her her heart.

Old Friends

Martinez sat waiting. He had always prided himself on his timeliness and his appearance. He checked his watch. *Past three.* He looked around, adjusting the sleeve of his jacket over the frayed cuff of his shirt. They were late. Unusual. Things were changing.

The waiter walked over, and Martinez covered the frayed cuff with one hand. He smiled as the waiter politely asked if he would like a drink now.

"No, thank you. Not till the rest of my party gets here."

"Fine, sir." The waiter nodded and walked off to resume his position with a full view of the dining room. He stood there with his hands behind his back, expressionless as if he were standing in front of Buckingham Palace.

Martinez continued to wait. It seemed he had been waiting for many things in life lately. What he waited for most was that one big break. If things worked his way, he'd be able to afford to eat in places like this more often. He looked over at the waiter and made eye contact. The waiter took a step towards him. Martinez shook his head no, gesturing with his hand. The waiter nodded and stepped back to his station. Martinez liked that. That was the way things should be.

But that wasn't the way things were. Martinez's hands started to pick at his face. Things were changing…and quickly.

His wife had finalized the divorce, saddling him with the tuition for his daughter, which he wouldn't have minded if she hadn't first taken a large chunk of his income and savings. The only thing that was still up for grabs was the house. The end result of that issue, he was fairly certain, was that it would be sold and the best he could hope for was a fifty-fifty cut. He doubted he would be so lucky.

At work, useless cases continued to mount. His career's downward trajectory was obvious to all of his fellow officers, and they gave him a wide berth. Once again, he needed to set something up.

The restaurant was quiet for now. Stealing glances at the other tables, he saw there were a few occupied tables, mostly people taking a respite from their shopping along Fifty Seventh Street. The City Diner was anything but a diner. Just off Fifth Avenue, it carried the look of the forties, but without the innocence of a postwar nation. All brushed chrome and marble, it didn't vary much from the grays in an old black-and-white movie. The menu reflected its trendy decor, no better or worse than a dozen "close to the top" restaurants in the city. What gave it its edge was the comings and goings of enough celebrities to hike it up a notch or two on the list of places to be seen in.

Martinez needed to be seen. Restless, he wanted to glance at his watch again, but was too conscious of it now. It might make him seem less important if he was obviously waiting for someone.

He knew he had had the chance years ago of making a major play. Christian had put an end to that with his gun slinging routine. With a little help, Martinez had pulled some strings, pushing Christian out of the force and saving his own ass in the process. If it weren't for that fuck-up in Brooklyn, it would have been other people sitting here waiting for him. Instead, he was backpedaling, trying to make up for lost time.

Martinez's fingers moved freely over his face. So far, Nestor had turned up nothing useful for him. He had a feeling that that bastard was holding back. He knew about the trip up to Tranquillity, but Nestor claimed nothing had come of it.

Martinez didn't believe him for a second. He'd never trusted Christian, and he didn't trust Nestor now. Martinez knew he'd have to take matters into his own hands. It was just with that screw-up in Brooklyn, he was aware of how quickly things could bite you in the ass. He didn't like to take chances with his own career, but it was time to bring him back in. *Funny,* Martinez thought. *Bring him back in.* He had always felt that he had never left; that he was always in the background some-where, simply waiting patiently.

Martinez reached over and took a sip of water. As he did so, he saw the maître d' guiding one of his late guests over to his table. He stood, extending his hand.

"How are you, James?"

"I'm fine," the smaller man said, taking Martinez's hand. "And you, Victor? How are you?"

"Good, good. Please sit." The maître d' pulled out the chair for James, and he sat down, thanking him. The maître d' left, wishing them a pleasant meal just as the waiter replaced him; a quick change of the guard.

"Can I interest you gentlemen in drinks?" The waiter turned first to James, then to Martinez, automatically sensing the peck-ing order.

"We're waiting for one more person," Martinez said, "but I think a drink would be in order... James?" Martinez threw it back over to him.

"Actually," James said, "while we're waiting, I'll have a beer. If you have it, a plain ol' Bud would do." James smiled up at the waiter. This smile had a certain down-home wholesome-ness to it. James had many smiles.

"Same here." Martinez said when the waiter turned to him.

"Fine, gentlemen, two 'plain ol' Buds.' I'm sure we can fill that order. Thank you." And he was off.

"Hell, Victor, I haven't had a Bud in a long time." Martinez ignored the homespun routine. His hand went back to his face. James had wondered how long it was going to be before that nervous habit surfaced. James spoke up again.

"So, it's been quite some time since we've seen each other."

"Yes, years. But you haven't aged." Martinez tried to mask his surprise.

"No, no. I don't suppose so. Not in my nature, you see." The waiter came back with the two glasses of beer.

"Excuse me, gentlemen," he said, placing the glasses down. "When you are ready to order, just let me know." The waiter smiled and walked back to his station.

"Well, Victor," James said, picking up his glass, "to old times."

"And to what the future may hold," Martinez added.

"Yes, of course, what it may hold," James replied, taking a sip. "Now, is there a reason for this face-to-face meeting? I was content with our conversations over the phone." He placed his glass down. The feeling of wholesomeness was gone.

Martinez drank slowly, taking a third of his glass. He looked at James, knowing he was another person who knew more than he let on. Martinez saw the quick movement of the man's eyes. *A hell of a lot more.*

"I need your help," he finally answered.

"Again, Victor? If I remember correctly, you made a mockery of it the last time." James reached for his beer. His polished nails gleamed like claws around the glass.

"Yes; I didn't know I had such a wild card with—" Martinez cut himself short as James' nails began to tap on the side of his glass. James didn't like excuses. "Yes, well..." Martinez continued, his hands going back to his face as he spoke.

James nails stopped their slow tapping as he listened to Martinez's rehearsed speech. The slightest smile touched his face as Martinez's plan unfolded.

"I see," James finally said as Martinez's eyes looked over his shoulder. James heard the maître d' guiding the third party over. He didn't bother to turn around.

"Finally," Martinez said.

"Sorry I'm late."

"Don't worry," Martinez said, standing halfway up doing the introductions. "This is Dr. James Kellogg." James slowly stood up and turned, extending his hand. "This is Detective Nestor Diaz." Nestor's hand swallowed James', but Nestor was surprised by the firmness of the older man's grip.

"Good to meet you, Dr. Kellogg." Nestor started to let go of his hand, but James held on a little longer.

"No, no, please…call me James," he said, letting go of Nestor's hand. "So, how are you, Nestor? I've heard so much about you…it's almost as if I know you." As they sat, James showed off another smile. Nestor looked a little confused at that statement, and turned to Martinez, wondering what he might be up to. Martinez nodded toward James.

"James is an old friend and has some experience with serial killers. I gave him a brief history of what we've been working on. I wanted you two to meet and eventually go over the information that has been gathered so far. I think things are reaching a point where we can go ahead with what we have. I'm sure James could give some guidance and insight to—" James raised his hand, interrupting Martinez. It was now Martinez's turn to be a little confused.

"Excuse me, Victor," James said. "Besides trying to get the correct information from all parties concerned, in all honesty, Detective, my motives are slightly selfish. I would actually like to ask a favor of you." James smiled, touching Nestor lightly on the arm. "I hear you are going up to Tranquillity tomorrow, just next to Menkerit. Both pleasant little communities. I have family up in Menkerit. I was visiting a short while back when my car broke down. I was forced to leave it there." James cocked his head to one side. "And the reason you're going up there is…?"

"A wedding," Nestor answered.

"Ahhh, weddings are such festive events. Very nice." James reached for his beer and lifted it as if he were making a toast. "More drinks, anyone?"

Uncertain at the turn of events, Martinez picked at his face for scabs that weren't there any more.

Time On His Side

Stephen wiped the dirt from the metal box. The sun was setting, and it brought a cooling breeze with it. It felt good. He shook the box. It was almost over. He had taken all that he could, pushing it with the last three. Still, his final number was eighteen. Eighteen. If their own count was correct, and if they hadn't exaggerated too much, he figured over the years they had accounted for over six hundred kills of their own. That was the number he arrived at even after taking twenty percent off for exaggerations. Now their tally belonged to him. He shook the metal box again.

Eighteen to six hundred.

The ratio wasn't that bad. True, some had been more productive than others. Only two had gone dormant, letting their numbers drop. Sometimes the urge to kill was quenched, something finally fulfilled within them. Rare, but sometimes. Stephen didn't know if this was the case for him. Hunting the others—his so-called peers—had given him a *different* taste for the kill. It had turned out to be more rewarding than he had expected. He shook the metal box again. Eighteen seemed to be the magic number. As far as he could figure, that was James' number too. He had been unable to find several of his fellow predators, and he assumed James had gotten to them first. He couldn't be totally sure, but he thought they were dead-on even. Either way, the game between them was over. It was apparent that Matt, his walking time bomb, hadn't gone off as he had hoped. Now, it was just a matter of time before the inevitable confrontation.

Stephen leaned back against the tree. In the distance, he could see the church. He was happy here, but something else drove him. He had taken a chance that James would come after him right from the start. He hadn't expected James to strike out on his own killing spree. And when he had finally realized what James was doing, he was caught off guard by the swiftness of it. James was good. Stephen now knew he might have to move everyone sooner than he had planned. Feeling the last fleeting warmth, he closed his eyes to the setting sun. He wondered what James did with the bodies he took. Didn't matter in the long run. He just needed to do one thing. He needed to break the tie—and he needed James to do that.

Stephen started to sing softly. Given time, he could have eliminated the entire Society. *Imagine that.* It was all a matter of time. And unlike James, time was on his side. It was just an unfortunate turn of events that James had taken so many from him. Still, once he took the aging killer, those kills would belong to him. Stephen understood that life was a compromise.

He opened his eyes and watched the glow of the sun as the day entered its final stage. Night would soon follow, and with it, that single volatile star would burn in the sky. He would extinguish it.

Stephen shook the metal box one last time. The plastic bags slid back and forth within, whispering to him. Yes, he would extinguish it.

Can Of Worms

Gigi was furious.

Nestor put three more unconfirmed black pins into his map. All were in a motel outside of Boston. All in one room. All killed within a twenty four-hour period. They had all come to the killer.

The police thought the victims knew the killer, since there hadn't been any signs of a struggle. They speculated it was drug-related, since the victims had been murdered in a ritualistic manner, perhaps as a warning to others. The report never mentioned what the "ritualistic manner" was. The report did mention, though, that they were still trying to identify the victims.

He now had sixteen black pins. He stepped back from the map.

It had been over an hour since his wife had spoken to him. He shook his head. He didn't like what he saw on the map, and he didn't like this argument with his wife. He knew he was missing some black pins. He just didn't know how many. It didn't matter anymore.

Gigi was right. Martinez was right. It was time to bring this to a head, to pass it on, to move on. Christian couldn't prove that Martinez had tried to set them up, but he was certain that Christian was also right. Nestor knew he was playing in waters he shouldn't be playing in, and Gigi was getting more concerned about it. He wasn't sure if he was trying to convince her or himself that he was a cop and that it was his job to solve things like this.

She had countered that he was going to be a father soon, and if things didn't change, he was going to be a father who thought more about serial killers than his family. "So how are you going to resolve that?" she had asked him. His ego didn't want to tell her that Martinez had practically pulled the rug out from under his feet with that Dr. Kellogg, so he had said nothing to her about resolving anything because, for all intents and purposes, he had nothing to resolve. She had stormed out. He had decided that once they got back from Christian and Katie's wedding, he would hand over his findings to Martinez. Most of them that was. He would hold onto the copies of his chats with Hymn101. That included any information about Palmer. Nestor rubbed the back of his neck. Palmer's involvement in this was another sore spot that he didn't know how to handle.

Nestor stared at the map. What did he really have? A bunch of colored pins surrounding a bunch of black pins scattered throughout the country. Police departments shrouded in their own secrecy and egos. People who didn't want to rock the boat, and who especially didn't want their own boat rocked. Rumors. Missing persons. Unsolved murders.

This was something that was happening every day across the country, whether he was solving it or not. Now, add to the mix some guy calling himself *Hymn101* that was what— suckering him in? Nestor didn't know. The only thing solid were the lipless bodies. But what did that even prove? Did that prove there was a society of serial killers? No, all it proved was that there was a sick bastard out there that liked to take lower lips. And it was someone who knew his victims. Someone the victims didn't fear, at least at first. He shook his head again. His mind was running in circles and it really wasn't doing him any good. He had a wife, a child on the way, and a good paycheck. *Fuck them.* He'd go back to chasing down cases that didn't feel like they were chasing him. Leave the glory to Martinez. Nestor clenched his fist.

"Shit!" he cried, jerking his hand open. A black pin stuck in the middle of his palm. Plucking it out, he tossed the pin

onto his desk. He squeezed the skin around the tiny puncture, and a drop of blood appeared. He brought it to his mouth
and sucked on it for a moment. Looking at the map again, he
knew exactly what he had; he just didn't want it anymore.
Too big a can of worms. He was a good cop. But he was afraid
now, afraid of what he could find—and of not being able to
handle what lay beneath the surface. He took his hand away
from his mouth. The blood was gone and he could hardly see
the tiny wound.

Nestor reached up and started to take down the black pins.
He had a good wife, good friends, and a good life. He was
happy. After handing the information over to Martinez, he
would put in for a transfer as far away from that prick as possible.

He put the sixteen black pins in a small plastic case. He
would remove the other colors later. Tapping his punching bag
lightly, he went downstairs to make peace with his pregnant
wife. He wanted to be a father before his child was born.

A Good Day

The gash above Christian's eye healed itself, but not before a
scar cut a wide path between the flesh it was supposed to pull
together. He turned his head in the mirror. He had lost weight
since the funeral, and it showed on his face, making the scar
more pronounced. The light in the downstairs bathroom didn't
help, either. One of the bulbs was out, and it made his features look harsher than they were.

Katie had evicted him from the upstairs bathroom before
he could finish shaving. Nestor and Gigi had called from their
car and said they were running late. Katie had taken the call in
the middle of trying to get herself and Amy ready to go, and
didn't speak long. She just told Christian that they had a little
errand to run.

"Christian! Come on!" Katie called from upstairs. She was
waiting for Rita to pick her up and run her over to the church.
But first, she needed to get Christian out of the house.

"All right, all right!" his voice echoed in the small bathroom. He touched the scar. Katie was right; he should have

gotten a few stitches. Nothing he could do about it now. He wiped the small spots of shaving cream from his face. Rinsing the razor, he made a mental note to replace the light bulb. It had been out for two months now.

Tugging on the lapels of his tux, he adjusted his bow tie, wishing Cecilia could have been here for their vows. The funeral had been two weeks ago, and it was a rough time for him and Katie, but not as bad as his sister had endured all those years. She hadn't even told anyone until two years ago that she even had cancer. That was just her way. Christian stepped out of the bathroom, wondering where Palmer was.

"*Are you gone yet?*" Katie called down to him. He kept quiet. "*Christian! This isn't funny! Come on!*"

"*Tum on!*" Amy yelled from the top of the stairs. "*Not funny!*"

Walking to the bottom of the stairs, he looked up and saw his daughter. She was dressed in a lacy, off-white gown that trailed down to the floor. Her wild curly hair was bunched up—slowly becoming un-bunched—and she had a mischievous look in her eye. Seeing her was like seeing a miniature Katie. He knew exactly what Katie was going to look like walking down the aisle. The thought brought a smile to his face. Christian waved to his daughter and she took off.

"Hon, Palmer should be here any second," he called up to her. "Besides, I've seen you before."

"I don't *care!*" He could hear her pacing around upstairs. "You can't see me until the church...now wait outside."

"It's cold outside!"

"It's sunny! Go work on your tan! Gigi isn't here yet—I told you that they called, right?" Before he could say anything, she continued. "Yeah, I did, that's right. Hey!" she yelled down. "You have me talking to myself and I have to finish! *Go!*"

"Okay, okay, going. I can take a hint. Bye." He heard a "bye" from Amy. As he stepped outside, Palmer pulled up in his patrol car.

"Hey!" Palmer called, rolling down the window on the passenger side. "Get in, it's cold." Christian opened the door and slid in.

"Going in style, aren't I?" he said.

"Hey, let the taxpayers cover your ride. You look good. Don't sweat it, going to be a good day." Christian looked at his deputy. Palmer was all smiles.

"You look pretty chipper."

"Yeah?"

"Yeah. You glad to see me make an ass out of myself today?"

"Naw, I got someone I want you to meet."

"That so?"

"Yep, at the church. Going to be a great day, Christian. A great day!" He slapped his friend on the shoulder as they drove to Tranquillity's only church.

Beyond The Shadowed Cross

John Roberts had finished the church exactly a year before he died. Nobody was sure why he started the building, not even his good friend Alexander Burns. Another source of wonderment was why he placed it so far away from the growing town. But since the church was built at John Roberts' own expense, few felt they had any say about its placement. The land he chose was open, no one laying claim to it. It was a rock-strewn piece of earth, not good for plant or animal. It's only saving grace, other then the church itself, was that the waters from the river were calm and shallow at this junction. Once the waters passed the church, the river regained its memory of what it should be. Beyond God's grace, it picked up speed and depth, twisting and turning in a slalom of its own. Some believed it was for the love of the river, the love of water, that he had built the church there. Some. Not many.

John Roberts had taken to ordering the wood for his church from adjacent Menkerit County, most times making the trips himself. He had asked for no volunteers in building the church. Whoever helped worked a hard day, receiving a thanks and a meal for it. Some said it was selfish pride that drove him, hoping for a final resting place for his soul. Others said he had the Devil in him since his son disappeared and was now trying to make amends with his Maker. Some thought grief had overcome him for the other children lost in their early years, or for the wife that ultimately gave in to her own death. By the start of the structure, most had forgotten about the bounty hunter William Reed. He had disappeared looking for John Roberts and Alexander Burns under a full moon. Most had forgotten, but not all.

It was rumored that William Reed had friends—friends that were of the same temperament as he was. It was also rumored that a few came looking for him, only to become rumors themselves. There was a belief that some of the evil from the bounty hunter remained after his goings. That John Roberts built the church as a holding place for the lost souls that still disappeared from time to time in Menkerit County. The people who talked never knew for sure of the killing of William Reed, even less about the Journal that he had carried. The truth was, with all of the talk, most couldn't figure on one clear cause for the building of the church. No one reason at all. Whatever was in John Roberts' mind or soul, he gave no hint of it even on his deathbed. The only thing that came to surface after his death was a rumor of a book, a journal that held pages of his flowing script. If this was true, the talk went about, the book was in the hands of Alexander Burns, and all knew he wasn't much of a reading man. No, not much of a chance learning anything useful from Alexander Burns.

When the church was finished, it was the tallest structure for miles around, almost three stories. The beauty of it came from its simplicity. The church was shaped like the bow of a ship, with the altar at its head. The pews were angled in, facing toward the altar. There were six rows on either side of the church. The first two adjacent pews sat four people each. As the church widened towards the back, the other pews feathered out, holding more people. The last pews were capable of holding ten people each. Keeping with the simplicity of it, there was only one set of windows that allowed light into the church. It was situated at the head of the altar. The original sets of windows were destroyed in 1969 when a twister touched down, sending a tree through the windows. They were replaced with four segments of glass reaching twenty feet high and eight feet across. The new windows gave a clear view of the fields that ran to the river and Father Toland's house on the opposite bank. On many mornings, the figure of Father Toland could be seen trudging over the stony field to the church.

In front of the window, a life-sized cross hung, made from the tree that had smashed through the old windows. As the sun made its way through the sky, the shadow of the cross also made its way through the church. On these sunny days, the parishioners would sit in the shadowed pews as the symbol of their God was projected on the church floor, slowly inching its way between them. It was as if Christ himself glided between the churchgoers of Tranquillity. On such days, the more reverent of the parishioners would reach out touching its encroaching shadow.

Here, at the head of the altar beneath the cross, Christian waited for Katie. In front of him, the shadow of the cross stretched out as if prostrating itself in confession. On either side of its arms, family and friends sat to witness the renewal of Christian and Katie's vows to each other.

Off in the far corner of the old church, beyond the reach of the shadowed cross, stood a small man in a double-breasted suit nodding politely at people. He was neither friend nor family.

There Was This Man

Katie was a wreck. Nestor had finally dropped off Gigi, and before Gigi could get a word out, Katie had her running around like a madwoman. The early morning excitement proved too much for Amy, who had fallen asleep. She was to be the flower girl, and now Katie hoped she wouldn't be a cranky one.

Rita Burns was, of course, on time. She was waiting downstairs looking her best in a dress that was, if possible, as red as her hair. Rita was in charge of getting Amy up and ready to go. At one point, she called upstairs to ask whether Amy had ever been bitten by a tsetse fly.

As Gigi and Katie finally came down, Rita looked up at them. Even with a four-year-old child, Katie looked every inch a new bride. The lacework wound up around her neck and ran down along her arms, completely covering her in the front. The back of the gown had an oval opening that bared most of her back. She had been a June bride, and the cut of the gown had helped keep her cool. Amy, who was still asleep, had a smaller version of her mother's dress, minus the train and the opening in the back. For a moment, Rita was envious of the years she had lost. But she was not one for dwelling on things, and it quickly passed.

"Woman," she said to Katie, "that sheriff of ours is one hell of a lucky man!"

"Thanks, Rita. You've been a doll!" Katie gave the older woman a kiss. Rita blushed, her face matching her hair and dress. Flustered, she pushed Katie along.

"I know that. Now, let's wake your daughter here and get this show on the road."

By the time everybody was packed into Rita's SUV, they were running twenty minutes behind schedule.

Amy woke up as Rita, speeding through a back road, suddenly wheeled off the road cutting across a field. Rita's shortcut saved them four minutes and gave Gigi a knot on top of her head as she smacked it against the roof of the SUV. Uncharacteristically, Gigi let out a stream of curses—mostly in Spanish.

Amy loved the roller-coaster ride, and as they came in sight of the church, she was raring to go. Katie, on the other hand, was beginning to sweat despite the coolness of the day.

Rita swung the SUV back onto another dirt road, and they shot over an old wooden bridge that spanned the river. She turned right, traveled a few hundred feet, and came to a screeching halt in front of the church. Sitting up front, Gigi's head snapped forward, almost banging the roof again. Gigi shot Rita a look, but the old redhead was already out of the car, running around and giving Katie a hand. Amy leaped out next and began to scatter flower petals from her basket.

Slowly climbing out, Gigi picked up as many of the stray petals as she could, managing to convince Amy to wait until she got inside the church before she scattered the rest of them.

Grabbing hold of Amy with her free hand, Katie slipped into the church behind her two friends. Knowing that Christian could see straight down the aisle from the altar, she had Gigi and Rita screen her as she stepped into a small alcove off to the right. A darkened doorway in the corner led out to the back row of pews. Amy kept trying to head for it as her mother maintained a tight grip on her hand.

With Amy cornered, Katie was giving her daughter some last-minute instructions about walking down the aisle when Father Toland came up to them. Gigi and Rita greeted him and excused themselves, heading for their seats. Father Toland smiled, watching them go. He looked back at Katie and Amy, his smile growing larger.

"My, my, my, Katie. You and Amy look beautiful. Just beautiful!" He had been serving the church as long as anyone could remember. His face was lined and deeply tanned from years of working on "the farm."

The farm was nothing more than an acre of land adjacent to the parish house where Tranquillity's priest took residence. The house had originally been the temporary living quarters of John Roberts while he worked on the church. It had also given John Roberts sanctuary from prying eyes for some other work. Despite its little known history, over the years the small house had expanded into a comfortable home for the clergy. Father Toland was one of the few that loved God and the feel of the earth in his hands. But his hands were a slight bit better with God than with tilling the earth. He had always admitted that if it weren't for the church, he would starve to death as a farmer.

He gave Katie a kiss. "Are you ready now?" he asked.

"Yes!" Amy answered before her mother could say anything.

"Well, well," Father Toland said, "out of the mouths of babes." He laughed. "I see we have a packed house." Reaching out, he touched Katie's face. "I'll see you down at the business end of the church."

"Thank you, Father," Katie said as he went back down the aisle. She was starting to get nervous again. It was beginning to feel like the first time she walked down the aisle toward the man she had fallen deeply in love with.

Christian had caught her eye six years ago at a New Year's Eve party. She had been moody over a two-year relationship that had come to an end, and a good friend of hers had thought it was about time to get her out and about. A party had been the last thing on her mind, but her friend persisted and dragged her off. Once there, she had found herself surrounded by four or five men all looking to be kissed at the stroke of midnight. At one point, Christian had walked by and, in desperation, she had downed her drink and handed him her empty glass. He had come back with two drinks.

By midnight, she had been anxious to kiss him.

A year later, right after the incident at Isaac's apartment, they had been married. It hadn't been the best of times for a wedding, but she loved him and had wanted to support him. Then things had started to snowball. A few months after the inquiry into the shooting had convened, he had been forced out of the department. By the time they had made their way to Tranquillity, she had been pregnant with Amy. As they had settled in, things seemed to turn around for them. Then, two years after Amy was born, the worm had taken another turn. His sister hadn't been able to hide her battle with the cancer any longer.

Katie was sorry that Cecilia hadn't lived long enough to make it to this day. She had wanted to call off the ceremony, but Christian had said Cecilia had been insistent that they continue with their vows no matter what.

Katie looked down at Amy and felt sorrow that her daughter would never really get to know her aunt. She still made paintings and drawings for her "Auntie Cec." They had kept Amy away from the funeral, not knowing how she would deal with it. Thus far, she hadn't brought up Auntie Cec that much, and they let it be at that. But Katie felt the loss, especially today.

Amy was running her fingers through the flower petals when the music suddenly started, startling Katie from her thoughts. Taking a deep breath, she leaned over and gave her daughter a kiss on the nose.

"Amy, hon—"

"Hi!" Amy said, kissing her back.

"Hi!" Katie laughed. "Now all you have to do is walk down to daddy."

"Ho-tay." Amy started to walk toward the darkened doorway.

"No hon, this way." Katie brought her to the other side. Amy looked down the aisle and started off. She had to pull her back. "Not yet, Amy. Okay?"

"Ho-tay."

"Now, when you walk, walk *slow* to daddy. Just throw a few flowers in front of you. Okay?"

"Ho-tay." Her hand was back in the basket, mixing the petals around.

"Okay hon…now go…Slow. Okay? Slow, Amy."

"Ho-tay." And Amy started to walk down the aisle, the petals flying. Looking back over her shoulder at her mother, she almost walked into a pew.

"*To daddy!*" Katie called out as quietly as she could, pointing and trying not to laugh. She could hear Christian calling their daughter, trying to keep her attention focused.

"*To daddy!*" Katie pointed whispering again. "*To dad—*" She started to say again when a voice behind her caught her attention.

"Lovely daughter. You must be very proud." There was something in the inflection of the voice that made her back arch up. Katie turned to the man in the double-breasted suit stepping from the dark doorway.

"Oh, I, er, we are…" She felt her blood pounding. *Nerves,* she thought.

"Lovely, *lovely* girl," he said, coming closer. He had a captivating smile, but, as with his voice, there was something there that wasn't right. She could see his eyes travel from her, to Amy, and back to her. For an instant their eyes met and—*a predator waits, watching until the distance grows too great between mother and wandering baby. The glint in its eyes takes on an extra awareness just as it knows that the young and inexperienced animal is beyond the protection of its parent. The predatory eyes dictate the fate of the young animal as it turns too late and sees in its own mother's eyes no hope of escape. A shared heartbeat between mother and offspring and then a snarl, a blur of movement. In the distance a young helpless cry cut short*—Katie blinked. It was over. For that fraction of a second, Katie was somewhere else, in another time, another world, feeling the hot, harsh sun on her. She was frightened. It was beyond her experience. She took a protective step down the aisle toward Amy, forgetting about Christian.

Behind her, applause broke out as Amy reached her father, showering him with the rest of the petals. But Katie couldn't take her eyes off the man that stood next to her. Wouldn't take her eye's off he man. Her fear departed as suddenly as it had appeared, replaced with a fierce protectiveness. Now she stood guard between her daughter and the beast. Amy's music faded. In that silence, Katie took a step towards the neat little man. The Wedding March started up. Katie held her ground.

"Well, Katie, they seem to be playing your song. Christian awaits you. Sorry I can't stay. I have another family affair to attend. By the way, you look *wonderful,* my dear." He walked toward the doors of the church. Cold air blew in as he exited, making her shiver. She felt a sudden tugging at her hand. It was Amy. She had ran back down the aisle to get her mother, accompanied by goodhearted laughter. Taking Amy's hand, Katie started to cry. The two of them walked hand-in-hand down the aisle, people touched by the show of tears.

By the time they reached Christian, she was feeling better, more in control. *Nerves, just nerves. Had to be.* She squeezed Amy's hand, and Amy squeezed back with both hands. She hadn't even noticed at the time that the man, whom she'd never seen before, had called her by name.

Christian reached over and went to hand off Amy to Gigi in the front row, but Katie refused to let go of her daughter's hand. Christian saw the look in his wife's eyes and let it be. The music slowly died.

"*You all right?*" he whispered.

"*Yes…but there was this man,*" she said, looking back down the aisle. The shadow of the cross almost reached the church doors. She felt Christian take her hand. Turning back, she smiled. *Nerves, that's all.*

"*I'm so happy to be here with you and Amy,*" she said, squeezing his hand.

"*So am I,*" he whispered as Father Toland stepped forward and cleared his throat. Katie turned and glanced over the faces that filled the church. There were sixty people or so. The man had not returned. Her shoulders dropped and she relaxed a little. *Nerves.* Continuing to look around, she caught sight of Palmer in the second row. A little shock registered on her face. Next to Palmer stood an attractive blonde. Palmer smiled and waved to her as he put his arm around the woman. Katie turned to Christian, yanking on his hand. He looked at her quizzically.

"*I told you so!*" she said, nodding her head in Palmer's direction, her fears all but forgotten.

"*Oh...that's Donna*," he whispered. "*I think they're engaged. I just met her.*" Christian smiled as Father Toland cleared his throat again, louder this time. Leaning forward, he unabashedly eyeballed the two of them.

"Er, sorry," Christian said.

Father Toland gave Christian a weathered smile. "We can start whenever you're ready. You can feel free to pay by the hour, or maybe a special parking permit," he said in a not-too-whispered voice that was met with laughter. He raised his thick eyebrows at the two of them. Christian and Katie got the message. Without the petals, Amy was bored.

"Well," Father Toland's voice carried and echoed in the small church, "we are all gathered for a most happy occasion. Over the years, I have helped to hatch them, match them, dispatch them...and, now, renew them." Laughter greeted his words. "I didn't have the honor of first marrying Christian and Katie, but I did have the honor of pouring Holy Water over young Amy." He patted her on the head. Amy looked annoyed. "But, as in all things in life, everything comes full circle. Like the seasons, we wind up where we first started out."

Palmer looked at his good friends on the altar. With Donna on his arm, he was beginning to feel as lucky as they were. He leaned over and gave her a kiss.

"*Hey!*" she whispered as Father Toland spoke on. "*Does everyone here call you Palmer?*"

"Yeah," he said out of the corner of his mouth. "*I warned you about that. Everyone except Amy...and you.*"

"So now," Father Toland continued, "bringing Christian and Katie's life together full circle, I have the honor and pleasure of renewing their sacred vows."

"*Amy's a doll!*" Donna said, trying to get a better look at her.

"Do you, Katherine Ann Lord, take Christian..."

"*They look good together. Amy looks like Katie though*," she commented.

"...for your lawfully wedded husband...?"

"I do." Katie's voice was full of emotion. Father Toland turned from Katie, addressing Christian.

"Do you, Christian Ste..."

"He doesn't look like one." Donna leaned over and whispered into Palmer's ear. He cocked his head towards her.

"Look like what?"

"...take Katherine Ann..."

"A 'Stephen,' that's what."

"...for your lawful..."

"Well, that's his name," Palmer said quietly.

"...I do." Christian's voice was clear and strong.

"Oh?" she said.

"Yep, just don't call that. He doesn't like that name."

"Oh? But it's such a nice name."

"...power vested in me by this church, I renew your vows to each other and pronounce you Man and Wife—once again. You may now kiss the bride."

"Nope," Palmer said when applause broke out as Katie and Christian kissed. *"Definitely wouldn't."*

"Why?"

"Well...I think he'd kill ya if ya did." He winked and gave her a kiss.

The applause resounded in the church as a cloud began to pass in front of the sun. Christian bent over and picked up his daughter. Turning with her, he took Katie's hand, and they stepped down from the altar. As they started down the aisle, the shadow of the cross faded. Father Toland's voice rang out.

"I give you Mr. and Mrs. Christian Stephen Lord!"

What God Gave Up

"I knew it!" Katie squealed, giving Donna a hug. The houseguests were thinning out. Earlier, the party had been a mob scene with more people than expected showing up. Christian had told Katie to be the social butterfly while he made sure all of the refreshments were out. Rita helped out as well, directing and moving people around like she was still delivering the mail. Finally, as things began to slow, Katie had more time to spend with individuals. She was dying to get to Donna.

"And you!" Katie gave Palmer a little shove on the shoulder. "What's with the secrets?" Palmer looked at Donna, hesitating.

"Well—" he started, but Donna put her hand on him.

"Actually Katie, it's my fault. I teach grade school in Menkerit and I was going through a messy divorce when I first met Bart...uh, Palmer here." She laughed. "Anyway, my ex was on the school board, and he's not a very forgiving guy. The last few months have been hell, and I'm sorry I pulled Palmer away so much. It was just that I was having such a rough time, and I—"

"Donna...it's okay," Katie said, taking her hand.

Donna smiled weakly. "No, I mean...I just wanted to say..." She took a deep breath, her eyes felt full. "I'm sorry about Christian's sister," she finally got out. "I know it was bad timing with him running back and forth all of those months. Seems like all the timing's been bad lately. I'm...I'm really sorry."

Katie shook her head, also on the verge of tears. "Donna, don't worry. Everything is over now. Besides, it's about time Palmer found somebody else to mooch off of!" She forced a laugh and gave them both a hug. "This is really great!" She was feeling better and gave Donna a genuine smile. The man in the church was far away from her thoughts now. With the help of several glasses of wine, Katie had managed to convince herself that she had overreacted.

Palmer tried to get a word in between the two teary-eyed women. "Wait!" he started off. "I still get free breakfast—"

"You wish! Come on," Katie turned to Donna, "I'll show you the skylight Palmer finally finished. Oh, did I tell you he tried to kill Christian with it?" Donna laughed.

"*Hey!* That's not right!" Palmer said as the two woman started to walk away.

"Ignore him, Donna," Katie said. "Now...are you moving to Tranquillity, or what? And what in God's name attracted you to him?"

Palmer heard Donna say, "It was his crooked little pinkies…" before the two of them became lost among the other people.

"*Donna, don't listen to her,*" Palmer called after them. "*She's evil…and Katie, I have great pinkies! She loves them!*" He laughed. He had worried about everyone hitting it off, but now there weren't any lingering doubts. Looking around, he saw familiar faces from town mixed in with Katie's family members. He didn't feel like socializing too much either way. He caught sight of Christian boxed in by a number of Katie's relatives. He had that nodding, polite smile on his face. Just out of Christian's reach, Palmer saw Nestor and Gigi.

Nestor had spoken to him earlier in the church, explaining why they had run late. Hearing the story, Palmer thought it was a little strange. The guy said he had been up a few weeks ago and left his car to be repaired, and now he was back up to get it. The strange thing was that Palmer had been in Menkerit just a couple days before, and the town's only garage was closed for the next couple of weeks while the owner was on vacation. Palmer shrugged his shoulders. It wasn't his problem. He worked his way over to Nestor and Gigi. Catching Nestor's eye, he smiled.

"…don't care, he gave me the damn creeps," Gigi was saying. "That was the longest ride in history!" Nestor nodded. He seemed uneasy. "And he's *not* riding back with us," she continued. "I don't care! Martinez or not!"

"What's up, kids?" Palmer said, wishing he had a drink.

"Oh, nothing," Gigi said. "Just wanted to make it clear to my husband that the ride we gave to that doctor was a one-way deal." Gigi looked at Nestor.

"Gigi, don't worry," Nestor said looking to smooth her feathers. "James is a big boy. He'll get his car and drive down on his own—"

"Don't think so," Palmer interrupted.

"What do you mean?" Gigi was quick to ask.

"The garage is closed for vacation. They're not opening back up until a week from Thursday."

Gigi shot her husband a look. "Don't worry," Nestor said. "He can take the bus. We'll have a nice, lonely, happy ride back down by ourselves."

"Better," she commented. Palmer thought it was about time to change the subject.

"Say, has anyone seen young Amy?" he asked.

"Amy? I think she's upstairs playing," Gigi said. She turned back to Nestor, whose sincerity had apparently not convinced her. "We're *not* giving him a ride!"

"Wait," Palmer broke in, trying to save Nestor. "Let me drag the groom over and we can all bitch at him." As he walked off, he heard Gigi continuing her harangue. He shook his head, laughing. Nestor's goose was pretty well cooked. He had to bring Christian in on this. Working his way through the small group that surrounded him, he reached out and grabbed Christian by the arm.

"Sorry folks, but I need to steal your in-law, outlaw sheriff for a moment. Police stuff, you know."

"Oh sure," a pretty young woman in the group said, "we know when someone is being rescued." She gave Christian a kiss on the cheek. "Congratulations. But next time you won't get away so easily. We have to run anyway."

"Well, thanks for coming by," Christian said as he allowed Palmer to pull him away.

"We'll just run over and say our goodbyes to Katie," the young woman said leading the others away.

"Thanks again for coming," Christian added over his shoulder.

"*Bad?*" Palmer whispered in his ear.

"Not too. Part of the day, that's all."

"Well, here, thirty seconds with some buddies of yours." He steered Christian over to Nestor and Gigi. Gigi threw out her arms to him and he gave her a hug. Stepping back, he looked at his old friend.

"You know, Nestor, I can see your belly more than your pregnant wife's! Ease up on the food!" Christian laughed a little more than Nestor. Nestor rubbed his hand over his stomach.

"Gigi?" he asked. She reached out and patted his stomach.

"Just a little, hon." He smiled weakly.

"Listen, guys," Christian cut in, "thanks for coming up. And especially thanks for everyone here helping out with my sister's funeral. I couldn't ask for better friends than you three."

"Well—" Nestor started, but the rest of his sentence hung in the air. "Well—" he tried again.

"Good, Nestor. Real good," Gigi said. "You have a real knack for expressing what everyone feels."

"Yeah, well—" he tried once more.

"Give it up," Gigi said.

Palmer jumped in. "Okay, one and all, how about drinks?" he suggested. "A little toast?"

"Sure, why not?" Nestor agreed. "Besides, I'm not driving back tonight and—"

"And we're *not* giving him a ride back!" There was no joking to Gigi's voice. Christian looked at her and then to Nestor.

"Give who a ride?" he asked.

Nestor sighed. "Gave someone a lift as a favor to Martinez." Christian raised an eyebrow to Nestor. Nestor held up his hands. "Please, I'm getting enough crap as it is."

"Oh? Who—" Christian started to ask, but Katie called over to him. She had the cordless phone in one hand and Donna in tow with the other.

"*Christian!*" she called again holding up the phone. "Said it's very important."

"*Okay,*" he yelled over. "*Tell 'em to hold on.*" To Nestor, he said. "Just let me get this."

Turning, he bumped into Katie as she handed the phone to him. She looked a little tipsy.

"Here," Katie said to him. "And here," she said to Palmer, "I'm returning Donna."

"Who's this?" Christian asked again holding up the phone.

"Don't know." She gave him a kiss. "Wouldn't say. Sounded nice, though." She kissed him again before starting to talk with Gigi and Donna.

"Excuse me." Christian put a hand over his ear as he said, "Hello." He was greeted with silence. "Hello?" he said again. Then he heard the name. Turning away from the group, he started to walk toward the front door.

"*Christian?*" Katie called after him, but he just waved her off and stepped outside of the house. The last of the guests were pulling away. They waved and Christian waved back. James whispered in his ear.

"Did you ever wonder what God gave up to create us?"

"No, James, I never did."

"You should."

"Why?"

"I was your God once."

"No, you never were."

"I find that hard to believe," the voice drifted back over the airwaves.

"Where are you?" Christian's voice was level. He closed the door to the house behind him. James ignored his question.

"Have you noticed, *Stephen,* that our gods are made in our image, and our devils in someone else's?"

Christian scanned the lightly wooded area in front of the house. All was quiet. "What's your fucking point?" He walked toward the back of the house where the two patrol cars were parked. Nothing.

"What do you think I'd look like now?" The answer came back smooth and silky.

"Where are you?" Christian asked again, going around to the other side of the house.

"A heartbeat away…"

"Why don't we meet, James? Could be just like the old days, just like old times—"

"I see," James' voice broke in, "like old times…before you started this, before you crossed the Rubicon? Oh no, we'll meet, Christian, rest assured." James paused. "Did you know Martinez sent me?" Christian was silent a fraction of a second too long.

"I knew…" he said knowing he was caught.

"My, my, you had no idea? Well, no matter. Martinez is a very foolish man. He thought he could use me to further his little plans. Too hungry and too stupid for his own good. But I was cultivating him. He would have been a good source of information if he had moved correctly. Isaac was a present for him, a little boost for his career. But he overstepped his bounds. He tipped Isaac off and set you and Nestor up. But of course you've known that all along, haven't you?" James laughed. "He actually believed Isaac would get the two of you and he would come riding in like the cavalry to the rescue with two officers down. Great headlines." James' voice faded for a moment. Christian knew he was on a cell phone. James would stay mobile. That was his style. James' voice came in strong again.

"I knew what he was up to. But you had your own agenda on the table, didn't you? Too bad you killed that kid. Who actually did it? Was it Christian or Stephen there that day...or *both*? I always wondered who distracted you." James' voice fell silent. Christian waited. He knew James didn't expect an answer.

Christian stood beneath Amy's room. He stopped and looked up. James continued.

"Did you know your buddy Nestor and his lovely wife gave me a ride up? You didn't know that either, did you? You do know that I could have killed them at any point."

"It was you who killed Richard," Christian said, trying to draw the conversation away from them. Nestor and Gigi had been lucky. The only reason they weren't dead was that it didn't suit James' plans.

"True. Not one of my proudest moments, but he was already half dead. I had a few things to set up around here, so I figured I'd stir up the home front a little."

"Set up what?" But Christian knew. James was setting up a safe house. His mentor didn't even bother to answer the obvious.

"And I'm sure you read the e-mail that Nestor and I shared. He doesn't really trust Palmer anymore, does he? I wonder how sure he is of *you*. It's so *easy* to mislead them. And you really can't tell them anything, can you? How do you stand their company, *Christian?*"

Christian knew he was no longer in control of the situation. James was setting up the game board and telling him who the players were. He was watching Amy's room. A figure moved quickly across the window.

"You want me, James?"

"Katie looked so pretty, didn't she? And little Amy, what an angel she'll make one day." The hairs stood up on the back of Christian's neck at the mention of his family.

"Where are you, James?" He kept his voice level. He didn't think James would have come to his house. It wasn't an environment he could control to his satisfaction. The only thing James would try to control by cutting it loose was fear.

"You know, my boy," the voice continued, "in the beginning, when you first started out on this adventure of yours, I didn't really mind in a sense. They would have had to be eliminated sooner or later. As I saw it, you were doing The Society a favor. But, you know what the problem was Christian? Do you know the real problem with serial killers?"

"No, why don't you enlighten me?"

"They just don't know when to stop." There was a long silence. Christian broke it.

"Why don't we just end it here, James? Call it a tie."

"It's not in our nature to do so, Christian. We both know that. Bit of a *Catch-22*." James almost sounded apologetic.

Christian looked around. "This means the end of The Society, you know that," he said. The late afternoon sky was clear, but Christian knew things were about to turn dark. Overhead, he heard Amy's voice screech from her room. Someone blocked the window. Christian watched.

"Oh, no. I've been busy. This just means the end of *you*. Pity, I almost miss the old Stephen. Well, we could go on for hours, but I think I'll pay a visit to the Murphys'. You know, get them in the party mood. Oh, by the way, there is a wedding present for you in the little angel's room."

The phone went dead just as the figure moved away from the window. Amy let out another screech. Christian didn't even realize that he dropped the phone as he ran for the front of the house.

Flying through the front door, he caught Nestor off guard at the bottom of the stairs. In one swift motion, he pushed him against the banister, grabbing his .38 from under his jacket. Before Nestor could react, Christian was at the top of the stairs, bursting into Amy's room. Amy let out a scream and a giggle as she saw her father charge in, stopping short. Palmer was in the room with her, holding a metal box. Christian heard Nestor hurrying up the stairs behind him.

"Christian...what the hell...?" Nestor said, catching up. He tried to squeeze past him, but Christian blocked his way.

Christian eyed Palmer and the box with the brown earth still stuck to it. Amy ran over to her father.

"Palmer, where'd you get that box?" Christian let the .38 drop to his side, away from his daughter. He patted her on the back as she hugged his legs.

"We were playing." Palmer sounded guilty, looking between Christian and the gun. "This was with Amy's coloring books. It was dirty, so I took it away." Palmer hefted the box. "What is it?"

"Did you open it?" Christian asked as Rita yelled up, wondering what the commotion was all about.

"No, it's locked." Palmer shook it. Something moved around inside of it.

Nestor cleared his throat. "Since you're not going to tell me what is going on, can I have my gun back?" he asked as he carefully reached over and took the gun from Christian's hand.

"Sorry," Christian said over his shoulder, keeping his eye on the box. "Can I have it?" he asked Palmer as he ran his hand through his daughter's thick hair.

"Sure," Palmer said, handing the box over. Christian felt a single object slide in the box. Someone in town was dead. He wondered what had happened to all the lower lips.

Rita yelled up again, sounding annoyed that her question had gone unanswered. Christian studied Palmer. He held the box in one hand and with the other continued to stroke his daughter's hair.

"Palmer," he said carefully, "seems we have to make a trip over to the Murphys'." Amy tugged on her father's pants leg.

"Murphys'? What—"

"Unta Bart can't play?" Amy asked.

"No," Christian said, looking down at his daughter. "Uncle Bart can't play. Uncle Bart and I have to do something." Christian looked back at Palmer and shook his head, nodding toward Amy. Palmer understood, and kept quiet trying to get at the dirt under his fingernails from the box. Nestor asked if there was anything he could do.

"No," Christian said. "Palmer and I can handle it." Palmer looked up from his nails and smiled.

Harm's Way

"Just wait here till I get back," Palmer told Donna as they stood in the living room.

"Sure?" she asked.

"Yeah. I'll be back in a flash." He leaned over and gave her a kiss. "Just give the girls a hand with things if you feel like it."

"*Bart*...of course I'll help."

"Good...I know. Let me run out back with Christian." He turned to go, knocking into Rita.

"Palmer! You damn fool! This room too small for you or something?" Rita had changed out of her red dress and back into her overalls. She sized Palmer up. "Don't be no damn fool with those boys," she warned. "And stay outta those woods by the house. Damn hunters crack their rifles at anything!" She reached over and took Donna by the arm, walking her off. "Come on, Donna. The other girls are upstairs. We'll get them and clean up some of this mess these boys left around."

Palmer watched them go upstairs. He knew Rita was worried. She wasn't the only one. With Richard dead and someone calling Christian's house threatening the rest of the Murphys, he knew something was going on. He wasn't sure what, though.

Christian charging into Amy's room with Nestor's gun in his hand made even less sense to him, but Christian had offered no explanation other than the threatening phone call. He knew it was more than that. Whoever was on the phone had to have said something about Katie or Amy. Palmer knew Christian would let him know in due time. Palmer took a breath. This could turn out to be a long night, and with Donna here, he wasn't looking forward to it at all.

Cutting through the kitchen, he saw Flea-Flea asleep on top of the fireplace. The cat opened its eyes and watched him. Palmer had an eerie feeling that the cat was the only one who knew what was going on. The two of them stared at each other as Palmer went out the back, looking for Christian.

"That guy you drove up, James?" Christian was questioning Nestor and Gigi. At the mention of James, Gigi took a step closer to her husband.

"Yeah?" Nestor answered.

"Did he say anything to you on the way up that seemed out of place in any way?" Christian needed to sow some seeds of doubt. He could ill afford anyone getting the whole picture. If that happened, he would find the killing that followed distasteful. James' little gift had very nearly put him in an unpleasant situation. It was all hitting a little too close to home. He knew James had been in the house planting the metal box while they were all at the church. But how he knew about the box confounded him.

"Anything at all?" he asked again. Nestor looked at Gigi and just shook his head.

"No, nothing," Nestor finally said. "He said his car broke down in Menkerit and he needed a ride up. I did it as a favor. But there's something else we need to talk—"

"Martinez is using my husband again." Gigi jumped in. "That guy spooked me, Christian. There was something about him." Gigi paused, searching. "It was like as we drove, his eyes were boring into the back of my skull. I made Nestor pull over, and I switched places with him." Nestor tried to interject, but she didn't allow it. "I didn't want that man behind me." Christian nodded. Nestor finally got a word in.

"Like I've been trying to say," he shot Gigi a look, "we need to go over some things about him that—"

"What?" Gigi snapped.

"Nothing that concerns you, *hon*." Nestor knew he was in for it later.

"What doesn't concern me, *hon*?" Gigi didn't bother to hide the irritation in her voice.

Nestor took a deep breath. "Nothing, Gigi. I was just going to tell Christian that he was pleasant, smart, and watched everything. That's all, okay?" Gigi was about to say something when Palmer walked over.

"'Bout ready?" he asked Christian.

Gigi looked at the three of them. "Too many cops here. I'll be in the house." And walked off in a huff.

Palmer shrugged. "Was it me?" he asked.

"No," Nestor said. "Just a little touchy, that's all."

Christian needed to keep things moving. He turned to Nestor. "Listen, before you wisely go after her, it's probably nothing, but while me and Palmer are gone, keep an eye out." He took Nestor's arm, leaning in. "And keep everyone in the house together, okay?" Nestor got the message.

"Will do," he said, looking to catch up with his wife. Christian turned back to Palmer, giving Nestor a chance to escape. Nestor hurried off.

"Murphys' now?" Palmer enquired as they walked toward the cars.

"Yeah, we need to head out. You got your vest in the car?"

"Yep, in the good car. You know, the one not bitten by a tree."

"Funny, Palmer. Gun?"

"Trunk."

"Okay. I want to take both cars in case we have to split up. I'm not sure where this is heading."

"No idea on that phone call?" Palmer asked, popping the trunk. He leaned against his car.

"No, not a clue. Didn't recognize the voice; it could be a prank. Could even be the Murphys setting us up for something. Don't know."

Palmer shook his head. "Naw, don't think it's them. They're too stupid, that's my bet. Besides, if it had been one of them, you would have recognized the voice. You want to take my car?"

"Nope. Wouldn't want to put you out."

"I'm sure," Palmer smirked. He reached into the trunk, pulling his vest out. Taking off his jacket, he threw it over his shoulders, adjusting the Velcro straps. He looked toward the house.

"I think Gigi is relieved Nestor is staying here," he said pulling the straps tight. "Bet Nestor would rather be going with us right now." Palmer grabbed his gun belt as Christian went over to his car.

"Well," Christian said, "she gets a little nervous at times. Best we leave him here to face the real music." Palmer laughed. He was surprised when he saw Christian pull his vest out of the truck. He hadn't expected that.

"*You're* wearing a vest?" Palmer asked, shocked.

"The tux is a rental," Christian responded. He watched his friend laugh, knowing that he was putting him in harm's way

I Can Feel It

Katie watched as Rita and Donna left the bedroom chattering, carrying the rest of the paper dishes and cups. Amy was stretched out asleep on the bed, still in the dress she had worn for the wedding. She had refused to take it off, saying she liked looking like her mommy. Making herself comfortable, she had been fast asleep in a minute.

Katie looked down at her daughter. She knew it had been a long day for a four-year-old, but knowing her daughter, she'd be up and about in half an hour. Fleetingly, Katie's mind went back to that man in the church. With all of the commotion of the day, she had never had a chance to tell Christian about him. Her thoughts were interrupted as she heard the guys talking outside. Walking over to the bedroom window, she saw Christian and Palmer below. They were next to the squad cars, getting their vests out of the trunks. She watched as they took off their jackets and slipped their vests on. Slamming the trunks closed, they started to get into the cars.

Katie ran downstairs, but by the time she made it outside, the cars had taken the bend in the dirt road out front and disappeared from sight. She drew her arms around herself, feeling the cold. Nestor came up from behind, putting his hands on her shoulders.

"Katie, it's no big thing. Just checking the on Murphys, that's all. You knew that. It's routine for them." Nestor's voice wasn't that convincing.

"I know," she said.

"They can take care of themselves," he added.

"I know that." Nonetheless, her voice was sad. "It's just that's the first time I ever saw Christian put his vest on." Katie stared at the spot where the cars had disappeared.

"Come on, Katie. It's getting cold," he said knowing she was right about the vest.

"I know," she said, a shiver running through her. "I can feel it." And they moved back to the warmth of the house.

Cain's Pain

Christian pulled up first, angling his patrol car a couple of yards from the steps of the Murphys' house. He waited until Palmer pulled alongside him before getting out. Keeping their cars between them and the house, Christian looked around not seeing anyone. The tailgate of the pickup stuck out from behind the house, and the Murphys' other car, an old Buick, was parked just beyond it.

Christian looked over toward the woods that surrounded most of the house. They were dense, but only just a few trees still had a covering of leaves. All was quiet until Rita's voice crackled over the hand radio. Palmer took the radio from his gun belt.

"Yeah, Rita?" Palmer answered.

"You boys okay?" Her concerned voice carried, filling the silence. Christian kept a watch on the area as Palmer talked.

"Yep, we're okay. How's the cleanup going? You scare Donna off yet?"

"Everything is fine and Donna is doing more than *you* ever do, Palmer. I'm outside now. Those boys there?"

"We just got here. Their car and truck are out behind the house. I'm sure they're around somewhere. We're okay, Rita."

"I'll call back in a few then. I'll keep the radio on…be careful, Palmer."

"Okay, *Mom*. Out." Palmer grinned, looking over at Christian, but Christian pointed to the Murphys' house. Kevin had just come out on to the porch with a hunting rifle cradled in his arms. Brian and Daniel stepped out behind him. Of the three, Kevin seemed to be the only one armed. Palmer dropped the radio on the front seat of his car, keeping an eye on the them. Kevin walked to the edge of the porch.

"God*damn* shit! Don't you boys look pretty! Tuxedo, suit, and wha's tha'? Oh, I see now, fuckin' guns. Those bulletproof vests for rent, Mr. Sheriff?" Kevin raised the rifle a hair. "Wha' the fuck you want now?" he called out. Daniel and Brian stood nervous at his side.

"Kevin," Christian said calmly, "do me a favor and put the rifle down. We're not looking for any trouble with you." Christian and Palmer stayed put behind the cars. Kevin just shook his head slowly.

"Christian, ain't fallin' for ya shit! This *my* house, *my* land, *my* family!"

"*Hey!*" Palmer yelled, walking around the car toward the house with his hands up. "No trouble, we just came to warn—"

"We 'ready *got* our warnin' 'bout ya! *Ain't takin' Daniel!* Tha' for Goddamn sure." Kevin started to bring the muzzle of the gun up. His brothers moved in closer to him. Christian spoke up next, trying to keep Kevin's attention divided.

"We're not here for any of you boys. We know it wasn't—"

"Christian," Daniel cried hoarsely, "I swear, I never did *nothin'* to my brother..." His voice grew more emotional as he walked in front of Kevin. Brian took a step to follow Daniel, but Kevin blocked him, yelling at his brother.

"*Daniel*, get the fuck out—"

But Daniel was on the move down the steps toward Christian. "Yeah, yeah, I hit on 'im," he said. "We fought, but Christian, I *swear*, I ain't never kill'im!" His hands were outstretched. There was a large bruise under his right eye.

"*Daniel! Shut the fuck up!*" Kevin screamed at his brother as Christian worked his way from the squad car toward Daniel.

"*No!*" Daniel turned screaming at Kevin. "He was my *brother! I didn't fuckin' kill 'im!* I loved 'im! We jus' fought. We *always* fought. Tha's all. He was okay. Said I *kill* 'im! *I didn't!*"

"Daniel, fuckin' warnin' ya, shut the *fuck up!*" his older brother called out.

"*No, goddammit, Kevin! No! It wan't me! I ain't no Cain!*" Daniel cried out, tears streaming. Christian stopped a few paces away from him and Daniel suddenly turned, taking a short hard breath seeing Christian so close to him.

"I swear it wan't me tha' killed my brother." Daniel took another step towards Christian.

Christian held out his hand, stopping Daniel. His other hand went to the top of his gun.

"Relax, Daniel, it's okay."

"No it ain't okay," Daniel said. "We got this call sayin' ya was comin' for me. I didn't do my twin!" He took another step towards Christian.

"Daniel! Daniel!" Kevin called out, bringing the rifle up a bit. Brian put his hands on his brother, but Kevin shook them off.

"*Kevin?*" Palmer yelled out warning, his pistol now in his hand. "*Kevin!*" But the older Murphy wasn't listening. Brian began to back away from his brother, down the steps.

Daniel sobbed. "We ain't murderers. I guess we hurt 'im pretty bad, but he was still okay. He was jus' beat'n down when I left 'im tha' night. He was jus' fucked up. He weren't dead." Daniel wiped the tears away. "I found 'im the next day in the livin' room dead. I cleaned 'im up. He was my brother...my *twin*..."

Christian spoke softly. "Easy, Daniel, easy. It's okay. You did nothing wrong here." He wanted to calm him down, but Daniel rambled on.

"We always beat 'im. We meant nothin' by it. Jus' way we was...family and all tha.' I didn't kill nobody...I don't know, Christian. I don't know..."

Daniel took one final step and Christian reached out to him. It was all too much for Daniel and it was all too much for Kevin. He felt he was losing another brother. He screeched at the top of his lungs.

"*Daniel! Shut the fuck up! Shut the fuck up! Get away from tha' fuckin' shit!*" The rifle was coming up to his shoulder.

"*Kevin! Kevin!*" Palmer cried out, taking aim with his pistol. Brian's head flew between his brother and the deputy. He started to back away from the house and move closer to Palmer. Kevin now had the rifle firm in his shoulder, angled just below his face. His finger eased over to the trigger.

"*Daniel...it ain't his business! Fuck him!*" Kevin warned. But Daniel kept on pleading with Christian, crying for his dead brother.

"*Daniel!*" Kevin screamed, but Daniel was beyond it all.

"*No Cain, ain't no Cain, here!*" he cried.

"*Daniel!*" Kevin screamed again, his voice filled with rage now. Brian looked from brother to brother. Kevin brought the rifle up to his eye. Brian froze.

"Don't, Kevin!" Palmer had him dead in his sights. *"Don't!"* he cried out, just as the echo of the shot reached them.

The bullet tore into Daniel's temple, knocking him off his feet. Daniel's hand flew out striking Christian on the mouth, bloodying his lip.

"Fuck!" Christian cried out. *"In the house!"* he screamed. He didn't have to check Daniel, he had seen too much of his head disappear. *"In the house!"* he screamed again.

But it was all too late.

The second bullet caught Brian in the temple like his brother, dropping him before he could take a step. The shock registered on Kevin's face as he looked from his two dead brothers back to Christian and Palmer. Palmer kept moving and was almost on the steps of the house when Kevin snapped out of it and swung his rifle at Palmer.

"No, Kevin!" The third shot drowned out Christian's warning. It rang out from the woods, spinning Kevin's rifle in one direction as his body and head snapped in another. Before the echo died, Kevin lay dead, his head shattered like his brothers'.

Palmer was low against the steps, firing wildly into the woods. Christian ran, firing at the tree line, trying to give some cover fire.

"Palmer! Get the fuck inside!" He emptied his .357 into the trees where he thought James might be. Christian had a speed loader out in his hand with another six rounds before he had fired his third shot. Three seconds after his sixth shot, his gun was fully loaded again.

He entered the woods hunting for James.

Just The Beginning

James hid behind a tree, counting the shots Palmer fired. *Panicky*, he thought. He ignored the firing that started off to his right from Christian. He had more than enough cover from the surrounding trees, but he knew there wasn't much time. Christian was hopelessly trying to draw his attention. James was a little disappointed. He wished Christian had run over to Palmer. *Oh well*, he thought, *sometimes you have to go with the flow.*

Palmer stopped shooting. Spinning around the tree, James immediately had him in the crosshairs of the scope. He could clearly see Palmer frantically reloading his pistol as he moved up the stairs, heading for the safety of the house. Another headshot would be a walk in the park, but he had other plans. James exhaled and steadied his rifle, waiting to fire between heartbeats. As he squeezed the trigger, the rifle kicked. The bullet hit Palmer just below the vest, shattering bone and ripping flesh.

James heard Palmer's cry pick up where the echo of his shot died.

He was pleased.

Christian moved through the woods trying to maneuver behind James. As he worked himself deeper into the woods, the Murphys' house was lost from view. As he moved, the fourth shot echoed around him. *Palmer!*

"*Shit!*" he yelled and bolted through the woods for the house, no longer concerned about his safety. As he ran, a panicky deer broke cover between two trees, heading straight towards him. Trying to anticipate each other's moves, both made the same decision. The deer hit him hard and Christian spun backwards over a fallen tree, his gun knocked from his hand.

As he fell, a broken branch slipped up beneath his bulletproof vest, ripping the tux shirt and slicing into his side. The top of the branch shot out of the arm opening and missed his face by a quarter inch. Christian twisted, the pain searing through him. He pushed against the branch, snapping it, and went flying to the side. Regaining his balance, he stood up, pulling at the dried wood. He heard a truck starting up.

Christian tore at the ground looking for his gun. By the time he found it under the fallen tree, the sound of the truck had started to recede. He ran for the house. As he neared the clearing, the sound of the truck had completely disappeared.

Christian slowed. His chest heaved and blood ran down his side. The pain was piercing, and he pressed his hand against his vest. He surveyed the area. The Murphys lay dead where they had fallen. Palmer was nowhere in sight.

He edged along the woods and saw that the Murphys' truck was gone, as he had feared. He broke from the cover of the woods and ran toward the house. He didn't think he would find Palmer inside—at least not alive.

Coming to the house, Christian saw Palmer's shell casings along the wooden stairs. Carefully stepping around Kevin's body, he entered the house. A clear trail of fresh blood made its way through the house. It led out the rear door and ended where the truck had been. He slammed his hand on the old rusted Buick. Palmer was gone. Out front, Rita's voice came over the radio.

"You boys okay? Over?"

Christian walked around to the front of the house.

"Palmer, where are you? Over?"

Reaching the car, he went to get the radio off the car seat. His hand stopped.

"Palmer? Christian? You boys okay…?"

He didn't want to say anything about Palmer to Rita.

"Answer me, dammit…you boys okay…Over?"

Pause.

"Christian…? Palmer…? Where are you…Over?"

Christian knew Palmer was just the beginning. He reached into the car and clicked on the hand radio.

"Rita…Christian here, I need to talk with you."

To Kill James

When Christian came back from the Murphys', he pulled behind the house next to Rita's SUV. Going through the kitchen, he ran into Nestor. Adjusting his vest, he shook his head. But Nestor had already read the expression on Christian's face. Before either one of them could speak, they heard Donna heading toward them.

"Later," Christian whispered, "just keep her away." And went directly up to the bedroom. Grabbing a change of clothing, he went into the bathroom, closing the door. Stripping off the vest and the bloodied tux shirt beneath, he didn't have to lift his arm in the mirror to see the ragged tear along his ribcage. As he was washing the blood off, Katie knocked and came in.

"Oh, Christian," was all she could manage upon seeing him. It was only a few minutes more before he was changed and back downstairs.

"I'll have him call when he gets done babysitting the Murphy boys." Christian stood between Donna and Katie. The twilight was passing, exposing the stars.

"Are you sure he'll be all right by himself out there?" she asked, worried.

"Sure, he's fine," Christian reassured her. "We just got a tip on some new evidence about their brother and we want to keep it intact." He put his hand on Donna's shoulder, leading her toward her car in front of the house. "I'm sorry about this, Donna. I'm afraid not a great first impression on my part."

"Oh, no. It's all right, Christian, just as long as Bart's okay."

"Palmer can take care of himself," Katie chimed in. "Besides, he's known the boys forever." Rita came around front, looking nervously between Christian and Donna.

"Okay," Donna said, pausing by her car. "I have to teach tomorrow. Just tell…*Palmer*, to call, no matter what time, okay?" She smiled.

"Will do," Christian said, matching her smile. "Are you sure you're okay driving?"

"Oh, I'll be fine," she laughed, getting into her car. "I use to sneak up here all the time to see Palmer."

Katie leaned over and gave her a kiss. "We'll have him give you a call, promise." Donna smiled and started down the driveway.

As she drove off, Katie waved. When the car disappeared in the night, her hand dropped by her side. "Christian, where's Palmer?" she asked, grabbing his arm.

"I don't know," he said taking her hand away. "Let's get in the house."

Rita stopped him. "Do you think he's all right?" she asked, searching his face. Christian's eyes were expressionless. That was all the answer she needed. She turned slowly on her heels and went back into the house, suddenly feeling her age. Katie turned and watched her.

"Go," Christian said, caressing her face. "I'll be right in. Just need a little air." Katie was troubled. "Go," he said again. She ventured a smile and left.

Christian scanned the horizon. A full moon was breaking above the tree line, an opalescent disc that shone through the bare skeletal branches. James waited out there, and Christian knew he had very little time.

Amy waved to her father from the couch as she played with the TV remote, switching the cable channels. Christian waved back from the bottom of the stairs. Nestor walked over with two cups of coffee. He offered one, but Christian just shook his head. Nestor put it down on the steps.

"Girls upstairs?" Christian asked.

"Yeah." Nestor said, taking a sip.

"Listen, thanks for watching everyone while I was out."

"Sure. What about Palmer? Any ideas?"

"I think James took him. There was a smeared trail of blood through the house. Two sets of footprints. Looked like he was dragged. Found his gun inside the house, and the Murphy's' truck was gone."

"What would James want with Palmer?"

"For whatever thing is in his sick mind." Christian knew this was thin ice.

"How long will James keep him?"

"You mean alive?" Christian asked.

"Yeah…"

"Too long, I'm afraid. I would think he's in a safe house by now. He needs his time with his prey."

Nestor was about to take another sip. He stopped. "Safe house? Prey?" He was perplexed, than something dawned. "*What the fuck!* You telling me you think this guy is a serial killer?"

"Don't know for sure, but I do know he's fucking with us." Christian knew he might have made a mistake. If Nestor had noticed, he didn't say.

"Are you *sure* it was this guy James?"

Nestor was feeling used, and Christian had to play upon that. He needed time to figure out what James' next move was. Christian continued to sow his seeds.

"I caught a glimpse of him before that deer whacked into me. Small guy, sharp features, hair straight back." Nestor was silent. *Good,* Christian thought. "I just don't know if he used Martinez or if Martinez is using us again. But that fuck Martinez is involved somehow. None of this is your fault, Nestor. We were both set up again. The prick is determined to get headlines."

"Way the fuck up here? How?"

"I don't know. I just don't know."

The two friends stared at each other. Nestor was watching everything run away from him. Reading about these killers was one thing, but this was something else. He knew he had hidden things from Christian, and now wondered what Christian was hiding from him. He also understood that this was a bad time not to be a hundred percent sure about people who could have your life in their hands—or the lives of your family. He lost his taste for the coffee and put it down. Christian broke the silence.

"Listen, Nestor, I need you to do me a favor."

"Sure, shoot."

"I need to drive back over to the Murphys' to pick up Palmer's patrol car. I'll take Rita with me so she can drive it back."

"Why don't I go with you?"

"No, no good. I think James is settling in somewhere, but I'd rather have you around the house while we're gone. Just in case"

Nestor heard the floorboards squeak overhead and looked up at the top of the stairs. Gigi spied down. "Yeah sure, okay, I'll stay."

"Worried?"

Nestor kept an eye on his wife as he answered. "Yeah, I'm fucking worried." He turned back to Christian. "Yeah—" The boards squeaked again. Gigi was gone.

"Listen, here's what," Christian continued. "When Rita and I get back, I need you to take Katie and Amy with you. I want them out of town."

"But what about you?"

"James called here, asking for me. I think I'm the only one that really figures in on this somehow. Martinez or the two of them must think I know something about them. It has to go back to that whole thing with this tattoo on the inside of my lip. Martinez knew I was a marked man from that day on. I've been racking my brain, and it's the only thing I can figure."

"Okay, then why didn't James pop you from the woods like he did everyone else?"

"Too easy. He's a game-player. Serial killer or not, this guy likes to watch his victims squirm. It's all a matter of control."

Nestor hesitated, weighing what Christian had said. "This is nuts," he finally said, shaking his head. "I can't leave you here."

"You can't *not* leave me. You have to go. I want Katie and Amy safe. I want Gigi safe. Nobody is safe here."

Nestor knew he was right. He also knew Katie wouldn't abandon him, and told Christian so.

"She'll go. She'll go because of Amy. I'll make sure."

"We'll leave," Nestor agreed with his friend. "But we'll leave in the morning. We can split the night standing watch. I don't know the roads all that well, and I wouldn't be able to tell if there was anything out there waiting for us." Christian objected, but Nestor held his ground.

"Christian, you have no choice. We're staying the night. Besides, a little time will help Katie get used to the idea of leaving."

Christian was trying to calculate what James might be up to. If Palmer were still alive, James would be occupied for a while. He tried to give his friend as little thought as possible. Palmer was a good man, but Christian knew he was a dead man. He had to deal with what he had left.

"Until morning, then," Christian said. "But once that sun is up, you're all out of here."

"Fine. But what are you going to do once we leave?"

"I'm going to kill James."

A Little Longer Than The First One

The fourth shot had caught Palmer in the right hip just below the vest, throwing him against the Murphys' house. He cried out, at first not exactly sure where he was hit. The pain didn't set in until he bounced off the side of the house, landing on top of Kevin. The initial shock of being hit turned bone-grinding sharp when he saw how much of Kevin's head was missing.

Biting his lip from the pain, Palmer rolled off Kevin. His hands went to the mess of blood and bone that had been his hip. His gun lay in the doorway, out of reach. As he tried to drag himself toward the door, the pain seared through him. It was difficult to focus. He wanted to stay put because of the pain, but staying put meant certain death. He needed to get to his gun and get inside the house.

Inching his way across the porch, he made it to the doorway and was within reach of his weapon when he was violently jerked up by his vest and slammed back down on his hip. The pain shot out, engulfed him. He thought he tried for his gun again, but he wasn't sure. He barely felt the muzzle of the pistol jammed into his cheekbone. Someone whispered in his ear.

"Keep up with me, or I'll kill you the second you slow me up." Palmer stole a glance at the man above him. He looked small, dressed in camouflage. A rifle with a scope was slung over his shoulder. The next thing Palmer was aware of, the little man was yanking him halfway to his feet. The pain almost made him black out. The man held on to him.

Palmer staggered, slipping on his own blood as he was pulled and shoved through the house. He was being propelled along and didn't stop until he was out the back door and slammed into the side of the Murphys' truck.

Palmer knew he was a dead man if he got into the truck. As the man opened the door, Palmer turned, making a grab at the pistol, but the man was too quick. The butt of the pistol hit him on his shattered hip. He tried to scream, but it stuck in his throat. He felt himself pushed into the front seat. In a last-ditch effort, he tried to fight back, but the pistol smashed into the side of the head.

The pain took on a different identity than he had felt before. He didn't get a chance to slowly come around. Instead, the pain raced through him, slamming him back into consciousness. It wasn't his hip this time. He was sitting upright in a chair, duct tape binding his chest and limbs—especially his arms. He realized what was happening and fought against the scream that was welling up in his throat. He couldn't. It turned out to be a long one, the back of his head banging against the wall. When he stopped, he was drenched in sweat.

The man walked around in front of him. Palmer watched with heavy, constricted breaths, the tape tight around his chest. He knew the small house he was in. It was Father Toland's.

"Why...why you doing this?" he managed to ask.

"Fear. I need the fear."

"Where's...Toland...the priest?

"Oh, just on the other side of the river in the church, where he's praying...forever. But excuse me, I have to finish this. Time is tight." And the man leaned back into his work.

Palmer started to scream again. It was just a little longer than the first one.

A Hunter's Moon

Christian and Rita pulled up next to Palmer's patrol car. Even under the full moon, the Murphys' house was dark, silhouetted against the night sky. Rita had fidgeted with her parka, looking for a cigarette on the ride over. Finally finding her pack, she lit one up.

Christian had asked her whether she had heard of anyone renting a house in the area. Rita had said she hadn't heard anything. He knew if Rita's nose hadn't sniffed out anyone renting, there'd be a few more people missing.

Other than that short exchange of information, she had been silent as they drove. Christian was sure that Rita blamed him for Palmer. Whatever other thoughts she had about Palmer, she kept them to herself. He looked over at the house and went to cut the engine, but thought better of it.

"Here." He handed her his gun. "Anything happens, or you see anyone other than me, empty it in their direction. Got it?"

"Yep." She sounded lifeless. Christian looked at her.

"Rita, stay alert. Please. We'll get Palmer. Take this—" He reached over to the glove compartment, grabbing a flashlight from it. "Like I said, if it's not me, kill it." Rita was still silent.

"You okay?"

"I'm okay," she said. But the vacant look in her eyes indicated that she was anything but. She held up the pistol and flashlight. Christian nodded, grabbing the shotgun from its mount. Getting out of the car, he pumped a round into the chamber and flicked on the small flashlight attached to it. He walked around to Palmer's patrol car.

Aiming the weapon, he ran the small light over the interior of the car. He was too hasty. Turning back to his car, Rita was already out.

"Keep an eye peeled," he said. She simply nodded.

Walking up toward the house, he shone the light around. The Murphys' bodies were gone. Christian moved carefully.

As he mounted the stairs, he saw the front door lay open. Christian moved quickly as the light reflected off the shell casings from Palmer's gun and passed over the bits and pieces of Kevin's skull and brain that were spattered along the porch. He aimed the beam of light at the door. It traveled in, absorbed by the darkness, reflecting back nothing. Stepping in, Christian swung his shotgun around, felt for the switch, and hit the lights.

The old and torn furniture sat empty, holding nothing more than depressions of bodies that would no longer fill it. From room to room, it was the same. It was what he had expected. Aside from the bits of flesh and bone from Kevin, the only other evidence of the earlier carnage was the trail of Palmer's dried blood. James was making good use of his time. *Too good a use,* he thought. James had to be close.

Rita waited outside the car with the gun and flashlight in hand and shone it briefly on him as he returned.

"Where are they all?" she asked.

"Gone," Christian said. The two of them scanned the area. The woods were dark and silent. "Time to go, Rita. You want me to take Palmer's car?"

"No, I'll ride it back." She put the flashlight and pistol in her parka and walked over to Palmer's car. Silently, she opened the door, the interior light casting a yellowish pall over the front seat. Something caught her eye; she wasn't quite sure what she was seeing. She leaned in closer.

They were pinkies...
Severed curved pinkies....
Palmer...

Rita broke the silence of the darkened woods that surrounded the house with a scream that matched her horror.
Slamming the car door shut, Rita muffled a second scream and
started to sob.

Overhead, the night sky sparkled with a Hunter's Moon.

Looking To Go Hunting

"Goddamn it, Nestor, I want everyone out of here *now!*"

Christian had just come from the bedroom with an extra
blanket for Amy. It was the second time he had said that, yet
everyone seemed to be moving in slow motion.

James wasn't.

He knew he had to get his family and friends out. They all
seemed stuck in the living room, and Katie was still trying to
argue with him. He kept moving as he put the blanket next to an
overnight bag for them. He was having no part of her argument.
Finally, he stopped what he was doing and grabbed her by both
arms. He shook her once and looked her straight in the eyes.

"*Katie...shut the fuck up! You are not safe here!* Take Amy and go
with Nestor and Gigi!"

Katie fell silent with shock. She had never seen this look on
his face, nor had he ever raised his voice to her like this. Hurt
and anger followed the shock in quick succession. She angrily
pulled away from his grip. She didn't want to leave him, and
didn't like being forced to go. As she started to walk away
from him, he reached out for her again.

"Just go," he said, more gently this time, turning her around.
"It'll be easier this way. *Just go...*I'll be okay." Katie looked at
him and turned away again. She snatched the overnight bag he
was packing and went upstairs. Christian turned to Nestor.
His friend just shrugged.

"Where do you think he took the bodies?" he asked Christian. Gigi was out of earshot packing their things in the guest
room and Rita was in the kitchen, putting together sandwiches
for the drive down.

"Don't know. Somewhere close. Someplace he scouted out when he killed Richard," Christian said. "Wherever he is, anyone in that house is dead. But I think he'd pick somebody who lived alone. Someone old maybe." He wished he knew where James was, but he knew he wouldn't until James made his move. It was a waiting game. Rita came out of the kitchen with a large plastic shopping bag.

"Here." She handed the bag to Nestor. "Mostly cold cuts from the party, and some potato salad too. A couple of sodas and some juices for Amy." Rita was still lethargic. Christian wanted her out for her own good.

"Rita, I want you to go, too."

"No," she said plainly to him. "Tranquillity's my home. I loved Palmer, in my own way. He was my friend."

Nestor stepped up to her. "Rita, there is nothing you can do. You know that. Come on down with us. It'll be better for everybody. We'd benefit from your sunny disposition." Rita didn't rise to his attempt of humor.

"No. I'm going home for now." There was a tone of finality in her voice.

Christian had had enough. "Goddamn it, Rita!" he snapped. "I want you to go with Nestor. It's not safe around here!" He wanted as few pawns as possible for James to sacrifice.

It wasn't working.

Something in Rita seemed to break loose, and she turned on them. "Listen, you two, I've been in this town all my life. I've taken care of myself all that time. I don't need no two Johnny-come-lately's to tell me how to take care of myself!"

Christian knew that if she stayed, she was likely to turn up dead—if found at all. He also knew that any further argument at this point would only cause her to dig her heels in deeper. It was enough trying to figure out what James was up to. He didn't need any more distractions.

"Okay, Rita, okay. Have it your way," he said tiredly. "Just do me a favor and drive with them over to the turnoff by the church. I'd feel better with the two cars leaving together. It's not much out of your way."

"Not out of my way at all, Christian," she offered a weary smile. "Come on Nestor, let's get this show on the road."

Rita waited up ahead in her SUV. Gigi and Nestor were in their car waiting to go while Christian stood aside with Katie. Katie had put Amy into the back, her daughter's eyes closing. Christian had rushed them so, that Amy still wore her dress from the wedding. Katie slipped one of her daughter's coats on her. She was patting down a blanket around her daughter when she felt the tears in her eyes. Smoothing down Amy's hair, she had turned to Christian.

"Christian..." she pleaded.

"No," he said firmly. "You and Amy have to go. I'm sorry about before, but you still have to go."

"But maybe it wasn't the man I saw in the church. Maybe he was someone else." She watched Christian shake his head. "You'll be alone," she said.

"I'm okay. I can't do what I have to do if I have to worry about you and Amy. Katie, think! He taunted you at our wedding! You know I'm right." Katie put her arms around him and started to cry.

"You're alone and you're hurt. The hell with this place, Christian, *come with us."* She held him close to her.

Christian stroked her hair. "Can't. It has to end here. Go now."

"No," she moaned. *"No."*

"Go," he said gently, pushing her away.

"Christian—"

He lifted her head and kissed her hard on the mouth. He could feel the tears mix in with their kiss. Rita gave a short honk on her horn and Christian broke away from the kiss.

"Go. Take care of our daughter."

"You sound like you don't expect to see us again," Katie snuffled, wiping her tears away.

"No, I'll see you soon. C'mon, in the car, hon," he said.

Katie got in slowly, putting Amy's head on her lap. She refused to look at her husband. "Bye," she mumbled, staring at the back of Gigi's head. Christian closed the door and walked around to Nestor's side.

"Nestor—"

"Don't worry, I have them covered."

Christian looked at his watch. "About three hours down?"

Nestor nodded. "Yeah, about, give or take."

"Call."

"Will do."

"Thanks." Christian gripped Nestor's arm.

"You don't have to—"

"No, I mean it. I owe you. Gigi, watch that man of yours, okay?"

"Watch him? He better watch me!" He could tell Gigi's bravado was forced. She half-heartedly smiled. Nestor had his cop face on. Christian knew they weren't giving him much of a chance of surviving.

"Katie," he turned back to his wife, "give Amy a kiss for me, all right?" Rita honked again.

"I'll save that for you," she said, facing him. "Christian?"

"Yeah."

"Feed the cat."

Christian laughed. "See ya," he said.

"Yeah...see ya." Katie reached over and touched his hand pulling back slowly when Nestor hit his horn for Rita to start out.

Straightening up, Christian heard Gigi warn Nestor that the "old bitch drives like a madwoman."

Rita pulled out ahead, turning on the road as Nestor followed. It was only seconds before both vehicles disappeared.

Christian headed for the house. There, he found Flea-Flea waiting for him. The cat meowed, wanting to be let outside.

"So, looking to go hunting?" Flea-Flea meowed again as if he understood what was said to him. Christian pushed open the door and watched the black cat blend into the shadows.

Second Best

James waited. The passenger seat in the Murphys' truck was sticky and stained with blood. When he had got back from leaving the pinkies in the patrol car, he had been surprised to find Palmer still alive. Although he had been bone-white from the loss of blood, there he was, taking those hard-earned breaths. Palmer wasn't giving up. James had to give the guy credit. He had turned out to be a tougher character then he had expected. It seemed a shame to let him die so slowly.

James considered putting Palmer out of his misery when he got back to the priest's house. *Maybe.* Right now, though, he had a lot of other things to occupy his mind. He wished the moon wasn't so bright, but he was sure the trees along the road gave him sufficient cover. With his decades of experience hunting man and animal alike, he did what he had done second best all of his life. He closed off his mind and waited.

Be Safe

The church was off to the right of the road, standing out eerily in the bright moonlight. Nestor knew the turnoff was a short distance beyond, and he didn't want Rita to go out of her way any more than need be. Besides, he was having a hell of a time keeping up with her, and Gigi's running commentary on Rita's driving habits was also driving him nuts. He knew it was her nerves, but he had had about enough of it. But what really worked on him was Katie's silence. It was a constant reminder of the friend he had left behind. He knew the guilt they shared.

Flashing his headlights at Rita, Nestor tried to get her to pull over, but she wasn't slowing up. Flicking his brights off and on again, Rita's red brake lights finally lit up the back of her SUV and she drifted over to the side of the road. Nestor pulled up, off to the side of her.

Getting out, he saw the river that ran parallel with the road. Its rushing surface seemed to sparkle beneath the moon-lit sky. Feeling the cold air, he walked over to her, holding the front of his jacket closed with one hand. Rita stuck her face out the window. She had been riding with her window down, as if impervious to the cold.

"Anything wrong?" she asked. Rita's face was red and her eyes swollen. Nestor didn't think it was from the cold. He knew she thought of herself as a tough, independent old woman and made no comment.

"No, everything's fine. It's just that it's late and I know the turnoff." Nestor motioned with his hand in the direction of the church. "We're okay here. Why don't you just head back home?"

Rita looked down the road. The church wasn't that far off and she could even make out Toland's house across the field from the church. There was a light on there. Something nagged at her.

"Rita?"

She turned to Nestor as if in a daze. "Uh, right, all right. You sure you're okay now?" she asked.

"Yeah, everybody's good. Try to relax. I'm sorry about...everything." Nestor wasn't sure if he should reassure her with a touch or not. He decided not to.

"Yep. Be safe," she said, rolling up the window. She avoided looking at Nestor, and pulled a U-turn, heading back.

Nestor waved and watched as she drove away. He felt for her, but couldn't express it. Leaving Christian gnawed at him, but he couldn't express that, either. If Gigi, Katie and Amy had been in a safe place, he would never have left his old partner. He just couldn't see any other way for now. Gigi called out to him, and he got back into the car.

"She's okay?" Gigi asked.

"Guess so," he said as he started to head down toward the church again.

He drove right past James.

Get Outta Here Now

James watched as an SUV pulled over to the side of the road a hundred feet or so from where he was hidden. Another car pulled a little to the side of it and James was pleased when he saw Nestor getting out. In the brief time that the interior light was on, he was equally pleased to catch a glimpse of Katie in the back seat. He couldn't see Amy, but where Christian's wife was, their daughter would be right there next to her. He had counted on Christian to try and spirit his family away to safety. He was pleased with himself. Sometimes, things worked out very well.

As Nestor spoke with the driver of the SUV, James adjusted his knife and checked the clip of his 9mm. He disliked handguns. If he was close enough for a handgun, he was close enough for his knife. For a distance kill, he preferred the M21

Sniper Rifle with an ART scope. With its power magnification set at nine, the Adjustable Ranging Telescope was a death sentence for a man at 900 yards. James preferred headshots. There was a certain connection between him and his target when he viewed it through his scope. He liked to take in the little details of the face: a twitch, a bead of sweat, a blink of an eye. It was like viewing some microbe underneath a microscope. A single focus. All else ceased to exist. It was—*God-like.*

He slammed the clip back home in his 9mm as he heard the SUV start up. He assumed that Nestor had been speaking with that old redheaded women, Rita and watched as the SUV spun a U-turn. James kept his lights off and waited until Nestor passed him before pulling out from the covering of trees. Pausing at the side of the road, he looked down to his right and saw the SUV speeding away. Turning the steering wheel sharply to the left, he headed after Nestor. James waited a moment before starting to flash his lights.

Nestor saw Rita's truck lights coming back after them, but there was no room to pull over without winding up in the river. Now the flashing headlights were lighting up the interior of the car like a cheap neon sign.

"Okay, Rita," he said aloud, "what's the problem?" He started to slow, looking for some room alongside the road. Gigi looked back over her shoulder.

"She take us the wrong way?" she asked.

"No," Katie answered, "this is right." It was the first thing Katie had said since they started. She sounded nervous.

"Listen, Gigi," Nestor said. "When I get out, slide over to my side, okay?"

"Why?" Gigi didn't like this little turn of events.

"In case anything happens, you get the hell out of here."

"No—" she started.

"Just do it," he snapped. Gigi held her tongue.

Seeing an open space ahead, Nestor pulled over to the side. The headlights behind them slowed, but didn't stop. They just inched towards them.

Nestor got out and stood by the door as Gigi climbed behind the wheel. Fastening her seatbelt, she looked over at him. He could tell she was extremely nervous. Pulling his .38, Nestor held it at his side and turned toward the headlights, shielding his eyes. They were still creeping towards them.

"I don't like this," Katie said, drawing Amy closer to her. She looked out the back window. Suddenly, the brights came on, flooding the car. Katie heard Nestor curse.

"*Fuck!*" Nestor was blinded by the headlights and screamed over his shoulder to Gigi. "*Get outta here now!*" He brought up his .38 just as the Murphys' truck pulled alongside.

Nestor squeezed off a single shot, hitting James in the side. James managed to get off four.

Lights Burning

There was something.

Her nerves were shot. Rita had never felt like this before. She didn't want to believe that Palmer was dead, but she had to face that possibility. Besides that, there was something else. Something that was staring her right in the face. She needed a smoke. Searching her parka for the rest of her cigarettes, her hand came in contact with the flashlight first and then the hard metal of the gun.

"*Aw, shit!*" she swore out loud. "*Christian's damn gun!*" She took the flashlight out of her pocket, tossing it on the passenger seat, but kept the gun where it was. She knew Christian had the shotgun from the patrol car and that .45 of his. Still, she would swing by her house, grab her own shotgun, and give him a call. She had no time to waste.

She intended to look for Palmer on her own. This guy had to be somewhere, and she knew the area better than anyone one else. There was a slim chance that she might get lucky. Finding her half-pack of cigarettes in her top pocket, she lit one up.

The emotional outburst of before was over. She felt better now that she had it in her mind to do something. Taking a deep drag from the cigarette, she held it in a second. Glancing in her rearview mirror, she exhaled.

Something.

That nagging sensation made her slow down a little. She was tempted to turn around and go back, but she needed to get to Christian and to look for Palmer. Besides, she had done her job. By now, Katie and them would be safely on the turn-off heading down to New York. But something nagged. She started to speed up towards home.

Nestor lay in front of the car. One leg was twisted under the other, his .38 in the dirt next to him. Gigi was slumped forward over the steering wheel where two of the four bullets James had fired had taken her life. There was blood everywhere in the car. A body moved in the backseat amidst the carnage. A slight moan escaped from its lips.

Rita was back home. She had just finished loading her twelve-gauge Remington and was searching for some extra shells. Rummaging through one drawer, she couldn't shake thoughts of Father Toland.
Something just wasn't right.
Finding a box of shells, she pocketed a double handful and was about to call Christian to let him know she had his pistol when it hit her. She checked her watch. It was almost eleven. Father Toland *never* stayed up past nine. Yet his lights were on.
She knew he wouldn't fall asleep with the lights burning. Toland was well-known to watch every penny, whether it was from his own pocket or the collection plate. No, something was wrong. She was annoyed with herself that she hadn't realized it earlier. She was wasting time. She dialed Father Toland's house. If she was wrong and woke him, she'd take his damnation that was sure to follow, but she had the feeling that she wasn't. The phone kept ringing. She hung up and tried again, with the same result. Rita was now sure she knew where James was, and hopefully, Palmer. She dialed Christian's number to warn him.

The River Rubicon

Christian ran the silvery steel blade of the hunting knife over the whetstone. Flipping the knife over, he let it slide over the stone. A few strokes, and he flipped it back. He did it rapidly keeping time with an internal rhythm.

The knife gleamed and the hypnotic metal flash. It had been a while since he'd used his old friend. It had been a while for many things, maybe too long. But now, he knew he had to wait. It was a game. A game that had been set in motion a long time ago. *Yes,* he thought, agreeing with James. *Like Caesar's act of crossing the Rubicon, committing his forces to civil war—an irrevocable course of action.* Christian was well aware of what he had crossed over.

He glided the knife back and forth, its razor sharp edge moved so quickly that it seemed to lick the stone.

The phone rang. His knife stopped singing along the stone, as if it too had heard the ring. The knife turned quickly in his hand, showing a different side.

He let the phone ring again. A waiting game. It always was. All of these years…finally. In the end, it didn't matter who actually killed all of the members of The Society. He had done his fair share. James had taken the others, he needed to take James. He put his knife down and reached over, taking a sip of warm Pepsi.

Thirsty.

Ring.

All that mattered to him now was that he kill the *soul* of the body. That he finally slaughter that "one fear." That he was finally to sleep dreamless nights.

He picked up the phone.

"Yes," he said. The quiet voice that returned seemed to drown out everything else.

The river Rubicon.

It wasn't the voice he had expected.

Two Shots

Rita got a busy signal. She tried again. No dice. "*Shit!*" She slammed the phone down, trying the police radio next to it. Her voice was drawn into the static. No answer. She wasn't even sure it was working. Precious seconds were flying away from her. It would take a few minutes to drive over to

Christian's, but those few minutes could mean Palmer's life. She stood, indecisive for a moment. Reaching for the phone, she stopped halfway, eyeing her shotgun. Making up her mind, she grabbed the gun and headed for her SUV.

It wasn't long before Rita had the church and the points of light from Father Toland's house across the river in sight. She had planned to take the side road that ran over the small wooden bridge, so she could keep the priest's house in full view. With the bright moonlight, she knew she would have to kill her lights to hopefully come up to it undetected. *Hopefully.* She searched her pockets for her cigarettes and came up with nothing. *Shit! Bet I left them in the house!* The lack of cigarettes didn't help her mood much.

Speeding along, she passed Nestor's car at the side of the road. Rita slammed on her brakes. In a flash, her mind had taken in the gory details as the headlights panned the scene. Screeching to a stop, she spun around in her seat, trying to see through the back window. A cloud of dust from her locked tires drifted in, obscuring her view. As it cleared, all she could make out was the darkened outline of the car in the distance. She reached over to the back seat and grabbed her shotgun. Laying it across her lap, she backed her truck past Nestor's car, stopping a few yards away. Angling her truck, she let the headlights light up the scene in front of her.

The driver's door to Nestor's car was wide open, the faint glow of the interior light washing down. The black hair of the woman slumped over the steering wheel was a dead giveaway—*Gigi*. Partially blocked from her view by the car door, there was another figure sprawled on the ground. *Nestor?* Shotgun in hand, she nervously got out of her SUV and made her way toward the car.

Her heart raced. She had to remind herself to ease up on the trigger, otherwise she was going to put a hole into something. Stopping short of the car, she could see that it was Nestor on the ground near the front of the car, his body twisted out of shape. She quickly looked around, half expecting to see the bodies of Katie and Amy. But as far as she could see, the area revealed nothing. Taking a deep breath, she started toward the car again, her grip tightening on the shotgun.

The moonlight and the headlights of her truck combined, giving everything a monochromatic cast, only the blood standing out black in the cold light. Rita could see that blackness covering most of Nestor's wife. Reaching over, she touched her. Gigi's body was as cold to the touch as the night itself.

Straightening up, she took a step towards Nestor. A moan came from the back of the car, and Rita spun in the direction of the sound, hitting her shotgun against the doorframe almost knocking it out of her hands. Grabbing it in time, Nestor suddenly moved and Rita spun back, her fear finally getting the best of her.

Her hands tightened on the shotgun and with a deafening explosion, she felt it pulling off to the left. The slug tore into the earth next to Nestor's face, tiny pieces of rocks embedding in his skin.

"*Oh my God!*" Rita cried out, realizing that she had almost killed him. Nestor was trying to turn over on to his stomach.

"*Gigi...*" he whispered, sounding like he was drowning in his own blood. He lay still. Putting her gun down, she leaned in and could hear the sucking sound as the air entered and left the open wound in his chest. His sleeve was also bloodied, but she couldn't tell if it was the same bullet or he had been hit more than once. All she knew was that she had to get him out of there and to a doctor. Rita looked down the road toward the church and Toland's house. She was torn, but there was nothing she could do. Now, she had to run Nestor either over to Richardson in Menkerit or Doc Knowles. The sucking sound in his chest made up her mind. She knew he wouldn't make it to Menkerit. Doc Knowles was about to have a new patient.

Working her arms underneath his, she found it almost impossible to move the dead weight of his body. Bracing herself for another effort, she took a deep breath and held it as another moan came from the back of the car. She snapped her head around. In the excitement of almost killing Nestor, she had forgotten all about it. Slowly, she lowered Nestor's shoulders back to the ground and picked her shotgun up pumping another round. Standing, she aimed the gun at the back of the car, swearing that if anything moved, she wouldn't miss it this time.

Rita avoided looking at Gigi as she stretched her neck over the barrel of the gun trying to see into the backseat. Walking around slowly, she went to peek into the side window when a bloody face suddenly slammed against the glass. It was Katie. But the realization came too late; she had already pulled the trigger.

He Took Her

Rita had a hard time getting the back door open. The shotgun slug had torn through the metal, destroying part of the lock. She finally managed to pry it open, and when she did, half of Katie's body flopped out lifeless. Rita mouthed a quiet, *"My God,"* as Katie's face turned toward her. A deep bloody slit ran diagonally from cheekbone to jaw.

Putting the shotgun down, she tried to work Katie's limp body out of the car. Katie moaned, and Rita stopped pulling at her, cradling her face.

"Katie, where's Amy?" Blood flowed onto Rita's hands. "Where's Amy?" Katie's eyes fluttered open, and it looked like she was trying to concentrate. "Katie, where is she?" Rita could see the confusion in her eyes. This was useless. She had to get her out of the car. Grabbing her shoulders, she tugged, but had no luck.

Looking inside, she saw that one of Katie's legs was wedged underneath the passenger seat. Placing her back down, she went around to the other side of the car and opened the door, almost slipping down the steep bank and into the river. Grabbing hold of the doorframe, she reached in, working Katie's leg free. Going back around to the other side, she yanked, and Katie's body flew out of the car with her. Rita's feet slipped out from under her, and she landed hard on her ass, dropping Katie.

"Aw, *shit.*" She got up feeling bruised. Katie lay there on her side, the dark blood running down. Rita picked up her head, patting her uninjured cheek gently.

"Katie! Where's your daughter?" she asked. Katie began to stir. "Katie…can you hear me? What happened to Amy?" Katie tried to sit up. Rita pushed, propping her against the car.

"Katie, listen. Nestor is hurt, and so are you. I have to get you both to a doctor. *Do you know where Amy is?*" Katie looked at her, struggling. "Katie, *where's your daughter?*" Rita was getting desperate for time. She still wanted to get to Palmer. Katie finally spoke.

"*Amy...Amy...*" She brought one hand up to her face, grabbing Rita with the other. "*He took her...*" She spat out the words. "*He took my baby!*" she screamed, and the blood dripped down from her face, black, lacking life under the moonlight.

She Heard Her Name

"Daddy," Amy spoke into the phone, her eyes wide, staring at the man in front of her.

"Very good," James said. "Now say '*hello*' to Daddy again."

"Hello, Daddy." She could hear her name over the phone as her daddy called back to her. Hearing her father's voice, she felt a little better, but she was still afraid of the man.

"*Mommy is—*" She wanted to tell daddy about mommy screaming and about the car, but the man took the phone away from her before she could. When he did that, she felt frightened again and started to fidget.

"That's good, Amy," the man said to her. "Now, go sit next to your Uncle Bart." Amy looked over at Unta Bart. He was sitting next to someone. For the first time in her life, she was afraid to go to him. He looked very sick, but not as sick as all the other people. None of them moved, and that made her more afraid. She started to rub her hands together.

She was afraid to go near any of them, but she was more afraid of staying next to the man. Every time she looked at him, he smiled at her. Dropping her eyes, she looked down at the floor. She didn't want to look at the man or at Unta Bart. She took a tiny step away from the man, but could still hear her daddy over the phone calling out to her. She wondered when her daddy would come and get her and mommy. The man was talking into the phone with daddy. He wasn't being nice. She took another tiny step away. She heard Unta Bart call her, but she wouldn't look. He called her again, and she started to cry, remembering how her mother had screamed her name.

The True Predators

"No! Get away from my daughter!" Katie screeched at James.

James thought the whole thing had gone rather well. The one shot that Nestor had gotten off had hit him in the side just as he had raised his arm to kill him. *Good for you, Nestor.* It was more than he had expected. He hadn't thought Nestor was going to be ready for him. Fortunately for him, Nestor's .38 round had had to travel through the side of truck first, taking most of the punch out of it before it had hit Palmer's vest. Still, the bullet had knocked the wind out of him, though it hadn't slowed his own rate of fire. Nestor had taken two bullets, spinning him around the car door. That had given James a clear line of fire at Gigi; the other two bullets resting in her. All in all, it had been a pretty easy shoot. But it wasn't until he had gotten out of the truck wanting to get to Katie that he had really appreciated Palmer's vest. Even though the .38 round had been slowed, he thought he might have a cracked rib. But cracked rib or not, he couldn't slow down for the pain. There was much to do. What he was really after was in the back seat of Nestor's car.

"Get the fuck away!" Katie continued to screech at him. She was covering Amy with her body. James reached in, and Katie kicked out at him. He pointed his 9mm at Amy and nodded. Katie stopped kicking.

"Very good, Katie, fight to the very last to protect her. Good, very good. But if you kick at me again," he said, placing the muzzle of the weapon against Amy's head, "I'll put a bullet into this little bitch of yours." Katie drew Amy in closer to her.

"Good…good. I like that." James slipped his knife out of its sheath and took the gun away from Amy's head, holstering it. "Know what else I like?" he asked. Katie was quiet. James put the point of the knife underneath Katie's chin, forcing her head back.

"I asked you a question…don't be impolite." James pressed a little harder and was rewarded with a trickle of blood along the point of his knife. Katie wouldn't move her head. He liked that too.

"What...what else do you like?" she asked. Amy began to squirm beneath her.

"Well, there is something special about the female of a species. Do you know what that is?" James cocked his head and pressed in the knife just a little more.

"What is special about the female of a species?" Katie asked trying to hide the fright in her voice.

"Well Katie, I'll tell you. They are the true predators when protecting their young. Ever notice that?" The small trickle of blood stopped, but James kept the point of the knife there.

"Yes," she said carefully, "I've noticed that."

"Katie, are you a killer?" James asked.

"No," she replied. "I'm not a murderer." Amy continued to squirm.

"Katie," James shifted the knife to another spot under her throat. "I never said murderer, I said killer." Another trickle of blood. Her breathing was rapid.

"No, I'm not a killer," she said.

"Oh?" James moved the knife. Another spot, another trickle. "Would you murder me now if you could? Would you kill for your young?" Katie was silent as his eyes took the unspoken answer from her. "Good," he said, enjoying what he saw.

Amy began to squirm more. Katie warned her to keep still.

"Ahhhh, always keep the young hidden and still when there is another predator about." Amy began to cry.

"*Shhhh*..." Katie said, the knife still piercing her skin. "It's all right..." Amy settled down.

"Yes, keep them quiet, too," James said. "That's very important." Katie watched as his eyes took her in again.

"Now, here's the deal," he said. "Nobody can save you both. That's just the way it is, so...are you listening, Katie?"

"*Yes*," her voice choked.

"Very good. You may now choose." James paused. "Your life or Amy's. One or the other."

"*No*..." Katie tried, but the point of the knife was pushed deeper into her flesh. She was aware of the blood and pain from her throat, but it wasn't as painful as the coldness that she felt inside of her.

"Katie, don't argue. I've spent too much time here."

"*Me!*" Katie quickly whispered. "*Kill me!*" She looked James straight in the eyes. She had never seen such cold eyes.

"That's what I expected. You're a good mother, Katie. But I have to decline your sacrificial offer. I have to let you go. You see, the unknown is more terrifying than the known, and..." James leaned in closer, whispering into her ear. "You would suffer more by leaving your daughter to me. By doing so, you will feel that you have failed her. And fail her you must. But Katie, deep down inside, you know you can have another litter, right? And that's good, because in an hour's time...I'll be eating her tiny little *heart*."

"*No!*" Katie cried out. "*Don't touch my daughter!*" She grabbed at James. The knife was quick, sure of its path across her face. The blade cut deep, and still Katie came after him. But James had had enough of heroics, and in a swift, hard motion, he brought the butt end of the knife down against her temple.

"*Amy!*" Katie cried out, continuing to claw at him. James struck again with a resounding crack, and Katie slumped back over her daughter. James jerked her aside.

"Hello, Amy."

Couldn't Be Better

Palmer leaned against Kevin's body. The tiny pinpoints of light hurt. They were everywhere. Kevin even had one in his hands. He closed his eyes to them. Palmer knew in a short time he was going to be dead. He had been slipping in and out of consciousness for a while now, and each time he was afraid that the next time would be the last.

His hands lay in his lap. They no longer hurt. As long as he didn't move, the pain in his hip remained a dull ache. His hands had pretty much stopped bleeding, but the wound in his hip was still oozing freely. He was bleeding to death. Palmer wanted to give in to it. He was about to when he opened his eyes and thought he saw Amy.

At first, he could barely make her out. *Hallucinating. Must be.* He was having a hard time trusting his sight. Yet there she stood, the moonlight throwing a soft shadow of the cross in front of her. It was the only light in the church other than the candles.

There were so many of them. *Stars, like stars,* he thought. He didn't know if they had been there the whole time. They flickered, blinked, winked, stabbed at him. Closing his eyes to the flames, he heard James come into the church. He knew he had slipped away again. *Amy. Hallucinating.* He opened his eyes. She was still there. She was real.

He called out to her, but she wouldn't look at him. He was tired, weak, and even the simple act of calling her name drained him further. He wanted to give up, to give in to his death, but he fought off the feeling. He called again, but she just stood there in her white dress, head down.

The effort was too much. He gave up and rested against Kevin. James was still speaking on a phone, but he couldn't make out to who. Palmer wanted to sleep. He looked at Amy again and tried calling her a third time, but all he could do was mouth her name. He let his head fall back.

He was in the front pew, and he thought he had seen Toland with the other two Murphy boys in the pew on the opposite side of the church. There might have been some other bodies, too, he wasn't sure. All he knew for sure was that Amy stood in the aisle between them, very still in her dress, her head bowed beneath the cross like she was waiting for a blessing from above. Palmer whispered her name. Suddenly, like an apparition, James appeared in front of him.

"How we doing, Palmer?"

"*Couldn't...be better.*" Palmer felt the hatred, bittersweet in his mouth. The loathing gave him strength. He welcomed it.

"Well, that's a lie," James said. "You look like shit, but under the circumstances, it's acceptable." James was quiet a moment as he stood regarding Palmer. "You surprise me, though," he continued. "I was sure you'd be like your prized, troubled friend Kevin here...you know, long dead by now. You're strong-willed. That's good. I'm most impressed."

Palmer looked up at him, saying nothing. The burst of hatred was ebbing, and with that, his body was dropping again. He was finding it hard to breathe, needing more of a conscious effort on his part now. He was also conscious of his heart. He knew less and less blood was returning to it with each heartbeat. Each beat seemed to rock his body now, the sound of it echoing in his ears like someone beating an empty metal drum. The hatred drained away, and his body beat with the rhythm of his failing heart. James sat down next to him.

"Strange feeling...*death*, isn't it? Well, my dying friend, as you can see, we have a little guest." James cast a brilliant smile in Amy's direction. "She's a good girl. Does as she is told...out of fear, I'm afraid, but it's the end result that counts, now isn't it?" James paused as if admiring her, but he was looking beyond her. He continued to speak to Palmer over his shoulder.

"There is something so...natural about her. A pity. I believe she would have done well. Be that as it may, her presence will serve to guarantee that the cavalry will come to the rescue. Actually," he glanced back over his shoulder to Palmer, "I had to hang up on Christian. He wasn't listening to me. He seems to have lost his focus. I'll call him back in a moment or two." James fell silent. He turned his head back, looking out the window over the open fields and Toland's house. In the glow of the moonlight, he saw a shadowy figure moving from Father Toland's house towards the depression in the earth where the river cut its meandering path. James got up and went over to Amy. He touched her lightly on the shoulder.

"Don't move," he whispered, and continued to the window. Standing to the side of it, he cocked his head watching the person use the contours of the land for cover. *Not too bad*, he thought. But it was an open field and the moonlight was quite bright. The only real cover was with the river.

"Foolish," he whispered. Whoever it was should have kept to the contours of the river. The person's actions screamed desperation, someone worried about time. He knew very well that such a mentality could get you killed. He tapped his fingers against the glass. He had a good idea of who the shadowy outline was just before it disappeared down to the river. It wasn't too long before the figure appeared again on the church's

side. Between the river and the church was a stretch of open space. Now closer, it was the way the figure moved that confirmed his suspicions.

"Ah," James said, turning back to Palmer, "our girl to the rescue! I'll have to greet her properly." He went over to where Amy was and took her by the hand. Picking up a roll of duct tape from one of the pews, he tore off a couple of long strips. Quickly wrapping them around Amy's wrists and ankles, he picked her up, laying her down on the pew.

"Here, Amy. I want you to be a good girl and be very quiet. I won't be gone for long. *Don't*, Amy, *don't* cause any trouble...do you understand?" Amy nodded her head. "Good. Now I have to see Uncle Bart for a second. Be good." Amy was too afraid to cry. James ruffled her thick curly hair and walked back over to Palmer.

"Palmer, need something from you." James reached down and grabbed his hands. As he squeezed them, they began to bleed again. Palmer let out a small moan, holding back his painful cry. "Not bad," James commented, releasing his hands. "You are a tough one. Now, not that I think you can, but I'd rather not take the chance of you going anywhere."

James' hands were swift as they punched into Palmer's shattered hip. Palmer doubled over and fell from the bench. This time, he couldn't hold back his cries. Neither could Amy.

Not What He Had Expected

Christian had been screaming into the phone for his wife and daughter when the line went dead. The last thing he'd heard was James saying he would call back once he could speak like a gentleman. James hadn't threated Amy or Katie—he didn't have to. When Christian had heard Amy's voice, fear for his family had skyrocketed to the surface.

James had his daughter, but at least she was alive. Katie was another matter. Christian didn't think she was dead. If James had killed her, he knew the old killer would have taunted him with it. No, she was alive somewhere. Whatever the case, in a strange way, at least for now, he knew Amy was safe with James. He wouldn't harm her until they were face to face. That was the key. James wanted that audience—*needed that audience*. He had to play to a house of fear. It was what he fed off. Christian knew his nature.

The other thing that Christian knew was that if James had his family, Nestor and Gigi must be dead. All James had said about them was that Nestor had given it a shot. That was enough for Christian to know their fate. He put the phone down and waited for James to call back. This was not what he had expected.

Rita's Decision

Rita finished fastening the seatbelt across Nestor. She was grateful that Katie had finally come around. The blow to the side of her head was nearly as nasty as the slash down her face. Rita was surprised that Katie was moving around at all.

Pausing by the side of her truck, Rita tried to catch her breath. She looked down at her clothes and couldn't believe how much of Nestor's blood covered her. Without Katie, she knew there was no way she could have gotten Nestor into her truck by herself. She felt bad that they had to leave Gigi where she was, but there was no sense in wasting time or energy moving her. Nestor's blood was beginning to feel cold and sticky. It was time to move.

"Katie?" Rita called out.

"I'm right here," she said, her voice thick.

Startled, Rita jumped and spun around. Katie stood there weaving like a drunk, not sure which direction to stagger off in. Unlike a drunk, though, Rita saw that she had her eyes focused on Father Toland's place. Rita wondered if she should have told her that she thought Amy might be there. Suddenly, Katie's legs gave out and she reached back for support. The older woman grabbed her arm, steadying her. Moving Nestor had proved to be too much for her.

"I have to go—" Katie said, her eyes still on Toland's place.

"Katie," Rita's voice was strained; she was having a hard time holding her up. "We'll go get Christian."

"Sure...sure Rita." Katie said, her face looking like a bad Halloween mask. "Go anywhere...anywhere. I just want my fucking daughter back...understand that?" Katie fell back against the side of the truck, fighting nausea. Despite the chill of the night, she broke out in a cold sweat.

"Come on, hon, I'll help you. Let's get going." Rita opened the door behind Nestor, feeling like she had forgotten something. "Here," she said to Katie, "let me help you in." Katie waved her off.

"Just gimme a sec—"

"Katie, we don't—" Rita stopped, remembering she had left her shotgun next to Nestor's car. "*Shit, be right back*," she said, running over to the car. Avoiding any looks at Gigi, she grabbed the shotgun and went back to her SUV, finding Katie bent over against it. Rita put the shotgun on the floorboard behind the front seats.

"Come on, hon..." She tried to help Katie in.

"I'm okay, I'll get in." Katie turned and started to climb in. Rita ran around to the driver's side, getting in. Reaching over, she checked the seatbelt holding Nestor. He was snug. Turning, she expected to find Katie in the back, but there was nothing but an empty seat. Rita spun around and saw her in front of the truck, heading down the road. She had the shotgun in hand.

"*Shit!*" Rita got out and ran after her. "*Katie!*" she called out, and watched as Katie stopped, turning on unsure feet.

"Not going with you," Katie said, her voice a little more steady than she was. Rita looked her up and down. Katie was a mess. She was sure she had a concussion, and she was about to get herself killed.

"Katie, please give me the gun." Rita reached for the shotgun as she spoke. "We'll get Christian." But Katie stepped away from Rita, having no part of it. She pointed the shotgun at her.

"He's got my daughter!"

"Katie, you'll be killed," she pleaded.

"No, I won't." Katie lowered the shotgun and started to walk down the road again.

"*Katie!*" Rita called after her.

"Take Nestor," she called back. "Tell Christian where Amy is!" Rita watched as Katie started out in a slow jog, stopped, and started again. This time, she kept going.

"*Shit!*" Rita yelled as she went back to her truck and climbed in. Nestor was still unconscious, his breathing shallow. "*Shit!*" She slammed the heel of her hand against the steering wheel. She could make out Katie's gray figure moving down the road. She looked like she was slowing. "*Damn shit!*" Rita screamed, and dropped her head against the steering wheel. "*Goddamn it!*" she whispered. "*Bad night.*" Rita raised her head, glancing at Nestor. *Really bad night,* she thought, and started up her truck.

Making a U-turn, she searched for cigarettes that weren't there. *Damn nervous habit,* she thought and stopped. She still had Christian's gun and the shells for the shotgun, but thanks to Katie, no shotgun. She looked over at Nestor as she drove. She should never have let Katie go off like that by herself.

Katie was going to die.

Amy was missing.

Palmer could still be alive.

Rita turned her face away from Nestor. Watching the road, she lightly touched his shoulder. Nestor looked to be as near to death as anyone she had ever seen. She knew he wouldn't make it if he didn't get some medical attention soon.

She said swore softly, dropping her hand from him. *A bad night.* She started to slow down. Finally, she stopped. Thoughts ran rampant through her head.

Katie...Amy...Palmer.

"I'm sorry, Nestor," she whispered, and turned the truck around heading back towards the church and Toland's house. "I'm really sorry." She knew she had just killed him, but she had to get to Katie.

Rita sped along the road. But Katie was nowhere to be found.

It was a bad night.

Nothingness

Katie tried to run. She had traveled only a few yards when she had to stop. The blood surged through her body, surfacing where James' knife had cut into her flesh. Tentatively touching her face, she knew there was no way she could stop the bleeding unless she stopped to rest.

Can't.

Feeling faint, she fought back the urge to throw up. She was afraid that if she did get sick, she would pass out. Fighting back the feelings, she took a deep breath, concentrating on Toland's house in the distance. The thought that her daughter might be there started her feet moving again. Keeping her eyes fixed on the priest's house, she tried to pick up her pace.

Her efforts were short-lived. Slowly, her running turned into a foot-dragging shuffle. The shotgun began to feel like lead in her hands. Finding the weight of it unbearable, she wanted to throw it away, but she knew that that didn't make sense. James wasn't going to just hand her daughter back to her. She needed the shotgun to kill the bastard. She clutched the weapon to her chest.

She managed to shuffle along another hundred yards before she had to stop again. This time, there was no fighting it. She doubled over, using the shotgun for support. She tried to hold everything back, but her body betrayed her. The nausea dropped her to her knees. There was an explosion of pain, but to her surprise, she didn't pass out. Instead, a wave of crippling anger and grief accompanied the nausea. The idea that her daughter had been ripped from her arms was too much for her. Katie broke down. James had been right; this suffering was far worse than death. She did feel like she had failed her child. And deep down inside, a dark voice was telling her that she could have another child. The nausea of it all swept through her.

"You motherfucker!" she cried out, choking. *"You motherfucker,"* she sobbed, trying to bang her fist against the hard road, not finding the strength. *"You evil motherfucker."* It was a whisper.

Sobbing, Katie got back up, wiping her mouth with her sleeve. Tears and blood mixed, running down her face. She stood hunched, her guts feeling like they were being ripped from her. Taking a step, she tottered on weakened legs. Her head hurt, her heart ached. She took another step, wanting to retch again, her breaths coming in heavy.

Slowly, she began to move again. Dragging the shotgun, she staggered toward Toland's house. In her pain and agony, she didn't notice that she had wandered off the road and toward the embankment of the river. Taking another hard-pressed step, she wiped away more of the blood and tears from her face. One more step, and her foot danced in midair for a moment looking for something solid, before she toppled down into nothingness.

Missing Pinkies

Rita pointed Christian's gun. She was terrified, but not by what she saw in Father Toland's bed. His bed was covered with dark brown stains, and she realized that whatever had happened to the Father had happened up here first. He had to be dead. The bed wasn't the only piece of furniture that screamed of sickening deeds.

It was the chair in the living room that actually terrified her down to her core. She knew Palmer had sat there, bound with tape, against the wall beneath a picture of Jesus walking with children. The duct tape around the wooden arms, legs, and back of the chair had held his body tight against it, but nothing had held his head. Right above the back of the chair, the sheetrock was smashed from what had to be his head whipping around in agony. The bits of tape that were still attached to the chair were curled up with caked blood.

Rita stared. Her sight was riveted to the thickest pools of blood on the seat of the chair and along the armrests. He had sat there. He had fought against the pain. He had screamed out. She could hear him in her head. She could see the four remaining fingers on each hand clench from the pain as each pinky was—Rita ran out.

The cold air hit her hard. Clenching the gun, she was glad to be out of that house. But in the distance, the church beckoned. She was terrified. She had the feeling that whatever had been done in the house was nothing next to what she would find in the church. Suddenly, Christian's gun seemed inadequate. She brought her hands up to her head, covering her ears.

She could hear—

She dropped her hands. *No,* she thought. *It isn't the gun that seems inadequate.* Taking a breath, she started across the field toward the river that separated her from the church.

She tried to stay low. As she went, she looked over to where she had parked her truck. Nestor had still been alive when she left him, but she doubted he'd stay that way much longer. That weighed heavily on her. She was killing him in hopes of saving some friends who might already be dead.

Rita knew her only chance at survival was surprising whoever was in the church. When she had driven up to Father Toland's house, she had cut her headlights the last few hundred feet and swung her SUV around, pointing it down the road toward the church just in case she had to make a quick exit. From the distance, she had seen flickering lights in the church and been torn briefly. Something was going on in the church, but she had felt her best bet was still the house. She had been wrong. All the house did was bring out more fears. Now, she didn't want to take the chance of being seen from the church. With that large glass window, she felt she had better odds on foot. Still, she gave herself less than a fifty-fifty chance. How much less, she didn't really want to speculate.

Rita found the going slow over Father Toland's field. She was an avid hunter, but usually she had trees to hide behind. Moving bent over like this took its toll on her aging body. The river gully between Toland's house and the church would be a welcome refuge. There, she just had to follow the path that Father Toland took every day. She knew it would afford good coverage, and she could stretch the kinks out of her body before continuing on. The river was just ahead.

She let the path guide her down to the stepping stones that Father Toland had placed in the water. Before going across, Rita straightened up, realizing how much all of this was taking out of her. She looked up and down the river. The moonlight reflected, glimmered, snaking along toward her. It all looked so peaceful, so tranquil. But it was an illusion. Other things were happening now, and she had to move on.

Carefully, she made her way over the rocks to the other side. She stopped and looked at the river again. She doubted it looked much different than it had when her ancestors had settled here. Suddenly, she felt like a weak, frail old woman. The only thing that was reassuring now was the .357 in her hand.

Making her way back up the bank, she crouched low, continuing across the field toward the church. Her body started to ache immediately. The field had never been worked and the ground was uneven, littered with rocks. She tried to look at the church and the ground at the same time, but couldn't manage it and tripped over a rock that sent her sprawling.

"*Shit*," she mumbled, her face skidding along the ground, getting a mouthful of dirt. Getting up slowly, she wiped the dark earth from her mouth and her gun. Suddenly, she caught sight of someone making their way to her from the church. The person was doubled over, hands held up in the air. One leg was dragging.

Rita wasn't taking any chances. "Who the hell are you?" she yelled. There was no answer as the person continued toward her. "Who the hell—" She took aim. She was about to shoot when she saw the hands.

No pinkies—

Palmer!

She wanted to cry out. She was shocked to see him alive. He was still moving toward her when he stumbled and fell. He tried to get up, but all he could do was to work himself up to his knees. Rita watched with her heart in her throat as he began to rock back and forth holding up his dark bloody hands. She heard the soft whimpering.

"*Palmer!*" She couldn't hold back. She kept looking at his hands and remembering how she had felt finding his severed pinkies on the seat of the patrol car. But he was alive! She started towards him, hearing the moans as he continued to rock back and forth on his knees, his head down in agony.

She was almost upon him when something caught her foot. She fell again, twisting her ankle. This time the gun went flying. She lay there a moment, feeling naked without it, but Palmer was right there. *A few feet, that's all.* She tried to get up, but her twisted ankle brought her back down. She rolled, grabbing it, crying out from the pain. Taking a breath, she looked around and saw the gun. It was in reach, but so was Palmer. *A few feet, a few feet away—*

She grabbed the gun as the pain from her ankle raced through her. She heard Palmer whisper her name. Her heart went out to him. Pocketing the .357, she crawled over.

"Palmer...you'll be okay. We'll get you to a doctor—" She was only three feet away from her friend when she saw the knife on the ground in front of him. It was a good-sized hunting knife. She looked up at the figure, seeing only the back of his hands. Slowly, two pinkies appeared and James raised his head. Greeting her with a smile, he turned his hands back and forth. It was one of his warmest smiles.

"Oh God," she said.

Rita watched the smile on James' face. Her shoulders dropped and she wrinkled her face up in her best smile. For a moment, they looked liked old friends. Her smile faltered as she suddenly made a grab for the knife. Her hand only managed to touch the cold earth.

The moonlight gleamed off the blade of the knife as it was wheeled in the hands of someone who has been killing this way for over a half century. From a distance, the cry in the night almost sounded like a coyote. Almost. But Tranquillity hadn't seen a coyote in over a hundred years.

Things Were Going So Well

Palmer heard James coming back into the church. He was still on the floor where James had knocked him down. He wanted to crawl over to Amy, but he just couldn't move. He had heard James say hello to Amy and then James' hands were grabbing him, lifting him back onto the pew. Palmer almost passed out from the pain.

"Palmer! You are something else!" James sat down next to him. "How do you do it? Most of your kind would have been long gone by now." James took a deep breath. Palmer saw that his hands were covered with blood. Palmer was sure it wasn't his blood; it looked too fresh.

"Well," James continued, "Amy is fine and actually we have another visitor. Sorry, let me correct myself. Not a visitor, a friend. Hold on, I'll be right back." James patted him on the legs as he got up. The pain raced through him and he threw his head back. As the pain settled, he lowered his head.

Palmer was as surprised as James that he had lasted as long as he had. There were moments when he wanted to succumb to it, to stop the struggle. There were other moments when he couldn't wait to draw the next breath. When James had first shot him, the problem hadn't been the pain so much as the image of his body being torn apart like that. He looked at his hands. He had taken such pride in his carpentry skills. *Things were going so well,* he thought. He tried to laugh, but it came out more like a cough. *Things were going so well. Love was in the air!* He loved Donna, he loved his work, and he loved his friends. *So well.*

Now, he was shot in the hip, missing his pinkies, and sitting against a dead guy bleeding to death. *No, not bleeding to death,* he thought. That was a done deal already. He was just waiting for death. Just waiting for his body to say, *"Palmer, that's it! We're closing up shop!"* And the real joke of it all was that he didn't even know why. He didn't know why he was bleeding to death in an old church filled with dead people.

Things were going so well. His lungs heaved up and down. It was the closest he could get to a laugh.

Palmer felt himself slipping away when something fell against his body. He felt the painful jolt, but the pain no longer mattered. Through glazed eyes, he looked over, not quite sure who he was seeing at first. He stared. *Rita?* His vision cleared briefly. *Rita?* James had been talking all the while.

"…so I figure, get the whole gang together for one last hurrah. My dear late friend Mr. Simon would have approved. Christian killed him—did you know that? No, I suppose not. Actually, it was Stephen who killed him." James laughed. "I don't know how those two stand each other. Anyway, that's neither here nor there." James sounded like he was chewing on something as he spoke. Rita's body started to slip in the pew, and James grabbed her, setting her upright.

"There," he said.

Palmer saw that the front of Rita's parka was sliced up. It had been a nondescript green, but was now a deeply saturated, wet-looking reddish-brown. "She's dead," he whispered.

"Slightly," James replied. "But it went well. Gave it her very best." James placed a candle in her lap and lit it. "Keep her company, will you? Just keep the flame burning while I'm gone. I have to make a phone call and bring this gathering to a head."

As James walked away, Palmer looked over at his friend. With an effort, he stretched out a pinkyless hand touched her. He couldn't understand how all of this madness had started. Weak, his hand dropped from her, hitting something in the pocket of her parka. As the pain subsided, he carefully touched the outline of it through the parka. He laughed to himself.

There is a God.

Slowly, he worked a butchered hand into Rita's pocket. Placing his fingers around the grip of Christian's .357, he took it out, trying not to hit the exposed knuckle where his pinky had been. Clearing the pocket, he laid the weapon on his lap. The weight of the gun sent spikes of pain through his hip. Taking hard breaths, he waited out the pain till it settled back down to a dull ache once again. His breathing slowed and despite the pain, the metal felt good beneath his hands. He knew he didn't have the strength to accurately take a long shot at James. What he needed was for James to come over and stand in front of him. He started to breathe heavily again but it wasn't from the exertion. His body was finally giving in and he fought it now.

Things were going so well.

As death waited for Palmer, Palmer waited for James.

The One That Made Us What We Are

Christian waited in silence. There no sound of metal singing against the well-worn sharpening stone. All of that was done. He stood outside, facing the cold night with an emptiness deep inside of him. His hand tightened around the knife he held, turning his knuckles white. The darkness held sway around him, and he waited within it.

After James had hung up on him, he had tried calling Rita, with no luck. Knowing her, Christian figured that she was probably driving around trying to find Palmer herself. For her sake, he hoped she failed in that endeavor.

He knew she had his .357 as well as her own arsenal at home. But against James, none of that would matter. She just didn't understand what she would be facing. None of them understood. Not Palmer, not Nestor, nor, for that matter, the other members of The Society. They had about as much of an idea as the countless ones that that fallen to his touch all of these years. Christian relaxed his grip upon his knife. He understood what he faced. He understood it well.

Watching the night sky, Christian caught sight of a meteor flashing across the darkness. It was close to the horizon and brilliant in its burning, but short-lived. With its passing, his eye went back to all of the other pinpoints of light that held their position in the sky.

Many years ago, it all had seemed so easy. Just pluck them out of the firmament one by one. Extinguish the lights until there was a starless sky with nothing to wish upon. So easy. In actuality, with or without The Society, there were many more pieces of cosmic debris on their way into the atmosphere all of the time. Like claws, they would streak across the sky, ripping at the fabric of the night. Some were seen burning bright, some not. But they were always there. That was the nature of things. That was the nature of his kind.

Christian turned from the sky. He no longer cared how many lit up the sky with their brilliance, their claws. He just wanted his daughter and wife back. The emptiness engulfed him. No stars filled the blackness within.

As he stepped into the house, the phone rang. He walked over to the coffee table, where the phone lay across from his .45. He put the knife down. He doubted the .45 would be of much use. Christian knew the killing would take place at close quarters. James was a cutter.

He let the phone ring two more times before answering. A waiting game. A waiting game to see who would make the first mistake. Christian picked up the phone in the middle of the fourth ring.

James' voice was clear, cold, like the night sky. "Hello, *Stephen.* I do miss that name so."

"I want my daughter," Christian said evenly. The anger was still seething, and the fear for her, just beneath.

"You know she is safe and sound...for now."

"Where's Katie?"

"Oh yes, the little girl's mother. Alive. You know Christian, she fought well. Tried, really tried. She will suffer at the loss of young Amy and of her husband. One sunny day though, I will visit and take her from her misery. A mercy killing, if you wish. Unless, of course, she takes her own life. I can see that. It's in her eyes. Did you ever notice that, Christian? Did you ever see that side of her?"

Christian ignored James' head games. "Where is she?"

"You should find her on your way here. Unless, of course...well, you know—"

"Where are you?" he asked, picking up the .45, seating it firmly into his shoulder holster as he spoke.

"It's becoming a full *house* here."

"Where are you?" Christian asked again. He sheathed the hunting knife that James had given him.

"Did I say *house*? I meant *House of God*. You know, the One that made us what we are. Come, Christian, pray with us before all of the stars go out." The line went dead.

Christian grabbed his jacket and the extra clips. As he went out the door, Flea-Flea bolted inside, escaping the cold and bearing another gift for Katie. He ran to the kitchen and effortlessly leaped onto the fireplace mantel, settling atop of the old beam. Dropping the headless baby rabbit, he stretched his paws over it. Blood from the rabbit dripped down into the carved quote. Content with himself, he was asleep in minutes.

As Flea-Flea slept, Christian sped down the road to the church. He wanted his family back. He wanted them safe, and knew in order for that, he would have to snuff out the very last star in the night sky.

The River

Katie held onto the rocks, trying to keep her face out of the frigid water. The cold bit into her skin, stealing breath and strength. It was getting harder to hold on, and she was slipping deeper into the river. The swift-moving waters had already carried her about thirty feet downstream from where she had first tumbled in. Now they threatened to wash her further away from her daughter.

Katie looked around frantically, but in the dark she was disoriented and uncertain. She had fished with Amy up and down the river. Once, Amy, in the excitement of hooking a fish, had ventured out into the water, away from the safety of the shore. The river had quickly knocked her over and threatened to wash her away, but Katie had rushed in and grabbed her before she could be swept away. Now, in her weakened state, Katie felt the river pulling at her as it had her daughter. She imagined it a malevolent entity bent on taking advantage of her weakness, as if it looked to finish the business it had first started with her daughter.

She had to get back ashore. She knew she couldn't hold onto the rocks much longer and before long, she would be too weak even to swim. Looking over her shoulder, she saw the dark outline of a high rocky bend a hundred feet or so downstream. *Amy's favorite fishing spot?* If she was right, that's where the sandbar was. She was sure she could crawl ashore there. If she was wrong, she knew she was condemning not only herself, but her daughter to certain death. She was afraid to act. Her hand slipped. She clutched at the slippery rocks. *No good.* It was no longer her decision. Katie took a deep breath and let go of the rocks. Indifferently, the river drew her into its icy embrace.

The rushing waters sped her along like a fallen leaf. Weary of fighting, she gave her body over to the motion of the water. The river carried her quickly; a few short seconds and she was almost there. Other than the coldness, it wasn't nearly as bad as she had expected.

She was close now, and was lulled into a false sense of security when her body smashed into a submerged rock. She cried out as the impact spun her around, the pain hitting a second later. Twisting and turning, grabbing for anything to stop herself, she lost her orientation as the water sucked her under. She fought for the surface, but the waters dragged her down. Her lungs were bursting, burning. She wanted to cry out for a child she would never see again. Water seeped into her mouth. *Drowning!* her mind screamed.

She fought it. Suddenly, her face hit sand, and icy water flooded her mouth. In desperation, she dug her hands into the sand, dragging herself hand over hand. *Air...soon... soon,* she told her body. She could feel her fingernails being torn from their roots. She fought on. Slowly, she managed to pull herself along like a creature of old crawling out of the primordial waters.

Breaking the surface, she coughed out water, and her lungs expanded with that first burst of air. Her breathing came in short, rapid, choking breaths. When her lungs finally filled with oxygen, it was only then that she realized she was crying.

Time

James was wrong. Christian didn't find his wife on his way over to the church. He ran alongside the river bank, barely making out the bend in the rushing waters up ahead, hoping to find them somewhere along the river.

"*Katie! Nestor!*" His voice carried along the water's edge.

"*Katie! Nestor!*" he cried out again. There was no time. He... no, *Amy* was running out of time.

His voice echoed along the river as he called for his wife and friend one last time. Nothing. Swearing, Christian turned and ran back towards Nestor's car. He had found Nestor's .38. Checking it, he saw that Nestor had gotten off one round. He wondered if it had been before or after James killed Gigi. For now, he gave very little thought to his friend's wife. From the wounds, he knew she had died instantly. He was more concerned about the shotgun blast in the side of the car. *That could only be Rita*, he thought. *Maybe she got to the two of them.* He didn't know. He could only hope. All he did know was that time was running out.

Christian jumped back into the patrol car, his back wheels spinning in the dirt until they caught. He shot off down the road toward the church.

A Moment

Katie heard Christian calling her and Nestor's names. She lifted her head and tried to call out, but all she could manage was a low, weak groan. Reaching out with torn and tattered fingers, she pulled herself farther onto the sandbar feeling the ground getting drier. She heard their names again, the desperation clear in his voice. Her mind screamed out, but her voice could do nothing.

Shivering, she pulled her legs up under her, attempting to stand. She managed to work herself up slowly. She tried again to call out, but the cold had racked her body so thoroughly that it came out a whisper.

Katie knew she had to make it over to Christian. She had to tell him where Amy was. But to get to him, she would have to get around the rocky bend. That would mean wading back into the frigid waters and risk drowning again, or climbing over the boulders that blocked her way. She knew she could do neither. She looked back at where the river had taken her. All she needed was a few moments.

Rest, that's all, she thought. *Then I can screech my brains out. Scream until they hear me in Menkerit. Just a moment or two of rest, that's all...* But she had none. Her legs gave out and she collapsed back down on the ground.

"Christian!" she called out. She could hear herself, but that was all.

"Christian!" Picking up a rock, she tried to throw it over the boulders, but it landed a few feet away, hardly making any noise.

A moment, just a moment, that's all. A moment to stop hurting...

The sound of the car caught her ear. She looked up toward the embankment and the road. The headlights started to brighten the darkness above her like a long-awaited dawn. The light quickly faded as the car sped down the road away from her. Katie finally found her voice.

"Christian!" she screamed. Her voice echoed, screaming back at her, accusing her of trying too late.

He has to be heading to Father Toland's, she reasoned. He had to know where their daughter was. He would set things right—

he always did. Then she could have a moment. That's all she needed, a moment. She paused. *But what if he doesn't know?*

What if... Katie forced herself to get up.

*What if...*Her mind reeled with it.

She needed to get to Father Toland's. She needed to get Rita's shotgun. She no longer had a moment.

Pushing herself, stumbling back along the riverbank, Katie found the shotgun wedged between two rocks. It was wet but it seemed okay. It *had* to be okay. She couldn't afford a "what if."

Katie looked back up the embankment to the road. It was steep, and the top of it was a good six few feet above her head. The dirt was loose, and she didn't think she couldn't make it back up with the shotgun. She thought of throwing the gun first, but was afraid she couldn't climb up at all. She looked upriver. She would have to make her way upstream to Father Toland's crossing. She knew she had no time to spare.

Following the river with the shotgun in hand, she couldn't wait to kill James with it.

Hello

Every year, Father Toland would whitewash the church in time for the Thanksgiving season. The wood was old and dry, and would soak in the whitewash as if it were ingesting the paint. The finish would last through Christmas, but by Easter, whatever whiteness remained on its surface peeled away like a body rejecting a skin graft. The church seemed to prefer showing its dark weathered wood. It was a constant battle between the house of God and the painting priest.

Christian silently walked around the buckets of whitewash that Father Toland had stacked outside the church for his seasonal task. He had parked his patrol car in front of the old structure next to the Murphys' truck. He knew James was waiting for him, but he needed to see inside the church before he went in. Cocking his .45, he headed around back toward the large window.

Leading with his .45, Christian was cautious as he turned the corner of the church. Working his way along the wall, he came to the edge of the glass. A warm, flickering glow emanated from the tall window. At first, he carefully looked into the church and then forgetting caution, quickly stepped in front of the glass window.

His daughter stood beneath the wooden cross, facing out toward him. Her head was down and a candle was cradled in her hands. She looked like a miniature bride in her dress—except for the dead all around her.

The dead flanked her, sitting in the pews, heads bowed, also holding candles. Even with their heads down, Christian had a good idea of who they were. *Palmer, Rita, Toland, the Murphy boys…all dead…all dead.*

Christian slammed his hand against the glass screaming Amy's name. His daughter snapped her head up in shock, her face and eyes puffy from crying. Seeing her father, she dropped the candle and ran to the window.

"Go to the door!" Christian yelled to her through the glass. Her face was pressed flat against the window, terror etched across it.

"The door! The door!" He pointed behind her and started to move, when Amy screeched, thinking her father was abandoning her. Christian froze in place.

"The door," he yelled again as one of the bodies in the front pew moved. Christian watched, eyes wide. The body moved again. *Palmer!* He watched as Palmer raised a bloody hand like the grim reaper and pointed across the church. Just as he did, another body slowly moved with its candle in hand. Christian instantly knew who it was.

James stood facing him from the pew, his eyes glinting, reflecting the tiny flame in his hand. Stepping on the candle Amy had dropped, he extinguished its glow as he came up behind her. Amy stiffened. Christian could see the wide-eyed terror root itself deep in his daughter. She started to bang against the glass.

James casually blew out the candle he held, tossing it aside. He placed his hands on Amy's shoulders, and she instantly stopped hitting the glass. Her eyes pleaded with her father. Flashing a smile, James mouthed a *"Hello"* to Christian and snatched his daughter from sight.

He's Going To Shoot Us

Christian burst into the church. James and his daughter were nowhere to be seen. Slowly, he walked down the aisle that Katie had walked a little over twelve hours ago. Looking off to his left, he saw Palmer in the first pew. His head had rolled back and to the side of Kevin. A familiar voice spoke from the pew on the other side.

"Always loved this church. Quite a history here." James stood, turning around, holding Amy in his arms. "I think she's grown quite attached to me." He walked out to the middle of the aisle, standing beneath the cross. "You don't think you're here by accident, do you?" Amy turned her head towards her father, and her arms flew out as she twisted against James.

"*Daddy!*" she cried out, but James pulled her back to him, pressing his 9mm flat against her back.

"Put my daughter down or I'll blow your fucking head off." Christian pointed the pistol at James. His hand was steady, but he didn't have a clear shot. James knew that, too.

"Now, now, Christian. Isn't that how you killed the last little girl you tried to save? I'm a lot smaller than Isaac was, aren't I?" Off to James' side, Palmer's head slowly rolled down as he spoke, his hands tightening around the .357 in his lap. James continued.

"Doubtful, Christian? After all, you don't have Nestor to work in from the other side. Nothing to say?" he asked. "No? Well, you know you owe me a lot. After all, I saved you from Martinez. Did you also forget I pulled the strings to get you this sheriff position up here? "

"Thanks," Christian said. "Now put her down, and we can go at it one on one." From the corner of his eye, he saw Palmer moving. He wondered what his deputy was up to, but knew better than to look directly at him. James ignored Christian's offer.

"You knew The Society saved your ass after you blew the back of that little girl's head off. Now, *Stephen*, is this how you pay The Society back? This little ego trip? This murderous little temper tantrum? Taking what I cultivated one by one?" James' voice was growing heated. He paused, his eyes searching about the church. Shifting Amy in his arms, he continued, calmer.

"You know," he said, "I never spoke about Isaac to you. Never took measures against you. You were more valuable than he was. But it was also time for him to go. That's why I handed him over to Martinez. I just never expected that you would get into the act." James smiled. "Of course, Martinez denied sending you. I knew he was lying to cover himself. So I said nothing, just ruined his career." James paused again. "The Society is greater than you," he finally said.

Christian watched him. "Thanks for the update." He wasn't really listening. He was trying to think of what to do. Palmer was having a hard time moving, and Christian still couldn't tell what he was up to. All he knew was that Palmer was attempting something.

Christian began to move to the right, to draw attention away from Palmer. James turned and faced him, cocking his head.

"How close do you think I'll let you get?" James asked. Christian stopped, not pushing his luck.

"I just want my daughter." Christian was calm. From his new vantage point, he could see that Palmer was trying to raise his hands. He held something.

"*Christian*...are you going to let this happen?" James asked, his tone mocking. Christian wasn't sure what James meant. But he could now see that the thing in Palmer's hands was a .357.

"Christian?" James asked. Amy was quiet in his arms. Palmer was working the gun up onto Rita's shoulder for support.

"*Christian...Stephen?*"

Palmer now had the gun pointing at James' back. James slowly turned his head over his shoulder to Palmer.

"*Stephen*—really now, are you going to allow this sort of behavior in the House of God?" he said in a voice full of wonder. Christian looked between James and Palmer.

"*Palmer*—" Christian started but fell silent to James' voice.

"That's a pretty powerful handgun Palmer's pointing at my back. I'd say chances are that the bullet would go right through me and into your daughter safe and warm in my arms. Chances are, that is. What do you think?"

Christian knew there were no chances about it. If Palmer killed James, he killed his daughter too.

"*Palmer,*" Christian yelled, "*put the gun down!*" He wasn't sure that Palmer understood. He stepped away from James and his daughter, trying to get Palmer's attention. "*Palmer!*" he screamed out.

"*Hey! Palmer!*" James yelled over his shoulder, watching Christian. "You couldn't save the Murphy boys could you? Just fired your gun wildly—"

"*Palmer!* Don't listen to him! Just put the gun down. You'll hit Amy—"

"Couldn't save them, could you? How about Amy here? Will you let her die, too?" The sound of Palmer cocking the .357 with his pinkyless hand echoed in the church.

"Stephen…I do believe he's going to shoot us," James said in a very calm voice.

"*Palmer!*" Christian yelled.

"*I got him…Christian, I got him…*" Palmer's voice was barely a whisper, but it shouted in Christian's mind. He watched as James merely smiled, taking a step backwards toward Palmer.

"Amy," James said, "say goodbye to daddy."

"*No, Palmer! No!*"

"Christian?" James' voice sounded bored now.

"*Palmer!*" Christian screamed just as his .45 exploded, jerking back in his hands. Palmer snapped from view like a bullet-ridden cutout duck at a shooting gallery. James and Christian watched each other. Amy sobbed against the old serial killer.

"Shhhh, Amy…Shhhh. Daddy did well," James said stroking her hair with his hand. "Thank you, I was getting worried. Nice shot, though. Very nice. Feels good, doesn't it, Christian?" Christian was silent.

Keeping Amy between them, James backed over to where Palmer's body lay on the floor. Bending down, he picked up the .357. The pew where Palmer had sat now stood between him and Christian. James moved over to the side a little more, using Rita's body to further shield him. He held up the pistol. It was still cocked.

"A bit bloody," he called out. "But once cleaned up, a nice killing weapon." He gripped the pistol. "As I said, it feels good, doesn't it? Not the weapon, the *act*, the *idea* of it. And it really doesn't matter who it is, does it?"

"It does to me." Christian knew he had been used. He had been James' weapon for killing Palmer.

James smiled. "Oh? Is that so? Is this what married life has done to you? Well, Christian, it doesn't matter to me. Just my nature, you see." James put the .357 to Amy's head.

"*No!*" Christian screamed, searching for a clear shot at James. There was none. James took the gun away from Amy's head.

"*No*," Christian said softly. "*I beg you.*" Tears streamed down his face.

"I beg you?" James had a quizzical look to his face. "I beg you? No, Christian, it's not in my nature to stop." James laughed. "*I beg you?*" He swiftly raised the .357 back up to Amy's head and pulled the trigger.

Amy's body jumped.

Left Bank

Katie was so cold, and the light from the church looked so warm. Standing on top of the embankment, she looked over her right shoulder towards Father Toland's house. She should have been on the other side of the river. Katie seemed to remember somewhere that Rita had said that Amy might be at that house. The lights were on in the house, and she just couldn't understand why she was on the wrong side. Things were a little confusing. All she knew for sure was that she was failing her daughter at every turn. Using the shotgun for support, Katie had begun to climb back down the embankment when she heard the muffled shot from the church. Twisting around, she stared at the church for less than a second before breaking out into a run. Fear of proving James right and failing her daughter one last time kept her feet going.

A Smile

Click.

Amy flinched again as the revolver's hammer fell on another empty chamber. James smiled. He pulled the trigger a third time.

Click.

Amy flinched. The smile broadened, and James tossed the gun towards Christian. It clattered along the church's floor.

"It's so easy to control them," he said. "I simply took the bullets out of the gun and put the empty gun back in old Rita's pocket. Say, by any chance, did you feel hopeless just now?"

Christian lowered his .45. James had ripped at his very soul.

"Hopeless for your child here, Christian?" he said. "Hopeless for your dear dead sister? How about for your wife, your friends?"

James was leaving him nowhere to go.

"Was it all worth it?" James was reproachful. "What have you truly accomplished? The end of The Society? I don't think so. Your family is going to die, and The Society will flourish again." He shifted Amy in his arms and pointed his 9mm at Christian. James' eyes widened and flashed. His body began to rock with the rhythm of his own heartbeat. Suddenly, he relaxed.

"Such a waste," he whispered. The gun drifted from Christian to the base of Amy's head.

Christian knew what was coming. James had his audience. Christian calculated the distance between them at twenty-five feet. But James held him hostage by holding his daughter.

"A pity, I kind of liked your daughter." Amy twisted in his arms, facing her father. Kicking at James, she started to scream for him. Over her voice, James yelled to Christian. "Aren't you at least going to *try?*"

His daughter's cries slammed into him. He sought the emptiness. Sought after S*tephen*. Reaching down beyond the dark, beyond the vile, he stood beside himself watching, waiting for the other person in him to act.

A dream, somewhere a dream. Fearful nights, fearful days. Amy cried out again. The sound of his child's fright dredged up a fear so deep in him, that as it rose, it shredded everything in its path. And within that path, Stephen disappeared. Christian's soul suddenly screamed, exploding to the surface with its rage. He moved quickly. The sound of his .45 filled the church once again.

Aiming low, he tried to hit James in the legs. The bullets tore into the pew and into Rita's body, knocking her and her candle over. James held his ground and dropped Amy in front of him, firing twice at Christian.

The first bullet took Christian in the shoulder, twisting his body and sending one of his shots wild. The second one found its mark, hitting him in the chest and knocking him off his feet. As he fell, he smacked into the side of a pew and lay still on the church's floor. The echoes of the shots died out around him.

James looked down at his feet. He watched as a terrified Amy curled up on the floor. The little girl was unhurt...*for now.* He let her be. He knew he could get back to her at his leisure. There was other work to be had.

As he stepped over Amy, the blood from his leg dripped on her. Christian had gotten off four rapid shots. The first shot had found its mark. He almost lost his balance as he stepped around Rita, ignoring the flame from her candle as it started to lick at the side of the wooden pew. The bullet had blown a splintery hole through the bench and Rita's dead flesh before hitting him. James knew he was lucky, as lucky as Amy was for the moment. If he hadn't dropped the girl, forcing Christian to stop firing, it would have been worse.

He held onto the pews as he limped over to Christian. Behind him, Amy sobbed. *In time,* he thought, *in time he would end that sound.* For now, though, between bloody steps, he kept his attention on the problem at hand. He slid his knife out.

As he drew closer to Christian's prone body, he admired the way Amy's voice played against the peace of the church. The soft sound of was a fitting melancholy requiem, joining the beauty of all the tiny flames around him. This must have been the way John Roberts had envisioned it. He wished he had known the seaman turned farmer turned killer other than through the Journal. Of all the entries, John Roberts' was the purest for him. He might not have been the most prolific of their kind, but there was so much of his soul, his pain on those pages—almost as much as his son John's. Father and son. Apple and tree. James smiled as he looked around at the church the seafaring man had built with his hands. He knew the church was an illusion, a giant headstone. Indeed, John Roberts had come a long way, marking his passage in the Journal.

The points of light around James seemed to reflect off his thoughts. In his mind, he could connect them like the fine dewdrops caught on the threads of a spider's web. It had been a long journey for him. Countless days spent hunting with his father. Countless more spent alone. The war and his years of imprisonment following.

All a long journey. But the journey really hadn't begun until the very first cleansing of The Society as he fought for dominance. A third of The Society had bled their lives on his knife or exploded in the crosshairs of his scope before they bent to his will.

So many years ago. So many other souls relieved of the restraints of their earthly body as he followed his nature. It had been a long, long journey to come to this. But James knew everything had its birth, death, and rebirth. Now, Christian was about to join the others. He had expected— hoped, in his way—that at some time in the future, Christian would have added his experiences to the pages of the Journal. He had been his hope, as James himself had once been for someone else. Now, he would be nothing more than a footnote.

James looked at the man he just shot. Regretfully, he would have to start anew. Unfortunately, the years weren't ahead of him. There would be another battle for The Society, but with nothing tangible he could press his knife into; it would be a battle against time.

He looked around the church once more. The flames from Rita's candle were eating hungrily at the pew. It was a pity. He knew the church wouldn't survive the night. And that wasn't all. *Pity.*

As he brought his knife up, the light from the candles reflected off its gleaming surface. He turned it back and forth. There weren't enough points of lights in the church to reflect off the metal for all the souls that it took. He moved steadily towards Christian, leaving a trail of blood.

Christian coughed.

James stopped in his tracks as Christian coughed again, turning onto his side. James realized his mistake.

"Smart," James said, and took another bloody step over to him, pointing his 9mm at Christian's head. Carefully kneeling down, he pressed the muzzle of his weapon beneath Christian's chin, tilting it back. Just above Christian's head, James stabbed his knife into the floor. With his free hand, he prodded at Christian's jacket, feeling the bulletproof vest beneath it.

"I should have known." He was angry with himself. Christian tried to move and James jammed his gun harder against his throat. Grabbing the zipper on Christian's jacket, he jerked it down. All he needed to do now was expose the chest. After that, the heart.

James yanked at the Velcro straps, pushing aside Christian's shoulder holster and flipping the vest back. He ripped at the bloody shirt, finally exposing the chest and shoulders. Blood from his first shot ran down Christian's side.

Snatching the knife from the floor, he took the tip of the blade and pushed it against Christian's throat switching it with the muzzle of the gun. Slipping the 9mm back into his holster, James almost hated to do this—almost.

"*Such a waste*," he whispered, taking the knife away from Christian's throat. Gripping it with both hands, he raised it high above his head envisioning the beating heart beneath its point. Soon, he would hold it, feel it beat in his hands. He would cut it out from between the two shuddering, gray-mottled lungs and, before the electrical impulses stopped, his teeth would tear at it. He would then place it back, upside down; a breach birth into the world of the dead. Over a half-century of delivering these stillborn births. Hundreds taken and given over to a world he created. He was their Maker. He was their God. James' fingers tightened on the knife.

A pity.

Christian opened up his eyes and looked up at the ageing serial killer. Constellations of candlelight played off the sharpened piece of metal above James' head. James smiled down upon him. Christian smiled back.

A Mind's Eye

Katie was less than fifty yards from the church when the warm candlelit interior flared up with white-cold flashes of more gunfire. The rapid concussions boomed, impossibly loud, seemingly threatening to implode the church. Katie slowed and stopped as the flashes died. The silence that greeted her was more frightening than the echoing gunshots. The sounds of the guns firing meant someone was alive. Its silence meant someone was probably dead. She redoubled her efforts.

As she approached the window, she could make out people sitting in the front pews. On one side of the church, flames were eating at the wooden benches and the bodies there. It was a strange sight. Touching the glass, she felt the warmth of the growing fire. She tried to take her hand away, but found that she couldn't. Suddenly—*the inside of the church was filled with the dead and the dying all lit by tiny flames. They were everywhere. They rocked back and forth in their seats in motion to some unheard choir or preacher's voice. Young, old, entire families, all were butchered. It was standing room only. They all seemed to be waiting for the next one to share their hell. It was an eerie, frightening sight. She was seeing into the mind of that little man. His inner vision of the world. A mind's eye to what God had warned about evil itself. Of what the Devil proudly viewed. These were James' victims. These were his memories. These burning bodies his purpose. He had no others about him but the dead and the dying—*

Among these decaying images, Katie saw the ghostly movement of a small white dress. The illusions of the dead faded from her. The white dress flowed along the floor anticipating the movements of the limbs beneath it. She watched as a young girl crawled away from the bloody bodies on the floor and the purifying flames. Katie's hand dropped away from the heated glass. Her mind cleared.

Amy! My God, Amy! I didn't fail!

Amy stopped crawling and slowly stood beneath the large wooden cross. Her body trembled as she faced down the aisle. Katie was helpless, the glass barrier between them.

As she raised her hand to bang against it, she suddenly stopped. She saw James down the aisle kneeling over another body. His knife was high above his head and it only took a fraction of a second for her to realize that it was Christian beneath him. With shotgun in hand, Katie slammed both hands against the window. The little man whipped his head around.

Moth

James stared down the aisle as Katie disappeared from the window. Christian moved beneath him and James' expression changed slightly, his hands tightening around his knife.

In a heartbeat, the knife cut through the air, and didn't stop until the hilt was flush against the side of the body. It had been sharpened to such a degree that there was little difference between the air it traveled through and the body it entered. The knife twisted, and James' hands tightened even more around his knife that was still posed above his head. He turned back to Christian.

Christian smiled and twisted his knife again. He had played possum and worked his own knife out from its sheath. Now, it was driven into his one-time mentor. He watched as James slowly lowered his knife, the smile on his face fading. Christian no longer smiled. He yanked the knife out. Blood rolled off the smooth metal. His hand flew back.

James' smile disappeared. With a low, guttural sound he arched back up, bringing his knife high above his head, and in a flash, it flew back down.

Christian quickly twisted to his side, letting go of his own bloody weapon. His shoulder screamed out from the desperate movement. James' knife missed its mark, harmlessly catching the side of the bulletproof vest that lay open. Reacting quickly, James brought his knife back up, using the motion to slash deep across Christian's shoulder. Christian cried out, but moved with the upward momentum of the knife, pushing against James before he could bring it back down. Knocked off balance, James fell backwards against the pew. Christian's knife protruded from his side.

James felt his own weapon slip from his hands and fall to the floor as Christian crawled away from him, propping himself up against the opposite pew. Bloodied, the two predators stared at each other.

Without taking his eyes off Christian, James reached across to his side and grabbed the hilt of Christian's knife, slowly pulling it out of him. James knew he might well be dying.

"This one is yours; I gave it to you once," he said in labored breaths as he tossed the knife back over to Christian. It bounced along the floor, coming to rest next to Christian's hand. Christian picked it up and looked toward his daughter. She was frozen in place beneath the cross, the flames from the pew dangerously close. Christian knew he couldn't go to her until he was finished with James.

"It's not over, you know..." James said, his voice labored. Christian turned back and saw James had slipped his 9mm out of his holster and was now pointing the weapon at him. His own pistol was beyond his reach. Christian shifted the knife in his hand, calculating his chances. Even with the short distance between them, his odds weren't good. He needed to get to his daughter.

"*Amy, hon, listen to daddy,*" he called out, keeping his eyes on James. "*I want you to walk to me. Get away from the fire.*" Amy sobbed and called for him, but didn't move. Christian knew she didn't want to come near James.

"*Amy!*" he tried again, "*hurry, come to Daddy. You'll be safe with—*"

Suddenly, Katie burst into the church, shotgun in hand. James' eyes and gun didn't waver from him.

Katie saw James and her husband across the aisle from each other. Both men were a bloody mess. But it was the flames around her daughter that brought the scream to her lips.

"*Amy!*" Katie started to run to her daughter not caring who stood between.

James cared.

Snapping the pistol around, he fired once, hitting Katie. The bullet tore into her cutting her cry short. Silently, she dropped to her knees and fell over onto her side, the shotgun dully thumping on the old wooden floor. Her hand clutched around the weapon and then slowly relaxed.

In a blind rage, Christian was on top of James, the point of his knife just above his heart. But James was just as quick. His gun was pressed against Christian's face, stopping the knife from piercing his chest. The last two surviving members of The Society faced off, predator to predator. All time seemed to stand still, the ancient crackle of fire, the only other sound. Heated blood raced throughout the two adversaries, carrying with it the need for the continuation of the self, of the species they represented. Theirs was a stalemate of purposes until Amy cried out. It was a cry that spanned eons. James listened to it. Christian felt it.

Amy screeched again, and Christian quickly turned to his daughter. The bottom of her dress was aflame. James jammed the muzzle of the gun harder against his face.

"Can't do both," James whispered.

Dropping the knife, Christian bolted for his daughter. The pain sliced through him as he ran down the aisle, waiting for James' 9mm to boom in the church. But the only thing he met was the fearful sobbing of his daughter.

The flames were riding up the side of her dress as he reached her. Christian snatched her in his arms, smothering the flames with his hands. Amy clung to her father, falling silent.

"Moths," James said as the fire worked its way toward the altar, reflecting in the church window, the dead in the pews staring back in a mirrored Hell. With a crackling like miniature firecrackers, the old church was giving itself over to the consuming flames.

"We're all moths, aren't we?" James said, his voice carrying over the crackling.

Christian didn't have to turn around to know that the 9mm was pointed at him. He pulled off his vest from under his jacket, wrapping it around his daughter. Slowly he turned, facing James. The pistol stared down at him, was solid in James' hands.

Katie stirred.

James waited for that second of rest that his heart took between beats before he fired.

Behind him, the shotgun scraped along the church floor. James cocked his head at the sound of its movement. His heart skipped a beat.

"Damn predators…" he said and spun around.

Katie pulled the trigger.

Brightest Light

Tongues of flame engulfed the church. Blackened ash twirled and floated, caught in the spiraling smoke. The black specks of burnt wood and human flesh rode currents of heated air high into the sky. Dense smoke eclipsed the full moon and hid from view the few stars that remained in the sky. Nothing shone through. The burning church was the brightest light for miles around.

The Dream

"Do you see them?"
      "No…"

The dream no longer came to Christian. His nights were empty. He no longer dreamt of the children in the white room. He no longer dreamt of Stephen. Still, the dream came and went, continuing its journey through the night…

One Year Later

Martinez sat in his car, picking at his face. It was cold, and there was a steady wind coming off the water. He had his heater going and his windows up, trying to keep the weather at bay. He let his hand drop away from his face. Glancing at his watch, he saw it was late. *Doesn't anyone show up on time anymore?* He swore the world was taking one bad turn after another. There was enough going on in his life that he didn't need to be sitting in Ferry Point Park in the damn Bronx wasting his time. Another five minutes and he'd be out of there.

Strange.

Not good. Something was wrong here. He glanced out of his side window.

About time.

He rolled down the window about to bitch. He didn't see the gun. Five rounds from a .38 punched into him. A hand reached in and pulled at his lower lip.

I Am Him

Waiting, Nestor hit the punching bag. There was plenty of room as he danced around in his heavy-footed manner. He had finally packed up all of the baby items that Gigi had collected. Since her death, he hadn't touched anything else in the house. All of her personal things—clothes, jewelry, photos, anything in the least pertaining to her—stayed in their original places. He had taken to sleeping on the couch, so at night when he turned over he couldn't reach for someone who was no longer there.

The loss of her and the baby she carried had wounded him more deeply than the two bullets from James could ever have done. There were days and nights when he was sorry that Christian had found him in Rita's SUV. He had been so close to death. On more than one occasion after Gigi's funeral, he had almost eaten one of his .38s slugs. With each bout of depression, he had brought the pistol up, placing the muzzle in his mouth, but memories of Gigi always stayed his hand. If he pulled that trigger, he would be murdering any part of her that he kept alive. With the gunshot wounds and the amount of blood he had lost, the doctors had proclaimed him a miracle.

A miracle of life...

His physical therapy had stopped four months ago. They were so proud of their skills. But Nestor knew that they had just brought back a dead man. There was nothing living inside of him but pain.

Two swift body punches rocked the bag, followed by a hook. Nestor pushed into the bag with his shoulder, stepped back, and followed with a left-right combination. He had never gone back to Tranquillity since that day.

At one point as he had sat wounded in Rita's SUV, he had come around long enough to see the church burning in the distance. The smoke was black, and he watched as the big window exploded from the heat inside. After the window shattered, the smoke billowed out from the church and into the sky. The whole building blazed red from the flames. He swore he saw the souls of the dead running from that inferno, but it was all in his mind. He was dying and he knew his wife was already dead. Watching the flames, he looked forward to seeing her, and closed his eyes waiting for the darkness. It never came.

Nestor danced to his right, faked with a right punch, and switched his balance throwing a left followed by a solid right. He moved into his imaginary opponent with his head low, throwing another left-right combination before wrapping his arms around the bag. He had been at it for a while, and his breaths came riding in hard. He closed his eyes. Memories of Gigi haunted him, but he welcomed them. Straightening up, he pushed away from the bag and took off his gloves. Walking over to the computer, he saw that Hymn101 was finally on.

Hymn101—How are you today?

Nestor sat down. The map was back up. So were the pins. There were none in Tranquillity, though. He didn't need them—he saw them all of the time. Nestor started at the keys, not wanting any small talk this week.

Ed.Hopper2—There was no tattoo on the inside of his lip.

Hymn101—I never said there would be. That didn't mean he didn't know what was going on. He set everyone up.

Ed.Hopper2—How do I know you aren't doing the same?

Hymn101—You don't. Then again, I didn't kill your wife, now, did I? Who sent James up to Tranquillity with you? It wasn't me.

Nestor felt no guilt at killing Martinez. He had deserved to die. The year he'd waited before killing him had been the longest of his life. Still, in some way, he needed to be sure.

Ed.Hopper2—There was no tattoo.

Hymn101—Who could have set this up other than Martinez?

Ed.Hopper2—There was no tattoo. He wasn't part of The Society.

Hymn101—I also never said he was a part of The Society. That doesn't mean someone in it didn't control him. Martinez handed out information to anyone who would pay. Think, Nestor. Money. Career. Kid in college. Divorced. He was in over his head. Pick one, pick them all. Martinez was hungry and didn't care who might be in his way. He used James just as he used you and Christian to further his own ends. James was supposed to kill Christian. Afterwards, Martinez had planned to kill James, coming off as the hero. Things just got a little out of hand. Besides, James was never part of The Society. He was just a thug. We've been through this, Nestor. Any other reasons died with Martinez yesterday, didn't they?

Nestor sat back, looking up at all the different colored pins. Hymn101 was right. They had been through this before. But Nestor was still looking. Was he right to have killed Martinez? All he knew was that it *felt* right. His wife and unborn child were dead and he knew Martinez's hands were dirty in all of this.

When everything had blown up, Martinez had had him transferred to another precinct and even pushed behind the scenes to get him off the force. But he couldn't push too hard without too many people prying. He wanted to stay as clean as possible. Tranquillity had turned into one big mess.

No, Martinez was dirty, but he wasn't sure he was as dirty as Hymn101 made him out to be. Even so, Nestor was glad he was dead. He had known in his heart that he was going to kill him. He had known it as soon as Martinez told him not to say anything about the meeting with James. He had told him that that piece of information wouldn't be any good for anyone's career. Besides, he would deny any knowledge of the man. And Martinez pointed out that the only other person that could put James next to him with any bit of certainty was the waiter from the restaurant, who had disappeared without a trace. The maître d' was also nowhere to be found. Nestor had just nodded as they shook hands, agreeing to silence. He was just surprised that he had waited this long to kill him.

Nestor leaned back to the keys, feeling each one take a breath from him. There was someone else that was dirty here. Nestor typed.

Ed.Hopper2—Should I look for anymore black pins?

Hymn101—Still doing that? No. Don't look. It's all over now.

Nestor read the last four words. He shook his head. "What about you?" He typed in.

Hymn101—It's over. Let it be. Go paint.

No, Nestor thought. *I'm not a painter, I'm a cop.*

Ed.Hopper2—Who are you?

Hymn101—You asked that question once before. I answered it.

Nestor had tried to trace the man on his own, but with no luck. He could have brought in expert help, but that might have involved too many people with too many questions, and he had had a police lieutenant to kill. He typed again. It was the cop in him.

Ed.Hopper2—Who are you?

Christian sat up in the bedroom and stared at his computer screen.

Ed.Hopper2—Who are you?

He was well aware that if Nestor really wanted to find out who Hymn101 was, he could. The pain of losing Gigi held him in place, but sooner or later, he knew the old Nestor would surface. He had a feeling that it was starting already. In the meantime, he had had to use Nestor to get rid of Martinez. He couldn't control Martinez, and he was fearful that Nestor would finally realize that Martinez was just a pawn in a game he knew nothing of. Christian didn't want to be put in the position where he would have to kill his friend. He had needed to work on Nestor's survivor guilt keeping him focused on that pain and making Martinez the ultimate cause of it. Now that Martinez was dead, he needed to sever the connection with Nestor. He no longer had to pretend to be Hymn101.

Ed.Hopper2—Who are you?

"Christian!" Katie called up to him from the bottom of the steps. He hadn't expected Katie and Amy back from Menkerit so soon. She had become good friends with Donna after Palmer's funeral. Each had loved Palmer in their own way, and they found solace in each other's company. Christian moved his cursor to "EXIT." The cursor blinked, waiting for a command. Katie was talking as she walked up the stairs.

"Hon, are you coming with us?" she asked from the top of the stairs. A long, thin scar ran along the side of her face. The plastic surgeon had done an excellent job. It was only notice-able when she tanned, which happened even less than before. Another heavier, thicker scar ran along her ribcage. It had taken two separate operations to repair the damage that the slug from James' 9mm had done to her body. Katie had her bad days, but for the most part, she was doing surprisingly well. In the end, saving her daughter had saved her sanity.

Amy was another story. She had become more introverted, and was having recurring nightmares, though they were not as frequent as they had been. She was getting better, but seldom did she venture far from them.

The funerals for Palmer, Rita, Father Toland, and the Murphys drew some media attention over the crazed madman that had shattered the peace of the small town. Newscaster after newscaster made clever reference to the town's name and the murders that had occurred there, ending their report with knowing looks. In actuality, they knew nothing. Christian had made sure of that. Since he was sheriff and controlled the crime scene, he was able to control the evidence as well. He kept all mention of mutilations out of the official reports. With Richardson's incompetent autopsies, the charred bodies took their secrets to the graves with them.

The church that one of the town's founding fathers had built with his own hands was never rebuilt. There were plans, but once the burnt rubble was cleared away and the old skel-etons discovered beneath the altar by the construction crew, all work stopped. Most people believed it to be an old gravesite, as the town council claimed, but not all. Twenty-one skel-etons were found.

Three deep graves held seven bodies each. Rumors from the construction workers had some of the remains with holes in the skulls. Other skeletal remains showed the marks of a sharp tool, like an axe or a saw that a carpenter might use. The remains were carted off to Menkerit County for further examination under the supervision of Joe Richardson. Some-how, they were misplaced. This incident added fuel to the fire for more talk. The remains of the madman James were also misplaced. Not long after, Joe Richardson, like Sheriff Adams, had taken off for parts unknown. Menkerit County was now in the process of looking for another medical examiner and local doctor.

So far, Christian had survived.

Ed.Hopper2—Who are you?

The question stared, asked in real time racing across cyberspace.

"C'mon Christian," Katie said, "Amy's raring to go. Get away from that thing." Another set of footsteps started to stomp up the stairs. Amy appeared next to her mother. They took each other's hands.

"Yeah Daddy, get away! Fish are waiting!" Christian started to laugh. He moved the cursor away from "EXIT."

"Okay, okay," he said, "just let me turn this thing off and we'll go. Be down in a sec."

"All right," Katie said, starting down with Amy. "I'll make some sandwiches. Don't take too long now. And wear a warm jacket. It's getting chilly out."

"Will do…hey, Amy," Christian called out. His daughter peeked back over the stairs to him. "Why don't you make some hot chocolate to bring with us?"

"Ho…" Amy hesitated, correcting herself. "Okay!" She beamed, and disappeared back down the stairs. Christian turned back to his computer screen. The question still waited for him.

Ed.Hopper2—*"Who are you?"*

"I am Him," Christian replied.

"No." Nestor wrote back. *"Something is different…Who are you?"*

"I am Him."

"Who are you?" The question demanded.

Christian watched his screen. If he wasn't careful, Nestor could push him in the direction he had fought so hard against. Hymn101 had to break with Ed.Hopper2.

"Do not push me, Nestor. You survived once. It's over." Christian signed off. Bending under the desk, he retrieved an old, worn leather book. Leather straps that had been replaced many times over held its loose pages together. Some of the pages between its thick heavy cover were quite old and worn, their stories

hard to decipher. Others looked as if they had been penned yesterday.

Christian had found it in Amy's closet that day, alongside where the box had been. He didn't know how Palmer had missed it, but he was glad of it. To this day, he didn't know what James had done with the lower lips he had taken from the metal box, nor whose heart he had left as a calling card. But he did know that James had had two reasons for leaving the book. First and foremost, James had intended to retrieve it after killing them all. But for some reason it didn't go according his plan, this was James' way of passing the Journal on. Over the many years of its existence, the Journal had fallen into various hands, but it always found a proper owner, a home. It was simply the nature of the book to do so. Within its new home, no new entries had been made between its dark covers. Christian didn't need to.

His hands ran over the book. He opened it at random, and it fell to a dog-eared page that had intrigued him. Careful with the pages, he ran his eyes over the writing. The entry he opened up to was dated August 15, 1836. The handwriting was strong, with a certain flair. The words were those of an educated and well-traveled man of the time. What amazed Christian was that it had been written in this very house.

The words lay before him, as silent as when they had first been written, but far from lifeless.

"It has been a Year now since my Father's Death. I have heard the Rumors, but believed Nothing of them until my Hands came across this Book. I have been shown many Ways and Manners of the World, but None, I Fear, such as each Page offers here. I have taken the Liberty of moving my Father's Body from his original Resting Place to one of greater Safety. That Act was undertaken by the Suggestion of Mr. Burns. I don't know if it was for the Safety of my Father's Remains, or if Mr. Burns wished Me to come across this Book. All I know is that a Fever has swept through this Town that has forgotten that it owes its Birth to the Sweat of my Father. It is a Fever not only of the Body, but one that also Inflicts the Soul..."

Christian closed the book. He knew he had better go downstairs before the two women in his life came back up. Getting up from the desk, he took the book over to the cor-

ner of the bedroom. With a thin pocketknife, he worked two
wooden planks up from the floor, placing the book beneath
them in an old metal box that he had wedged between two
thick support beams.

The Journal was a Rosetta Stone of Death. It spanned cen-
turies and cultures, but ultimately it spoke a common language.
He understood the spell the book could cast and the danger it
posed to him. He had to either find a more secure place for it,
or destroy it...

Destroy it.

Christian touched the cover.

Destroy it.

Maybe.

He had a new life, and they were calling up to him. He
closed the lid of the box and replaced the two floorboards.

Soon.

Maybe...

Christian smiled and went down to the kitchen.

Good Kitty

Flea-Flea trotted from the woods that surrounded the house.
His jaws were firmly clamped on the tough piece of meat.
Behind him, uneven footsteps crushed leaves and twigs, retreating deeper into the woods. Suddenly the footsteps stopped
and turned. The crippled body settled in and the dark fleeting
eyes followed the movement of the cat.

"Good kitty."

Just A Madman

"Amy!" Katie called from the kitchen. She heard her daughter
drop something in the living room and come running with her
coat on, ready to go. "Be a good girl and bring your pole outside
for me." Katie handed the small fishing rod to her. Turning to
Christian, "Pass me some of those sandwiches," she said as
Amy opened the door. Flea-Flea streaked in and ran underneath the kitchen table. Startled, Amy screeched, then started
to laugh.

"Here, hon," Christian said straightening up. He held out the sandwiches she had dropped when Amy let out her scream. Katie was looking over at her daughter.

Amy had forgotten about her task of bringing her fishing pole outside and was now trying to get Flea-Flea out from under the table. The cat wouldn't budge. Christian touched his wife's shoulder and she jumped as if she'd touched a live wire. Katie's hand shook uncontrollably as it took the sandwich from him. He took her hand and held it. Her eyes were wide with fear.

"Tell me he's dead." Her voice reflecting her fear.

"It's over. It's been a year now," he said reassuringly. But the terror wouldn't leave her face.

"Tell me," she pleaded.

Christian drew her in. "Katie, he's dead. It's as simple as that. There's no other way to put it. He couldn't survive all of those wounds. Besides, the remains—"

"But were they *his*, Christian? Everything was so screwed up. How do we know?" Amy was laughing, still trying to get to Flea-Flea.

"Katie," Christian started slowly, "you shot him. You understand that? *You shot him.* That blast tore him apart. The fire took everything else. He died in that blaze." Christian brought her closer to him. He spoke softly to her. "He's gone. *All of it is gone.* It's finished."

Katie's shoulders dropped. "Christian, who was he?" She sounded lost.

"A madman, just a madman. That's all. Other than that, we'll never know. *It's over*, hon, that's what counts now." He leaned in and kissed her, taking the sandwiches. The expression on her face didn't change much. "Come on," he continued, "let's go before it gets too cool outside."

Christian turned to Amy, who was halfway under the table. "Amy! Leave the cat alone. Get your pole."

"Flea-Flea has somethin' in—" She started to protest from under the table, but her father cut her short.

"Young lady, if you want to go fishing, I suggest you pick up your pole and get outside with it." Amy popped her head out from under the table, quickly grabbing her fishing rod from the floor and making a beeline for the door. Christian prodded Katie out the door before any more questions or protests could be uttered.

As soon as the door closed behind them, Flea-Flea walked out from under the table and sprang to the top of the fireplace mantel. Settling in, he dropped the tough, raw meat from his mouth. Wrapping his paws around it, he arched his back, stretching. Yawning, his teeth were like polished ivory, with just the slightest traces of blood staining them. Settling back in, he held down the meat with his paws, angled his head and tore into it. Flea-Flea left the rest of the heart under the kitchen table as a "thank you" for Katie.

As he chewed, he purred, slowly closing his eyes, contentedly working the heart tissue with his back molars. His claws flexed around his meal with enjoyment as a single shot rang from outside. Flea-Flea's head flew up, eyes wide. Katie's voice cried out.

"Christian!"

Another shot echoed from outside, but this one didn't disturb Flea-Flea. Looking around the kitchen, he blinked and went back to chewing on the tough meat. He began to purr again.

Epilogue

The dream came and went, seemingly sporting a will of its own. Sometimes it would end as soon as it began, only to pick up at the point it had left off to continue its journey through the night. As it held onto the dreamer, its details would vary a little, in the way that a commonly known story might take on characteristics of its narrator, emphasizing certain points, but still sticking to the general scheme of things.

In the whiteness of it, they were always there in one form or another. Within his dream, he knew he fought the demons that were his. He watched as they entered. The voice washed over him.

"He forgives you." The pain was there...

"...Shhhhh," she said, "You cried out. You were dreaming again."

"Sorry I woke you," he replied, concerned.

" 'Tis nothing. You talked in your sleep too."

"Did I, now?"

"Yes."

"What did I say?"

"You said, 'He forgives you.'"

"Strange thing for a man to say."

" 'Tis," she agreed. "Who is he?"

"I don't know." Confusion replaced concern.

"Were they there?"

"Yes."

"Strangely dressed?"

"Yes." He was troubled.

"How many this time?"

"Too many."

"Come then, try to get back to sleep. In time, it will pass."

"I don't know. I can not be sure of that."

"Sleep, then," she said.

"Soon," he said, and got out of bed.

"Younger" John Roberts put the quill down. It was mid-August of 1836, and he was tired. The candles were burning low, and his wife called again for him to come back to bed, but he didn't want to face the dream for another night. He read the last part of the entry in the book.

"...*this Town that has forgotten that it owes its Birth to the Sweat of my Father. It is a Fever not only of the Body, but one that also Inflicts the Soul. A Madness grips a mind—*" Younger John put the quill down.

He had gotten lost in life. Through no choice of his own, he had become what his father had run away from—a sailor upon the high seas. But from what he had read in the book, his father had also lost his way in life.

He had found the book buried beneath his father's coffin, sealed in a metal box. He was sure it was Mr. Alexander Burns who had placed it there. He was saddened that his brothers and sisters had all moved on, not wishing to be part of this land anymore, but he was grateful that Mr. Burns had taken it upon himself to maintain his father's home.

Younger John touched the page he was writing upon. He knew Mr. Burns to be a good and Godly man, but what Mr. Burns knew of the book wasn't certain in his mind. He would have to find out.

Before his wife could call out to him again, Younger John blew out the candles, casting the house his father had built into darkness. With that darkness, his spirit felt heavy within him. It wasn't the hard work of the farm; he was used to the harshness of work. It was when he should be at rest that the troubles came upon him. The dream anchored itself to him. Next to his wife, he would toss and turn, held tight in its nightly grip. The dream came and went, as if it were a creature with its own free will. He couldn't understand it. Young John had a fear that it had something to do with the book. But what he feared even more was that it might have nothing to do with the book. That what visited him during the dark hours was within him and came from nowhere else. He had seen madness before. He could only dream and hope to keep his fears bounded within the night.

Younger John listened to his wife's advice and slipped back into the bed with her as his newborn son slept a few feet away. He waited for the dream to come upon him. He was soon asleep and within the whiteness of it. There was the black door and there were the cries of the children.

He heard them. And for him, it was a most fearful dream. A most maddening dream. And within the house his father had built beneath constellations that formed beasts and gods, he slept.

John F. Conn, A Biography

John Conn was born in the South Bronx in 1949. In High School, John became captain of the gymnastics team and helped to lead them to victory in the New York City championships. During this time, he also started to study Jiu-Jitsu, Judo, Karate and eventually Kendo.

From 1968-71, he interrupted his martial arts studies, joining the United States Marine Corps. There, he graduated from the Combat Still Photography School and was also a graduate of NBCD School (Nuclear, Biological, and Chemical Defense School). During his tour of duty, he became a Presidential Photographer for the Marine Corps.

Once honorably discharged, he attended the School of Visual Arts in Manhattan where he earned a BFA in photography with honors. During this time, he continued with his martial arts studies. Since graduating he has worked as a freelance photographer covering just about everything from riots in South Africa, underwater photography, interiors, corporate, and even his ex-wife's wedding when she remarried. His work has appeared in the New York Times Sunday Magazine, Imax Films, Time/Life Books, Village Voice, Shutterbug Magazine, American Photographer, Ocean Realm Magazine, Discover Diving Magazine, Dive Travel Magazine, Human Rights Magazine, Africa Report Magazine to name a very few.

John currently lives in the east Bronx and shares his home with an albino ferret, Monty.

A 5th degree Black Belt in Jiu-Jitsu, John painfully passes on his knowledge to his students.